Scann

Robert Harlow

Introduction by Robert Diotte
General Editor: Malcolm Ross

New Canadian Library No. 142

McClelland and Stewart Limited

This book was originally published by The Sono Nis Press in 1972

*Time is force; give a man some for his own
and he will try to play God.*

*Space is the great healer; a man with
enough of it will get well.*

The Canadian Publishers
McClelland and Stewart Limited
25 Hollinger Road
Toronto, Ontario

Printed in Canada by Webcom Limited

Introduction

Amory Scann looks over the galleys for the issue of the Linden *Chronicle* which will mark the town's 50th anniversary. How apt is this introduction to the little world of Linden where the commonplace recurs daily. The commonplace is a repetition that belies a history of adventure and struggle and a present of serious social problems for the small town. So, it is fitting that Scann be intent with Linden's history as a prolegomena to its present.

More than any single book to emerge from the literary nascency of the '60's, Robert Harlow's epic novel, *Scann*, is a book about history. In fact, Harlow admits to a sense of history and his personal approach to his work reflects it.

"Fiction's business is to deal with the 'times' in terms whose bedrock is time itself," Harlow has written. "Fiction is *of time*, *about* time and *all* the subtleties of time are its tools." (Harlow's emphases.)

In an interview with Geoffrey Hancock, editor of the *Canadian Fiction Magazine*, Harlow insisted that "the actual pure novel form now is perhaps what we laughingly call 'the historical novel'."

> Eventually the novel is about time: it's about how time operates on the times. . . . I mean time itself: actual chronometric time, sex time, life time, all sorts of things are going on and they are the different kinds of times. How they force the times to become history.

These last remarks are excerpted from a conversation I had with Mr. Harlow.

Their important to *Scann* will be self-evident to the reader for, in this book, unlike his two earlier novels, *Royal Murdoch* and *A Gift of Echoes*, Harlow explores the relationship of the times to time, of human consciousness to the times, and of consciousness to time.

The times for Amory Scann are post-modern: the 50th anniversary of Linden. It is time to take a nostalgic glance at the heroes who have founded and defended the town. But then, of course, the nostalgic 'scanners' have troubles of their own to harry what ought to be, what they would certainly like to be, a relaxed pleasure.

The novel is structured around Amory Scann's Easter weekend retreat with the fictional impulse in room 322 of the Linden Hotel on this historic occasion. We may understand this impulse, the fictional impulse, as the old desire to tell a new story. Scann is the editor of the Linden *Chronicle* as well as a writer of fictions—good or bad is hard to say. He lies to his wife, telling her he is at a convention in Banff. The three days of creation—Scann's creation of his novel and his creation as a character in Harlow's novel—begin.

Harlow uses the Christian, 3-day Easter cycle of death to re-birth with an unobtrusive grace to establish a structural base for the novel in addition to giving it a grounding in Christian mythology. There is an irony, however: he presents us with the birth of David Thrain on the first day of the cycle and the possible death of Mary Ann, the Indian girl, a character borrowed from the *Royal Murdoch* book, on the final day; the Easter context reversed.

Overseeing Amory Scann's story telling ambitions is a narrator, the real muscle in the book, who narrates Scann narrating. This narrator can and does become a character in the book. Carrying on an intelligent interplay with the novel, the voice of that narrator mixes three distinct stories within the chronological framework of the Easter weekend. The voice is, in fact, the bridge from day one through day two to day three. Day two, the war sequence, Scann's visit to the underworld or hell, does not fit into the clock of that weekend.

Each of the three stories, which Harlow has called novellas, is discontinuous within the book. The principal tale is Scann's efforts to chronicle the saga of trapper Linden and settler Thrain, two men central to Linden's history. One loaned the town his name while the other built the first building, the Linden Hotel, on the site that would eventually be Linden. The town is also the setting for Harlow's first two novels.

Into Scann's efforts to write the Linden-Thrain adventure the personal details of his life intrude. We learn of his faltering marriage, his affair with his secretary, his attempt to seduce the aging chambermaid, Mary Major, the plight of his dentist, George. In short, we see Scann's social ambience and listen to his phobias and those of the characters around him. These details become the frame for the three stories.

The Philippa Morton story, at least our initial glimpse of it, evolves out of Scann's efforts to seduce Mary Major. Later, we discover that Philippa has more reality to her than Amory Scann's incredible narrative would suggest. Philippa is the mother of Amantha, Thrain's second wife whom David Thrain is tried for murdering. We are given the elements of the classic thriller a bit at a time.

Finally we have Scann's Second World War experience and the story of his first acquaintance with David Thrain, everybody's idea of the basic war hero. Harlow uses Scann to exploit the popular cliches which the war period gave us. The lady in red, the female jinx and other characters popularized by American films, Harlow casts in the traditional realism of time, place and character. It seems to me that Harlow has nothing to tell us about the stereotypes in themselves. Rather they enhance his conception of history, a conception rooted in the human drama and the loss of control, actual, physical control on the individual level.

In fact, the war story is certainly Harlow's finest technical coup. Grafted to the novel in a lengthy, conspicuous chunk, a kind of flashback, the precise chronology of the section to the Easter weekend is never clear. As a result, it has the quality of a vivid memory. If we allow that it works, and I would argue that he does pull the lapse of time off on several levels, structural and thematic, then the book's scope is simply awesome.

Counting the brief reference to the parentage of Thrain's first wife, Erica, the book spans four generations. It includes a world war. It deals with the rise of the Thrain family, a family which partakes of the power aura shared by the self-made North American elite. It plays with myth and gives us a clean look at the people belonging to three periods of Canadian history in the process: the pioneer past of the Linden-Thrain saga, the war period of Scann and David Thrain, and the contemporary, domestic drama of Scann and George, his dentist.

Perhaps, then, it would be pertinent to look briefly at Harlow's conception of history and locate our Amory Scann within that conception. We may recall from a previous statement that Harlow conceives of time as a phenomenological multiplicity, a quantum time. Sex time, life time, actual chronometric time structure the drama of men and women moving between their beginnings and their ends on the stage of civilization.

The idea of civilization I have in mind here is the physical properties of a way of life as well as the kind of mind arrangements, rational structures, a people carries with them to confront and engage the phenomenological environment. In fact, the problem has always been to decide how valid the final mapping of the predominate ideas, values, etc., into the total environment is.

For Harlow, the drama of Linden and Thrain around Linden's trapdom shares a basic reality akin to Amory Scann's comic antics in the town of Linden. The common denominator is existential: a humanity looking about for space to live. The kind of space the characters find to extend themselves in distinguishes them. Again, the characters live the 'times.'

But they do not play on an empty stage. The stage accumulates props in the name of progress, a linear, temporal overview which is the rationale of increasing technological innovation and physical diversification. Linden and Thrain act in a forest filled with ice and snow but Scann has the Linden Hotel. Carcajou is the third in the triangle for Linden and Thrain; Scann has a wife, a mistress and Mary Major.

Harlow does distinguish between the generations on moral grounds, however. In a conversation I had with him, Harlow referred to the characters of the post-pioneer phase as "second generations pioneers." He finds them "less worthy" than the original pioneers. He sees in his father a representative of the earlier, pioneer phase.

"When my father's generation went to that part of the country (northern British Columbia) they had control," Harlow said. "They were civilization, they were culture, they were whatever was there. . . . But I was writing about a generation in which the heroes, the protagonists, were people who were losing control, had lost control. In fact, they didn't know what in the hell they were doing. Murdoch (Royal Murdoch), the pioneer, knew precisely what he was doing, despite the fact he staggered there (to Linden); he knew who Murdoch was. But his son didn't. His son was quite willing to go in any direction at all."

In *A Gift of Echoes*, Harlow refers to the generation which followed the Lindens, Thrains and Murdochs, the pioneers, as the "generation of caretakers." Land space, the physical dimensions where life was to be carried out, had been built up for them. Their duty was to look after what was already there. They failed to do it.

Thus, when Harlow interprets the course of history in terms of the response of characters to the demands of their civilization, the key word is control. The context is no longer individual

Lindens and Thrains pitted against a seemingly infinite amount of land space and its content of wolverines, ice and snow. The human universe has filled itself in with a manufactured content of fighter planes, hotels and Parliament. To Harlow, the caretakers, the people who followed the Lindens and Thrains, didn't accept the terms of the changing circumstances and so they lost control. The assumption is, of course, the western-Christian idea that they could exercise such control.

Accordingly, we see in Scann's war individuals with no real control. Control resides for the most part beyond the individual. Beyond the Stephanies, the members of Flight-Commander David Thrain's flight group who scale their chair mountains to map the ceiling, and beyond the neurotic Maries, who are encumbered with visions of hard luck. Only the David Thrains still seem to maintain some vestige of control.

In Amory Scann's Linden, a new kind of control proliferates. The characters are resigned to the reduced physical landscape, a resignation which, in some cases, is complacency. Linden is a mind world playing on a stage stuffed with props. "By the time you get to Scann," Harlow has said, "Scann is trying to make myths."

A man's space, the land he patterns his behavior in, is now defined as head space, a neutral world of rational structures. Minds do the exploring and the warring in domesticated Linden. The predominate conflicts are thus verbal: arguments between Scann and Mary Major, Scann and his secretary, Scann and his wife. The tone is comic.

We have only to locate Amory Scann in Linden. Scann is certainly a coward, frightened to the point where his capacity for fright is exhausted in the flight with David Thrain. Irresponsible, obsequious, he is a voyeur, peering through key holes and titillating himself with images of lolling mammaries. He is a clown falling from the chair he uses to prop himself up so he can roar at the world contained in the hallway of the Linden Hotel.

Scann schemes and plots to manipulate Linden to his best advantage. But love stories threaten him. In the Philippa Morton story, the version he tells Mary Major reveals a fear of overbearing women symbolized in the threat of castration. Scann searches for myth and he finds the romantic figure of Thrain, the paragon of pure adventure, the continuous argosy of exploration and conquest. Scann's own adventures consist of his women.

In the end we cannot say the three days of creation have

taught him anything about himself despite the fact he has walked that 8x9 carpet in room 322 of the Linden Hotel in the same way as Linden used to walk the boundaries of his trap-dom. A Chaplinesque figure limping from the hotel, Scann owns at least the dimensions of that carpet.

The aesthetic here is epic. Neither comic nor tragic, life goes on. We are not told if Mary Ann has died. We are left with a look at ourselves which is not complimentary. But it tells us this much: if we are victims, a child-like state too often given to self-pity among a people so affluent, then we are victims because we have allowed ourselves that escape. We shouldn't overlook the fact that people are shouting at David Thrain, the Parliamentarian. Or that old Thrain burns the manuscript of the story which features him as its principal character.

Post-modern in spirit, frequently touched with a rabelaisian sense of delight, Scann as a novel has problems in places: a narrative too protracted at times, an abruptness of transition which can be confusing. The pitch-catch metaphor seems to me overly gratuitous. But, the head of the creative writing department at UBC and a teacher who has had a hand in the development of an upcoming generation of writers, Harlow has given us a book which departs from traditional realism. It deserves our attention.

Robert Diotte,
Vancouver

EDITORIAL INSIGHTS. One: pitching and catching. The editor of the twice-weekly *Chronicle* writes on scratch-pads that float like open rafts on the river of copy that runs across his desk. He is speaking to himself about history: the fiftieth anniversary of the town of Linden. He makes notes. Dry, but personal. A forty-page special issue of the *Chronicle* is before him. LINDEN 50 TODAY, and under this headline a half-page photograph taken with a wide-angle lens from a Beaver aircraft flying at 5000 feet. Not too high to miss anything important, but no garbage, cracked cement, peeled paint or wear-and-tear show. The new pulpmill gleams — the sun is carefully on it — and the new hotel, civic centre, city hall, golf course, shopping plaza. Also, planing mills, a cement plant, a brewery and the suburb of Rainford. The great curve of the Linden river flows from the east and runs south out of the picture. The big picture. Seven billion board feet of spruce. Twenty-two million tons of pulpwood. Thirty-thousand people within easy driving distance. Molybdenum. Natural gas. Boom.

The editor of the *Chronicle* is Scann. Amory Scann. He is studying himself studying this issue of his paper. The jumbo edition, as with most other products of himself, is now an excuse, something to concentrate his attention on so that the view of himself viewing is focused and clear. There is a wildness in everything he does that is beyond domesticating; it terrorizes and fascinates him to observe it and to see what new embarrassment it will reveal. His animal is out there acting. Scann sits inside his skull and watches, using himself as bait to try to trap it back inside the cave of his mind where he can silence it with reason. He doesn't believe it can be done; this watching and waiting is merely habit. He understands that the separation of himself from his acts is a madness, that perhaps continuing to act at all is insanity. Still, he is plagued by hope and damned with new and grander designs, and each exploit in his life is begun as if the raving beyond himself is contained or asleep, but what follows always degenerates into a performance, a dialogue between Scann watching and Scann doing. Lately, he has discovered that there are a number of Scanns watching, and some of them urge the animal on. "All my Scanns," he notes, "are divided into three galls: genital, excellence and levity, and each draws blood." He has, finally, only words to believe in, and the notes he writes down seek at once to render despair and to lock it away so that it will not contaminate the belief in words that forces him to write notes designed to contain despair. He is interested in circles. And straight lines, hyperboles, the geometry of existence.

The paper was designed to *be* Linden. A work of art. He dreamed its exhibition in distant places, festooned with ribbons of merit. He wrote it, designed it, chose the fonts of type that printed it. But it is neither biography, *aide memoire* nor journalism. It is literature of a kind, a private thing that only puzzles his readers. And incomplete it lies crippled somewhere between fact and truth: a confused audacity. Marion had praised it. But when had she not praised his work, as if it were part of a wife's contract? Or maybe hers was always the kind of encouragement she would give to a retarded child who had tied his shoes but had got them on the wrong feet. "There seems no beginning," she had mildly said. Nor had she much appreciated — along with the Reverend Lucas and others — the essay on Flat-Ass Annie whose doyenship of the whorehouse had lasted well past the war and the influx of amateurs during and after it. Other than that, wide quiet, part of a continuing silence he feels around him more and more every day, a silence that grows deeper each time someone tries to speak. He gathers words on copy paper, accumulating new evidence of his competence even as the anniversary issue of the *Chronicle* rests its case. He is closing in on other designs, other possibilities. Necessities. It has come to him quite clearly, as something that must transfigure him, that he should not fight his animal now but use it. The surprise of this new tactic might tame it. It occurs to him that he has planned this for a long time. "I begin," he writes, "and therein lies a clue to our confusion about causes and effects."

The city is named after a trapper. This fact especially must be written down. It is a beginning. Of sorts. One hundred and fifteen years ago Linden, the trapper, was born in Truro, Nova Scotia. Eighty years ago he arrived by canoe. On this his fame rests: alone he came. A madman. Paranoid. Certifiable. But free. He sired a log cabin at the confluence of the two rivers, the Swifter and the Linden, and in the spring there were floods that made his madness worse. In the winter he froze. In the summer he gasped. In the end, railway cache 23 became a town and was named after him. An ending, of a kind. But he walks yet. The picture of the city on the front page of the anniversary issue is also his: clear-eyed, simple, obsessed with survival.

Editor Scann knows more than this, much more. He, too, is now obsessed. Like any good editor he knows almost everything, and when something by chance happens to escape him he knows where to find a woman who will research it for him. What he doesn't know is how to create, compose, shape fiction. It bothers him. But it is helpful honesty that he knows this. He thinks, scratches on a new sheet of paper from another pad, a yellowish one, lined with green: "Pitch-catch." What happens between the pitch and the catch is the main fact of composition. Of course, there is a hitter in there too, and that's important. (The way he is putting this down is important.) That moment of waiting for the time of the pitch to culminate is where composition and life touch. It includes the pitch and the catch, but it excludes them too (they should be forms only), because they are beginnings and endings and therefore false: there are no beginnings or endings.

Once upon a time there had been a mayor named Murdoch who ruled Linden for twenty-seven years. Was Murdoch a beginning? He is only rotting history, although what he did is all around Editor Scann at this moment. The *Chronicle* at whose editorial desk Scann sits, for instance, is by Murdoch out of old Abbot, the itinerant printer, who was sobered and given money and then commanded, encouraged, even loved, but reduced: to man-made truth. Trapper Linden, however, did nothing: he obsessively was (and is). He was, unlike Abbot, pitched past the hitter and was caught. It is important to get the pitch past the hit to the catch. The catch: the catch is what makes the whole thing meaningful. A hit is a fact: recordable, ignorable, changeable, reducible, directable: sane. The instant past the hit is therefore important. It is where life happens; it is us in a moment of deathless mortality. Genesis, Exodus, Leviticus, Numbers, Judges, Kings, Chronicles, Proverbs, Prophets: a catch and a new pitch to prove the futility of History. Had there been a hit, it would have meant the end of the world, and ends of worlds are not our business. The Great Beast, the Seven Seals, Judgment, Separation, the Stopping of Time. Only bad writers go in for endings. Or beginnings. Beginnings are gardens. Endings are revelations. Editor Scann's work must have neither: it must grow every which way out of the only time there is, the time between. Pitch . . . catch. And there, suspended, infinite, fated, some of us will be brought out of time: Trapper Linden. Yes. But not Murdoch, Acton, Droggan, Abbot, Oaks, Grandy or, sadly, Editor Scann himself, although all of these are in the anniversary issue of the paper. Murdoch, the mayor for twenty-seven years; Oaks since then. Acton, the eastern mill man; Droggan, the western. The elder Grandy, merely representative; and Editor Scann on the masthead. And Thrain. Why is he mentioned as simply the builder of Linden House and the father of David Thrain? Because Scann is saving him for himself.

Trapper Linden. Yes. His name — as if the essence of the town were in a name. This place is not, after all, called Longfellow, Bentham, Milton (although simple romantic minds did vote for these), or Ur or Troy or Storyville, each with a living time that could not apply here. No. This is Linden, named after Henry Auguste Linden — the bastard was a German with a Scottish accent. The accent is a fact, largely ignored, but adduced from minor scholarship and from earwitnesses, reduced from memory to a recorded note, but nevertheless a fact and intriguingly sane and unchaotic.

But in justice, why not Thrain? There is not even a mention of his wife Erica, or Amantha, Cecilia, Philippa Morton, or of Trapper Linden's Ro. They don't belong: they are Scann's now. And what about Dorothy, who makes a home for Thrain's old age and is the only person who will put up with what he calls his freedom, and who is at this moment across the hallway writing for Editor Scann's newspaper on a 1928 Woodstock? Her father was a gunslinger of sorts (Carmoddy) who, drinking one night in the old Rialto bar (in 1914) with his money tied for safety to his testicles, raised his rifle to shoot a joyhole through the ceiling, missed even that great expanse, hit the wallsafe causing the bullet to boomerang and lodge in his brain. Three men dived to take his pants off. Dorothy, who was seven and who went everywhere with her father, even where she shouldn't, grabbed for his money and held tight. When he didn't rise up fighting they knew he was dead. A true story. Once upon a time. Beginning, middle and end. But Scann understands that chance ruins it. Stories abhor chance. Fictions are supposed to control chaos: that's why we like them. They make us feel safe — or safer — even the tragic ones.

PRACTICE SESSION ONE: CATCHING. He is born — which is not a beginning — David, the first and only son of Thrain, on his father's birthday under the sign of Scorpio and with Leo rising (the most difficult sign, demanding, successful, rewarding, damnable, exalted, potent, uncertain, selfish, secretive, charming) on a paddlesteamer as it turns terrifyingly but routinely end-for-end down the long rapids eighty miles east of Linden. Thrain delivers him himself. Everyone else is manning ropes, pike poles, the wheel and the engine. Erica, her nordic bones separating and her long muscles heaving, shoves him out, and Thrain catches hold of him, after miles of whitewater labour which had started when her own water had broken as she had leaned against the railing amidships near Thrain who was standing, head tilted back, looking up at the tops of mountains through spray scooped up by the paddles aft and blown by the wind across his line of vision. It had been cold. Quiet water along the edges of the river had turned to ice, but during her whole preganacy she had felt too warm and carried a fan which she had held even then in her lightly mittened hand. Inside, on the bunk, she had held it like a relic over her heart, and during the last deep, desperate and exhausted heaves to get the baby born the fan had broken, shredded, disintegrated, and pieces of it had become tangled in her hair — bright yellows and blues and reds. Thrain — it is a new thing — is charmed as he looks down at her while he holds the boy for her to see.

It cries and then Thrain reaches into his pocket for a knife to cut the cord that is still joining the mother and his child. He folds both ends over as if he were stopping the flow of water from a hose and ties them with pieces of torn sheeting. She has swaddling clothes for the baby. He wraps and hands it to her, expecting that now his job is done. The moment is private; he touches her free hand and watches her face come back to life. Her eyes fill with moisture that gives them depth. The mouth lies swollen against the pretty exhaustion of the rest of her face. Her brown hair, with the shards of fan in it, curves down over shoulder and arm. Then it is her turn. She looks down at the boy held by her wide long hand against the great stores of his food. "He pushed and pushed to get out," she says in a low voice. "Just at the end I loved you. Do you know?"

He nods his head, grasping at the deliciousness of her meaning, and then looking at the black-haired, red-faced, blood-stained boy. He does not feel a father. He denies this and forces himself to hear the paddlewheel pushing them through calmer water. "We must get the book and find out now what to do," Erica says. The baby cries his loud damp-reed cry, and Thrain shrugs himself back unconsciously into his new rôle, thinking: This is the only miracle we're allowed. He gets the midwife book and begins to turn its pages. "Hurry," she says precisely. "There is more to come."

EDITORIAL INSIGHTS. Two: full moon at noon. It is easier to be a writer — to become one — in old towns, countries, civilizations. There, one knows who counts: who could write about Italy without feeling even now the weight of the Borgias, poison, popes and painters and great comings and goings in the night? Who cares there about seven billion board feet, twenty-two million tons, population per square mile? Or girls who are only statistics? 44-18-37: the new math. There's only one kind of going and coming in the night here. There, Editor Scann notes, the building has been done. Mention the Forum: Christians, lions, emperors, malaria, martyrs, life and death — the whole human condition. Mention the Forum here and it's Hockey Night In Canada. There is something ridiculous about a gladiator with a jockstrap. And while Editor Scann isn't getting any younger, Linden doesn't seem to be getting any older. The Borgias are still alive in Linden and are still contingent; no recognizable patterns have formed; the historiographers haven't yet facted the fictions. There are no critics, only reviewers. And the Dominion Bureau of Statistics. Critics are necessary: they are a sign something has been said that does not make us feel safe. Think about this. Fifty years ago in Paris a statement was made: young women were dressed as angels and stationed in public urinals. Could any man stand among them there without feeling the terrible rumbling of the world beginning to turn over? The reviewers shouted alarms. The critics took a more-or-less positive view. They could afford to. In Europe angels *belong*. See Swedenborg, Mons, etc. Here, it's difficult enough for a man to go to a public urinal without being arrested for attempted gross indecency. (Maximum sentence 2½ years.) No angels among us and very little consciousness: no statements of our own to make us that way. What we're concerned with even now is birth in all its forms. Mere historians and reviewers feel safe with birth and its attending tortures where everyone is helpless, mother pinned down by pain, sweat and the business at hand, father immobilized by fear, wonder, awe, and baby held tight in the cervix, then the birth canal and then stunned by light and jubilation and a cut across his hind flank. The mystery of it all. The violence, noise, blood, suspense. The security of it. Tell it over and over again and it never loses its unity and variety in time, place and action. Primitive. Universal. Borgias are born. And Mortons, too, who are as yet unknown and must be remembered soon by Scann. Already he is beyond the mere historians and reviewers with their name-the-baby contests, their beginnings and endings, their gardens and revelations. He has written down and found irrelevant still another birth. He goes back to it and notes the sentence structure, the easy metaphor of wild nature laid over against the small human concerns of the Thrains, and sees also the small and subtle conflict of man and son already begun. It is a lesson to him: a tiny explanatory fiction. It pleases him to be through with it, to understand that it is too lyric and too sentimental. But it saddens him, because he is in the middle of things now, without maps. He picks up once more, painfully, the special anniversary edition of the *Chronicle*, folds it, puts it in his jacket pocket and goes out to attend a Board of Trade luncheon. It is Monday. Tuesday, Rotary; Wednesday, Lions; Thursday, Kiwanis; Friday, Gyro. Advertisers are important to an editor, even more important to his publisher; the birthday issue of the *Chronicle* is important to the advertisers, those builders, those ebullient second-generation pioneers. To a writer nothing is more important than anything else — until he begins to write. Editor Scann's own birth as an author is imminent and he struggles to keep it that way. He walks down the street and the creator is within. But: "Watch out," he says, broadcasting a blind smile and not moving his lips to any who greet him, "Watch out, the full moon of my lucubration is rising. I may go mad at any moment." Editor Scann. Editor Scann, they say to be a real writer *you* must disappear. But now he remembers to go to an appointment with his dentist.

George's office is in an old building on Fort Street. Through its bay windows the town's main intersection can be seen at a little distance. Scann's appointment is the first of the afternoon and he is early. He walks through the waitingroom and sits in George's new chair. This is ancient privilege rather than real familiarity. On the roof of the store across the way is a clock that is surrounded by a cigarette ad. It has a minute hand that jumps forward every sixty seconds. Waiting for George to hurt him for his own good, he stares at its white face and when the big hand leaps his anxiety responds. His animal is inside him now; it will not succumb to reason, only to the imminence of pain, but even then it whines. It would be much worse, Scann thinks, if George did not love his teeth — if every large cavity, every rebuilt molar, every root-canal job were not a crusade, and every extraction a rear-guard action, scorched earth in the face of the possibility of total defeat. Only once in two decades has George lost a battle, and that was with a wisdom tooth that started to grow when Scann was forty. Impacted, it had come out in pieces, a curse at a time, and Scann had bled for a week from the mangled sutured hole George had been forced to make. Awake or asleep, he had sucked blood from the wound until he was sick with it. He had involuntarily kept the hole open as if it were producing something valuable: the happy proof that even super-George could be forced to bungle. Seldom do experts get negative publicity.

George's assistant arrives from lunch and says good-afternoon. She is not young any more. He has seen her mature over fifteen years from a thread of a girl to a parcel of toothpick bones dangling from a skull smile — the eager grin of one who has been left out but who hovers nevertheless and gives hope a bad name. She has seen often how he reacts to pain. She puts her coat in the closet and washes her hands. George is behind the partition where he keeps his appointment book and accounts. Scann imagines that little room to be a vestry where he robes himself and waits until his acolyte has prepared the instruments of his divine service. Hermione does her tiny businesses: fixes a paper bib beneath his chin, adjusts the chair so that he is lying down, fills the paper cup for rinsing, puts out picks and mirrors and the big needle on the moveable tray. Hermione begins to flutter. It means George is approaching. "Mr. Scann," she tells him as if identifying a body.

Scann has no friends. He has always understood that closeness requires a certain free formality if it is to be saved from depravity or abrasiveness, and he has never found that possible. Depravity he has hoped for in an isolated form, and abrasiveness is to him inevitable in prolonged human contact, one of the observable laws of human nature, whose momentary amelioration brings on a euphoria strangers call love and the world's rare intimates have no precise word for, or refuse to utter it, as the ancients rightly would not speak the true name of God. George has always understood. Scann is, to him, upper and lower jaws lined with gums into which teeth are implanted. They have shared them for two decades, forging a unique relationship which has brought them pain and joy and trial and triumph without allowing their actual lives to impinge one on the other. Scann waits as usual for George to settle beside him, feeling relief and fear and true sentiment at once.

George sits on the free-swinging stool attached to the chair. He used to stand, reach for instruments and attack immediately, a tiger at the gate, but he has settled into middle life and now he puts a hand on each knee and Scann feels his gaze before he returns it.

"Amory," he says and pauses, licks his big nervous lips. "Christ, where's it going to end? Everything we've slaved for down the drain. Inflation, stagnation, outrageous taxes, a whole generation dropping out."

Scann lies carefully stretched out on the chair and says nothing. He looks hard and forces George's eyes to stop staring. Unwillingly, his hand reaches for mirror and pick. Scann opens his mouth; there isn't a tooth that isn't somewhat sore when it is probed or knocked. "You're a mess, Amory. We should cap them so they'd at least be pleasant to look at." He sits back on his stool. Scann says, "The job'll put you in a new tax bracket." George returns the instruments to the tray. He pulls a lever. The chair forces Scann to sit up. George points through the window. "Look at them." Scann does what he's told. On the corner opposite are a half-dozen young men with shaved heads and wearing saffron robes. They walk in random patterns on the cement sidewalk. Perhaps they are chanting.

"Is nothing sacred anymore? They mock us, Amory. Mock us. Everything we've done and built, a whole world full of the most wonderful things and they: Amory, they piss on it. What did we have? A depression. A war. Deprivation. Struggle. My father worked fourteen hours a day to put me through school. I lost five years private practise while I was in the army, and it took another five to make this one go. Marriage, a decent home, a decent home, by God, insurance policies, investments in good Canadian companies, extra duty on professional and public committees when I was called on. Amory, we *served*, and that's the thanks we get. Pigshaves in women's dresses."

Scann takes a deep breath. "George," he says and stops. There is too much territory to cover between them, lifetimes each have lived in ignorance of the other and all at once George has built an imaginary bridge between them out of imaginary sympathies and real presumptions. Scann lies confused. The situation is delicate and suddenly out of plumb: Who are you, George Dockerly, to think I must agree? I have suspected you of insurance policies and investments and a decent home and of thinking the world full of the most wonderful things, but they are irrelevant to our teeth in my mouth. "George," he says again, "there's nothing wrong with buying a

17

yellow robe and joining a religious order." He pushes back in his chair, a double gesture.

"Religion? If they want religion let them go to the church up the street. There it sits tax free on the most valuable piece of land in town." He jumps up and goes to the window. "Hare Krishna, who cares?" he shouts down at them and then turns again. "It's their *influence* that counts. Hippies, yippies, communes, foreign thinking. The kids they corrupt, lead astray." He comes back to the chair and stands over it. "They're taking it all away from us without moving a muscle, Amory. Our money, our decency, our kids, even some of *us* are beginning to doubt. Hank Lewis, my own brother-in-law, turned up at a Dental Association meeting in Banff last week wearing love beads and one of those jewelled crosses where his necktie should have been. I'm telling you, Amory, if I had a rifle up here I wouldn't advise buying futures on their lives." His voice halts as if he has run up against a wall. He sits on his stool and works the lever to allow Scann to lie back. His breathing stammers in his nose.

Editor Scann feels violated. Hermione has disappeared. He understands now that there has always been a flow of resentment beneath his admiration for George. "Maybe they're good people," he says, trying to make those words remind his dentist of his real place.

"By God, where I come from what they're doing out there is sedition and shooting's too merciful. Amory, they've — that kind of dirty thinking's got Johnny. He's gone." His eyes don't glare, they shine. "Doesn't a man have a right to protect his family? Isn't that the first law?" Scann refuses him. He must. "All right," George says. "Open up." The pick probes a lower molar on the left side, then it is reversed and the butt-end of it taps the tooth sharp three times. Scann rises up to meet the pain. George reaches for the hypodermic and snaps a vial of anaesthetic into its barrel. "Open wide. Breathe deep." His fingers hold Scann's cheek and shake it violently as the needle sinks into the flesh above the point of the jaw. The syringe plunges. Nerves vibrate in pain down deep in Scann's throat. Then George puts the empty hypo back on the tray and sits once more with his hands on his knees. It seems to Scann that this might be the end of a world, but he must produce a shocked smile for George while he can and give him, as humans always do, a little of what he wants. "Johnny's gone," he says. "Where?"

"How the hell should I know? I sent him out for a haircut and he never came back. We've tried everything, friends, relatives, the

Children's Aid, the police. The police." He jumps up again. "The goddamned police just smile. They say thousands are on the road and maybe he'll be back when he's got it out of his system."

"How's Helen?"

"Sick with it. She shouted at me. All for a goddamned haircut, she said. I've never heard her swear before in my life."

"She's right," Scann says, forgetting himself. "You could've saved putting that between you. He'd have gone anyway."

"But a haircut's important, Amory." He points out the window. "They've made it important. It's a badge."

Scann swallows around the dead lump that his jaw and tongue have become. "Hair's not your line, George," he says, leaving the words to hang between them. The man who may not be his dentist anymore says, "I thought you might have had some advice." Scann shakes his head. "Just sympathy for the kid. I hope he makes it." "Where?" Scann laughs awkwardly. "How the hell should I know?" "You're like all the rest, Amory. Can't or won't hold the line. Where would we be with your teeth if I had that attitude?" He turns away and opens a drawer in his instrument cabinet.

Scann says uneasily, "You can't make morals out of teeth."

"Prevention," George says. "That's what dentistry's all about. Diagnosis and prevention." He sets a stainless steel basin on Scann's chest and holds forceps in his right hand. "An effort to conserve the investment nature has in us. How do you know that isn't morals?"

Scann stops thinking. "You're going to take it out?"

"Yes, Amory, I'm afraid the battle for that one is over." He consults Scann's chart which is lying on the tray. "We put the first big filling in it in 1952, then another in '54, and again in '57, rebuilt it in '64. It hurts, doesn't it? It's poison, Amory, pure poison in your mouth. Better to get rid of it now than go through a major flare-up, abscess, perhaps a chain reaction all along the jaw." He is calm again. Scann sees his point: a pound of prevention and a fillip of cure. He prepares to open his mouth. Hermione is by his side pressing her lower abdomen against his elbow as she always does. But things aren't back to normal. "We're going to have to face it pretty soon, Amory," George says. "With a mouth like yours the chances of still having your own teeth in five years are slim." Editor Scann sits up and hands Hermione the basin from his chest. He removes the paper bib and puts it over the instruments on the tray. George says, "What's the matter, Amory?" Scann gets up. "I don't know. I want to think about it." His tongue won't work. "We covered a lot of ground today." He holds out his hand, but George doesn't take it. Scann's animal is loose again, and perhaps it is saving him. He watches himself half-smile at George. "Apocalypses scare me." George doesn't understand; he likes him for it and forgives him his trespass. He drops his hand. "I'll be back again, I guess, George." And he walks away through the waitingroom and down the stairs to the street, knowing as he goes that once again he has caught himself in time.

PRACTICE SESSION TWO: PITCHING. Editor Scann clears his desk onto the floor: a lunge, a sweeping motion in opposing directions with both arms, scratchpads and all. U.P., Reuters, A.P., C.P., dispatches from the teletypes. He has done this before to spite reality and when nothing else made sense. Once he published a whole front page without using an outside source. Four people congratulated him on the street the next day. The train wreck in Bolivia which had killed two hundred people particularly caught their fancy. They wanted pictures. There was the same reaction to a girl in an iron lung whose only known movement was her eyelids; she was being taught to paint with her lashes but it was difficult because no one knew her reaction: "Once when I spilled paint, a little bit on her lid, there was a horrified look in her eye, but that's all," the arts and crafts therapist at Scann's German hospital had said.

Scann picks up one last piece of paper. The head on the story says: Quebec authors get rave notices and prizes in France. He can't read or write French. He drops it in the pile on the floor, rescues a lined pad from the debris there and doodles, draws, writes notes on no known subject, composes dispatches of his own, fights simultaneous urges to urinate, defecate, eat, drink and put his head down on the desk and go to sleep. His molar aches a little. It is 5 a.m. The sun is only a light under the eastern horizon and there are no shadows. History is mortal. It does not live. It dies and rots and stinks up the present. Henry Auguste Linden, the German with the Scottish accent from Truro, Nova Scotia, walking the log-fenced edges of his acre or so on top of the little bluff overlooking the confluence of two rivers — the Swifter and his own — considers the horizon and makes his hands into fists. Editor Scann stands him where he must have stood a thousand times to look up at the Rockies, the saw-toothed edge of his world, and he must have made fists there as he did in other places in front of witnesses. So much for research. Is the river high or low, flooding or receding? Is the railway through or is it still to be built? Are the salmon running? Is there a dugout canoe full of Indians from their village at The Crest floating before him on the water? A moose, a deer, a bear in the picture? Canada geese going north or south along their ancient flyway? Snipes, bluebirds, robins, ospreys, eagles fluttering or circling? Is there a pet squirrel or a chipmunk with him on his sleeve? A mouse at his feet rustling through the tough grass? A packrat angling toward his cabin? Is he buzzed by hornet, bee, horsefly, black fly, wasp? Does he endure or ignore mosquitoes and no-see-um? It would be odd if a weasel were near, or a porcupine. (Try to keep the porcupine in mind.) There is no history around him: people make fists at chance, not at history. The fist is history. Trapper-prospector Linden makes a fist.

The river is rising, cutting a little at the foot of his bluff. Geese are flying, a moose paddlewheels from island to island in the backwaters of the confluent Swifter and an eagle circles looking for cutthroat. There is a squirrel on his fence, a packrat does angle his way toward the cabin, and a canoe with Indians sits solemnly out on the swollen water. It drifts on a cross-current, its occupants gazing at Trapper Linden. He reaches for his gun (a Lee-Enfield of which he is very fond and by which he lives off the land) and fires a shot close over the heads of the Indians. He lowers the gun, sets it on its butt and leans both fists on the fence-railing while the Indians still stare at him unmoved by his violence. The moose, the eagle, the squirrel, the formation of geese startle, whirl or hide, but the Indians cut for the bank of the river and glide back upstream on a reverse current.

Trapper Linden shouts down at them, waving them away with both arms. He climbs his fence and descends to a prominent boulder twenty feet above the water and his own canoe. He sits, clinging to the rock and raging as if it were spiked there, but the Indians dock at the narrow ledge below and one of them lifts a boy, who might be three or a small five, in his arms and walks steadily, looking always at Trapper Linden and not at where his feet are having to find steps in the clay and on the rocks of the steep pathway up the bluff. The others in the canoe follow, four of them, three men and one woman, up the switchback to the rock where Trapper Linden sits. He is not calm, but rather he is immobile, stunned by their invasion and their foolhardiness in the face of his Lee-Enfield. They stand in a half-circle around him. The woman, young enough, square, and with a sore on her jaw covered with a poultice of leaves, holds the boy's hair back from his face. He is red-blond, palomino.

Henry Auguste Linden stands upon his rock and looks down at them all, the six of them, his white hair standing on his head like dandelion seed. They point at the boy, at him. The boy is sick, fainting, his small chest rises, falls, rattles. Linden points at the poulticed woman. "Yours?" She shakes her head. The mother is back there, high up on The Crest, fifty miles north, dead. He glances at the boy. He does not ask, Mine? or leave himself open to confession. They move closer; the leader holds the boy out and up. Henry Linden turns and goes back over his fence, holds his gun again. The brave with the boy follows him. The gun points, impotent as guilt. They all smile.

And now history asserts itself: Henry Auguste Linden takes the boy. Raising his gun and his fists at chance did nothing to fend off the fact: he took the boy over the fence and followed the packrat to his cabin where he made the child drink river-water and pot liquor, and eat a little food mashed to gruel. The old man, Editor Scann believes at eight o'clock in the morning, saved the boy as proof that no matter how far you travel, how high your fenced promontory, stout your cabin, or solitary your existence, no matter how carefully you plot against the plot you know is being plotted against you, nothing, absolutely nothing can prevent you from being forced into a guilty association with life and a prankish partnership with contingency. Obsessed, persecuted, at the end of his wit as always, as he tries to stem the invasion of man — the only animal except the wolverine (remember, please, the wolverine) he detests — Henry Linden has no sense of time; his only greed is for space. He stands inside his cabin and looks down at the boy sleeping, probably getting well, and he shudders, begins to heave at the chest, his knees start to bend, straighten, bend, until he is leaping, crying, leaping as if he were Rumplestiltskin hearing the sound of his name.

Henry Auguste Linden: a river, a son, and soon a town. Men are approaching from east and west. Rails are being laid, trestles built, and the bridge a half-mile below his cabin will run across the two rivers where they have already met, five hundred yards of black steel and grey concrete with lifters balanced a hundred feet in the air which will jackknife the east span to let paddle steamers go through. And up at The Crest, dead, is an Indian girl he can't remember, perhaps the half-breed daughter of an itinerant evangelist missionary. Or, if Linden does remember it is not with his brain. He sucks air through his teeth, grabs himself, looks, stares, takes himself outside, cleans the offending member with its own water, and with his Lee-Enfield shoots the moose as it stands fifty yards below him at the edge of the confluent Swifter. He runs, kneels, plunges his knife into the warm belly, spreads the guts out onto the ground for the carrion birds, slashes off the head and leaves it too, skins and butchers, hauls and sweats, cries at God and cuts his finger and shouts again. He strips and salts and racks it up to dry. He pickles and boils and finally fries, chews, then, ruminating, looks once more at the boy sleeping. The soft groin of this young one's anonymous mother is now a faint musk rising above the smell of food and the stink of the cabin. He remembers her: the time, the place. He feels his knuckles tingling as if he had only just stunned her a moment before, and already their offspring lies rattling and restless on the bunk in front of him. That there has been no escape thrills him full of laughter — and relief.

This last puzzles Editor Scann. The relief seems not so much wrong as too right. It is a fact that by this time in Henry Auguste Linden's day, after the early visit of the Indians and the slaughter of the moose, the sun would be setting and the tensions between light and shadow would be resolving themselves down through the chromatic scale of the spectrum, toward black, toward deliverance and a moment of neutrality. It is true that Henry had lived long through the obsessed and timeless day of his escape and now his own light was fading. But would it bring relief that his monster had caught him and that it was a forerunner of more beasts to come? Perhaps not relief so much as a sudden focusing on the result of his simple endeavour, not quite relief but certainly deliverance whether he liked it or not — hence the laughter.

H. A. Linden goes out into his garden and has a revelation. He sees himself killing the boy. And now he feels relief. Without laughter. He walks to the remains of the moose again, to where the gun stands stock-still, loads it, breathes shortly, sharply in his accustomed manner, enters the house, and leans the rifle against the door. On the bunk the boy is awake and looking around. His long hair lies against a bear-skin's fur. His face is small, tense, his eyes suddenly blank and watching. Trapper-prospector Linden leans over him, and thinking that the bullet in the gun would be wasted, he reaches with his hands and his already cut finger is torn again by strong white teeth, crowded teeth that lie along both jaws in the Linden manner. He withdraws, holding his finger and seeing the blood drip from it. Beneath him the bunk is empty. The little skinned animal is behind him and he turns to see it falter, its knees buckling beneath a weight of sickness. Tiny, not much more than three feet high, it scuttles, making pinched growls in the back of its throat, across the dirt floor to the gun. It stands again, facing Henry Auguste Linden, its face purple and hunted, and takes the gun from its resting place by the door. It is too heavy; it falls, firing, and man and boy scream together, looking remarkably alike as they lie on the floor, the one unconscious, the other stunned and for the moment paralysed by a bullet through his left shoulder.

Trapper-prospector Linden lies deaf from the noise and feels shame, confusion, pride: sobs embalmed in laughter.

Editor Scann watches the blank wall of his office, listening. The moment is so important it almost escapes him. A world is precisely in balance, has ceased to move or breathe. It may die. But it doesn't. That's history: a note in Editor Scann's files. Henry's long first pitch has culminated. The world indeed is in balance. All forces are equal. The actual has become real. H. A. Linden knows why he feels shame, confusion and pride. He has become a father. The distorted miniature of himself lies, breathing, not six feet away, a deathless mortality. Trapper Linden lives. The arrogant clappers in the bell of his scrotum rang in lust, in violence and in victory and the reverberations have culminated in the whine and shatter of a bullet through his flesh. He is responsible for his own dying; were he without the power to give life he would have to live forever. But now he doesn't die. The moment is so profound that Editor Scann momentarily abandons his pen. There are no beginnings or endings. Trapper-prospector Linden has been caught. He must get up and be pitched again. He crouches beside the boy and turns him with his good right hand so he can see the face. In repose it still has an intensity which disturbs the old man. The scene is sentimental. After epiphanies, curtains should always be drawn to hide the insipid emotional results of these sudden insights. What can Henry do? Carry on with killing the boy? No. The little bugger has almost suceeded in killing him. Shame. Confusion. Pride. It's enough to make anyone sentimental. Now that he feels the child deserves to die and lies helpless on the dirt floor, something soft in Trapper Linden's chest and throat expands and affects his vision. He *sees*. Or he thinks he does. The picture is at once complete and incomprehensible. It forces him to act, because now the boy must live and so must he if this new time is to survive. Once more there is imbalance. Unequal forces opposing. Actual event following actual event. Trapper-prospector Linden feels comfortable again as he contends with blood, fever, hunger. He thinks no more. The boy is *himself*. He lets him hold the Lee-Enfield while he gets better.

EDITORIAL INSIGHTS. Three: The long afternoon of the faun's father. Editor Scann sits at his desk again, letting the *Chronicle* edit itself and draws diagrams and maps and nurses his vision. There are no techniques to communicate the complexity of it. All of its time, space and action should be represented at once as in an infinitely exposed colour film. In his mind it is like that; it is his own vision and he is free to let it flow and break and form again. It lies in all strata of his consciousness, and at night it expands and he moves through it, a dwarf in a landscape that is at the same time Henry Linden's, Thrain's, Erica's, Philippa's, as well as David and Ro's, even Mary Ann's, the whole town's: a place where everything impinges at once, and its dimensions don't exist except as a co-efficient of change. There is nothing innocent about Editor Scann's eye. Its guilt is tangled and consummate. It is ready to lie for effect, bully a fact to make it perform, cut corners, smooth edges, and feel noble because it is searching for truth. Muckraker. He sweats. His bones melt. His viscera flow and rumble. He dances inside of himself with impatience. He wants the moment when everything comes together with shattering significance to happen now. And all he has down on paper are two practise pieces which aren't in sequence, because David's birth happened seven months after the arrival of the young Indian at Trapper-prospector Linden's cabin.

Editor Scann picks up his special anniversary issue of the *Chronicle* and turns to page twenty-two where there is an old faded and grainy picture of Linden House taken during the period of its construction. Beside it is another picture taken the same year from the top of the lifters on the bridge across the rivers. The view is north and in a circle Scann has drawn is the cabin where Trapper Linden lived. It is an extremely clear picture whose detail is remarkable. He takes from his drawer a magnifiying glass of considerable power, changes spectacles, and looks down through the bright air above the river, down past the tops of the cottonwoods and high willows to the enclosure that surrounds the cabin. There are two figures leaning against the fence. They are of equal size and shape, although one is not wearing a hat; his head is white against the darker background of the picture and there are no features to distinguish him: Linden. The other is pointing north and east; his face is in profile, the nose canted in the direction of the arm — up and away. The next gesture and the one before the picture was taken are hidden even from Scann's imagination, but there can be no mistake: this is Thrain. And the finger, the hand, the arm, the chin, the nose are all pointed toward the country Trapper-prospector Linden alone, of all the people in the settlement not yet called Linden, knows anything about. He knows his own river. He knows its tributary, the Bear, from its mouth to its source fifty miles north where The Crest Indians have lived for perhaps a hundred years. He knows the creeks — the Squirrel, Moose, Twelve Mile, Mosquito, Toebroke and Windfall — the rising, undulated land on both sides of the Linden. He knows the animals, the birds, the flies, the devil club, nettles, the spruce forests, the fir and hemlock, the birch and poplar and cottonwood stands. He knows the swamps and the moose pastures, the sudden hundred yard prairies where blueberries and wild strawberries grow. And he knows — or Thrain thinks he does — about what lies beneath the ground and in the gravel bars of the creeks and along the rivers. Trapper-prospector Linden is silent, and his gun is hanging from the roof of the cabin out of reach of the boy who he has found is no more to be trusted than when he first arrived. But even in that pictured silence between gestures, the bargaining has begun: Thrain's soul for Linden's land. They stand statues at the fence over-looking the river where they are caught slightly off-centre in the official railway photograph. Northwest the photo lens looks into the face of the clay cliffs that force the Swifter to converge on the Linden beyond Henry Auguste's cabin. North the men look and point. North they go, god and hero, and Erica Thrain takes the boy for safe-keeping and is left with him and David at the nearly-built hotel which will become Linden House when the town is named.

Editor Scann knows now the place where his own private vision is leading him. He swivels his chair and looks out of his window and into the street: cement, blacktop, chrome, paint, plastic, glass, steel, brick and wood. A mini-skirt or two, hot pants, a hard-hat, a delicate summer frock and then his own eldest daughter walking toward the post-office with the first mail of the day from the legal office where she works part-time. She doesn't stop pedestrian traffic but she makes it turn its head. Editor Scann stares too, trying to think how it is that she is pretty, and wonders if it is simply good health, good feeding and a certain stupidity that passes for innocence in her face. She has the look of a faun: eyes set too wide apart and slanted up on a head that somehow has little substance from crown to neck. It would, however, be wrong to put a tail on that perfect rump. Scann is disturbed. It occurs to him that it is his daughter he is looking at. He doesn't so much feel old as he does marked out for probity. Soon his eyes are to be blinded, his hands stiffened and fettered, and his mind Sani-flushed to ensure better, more serious, fatherhood. It seems only a moment since Marion had given herself up to him while they were sitting — eyeless — in a Betty Grable movie in London during the late spring of 1944. Afterward, they had gone to the Strand Palace Hotel. Or perhaps the Regent Palace. One or the other. He remembers the bill clearly. He stands up and takes his jacket and hat from the coathook on the door and goes out past his receptionist-secretary-coffeebrewer-etc. Etc. He says to her, "Linden House." She is the only one who knows what he is doing, feeling, thinking. Privileged, she nods, and he knows her gaze follows him out, watching over him. He feels safe and visceral and rotten and justified and tempted and defensive and when he sits at the bar of the Linden House Lounge where everything is discreet and fashionably hypocritical, he orders a Cutty Sark on the rocks, adding a little water because it is only eleven-thirty, and sips a toast to the half-century of the hotel's existence. The eighty-five cent tab is laid before him in a black discreet saucer and he puts the exact change into it. He likes this room, although in the dim light he can just see across it, because it is the only part of the hotel where the original logs show through. Elsewhere they are crusted over by the sugarcandy plaster of progress.

Editor Scann takes out his travelling notebook, the one filled with scenes, sketches, prose line drawings, and sits, as all creators think they must, at the centre of his vision. It is a web. There are strands of time, planes of space. And there he is himself, manufacturing it all and seeing it all at once. But it is not a picture to stir a strong positive faith anymore. He drinks and orders another and lets its tab gleam whitely in its black saucer beside his elbow.

He writes in his notebook: i-n-g. ing. A feminine suffix: regenerative and on-go(ing). A tend(ing) toward; in the ideal sense, a yearn-(ing). For instance, the act of, the art of, the documentation of becom(ing) is not a straight line but a web of ing. Sleep(ing) eat(ing) work(ing) lov(ing) etc., which gets rid of the special category for be(ing) small 'b'. Watch a web expand(ing). Picture it. There are rhythms of forward motion: spac(ing) tim(ing). Rhythms of composition felt, laid over and creat(ing) tension between tim(ing) and spac(ing). Tension each with the other, but control is always in perfect tim(ing) and spac(ing): and the even measures of that effort are the same as the cadences of (my own) pitch and catch. And in the interstices formed by spac(ing) and tim(ing), where life and composition happen, is there a Be(ing) capital 'B'? Perhaps not. No. That jump is a leap of faith. Too comfortable. Let Be(ing) remain unnecessary to becom(ing) or otherwise there is no horror, no humour, no 'other' possibilities. Thrain would agree.

In the dim light his notebook lies pale beside his elbow like the tab for another larger drink, one he has concocted himself. It inebriates, and on that tab are his most guarded moments. Receptionist-secretary-bookkeeper Shirley comes in and sits beside him at the bar. He feels euphoric, in control. She reaches out and touches his open notes. He wants her to look at them, and he watches her read and thinks about how he loves her, what he loves about her. What he loves most about her is that she is his own discovery. He believes he came upon her suddenly one afternoon sitting at the desk outside his office in a vertically striped blouse, a dark skirt, ginger nylons, shoes to match one of the colours in the blouse, her hair styled so that the lobes of her ears were laid bare, her eyes ringed with black and haloed with turquoise and her lips pale against small teeth. He would have preferred to have discovered her tiny; he would have liked to have found her perfectly slim with tapered hands and little feet, firmer buttocks, larger breasts, fewer years and smoother skin. As it is, he feels it took a man of considerable insight to penetrate her camouflage and find what Prospector-trapper Scann likes to call her sexual integrity: an honest supply of precious metals in the broad vein of her womanhood. That, too, is in the notebook and he hopes she won't turn the pages and find it, because it isn't altogether true nor does the phrasing make precise sense. She finishes reading and says, "You have a very complex mind, Amory." He picks up his glass and drinks from it. "Do you like it?" "I don't understand very much of it." Her voice hangs, as if she hasn't quite finished. "And?" he says. She closes the book and puts it into his right-hand jacket pocket. "And it doesn't sound at all like who you are." She stands up beside him and says, "I've worked three nights in a row overtime. I'm going to take a long lunch. Maybe you should too." "Yes," he says firmly, and she lets him see her eyes again before she turns to leave him to the slow device of another drink.

Behind the door marked Men he looks at his forty-eight years in the mirror above a short line of basins. If it takes arrogance to create he finds none in the face confronting him. One might be suspicious of something devious behind the frank set of the eyes, a measure of vulgarity in the slope of his lips, a weakness in the chin and a narrowness of cheekbones which rise to a slightly balding forepate. Like Shakespeare. He smooths his tie and feels for the top of the new Lightening his wife has sewn into his pants, pats his pocket to rediscover his ballpoint and leaves the lounge. In the lobby, he exchanges nods with Burke, the new manager David has hired, and wonders for a moment how discreet he might be. It is as yet rootless thought. Shirley lives in an old section of town. A cottage, shingled, stained brown by intention and by rain and weather, left to her by tragedy and sustained by fiscal continence. He drives to its woody seclusion and parks in a nearby lane, approaching the house at an angle that takes him to the treed and hedged back garden where he waits on a dappled lawn in front of an old pine beneath which he sits. He takes out his notebook, reads, thinks. Time. Separate moments impinge, lapse. The sun cuts its engines and begins to lose altitude.

Shirley appears to him and the light descends on her as a gold rain. Her hair is loose, just washed and shaken dry. What she wears is long, a pillar, light; her pale arms and legs are shadows, the double bodice innocent and high. He rises from beneath his tree and, in sudden violences, forces her. Down. She goes down beneath him; the bull-swan settles. Her face is lined with surprise, even outrage. Scabbard, sword, hilt hitting, sheath sheathing, a god belly-dancing. Chaos. Beneath their tree a small echo: a spasm of wind spurts and flows. They lie on moss, deciduous hands moving above them; they savour the spices of violence and their good ointments better than wine. Resting beyond noon between her breasts, he feels her fingers in his hair. His lips tug at her. "Sometimes in bed I reach out for you," she says. "Never mind, I'm here now," he tells her, "and so stay me with flagons." "You'll have to come in," she says. He does, and now that she should be surprised, she is not. "I meant into the house," she calls softly, but the black saddle is already moving beneath him, loping, cantering. He posts. Timing. Spacing. Controlling. God. Running at full gallop he lies his face along her neck and holds on. Low bridge. Open country sloping up and then down and up again. The landscape closes in. Wind sobs in his ears. The saddle launches him. For a moment he is free. Terror wracks him. He is held again. Chaos. Gallop, run, canter, a long sensuous walk. Cooling out, he blankets her until only a little momentum remains. Ceases. She is weeping and smiling.

He lies beside his fancy and looks, stares, choked with love for their lust which hovers nearby only slightly weary and breathing deeply of the oxygen of their adultery. She rolls her head against the moss, blinking her eyes to dislodge the last of their tears, and looks up into the sky as if she were longing to disappear into it. He understands and makes up some words for them both. "God bless," he says, "God bless you gentle Beatrice. Rise to the stars and find your native bliss, but leave this doggerel boy, who stays behind, amendments to the scripture of your soul: gross entries, obscene addenda to your physical whole. I love-hate you." She rolls toward him. "Love-*hate*?" "Of course, I am a worshipper." She rises to her knees, breasts pendulous, belly taut, thighs muscled, hair snarled, a bawd pummelling him with fists. He grabs at this new century of her, but she runs free and with him after her. Pale buff she goes, around the pine tree, along the hedge to the blind switch at the gate to the front garden, swings, dives at him and he feels cool flesh pass him by. At the steps to the back porch he holds her, lifts her against him and slides her down, hooks her neatly and walks step by step up out of the garden into the bright glare of possible scrutiny from distant neighbours. But she rises, leaps; she frees herself once more and pushes against his chest sudden and hard. Arching back over the step's rail, he loses both balance and will and plunges down headfirst into the soft water of her fifty-gallon rainbarrel.

Brown-stained liquid envelopes him like a flash of pain, and his head scrapes the side of the barrel. A hand above him absorbs the shock of hitting bottom. His member — above him now, afloat, awash — feels the cold acutely but inaccurately and discharges, hiccoughs as a salmon at a trenchful of roe, or perhaps as a hanged man is said to make, sometimes, this last gesture toward immortality. There is water in his mouth, his ears, his nose; his sinuses are flooded and he is sick with shame. As a husband he is trapped. As a lover he is lost. As a newspaperman his final headline will have to be bowdlerized. He is unable to move. A moment of devilish perfection: the ultimate absurdity of death transfigured into an infinitely absurd posture. Then there is another pain. His one testicle (the other, withered at thirty-two by a late attack of mumps caught from his eldest, is immune to hurt) is being assaulted. He moves. His fingers claw for the lip of the barrel and he rises like a *leit motif* from the unconscious water, straight up and over, following the source of the pain and trying to keep ahead of its killing pressure. His feet touch the ground, water cascades and he looks, coughing and sneezing, into a laughing face, a face crumpled with mirth and which is below him because she is crouching, her hand still extended as if in suppliant attraction to his apple, his essential core, his seat of learning and living. She rises and he worships her again, for she is wondrously wise and has saved his life. He grins, and she loses control, gargles deep inside herself, snorts, looks at him out of eyes green with struggle and begins to turn and turn until she collapses against the railing on the stairs. Then she watches him, watches him with tenderness and anger. "You might have drowned. What would I have done?" "Buried me. Burned my clothes and buried me." "You," she says, "you practical bastard, I didn't mean that." It is difficult to be regal in the nude ascending the back porch stairs, but she is, and she goes into the house. He gathers their clothes and goes inside, and finds her in the livingroom on a divan smoking a cigarette. She blows smoke at him. "You're one up on me," she says.

He closes the notebook, looks up through the branches of the pines beneath which he is sitting, and then he opens it again and writes some more. Pretty good attempt, even if out of any real context. Still, it is sentimental fantasy. Lacks metaphysical base. See notes on Thrain adventure. Also check Robbie Burns, our patron saint, who, if memory doesn't fail, says someplace that bawdry is truth and "a standing cock has no conscience." Such acceptable universals make us believe in history: a nervous faith in repetition or, at best, spiralling causes and effects. So, a standing cock *with* a conscience makes a story with a start and a finish that, blessed relief, stops history and makes us feel secure. But seminal events can happen only in the absence of conscience. Conscience requires compromise. God knows. He built the standing cock to remind us.

The real Shirley appears in a sheath of many colours. At this distance she is pretty, and she walks toward him with all the tension gone from her. This is her territory. She sits beside him and smooths the dress. He reaches for her, fondling. "Out here in the garden, Amory? What are we, apes?" He hears his laughter arrive uneasily. "You know what drink does to me." She purses her woman's magazine lips and opens her true-detective eyes wide, but then she says, as if recounting the obvious roundness of the world, "You really know how to make a girl wait." His belief in contingency falters. She is ultimate order, and he ceases, thankfully, to think.

THE FIRST DAY OF CREATION.   Camera pans three hundred and sixty degrees through chaos. God has shot off his explosion into the void. Long and short-tailed comets. Balls of fire. Move in for medium close-up on gathering granules of matter. Cut close to further formations of atoms lying in pregnant gaseous wombs. Dissolve through core after core of heat to reflections on a dark thunderous cloud: stereopticon images of the accident of eternity. Camera cranes and tracks, bumping against unexpected solids and whole spectrums of refracted light. Sheers off into quiet, spaceless, timeless nil. Quiescent. No movement. Then explosions in the distance measure timing, spacing, becoming. Dawn after dawn breaks against the wide angle of the lens as the camera moves forward and establishes direction, forces vertigo through depth of field, becomes obsessed with a single object on the horizon, joins it, is part of it. Camera again pans three hundred and sixty degrees through new chaos. Flickering lights. Camera begins to move forward, crashes against a blank wall, turns one hundred and eighty degrees on its own axis and backs through labrynthine corridors, drowns in red, surfaces, drowns and, escaping, breaks through into perspective again: an ear, a shoulder, an arm, a hand holding a ballpoint pen over yellowish lined paper, writing. The script is Scann's who draws pay from the *Chronicle* but no longer edits it, who is married and has three daughters but no longer lives at home, who is the lover of Shirley who may or may not know where he is. His intentions are good: he will edit the paper, he will go home, he will lust for Shirley. But first

The emptiness that follows commitment. Visions. Pretentions. Fantasies too big for foolscap paper. Sentimental struggle with plethora to try to achieve the irony of simplicity. Distance between reporting and meaning becomes infinite. Everything is simple: just one thing after another, behind another, beside another. Only Nothing is complex: in its demands on Scann himself. No escape now because he has escaped. He is caught, as it must have been in the beginning: God guiltily harbouring Void, Nil. God again. Temptation. There is a temptation to reverse the process, take a day of rest first and then create man and woman and watch them work their way back through the gates to the Garden and beyond, back to birdless, beastless, waterless, lightless void. But this reality must not be allowed to prevent creation, the necessary search for consciousness, for meaning. It is Eastertide, Good Friday to be exact, a time of hope, of glory, of confirmation, of culmination, of retreat in order to advance, of cruelty in order to free love, of no conscience in order to act significantly. The room is twelve by fourteen, as are most of the rooms at Linden House, and it is numbered 322. There is a bed, a night stand and light, an 8 x 9 rug on the floor, a bureau with three drawers with a glass-covered top on which sit a drinking glass, a piece of soap and a Bible. There is a mirror over the sink, a window (with a green shade) looking out over Fourth Street and a desk and standard lamp and a chair on which Scann sits. He has brought paper, six ball-points, pyjamas, shaving gear, toothbrush, comb, sweater, extra drip-dry shirt, the clothes he is wearing, his briefcase and a dozen depravities in case Shirley

His wife thinks he's in Banff at a conference. The owner of the paper, his publisher, thinks he's on holiday. He is trapped. Only someone else playing or being God would understand. But if he is to be committed, this is the best place for it to happen. He lets his camera move again, this time to the horizon so that it tracks around the rim, gazes down into the empty bowl at the place where the rivers Linden and the Swifter meet. It is not quite empty anymore. Steel tracks run east and west. A roundhouse is rising above the alluvial gravel beside the main line, and houses, buildings grow like dragon's teeth sown south and west. All the dull detail of events repeating themselves, of man fouling yet another nest. Thrain is

33

part of this invasion of Trapper-prospector Linden's territory. They pass each other, these two, because Thrain meets all of the paddle-steamers as well as the trains. He sees Linden and the boy, Ro, at varying distances, the old man carrying his Lee-Enfield and with the young one behind him on an invisible leash. Ro sees David. David sees Ro as he looks down from his strapped-in position on his father's packboard. He rides backwards and does not know where he is going, but knows perfectly where he's been. There are few children in the village. David smiles, laughs, waves his two-year-old arms when Ro spits at him. The boats, the trains, arrive. Thrain takes from them what is his, loads his wagon and squeaks back to his stoppinghouse, with its corral behind, its hitching rail in front, and its gothic vastness rising log after log slowly towards the heavens.

Writer Scann pauses, opens his briefcase and takes out the drawings he has made of the original stoppinghouse Thrain built and called Linden House when the town was named on Easter Monday, 1919. Archeologist Scann has talked to survivors of that time, has a copy of the one known picture of the original façade of the building (there was a fire only months after it opened for business), and has listened to Thrain talk, although speaking with the old man enlightened him not at all about the detail of the first structure. "It was to be the biggest place in town. Erica was madder than a she-bear with a stick of carbide up its bung. She figured a boarding-house would do, but I just kept building, knowing in my own mind what I wanted. I'd get it up there no matter what anybody said. And I did. The chimney was a little off plumb. You can write that down if you want, but in the end that was a real victory. The son of a bitch was — is, damn it — field stones and she fell three times before I got her wide enough at the base to hold the height. What's a little crooked? Four fireplaces in the main lobby and everyone of them takes eight-foot logs. The wife needn't have bitched. She had a comfortable place to live. I built that and the bar first thing we came west and then put up the stoppinghouse adjacent. Adjacent," he had shouted as if Scann were deaf: "butting on to it. Part of it's still there. It didn't go up all at once. It took a few years on and off. I wasn't rich. I had men bring me in three-four acres of logs and I peeled and bucked them, put the corners on them and used anyone I could get to help me raise the walls and put on the roof. I saw the old Papineau place in La Belle Province once and that's what I wanted it to look a little bit like, only a lot taller. Erica helped too,

34

when she wasn't mad at me. You see, the trouble was I never told her what I had in mind. She wanted to plan it down on paper. A woman'll never do a stupid thing for good reasons, but she'll do good things for stupid reasons. Practical as hell, I guess. Well, life is full of idiot things that have to be done for good reasons but my stoppinghouse wasn't one of them. It was pure mischief, that's what it was, the kind that used to make the world go round. It was a luxury that came with being able to be ahead of my time. You don't have that little gift anymore. Time's caught up and passed you and you're all running tightassed after it. Look at me, I'm eighty-two. Been dead for twelve years according to the Book and the scytheman is still a long way back. Now, take my bar. It was real mischief. You've heard of it. A hundred yards long, with six waiters on roller skates and a snakeroom big enough for fifty drunks. It made Ripley's Believe It Or Not later on in the middle of the thirties. A great mischief when I built it, but that's the thing about mischief. Ordinary men can scarcely believe it and if they do they don't know why. Without my place two-thirds of the people passing through here wouldn't have stayed and Murdoch never would have had a town to give city status to so he could be mayor. I remember him when he first came here, staggering around like a blind man in the swamp down by the Linden, damned near starving and just waiting for this place to get big enough so he could suck its blood. Now, I admired him. He did more mischief than any man in town — good and bad. But his biggest was he held the place back so he could run it easier. Maybe he was right. It sure isn't much of a town with the kind of buffalo hunters we got here now."

Writer Scann puts away the data he has gathered on Linden House and considers mischief as an operating principle. It is a positive philosophy, with neither ritual despair nor ceremonial hope. It also resurrects the slain illusion of the centrality of man by saying that he can control his life-style within his environment. It offers man a sense of proportion, humour, and an antidote to contingency: a happy violence which allows each and every man to revolt against chance and manufacture his own personal absurd systems. Why rely on God and technology? Scann gets up from his desk and begins to pace. The Spanish say that the only revenge is to live well. Let us enunciate our own revenge: to live mischievously. He pees in the sink, washes his hands there and considers his own project. He feels a certain kinship with Thrain as well as a common insight; half an equation forms: i.n.g. plus mischief equals. . . He halts, regretting a tendency to require answers. He is afraid of remaining a journalist or only becoming a scholar. He sits again and takes out his notebook and begins reading. Soon the waters of his fear cease to roil. In the distance he hears waves of confidence begin to build and crash against that shore where his expedition must land.

Author Scann sinks into himself. His ballpoint starts to write on the yellow foolscap: he follows it, eyes wide, nose down as it digs into the page, tense, jerky, scribbling after the image of them in their canoe — Thrain paddling at the bow, packs sitting as ballast amidships, Linden astern setting a course upstream across the boiled surface of his early winter river toward the Bear whose cold green fifty-mile bowel empties into the silty Linden. The canoe bullets along on back-currents; the sun is a fielded ball thrown across the sky toward the flat plate of the Pacific. They land at the Bear's estuary, beach the canoe, eat, sleep, eat again, shoulder their eighty-pound packs and head off up the trail that cuts along the edge of the Bear for ten miles before it swings west to catch Toebroke Creek at an acute angle just above its hundred-foot waterfall, the natural barrier behind which Henry Linden traps his winter furs.

Campfollower Scann is already very tired. The men, Linden well past his half-century and Thrain within a week of his twenty-ninth birthday, lie on opposite banks of the stream with their faces deep in swift water, drinking. Temperature, thirty-six degrees above zero and falling. A small wind is dragged along by the creek and over the falls a few yards below them. There is no sun, only a diffuse light from somewhere south; the trees stand near them like troops guarding a dead riot at their feet. There is blue-green spruce darkness along the trail ahead. The noise of water cascading lulls Thrain. He pulls his head up to an inch above the surface and stares at the stones beneath it: yellow, green, grey, black and with coarse sand between them. He reaches for a handful of the sand and lets it trickle between his fingers, wondering. Bonanza Creek. A dollar is caught for every shovelful thrown into the sluice of his imagination. His belly, empty except for cold water, speaks. He looks to his pack where there is food and sees Trapper Linden disappearing along the trail leading from the other side of the creek. They have walked through four hours.

Scann picks up the phone and orders an egg-salad sandwich and a pot of tea: the only author in the world who doesn't drink coffee.

He unlimbers, walks to the window and looks down into Fourth Avenue, peering from behind the drawn shade. From here he could shoot five of the *Chronicle*'s advertisers in the next twenty seconds. Mischief. But Trapper Linden is half a mile up the trail walking, as always, as if he is pursued. Thrain is strung out behind him like taut gut. His feet slip over a rug of needles on the small incline of the pathway. After three miles he sees Linden again, a shadow moving along a ridge in Thrain's future. After seven miles a hundred yards separate them. Thrain's pack sways and tilts and pulls at recently discovered muscles, and the headstrap chews his forehead like a weasel at an egg. Three miles further on they cross the Toebroke again and Thrain falls in, soaking himself beyond his waist. Trapper Linden breaks his twenty-four hour silence. He grins until his rusty teeth show. "Another seven miles," he says, looking up into the warp of the failing light and then ahead at the weaving shadows of the trees in whose crowns the wind gusts and shifts. "I guess we better keep moving," and they move no slower than before, temperature twenty-seven and the wind against them for half the distance. Thrain sweats and chills, his clothes stiffen, his feet blister in his wet boots, and by the time darkness arrives and the wind stops and the calm snow begins to fall and melt and run between collar and skin he has been without guts, feeling or sense for over an hour. Trapper Linden walks, strolls at marching speed, his head high now as he peers in front of him and shifts his rifle so that he is carrying it in one mittened hand by his side. He sees downed timber, curses, charges it like an infantryman, leaps from its farther side onto the trail. Eleven hours of their march has released him. Thrain walks stiff-legged through black snow, an infinitely clogged pattern of spacing and timing that finally focuses on a single erotic trickle of water across his chest, down his belly and over his testicles — at once a hint of eternity and a tiny mortal thrill. The rifle cracks, its flame real, the bullet's whine concrete before the instant scream of an anguished animal. Branches carve the air, split and shatter. Thrain's muscles pull him forward, refusing to halt him, knowing that they may not move again if they stop. His mind clears and he sees, as if the gun's lightening has produced the dawn. He might reach out and touch Trapper Linden but he doesn't; he walks into him knocking him out of the way as the badly wounded body of a great cat falls finally from its tree. Thrain goes down beneath the cougar and listens to the sound of Hunter Linden's yelling rifle plug

37

his ears. He lies, twists his head to see upward and understands how Linden could have seen the outline of the animal. The snow-sky holds a little light allowing shapes to form against it. A bullet pierces all the layers of his pack and he feels its crazy heat against his ribs. He shouts at Linden, tries to reach him in his rifler's ecstacy, calls him and curses him and then panics out from under the double load on top of him. In the darkness beyond pack and body he hears a sound that can only be Linden dancing to the rhythm of choked laughter. The snow swirls and Thrain sees nothing. There is no distance and no direction and no new sound. Trapper Linden has vanished with his laughter. Thrain's call is an unexpected whimper that squeaks out between pain and exhaustion and fear: "How far?" Linden's voice comes from just above the ground. "Fifty paces." Thrain goes near. The older man sits hugging the cat's head to him and rocking it. "He knew I was on the way and I knew he was waiting." Linden is on his feet and dragging the cougar by its scruff. Thrain only wants to get there. He finds a paw and then a leg and holds it feebly, leaning his weight in the direction Linden is pulling. The big cat slides over the new snow along the trail. They emerge abruptly from the jungle and into an expanse of darkness Thrain knows is empty of trees. The shape of the cabin confronts them. Thrain relaxes his hold, stumbles, falls against the logs and lies there knowing he must get up and go back for his pack or die. His clothes, caked with snow, are rigid around him. Even his eyelids are a weight he can only just keep from crushing him.

Writer Scann sweats and strains and wishes the scene would end. He sits with the upper end of his ballpoint probing a dry nostril and knows it can't stop here. There is the pack to fetch; the door to open; fuel to bring in; the fire to kindle; water to boil; tea to brew; Thrain must change his clothes; he must eat; he must be sick in a linear pattern on the snow outside — a small exclamation mark of vomit against invisible white and overpowering tangible black. He must faint rather than go to sleep, a fever building in him; Linden must throw the bloody pelt of the skinned cougar over him, its skull lying against Thrain's shoulder so that perhaps the dead tongue carresses the lobe of his ear; and outside, a wolverine slanting across the clearing on a line of least resistance toward the lake sniffs the air and smells food. It is late fall, the snow is here and drifting, the stolen eggs of spring, the summer's larvae and the autumn berries are all gone. His best season has begun, a time when suddenly he is the fastest hunter in the territory. In the snow he gallops when all else struggles. Perhaps three feet long and weighing a third of Trapper Linden's pack, he can slay a moose or an elk, drive cougar and bear from their kills. Writer Scann gets out his notes again. *Mustelidae; genus Gulo, Pallas.* Colour: blackish brown with a light band of creamy fur that runs from its shoulders, along its sides and meets over the base of its tail. It has wrestler's ears; close mean eyes; a nose like an angry bear. A trap of a mouth curved down and mad, like Hunter Linden's. But unlike Linden, or Thrain, he is not obsessed. He does not push himself along straight lines. He cruises his own hundred square miles challenging accident with chance directions; confident, playful, strong, smart, cruel, cunning, he is a wit and a sick joke artist. He is man without any awareness of mortality. He seduces his world from a position of strength. He uses nature without identifying with it. He lives his dozen and three or four years alone in a freedom that fascinates but terrifies Trapper Linden, who knows him only by his acts — sprung traps, tattered pelts, plundered supplies, downed and half-eaten animals, meat stashed in the crutches of trees, and tracks in the snow.

Scann writes a note beneath his notes: if you can't be a wolverine be a priest. Wolverine wonderfully insane, moreso than the world he lives in. Priest beautifully insane because he can live in no world at all. Newly-ordained Scann rises from his work. The calling is strange. The walls around keep falling in on him. There is no anteroom where he can prepare body and soul for servitude, and no assistant to make drudgery into ceremony. George, you are right: pain requires ritual. Or insanity. He walks the room from door to window and basin to closet, the only ceremonial observance he is allowed. He understands that he is taming the room, making it his, but his stamina is still small and, at the door again, he gives in to necessary temptation. He opens it and looks out into the dimness of the hallway: beige walls, blue roses in the pattern of the carpeting. To the right is the stairway down to the lobby; to the left, far to the left, is the emergency exit to the fireladder. Halfway there is a bathroom. Cleanliness is next to godliness. He steps out, closes the door behind him and walks in the gloom to where the tub is big and stands on claw-feet, its porcelain finish gray with use and daily cleaning. He leans against it for support. He has come a great distance, and as he watches the water climb the sides he feels weariness rise up in him. He strips and settles himself into its warmth. It is a physical release. He gradually begins to drift into a shallow sleep where he dreams of fast movement, brittle sounds; he nearly wakes and then falls away again to where images pass by as he edges toward a dream where he is driving his Volks across a desert. There is no track to follow. The wheels spin twice for every tire-length he progresses. Still, there is green ahead, moving toward him. He drives to it and then through it. The cabin is there just beyond the tip of the lake. It is a very small cabin, low at one end — perhaps three-and-a-half feet from the foundation log to the sod roof — and not more than two feet higher at the end where the door is. Inside, there is a dim orange light from the fire at the back of the room. There is a bunk on one side, utensils and shelves of supplies on the walls near the fireplace. And on the floor is a man; he is alone, wrapped in fur, his face pale and his breathing shallow. He kneels beside the unconscious Thrain and speaks to him. He will not reply, not even when he is grabbed by the shoulder and shaken. Scann rises, grazes his head on the roof, finds he can't stand. He sits on the bunk for a moment and then goes outside again. The Volks is gone and he is trapped here. The lake is black. There is snow on the branches of the evergreens. He is puzzled. This is Thrain's and Trapper Linden's problem, not his. A small wind that is more painful than it is cold drives him back inside. He sits once more on the bunk and stares at Thrain. He is going to die. Sick and alone, he will die. There is no way out of it. He watches the unconscious man for a long time. The fire shifts and burns more brightly. The creased face of the ill man lolls as if disconnected from its body and only cradled by the fur blankets. He listens but there is only hermitic quiet. Now there is an artificial light from the fire that holds the scene stiff and makes time redundant. Stasis. The scene denies movement; it is a small roped-off section of a wax museum, part of a celebration not defined. The drama is there in that refusal of consciousness to allow action. This is memory as memory always is: fixed like light on a film, and denying the rational need for connection, movement, culmination. Scann sits inside the memory of a vision that will not yield to necessity. Thrain is there, simply there. Scann is the Red King dreaming him. It occurs to Scann that he is dreaming, and that he dare not wake. He lies down on the bunk and watches the steady orange light caught between the shadows at the higher end of the room. It is a relief not to look at Thrain but to leave him until he sometime soon finds a way to make the vision move again.

But Thrain's Erica moves. She takes a new vision in her hands and ropes it into twin strands: David and Ro. Ro is six, David will be four next month. She stands at the door of her kitchen and watches them play among the stacked logs Thrain has had hauled from the bush. He has almost finished building a hotel out of that timber. She remembers doubting that he would, but that doubt died immature. What Thrain says, Thrain does. Yet, he is in trouble now. This, she doesn't doubt. She leaves her kitchen door and walks toward the children, wanting to be close to them for protection from the small swells of fear that press up against the shores of her breathing. She feels guilt too. She had wanted him to go. Not for his sake, she knows now, but to test her own ability to live alone. Yet, since he's been away, little has been different; he is not there, not across from her at table, not beside her in bed where he was some use, not a noise in her ear as she bakes and cooks. Instead, he is another kind of presence: perhaps a fear. She sees him missing and feels him not there. He is a voice inside her head telling her he is in trouble but her anxiety is for herself and the two boys.

She crouches beside David. The snow makes the morning crisp and cool and brilliant. She touches his arm but he ignores her and climbs up on a log and throws a spray of dry snow at Ro who ignores them both because he is chipping bark with the blade of his six-inch knife. Erica has a bandage on her finger where it was slashed when she tried to take that knife from him the day he arrived. Already she loves Ro. It is her way. Already she has plans not to give him back to Trapper Linden when he returns in the spring. He is company for David. Together they seem happy and David is freer of her. When Thrain returns she will tell him of her plan. She moves to Ro, turns him by the shoulders and gently hugs him to her. "Ro," she says, "It's so nice to have you with us." He grins and puts the point of the knife on her belly and pushes. She backs away and stoops to the level of his eyes. "Don't," she says, smiling, "or I'll kill you." Ro laughs and puts the knife away in its sheath at his belt. "Just like a goddam woman." She holds her ground. "You've only got Mr. Linden's word for what a woman is. Do you really think I'd kill you?" This is the first hurdle to help him over. He looks puzzled. "I put the knife away so I guess you don't need to now." "Do you know something?" she asks, "when I said I'd kill you it was the first time you looked at me, really looked at me." "You tell me you're going to kill me, I'll look at you," he said. Erica stands tall and folds her arms over her breast. "You keep an eye on me, make sure I don't, eh?" Ro takes out his knife, watching her. She turns from him and picks up David. "What are you telling Ro?" he asks. "Silly things," she says, "jokes. Play, have fun, I'll call you."

The boys head north beyond Thrain's property, held on course by who knows what combination of purposes and intents. They will arrive eventually at the slough which is a parasite feeding on the Swifter. The ice there is strong enough near the edge to hold them and they will toss boulders toward the centre to test the thickness there. It will be late before they are remembered and found and brought home for food and punishment and sleep. And inside, beyond the cooling bread and the warmth of the kitchen, Erica sits at her dressingtable and writes in a book that has a purple cloth cover and, inside, buff paper ruled over with twenty-five pale green lines on each page. She has been taught calligraphy — a cosmetic craft to complement embroidery, dressmaking, cookery, a little music. She practises, writes her name on the inside of the cover and then:

I see much of God's handiwork here in this land but not God at all. Maybe I think this is why Thrain (even any man) comes to this place. It is to escape Him. But for me He is just something more to miss. Thrain is not enough. His plans wobble. When the hotel is finished who will run it? It is beyond anything. All I wanted or needed was a house big enough to keep boarders, maybe half a dozen rooms more than the four we need ourselves. But not my husband. He wants this thing, this wooden statue to himself. Still, I will say this for Thrain, I think he senses the big joke behind these things that make him mad, but that doesn't stop him. Someday he hopes it will not be something that maybe people will laugh at anymore. He thinks the country will be his and if God comes back to look at His handiwork, there will be very little left of it, and He will be kicked out. I can see Thrain now in my mind. He is standing on the top of Sugarloaf Hill, pointing for God to leave and shouting that he has built his own paradise and has no need for Him anymore. But I hope God tells him that's okay, because there's still death. Thrain is so young inside himself that I don't think he has thought of dying. And now he is out there in the wilderness with old Linden mapping the country in his head, doing what he says is "making a deal with nature." I don't know what that means but it frightens me anyway. What is this making a deal? We do not make deals with nature. It makes deals with us. It says to a man, "Move fast or I will bury you." And it says to a woman, "If you do not move at all you can be part of me and I will be part of you." Separate deals — that is the really big laugh, especially if we don't even know if we've heard right. We live trying to hear what it is being mumbled at us. So, maybe Thrain is right to come to where there is silence and maybe a better chance to listen for the real words that are being said. Yet he is wrong to think he can make a new deal. He is out there in the wilds and he is in trouble. No wonder. But I am in trouble too. For me there is just silence, except when I work as hard as a man. It will be a long time before a woman will be needed to be a woman in this place.

Erica moves away from her lined pages and out into the dim cave on the main floor of Thrain's hotel. It makes her think of a cathedral, except that the light is not stained with the purple and amber and red of the church. Empty, cold, the building groans as if it were giving birth to itself. The chimney squats on its wide base and rises like a monument through log rafters to the roof, and around her the galleries run rigid against shadowed entrances to the rooms. She climbs the stairs toward the noise of carpentry. A dozen tubs came in on the last boat before Thrain left, and Ole Johnson is making the bathrooms ready for them. She begins to help him. It comes naturally now, this bull work. She tucks her sleeves and skirt up and holds, measures, saws, hammers, watching Ole thinking about her, his mind bubbling like cooking porridge over the heat of his desire to cuckold Thrain. She thanks him for this. Thrain would kill him if he touched her. She might kill him herself.

Scann watches and feels the cold insist against his need to remain alert. But they only work, plotting just the bathroom and they do not yet reveal any of the intricacies of Scann's vision. He shivers and wakes. The water is cold. The window, the toilet tank, the mirror over the basin are washed with condensation. He pulls the plug with his toe and feels the warmth of the room touch his skin as the water drains away. He sits up, climbs carefully out of the hard-edged tub and stands on the bathmat in front of the moisture-beaded mirror. He looks at his fragmented reflection and hears a silence within himself that is a signal. He is frightened and excited.

43

The motor of his ambition no longer functions; he is in orbit out among the moments and spaces beyond the refracting atmosphere of his initial vision. He laughs thinly. All is there, in place. He has worked for this, planned for it as if he had honestly thought it might happen; and now, here he is scrubbing the wet mirror with his hand so he can see himself, comfort himself with the reflection of himself. He doesn't look wan or afraid. He glows in health. The reflection is bright-eyed, confident, congratulatory. It disappoints him. He wants to be sick, or at least sickly. He wants to need a drink, companionship, more sleep. He even wants to consider going home. Instead, his own Red King in the mirror is dreaming him dreaming Thrains and Lindens who dream themselves arbitrary dreams of conquest and dominion. But only he, Creator Scann, knows that all dreams are arbitrary and therefore futile, and that dreamers dreaming dreams dream only partial fancies before a last nightmare. Dreams are straight lines in the great-circle world of experience. Dreams are little animals walking their undevious paths into the mouths of traps. Dreams are marten, fisher, fox and lynx who, trapped, are skinned and left as guts. We dream and are dreamed. But the world isn't. Writer Scann walks without thinking, and without dressing, to his room cradling dichotomies in his mind and his clothes in his damp arms. His vision contains his mind and the world. He stands naked between the bed, the basin, the window and the writing-desk letting logic do what it must: destroy itself. And beyond Toebroke Falls, at the cabin beside Water Lake, Trapper Linden waits, sick Thrain lies, marten, lynx, fox and fisher run their true lines toward their jawed futures, the porcupine feeds quietly in his tree, rattling occasionally the quills along the top of his tail, and the wolverine cruises indefinitely, refusing the temptation of a fixed route, knowing that the mighty always move in mad reverberant ways their mischiefs to perform. And outside the cabin it is snowing angel-feathers. Amid this quiet drift, Scann dresses and sits lightly on the edge of his chair. Then he holds his ballpoint ready, and sees.

Trapper Henry Auguste Wallenstein Linden — the Wallenstein is for his grandmother, his mother's mother, whose origins were dim but whose obsession was famous: she believed that what she knew of counties Truro (Ro is named for Linden's Truro) and Hants and Colchester and Pictou, was the world, and she walked them from Cobequid Bay to Pictou Harbour and from Tatamagouche to Shubenacadie (in bare feet in the good weather) "to keep in touch"; fearful of change, suspicious of strangers and preyed upon by the notion that the land would shrivel up around her like burned pastry if she did not "roll out the country" to keep it "as half-flat as it is"; thus, in a day, she might walk from the harness shop in Truro past Old Barns and Beaverbrook to Princeport before most people had digested breakfast, and come back the dozen or so miles in time to eat dinner and tell her daughter and son-in-law that the hills were "making mountains that soon are going to fill the sky", and Henry believed her, believes even now that he keeps his land, makes room for himself in it, by walking it, that it will shroud up around him if he fails one year to master it with his feet; yet, he is more sophisticated than Grandmother Wallenstein (who was born in 1789 and died one hundred and one years later, the year Henry arrived here) because he doesn't anymore think that the world stretches west only to the far reach of Colchester county: he proved this by moving in easy cautious stages through three thousand miles to the valley of the Linden, and now he knows that he could walk west and the land would unroll before him at the horizon forever — H. A. W. Linden is tramping his woods, the snow easing but blowing in his face from the northwest, and he is talking to the trees, telling them of himself. They don't talk back, or if they do he doesn't hear them. He tells a random sampling of them, "He's here, carcajou's here." He stomps forward in his mocassins and snowshoes and senses the contours of the earth beneath two feet of early snow. He raises his face so that blown crystals sting his cheeks. A wolf, he howls: "carcajou." But even wolves can be driven from their prey by the Glutton. He stops, holds his gun like a shield, says to a two hundred year old spruce, "He came after I skinned the cougar, never even heard a snuffle. Eats. Stashes chunks to freeze in trees, in trees to freeze." Linden snorts, walks again, halts. He spies out a rabbit not quite camouflaged in winter white. Marksman Linden holds his rifle to his shoulder and blows its head off. He waits for the twitching to stop. "It's him or me. My trapline or his. Which is it, eh? Do I pick marten heads out of trees or do I get skins? Do I have safe cabins or do I come back to stinking wrecks?" He shakes his fist at the trees. "Can't you smell him? He plays with trees too, you know. Puts meat in your crotch and sprays your feet like a skunk. You'll get bloody lonely with a stink like that around you."

He kneels beside that dead rabbit, upends it, and lets its blood trickle over his bare hands and wrists until there is enough to massage into his skin to kill the scent. He bloodies the gun. He is meticulous. With his knife he cuts off one of the rabbit's feet. The snow is stopping: the sun is breaking through clouds to the southwest. His shadow runs beside him off his right showshoe. He holds the gun and the rabbit's foot and feels in his pocket for the bacon and the fishline that are there. The trees have thinned out, the land slopes, breaks, flattens to a quarter-mile of willows bordering the middle reaches of Mosquito Creek five miles north and west of his Water Lake cabin. He cuts a branch from a spruce and moves in long slow careful steps to the first configuration of willows. The wind has drifted the snow into a gentle mound against the brown stems. He crouches, looks around. He works, saying a litany that curses the wolverine. The fishline is fixed to the bacon; the bacon is fixed to the muzzle of the rifle; the line is fixed to the trigger and around the gun's butt and the smooth hide of the willow. The rifle is buried in the snow with only the bacon in sight. Safety catch off. The spruce branch sweeps away his tracks, and as it sweeps he makes new tracks with the rabbit's foot to lead the enemy to the willows, the gun and the bacon: one yank at it and

Trickster Linden stands again in the shelter of his trees. He looks back across the snow and along the line of rabbit tracks. Linden is satisfied. "Let him read that," he says to the trees, and he begins to circle for home, pausing after a mile to wash the blood from his hands. It comes off easily.

With the darkness he arrives at the Water Lake cabin. The fire is embers. He brings in kindling and split wood to make it up. He too is a good chimney builder; this one draws well and the fire burns easily. The heap of furs beside it groans. Linden stares down through the spastic light of the fire at Thrain whose hand reaches out of the pile toward a birch bowl of water. Linden sits on the bunk, a hand on each knee, head cocked forward, watching. Thrain sucks in the last of the water and puts the bowl back on the floor. He coughs and Linden hears his breath scrape against the back of his throat. Linden rises and goes to Thrain. After a moment he pushes at him with his moccasin. The body sways as a foot-cradle might under the same pressure. He does it again. "Thrain, you rock fine. Are you there? Maybe you died just now." He prods with his foot. "No? then tell me this, when you do die do you want to be put in the lake?" He listens for an answer. "Or do you want it Indian style, the top of a tree? I'll be damned if I'll dig a hole in this weather." Thrain comes awake. He almost sits up and then he collapses again into his pile of dusty furs. "I asked you a question," Linden says. Thrain grunts. "I heard you. You'll die before I do." His thick voice scrapes like a sled over gravel. Linden smiles and prods him more gently with his foot. "So you got a little strength in you yet." He crouches down. "No matter if I put you in a tree or in the ground old carajou'll get you. He can climb them trees and he can dig." There is a long silence. Linden crouches; Thrain's breath rattles softly. "You're scared, Linden."

Linden holds the possibility in his mind for a moment and then shakes his head. "There's a surprise for him out there in the willows just this side of the Mosquito." He lets himself laugh. "If I die," Thrain says, "you put me on a sleigh and drag me back to town so they can see it wasn't you who killed me." "Can't do that." "You better. They'll come after you with a rope." "Maybe you won't die." "I will if you don't help me." Linden rises and kicks the fire to spread it a little. "I told you not to come. I told you you'd be on your own." "I got sick. If you were the one sick I'd look after you." "Never been sick." "Your trapline is, it's got a wolverine." "It'll be well by morning." "Turn around, Linden." He turns from the fire. There is a pistol pointing at him, shaky but mean. "Where'd you get that?" "My pack." "Put it down, boy." He takes a step forward and feels a bullet go past his face before he hears the explosion. Thrain says, "I don't want to talk." Slowly Linden sits before the fire. "When you pass out I'll take your gun." "We'll go together." Thrain's voice bothers Linden. It sounds strong against the sparking of the fire, and now Thrain is laughing. It's an uncontrolled giggle mixed with gleeful sobs. "Linden," he says. He chokes it out; the gun still glints in the firelight. "I had a surprise for you too." Linden laughs with him. "Yes, you did, yes you did too." He gets up knowing the gun is on him. "So put that thing away and let's eat." Stalker Linden prepares a thick soup from the beans and meat in the pot beside the fire and feeds it to Thrain. The gun has gone beneath the furs. Linden knows where, and thinks of his own rifle held under the snow in the crotch of a willow. He feels calm; the encounter with Thrain has stopped up a fierceness in him. His shoulder, where Ro's bullet tore it, radiates a sore tenderness. "Your wife will look after the boy no matter what?" Thrain chews and sluices liquid between his teeth, swallows sorely. "She's that kind of a woman." "Even a half-breed?" "Especially." Thinker Linden nods. He sits on the bunk and smells above the normal stench of the cabin Thrain's sick human body. Then he smells his own. Different. He is puzzled. All carcajous smell alike. He listens across the silence for the sound of a rifle. Everything smells the same dead, man or wolverine. It seems he is waiting for an answer. Thrain's gun comes out from under the furs. He stares at it. One wolverine and one man on his trapline. Two stinking presences. "Put it away," he says. "It's safer between your legs."

"I want to take it outside with me," Thrain says. His eyes look empty, hollowed out. Linden tells him, "It's cold out there." "I have to go." "Then go." Thrain pushes back the furs and emerges from among them. Linden watches. He has seen animals alive in traps with eyes like these: rage, pain, fear; but in Thrain's there is something else. Animals go quiet waiting for instinct to give one last order. Thrain is not quite animal. He crawls, reaches the door, pushes it open, turns back out into the darkness; Linden follows, sees him crouch in the snow, strain: and now he is animal, helpless. Even the gun droops softly. Then he is man again. And Linden thinks that if he wanted to kill him and be innocent of his death he would help him. But he plays God and does not help. He lies back on his bunk and listens once more for the crisp quiet air to bring him the report of his rifle. He hears it distantly. He even hears its echo. Thrain, upright, comes to the door, and then for Linden there is a dreamless moment before it is dawn.

Editor Scann's room — perhaps no bigger than Trapper Linden's cabin — is a place where the light holds. He stands at his window and looks past the edge of the blind into the street. The sunlight hurts his eyes after hours of staring at yellow paper beneath a hundred watt bulb. Linden's horizons retreat infinitely in Scann's mind, and below him strangers he has known for more than twenty years walk single or in groups. There is his wife. He has to think a moment to remember her name. "Odd," he muses, "a girl I know so well." Marion. He remembers her. She still has an accent. A country girl from Yorkshire, a sweet thing then in the midst of the war, but a bit wooden up close. He supposes he must have seen her as a challenge. He watches her stand at the corner with Jane Fairfax, talking as if in fact they had not spent an hour on the phone in the morning. Her broad, forty-six year old figure beams through the flare of her new spring coat, and he thinks he must love her: she has been a fine antagonist for him. The Maginot Line of her devotion has held firm against assault and yet has been blind to all movement around its flank. He has silenced everything except her tongue's quick gun, which has never ceased to chatter above the comfortable suicide of their conjugal contract. He loves her because she is so there, and he is so *here*, finally for these moments empty of the duties of their marriage and standing in this blinded room with this desk and this pen and those scratchings on that paper on this Good Friday. My God: I do know what I do.

He goes to the desk again, understanding the epicentre of Linden's energy. In him there is a man for whom existence is a rear-guard action which erupts with beauties: violences, watching the enemy destroy himself as he destroys you, and ravaging and burning one's own territory before it can be conquered. Life is total war whose essence is defined in acts of endless cunning retreat. The act of advancing, freeing, conquering, brings only the illusion of mastery over contingency while it distracts the mind from the certainty of tyranny and bondage. Victory is for mobs.

Thief Linden balances Thrain's pistol on the palm of his hand for a moment and then, free from reason, tosses it lightly into the bush. It makes a hole in the snow, a blurred image of itself and all the more meaningful for that. The space it has carved during its descent is hollow but filled with light. Snowshoer Linden gazes at it for an instant and then goes on silently down his trail toward Mosquito Creek. There has been a little new snow but no wind. His own breath, the swish of his showshoes are a sin against the quiet. He rebels, shouts, then laughs. The place is his. He begins to trot, swings at tree-trunks with his axe and ducks away from falling wads of snow. Then he walks more slowly, paces himself until the willows appear on his horizon beyond the edge of the forest. He stops where he must turn to retrieve the rifle and the wolverine. It is a delicate moment. He squints over the new-laid counterpane; he looks across the live crystals of light and reads: Once upon a time, maybe ten hours before, an animal, a rusty black one with a creamy stripe from skull to flank to butt came from the west along the line of willows and sniffed the gentle easterly, the air that would bring more snow soon. The temperature was up suddenly, and the moon was hidden in the south by clouds. The animal drifted, scudded along the bank of the Mosquito, held communion with a patch of open water, listened for the sounds and documented the odors of the hunts that were going on around him. Then a new smell challenged him. He followed it upwind, as if disinterested. He wandered, his direction secret except to himself. In the darkness his eyes lost their bloodshot blindness. He crossed the creek, sniffed the remains of a hawk's rabbit and chewed its bones and bits of flesh. *Hors d'oeuvre.* Again he crossed the creek and paused, his leather snout hunting through a library of smells before coming upon the sweet smoke of bacon. He listened, moved forward and came upon the meat. He sniffed the foolish morsel. Closer. It was a new kind of carrion. He sprang, snapped, pulled. The gun went off. The bullet pushed flesh, blood, bone, brain in flecks across the snow. Carcajou, the wolverine, lay dead, and in a while new snow came and covered him.

Linden mushes the yards between the trail and the clump of willows and crouches beside his buried gun. The power of its recoil has lodged it further beneath the snow and back in among the brown and yellow stems. He feels with his mittened hand for the wolverine. Nothing but bits of bacon when he disturbs the bright loose snow. He stops, astounded. He reads the passage again. The images form new meaning: circling, carcajou had crouched in the willows where the bacon smell was least and where he could watch, listen, feel for movement. Springing, he landed on the rifle, the string pulled the trigger, the gun exploded, and carcajou, astounded too, leaped up and back. His trail goes north and east on the far side of the willows, across the creek again and into the scrub beyond.

Henry Auguste Wallenstein Linden stands holding the rifle still tangled in fishline. The thousand square miles of his trapdom shrink to the dimensions of his eye. "Now," he whispers, "the bastard knows I know." He crouches with the rifle to his nose. He sniffs at the frozen rabbit blood that still fouls its barrel and butt. In the high cold air he detects no specific odors but his own moosehide mitt and the sweat of his armpits. His eyes dream violence over against the scrub forest's wall beyond the creek, and his hands slowly wipe snow over the gun, cleaning its surfaces of rabbit blood and cordite. This glutton would be a young one, born maybe three Aprils ago, suckled till that next July and trained by its mother for two summers and two winters after that and then, this past spring, was driven by her from the territory north of the divide. Linden looks at his rifle in his hands. It will shoot the habitual cougar, even at night. Habits betray. Carcajou you bastard. He unbends, walks, thinks. He slings his rifle and talks to the trees. He tells them of the proper balance of nature: land, water, trees, birds, fish, animals, insects, and he himself who has walked the land, drunk the water, built with trees cabins and a bridge across the ravine south of the headwaters of the Moose, who has eaten the flesh of birds, fish, animals gratefully and has always taken skins politely to trade for flour, rice, beans, salt, bacon, raisins and prunes (he loves prunes). He speaks of the coming of the white man to his other territory at the join of the Swifter and his own river, and of Thrain who has followed him from there. And now the wolverine.

"It is time to move on," he says, and stops snowshoeing when he says it.

He has said this many times before, always with freedom and without serious meaning. The words echo. They are like curses without honest strength or force, but he compels them to make a picture form in his mind: himself heading west over the divide, past Cariboo Lake, and carcajou sitting in a forked tree blinking his day-blind eyes slowly and sniffing the light airs to check the gradually fainter smell of the man he is forcing from the land. Linden sees what the wolverine only smells. He looks around him, down the trail toward his cabin where Thrain is lying sick and then back in the direction of his defeat. He stands against a wall of spruce and hemlock. His mind is shocked at what his mouth has said. He glances around as if someone might have heard. Then he begins to walk again, softly, almost with stealth toward Water Lake and his number one cabin.

Thrain is alive and awake. Trapper Linden knows the other's eyes are watching him in the dimness. He hauls traps in from the pegs outside, checks and springs them, packs bait, food, nails for trapping marten, takes up his gun and axe and looks around him. The ritual makes him safe. Except for Thrain — and he can ignore him — all this is normal. He would sing if Thrain weren't there. In Truro there had been plenty of singing. Old John Morrison's father had been drunk with Robbie Burns himself and knew the songs he sang when he wasn't writing his own. "Oh . . . they were screwin' in the wagons, they were screwin' in the ricks, you could na' hear the music for the swishin o' the pricks." There were others, worse. Linden laughs and hums a little, but without the words it isn't the same. It's like trying to cure warts with spit but no spell. He turns on Thrain: he is only a head that lies among the furs. "Stop your damned looks," he shouts. "Take your eyes and get the hell out." He points to the door, unable to explain his feelings or why he is at Thrain's side kicking him hard enough to hurt his own mocassined feet. The man can't move by himself. He is too sick. He moans as he is kicked and his chest rattles. Linden picks up his pack and goes to the door. "If you're here when I get back," he hollers. He staggers under a great weight of pleasure and runs again to Thrain's side. He kneels and hits the body with his fists. "Speak . . . do y' hear?" He sees Thrain watching him, and his anger breaks. He stands abruptly and his dandelion head hits back against the packboard. A vision forms. Carcajou is in the empty cabin, wrecking it, tearing up the place with his claws just for the hell of it, and then he backs and sprays the bed, the food, the furs. The stench rises in Linden's memory and sickens him. "Stay," he says, as if to a dog. "He won't come as long as you're here." The strength in Thrain's voice surprises him: "You didn't get the wolverine." The head rolls away as if to watch the wall. "Too bad." Linden goes to the door and looks out. "He got lucky. It's just a matter of time. I'll give him a few free meals until he gets careless. I got tricks he never heard of."

"Yes," Thrain says. Linden tells him, "It's him or me." He waits for Thrain to reply but inside as outside the cabin there is silence. He closes the door and looks across the clearing and up into the trees. Nothing seems to move. The mid-morning sun is low and its light is weak and grey. The lake is flat white, unfamiliar. The trees creak slowly in a small wind. Snow blows from the roof of the cabin and down his collar. He shifts, slaps at the cold wetness at the back of his neck. He smells himself sweating. At the edge of the clearing he stops, takes off his mitt and finds his watch. He winds it tight and then begins to snowshoe forward into the corridors of moving air that slant between the trees. At intervals he pauses to set a trap or chop a narrow vee into a tree-trunk and fix two nails to catch a marten's skull as it tries to draw back from the bait that Trapper Linden stuffs below and behind the nailheads. There may be nothing left of the marten but a crucified skull after carcajou happens by. Or he might just rip the body with his claws until it hangs tattered and useless against the chopped trunk. It depends. Carcajou is accidental, and trapped Trapper Linden feels the coiled spring of this injustice spang painfully in his gut. He drops a trap, fixes it, tests it and baits it, knowing that when he returns there will be only a leg or maybe a scrap of bloody fur frozen to its snapped jaws.

He goes across his land slowly, stops, plants, chops, nails, baits. He doesn't speak and in the silence he hears hope muttering at the edge of his consciousness. This could be the extreme of Carcajou's territory, the southern side of it where he comes to hunt only occasionally. He could be gone for days, weeks. If the rhythms of setting and gathering were lucky they could force him to pass empty traps and make him follow the wolves on the slopes and pastures of the other side of the divide. He had run north last night, ejected by the rifle, Linden is going north and west himself, his usual route, and he wonders why he hasn't thought to set the south side of his line, up the Windfall to the tributary Moose and beyond to his number three cabin on Cariboo Lake. But what he is doing now is as safely close to his old self as he can get. He will not be driven. The wolverine is not here. H. A. W. Linden sets traps; he chops vees in trunks of spruce and hemlock and fir and drives nails into them. Down by the swamp three miles below his number two cabin he stops and crouches by marks in the snow that tell him a porcupine has plowed by within the hour. He could have gone by a minute ago. Linden stands up and looks around for him. He cocks the rifle and feels angry.

Writer Scann's head rises out of his hundred-watt pool of light and he goes over to the closet on the east wall of the room, opposite the sink. His overcoat and jacket are there; they make the space more empty than if all of the hangers were bare. In one of the pockets are notes on copy paper. He searches and finds it after going through all of his pockets twice. The paper is worn and wrinkled. He stands facing the closet. Between the coat and the jacket he sees the wall — white rough plaster against which the skeleton closet has been nailed. There is a dent in the plaster where someone's suitcase or a flung shoe has struck it. He goes forward and stoops to pick at it with a copypencil. Behind are the original logs with which Thrain built Linden House. He pries once more with the yellow pencil and a chunk of plaster falls away. Beyond is not a solid log but a space between two of them. He stoops closer. He can see into the next room. Still holding the paper he has found in his coat, he puts his eye to the hole. The aperture looks out beside the basin in the other room. He widens the hole. He can see the bed, the desk, the closet opposite. The room is identical to his but it is empty, made up by a careful chambermaid. The extra blanket on the bed is folded exactly like his own. The counterpane is nubbly and without wrinkles. He looks behind him and then puts his eye to the narrow hole again. The closet is bare. He can't see either the top of the desk or the mound of pillows at the head of the bed. He turns, still sitting on his heels, and he smiles. The note in his hand says: "Erethizon dorsatum (the Canadian porcupine). Largest rodent. Blunt round head: fleshy mobile snout. Quills mixed with long soft hair which sometimes hides them. Short stumpy tail. Four front and five hind toes. Terrestrial; can climb trees, but does not live in them as does his South American cousin who has a long prehensile tail. Trappers dislike them because they raid their cabins, but they die easily." Peeping Scann walks out of his stoop and into the room again and drops the note onto the desk. He traces his cubicle with his eyes: the room is his; it no longer caves in on him; the wall against the street is blocked by nightstand, bed and blinded window; the west wall is smooth except for sink and mirrored medicine cabinet; the north wall, which cuts along the corridor behind his desk, holds the phone and the transomed door; and then he sees again the closet-wall with the new hole in it. He wonders if now he has tried to pencil himself out of here: an unconscious escape plan surfacing at the hint of an opening in the closet's plaster. It occurs to him that the thought of escape is morally meaningless except to the oppressor. Incarceration is a form of revenge for which jailers pay. He goes, his own jailer, to the window and looks along the street. He is free to go. But the object of his being here is to confine his own consciousness. And now there is a hole in the wall out of which some of it has already escaped. As its oppressor he tries to hunt it back, but still its east eye is pressed against the white plaster taking possession of an empty room and dreaming possibilities, coincidences, subtleties, flagrant violences against documentary life, and manufacturing delicious subjunctive presences. His mind runs confused. He has lost control.

He moves to the desk again and grasps the back of the chair to lean over the lined yellow paper. He sees and feels nothing. He is surrounded. He takes the chair to the door, steps onto it and peers through the acute angle of the open wooden transom. The hallway is empty. It has cream walls, walnut-stained doors and carpeting which is a deep red slashed by light blue roses. He watches east for someone to walk toward him. His other eye is still at the plaster hole waiting for the door of the next room to open. "The porcupine," he says aloud, "has not the knack of rapid transit. He dies easily. A small blow with a stick between the eyes will do it. This is not

54

true of the water buffalo. The bone between his eyes will often take a 50 calibre bullet as granite will, simply giving up a few chips. The water buffalo is a herd animal, a public personality. The porcupine, however, is a private individual, shy and easily frightened. He need only be turned over to render his quilled armour a sham. He can even be picked up by the tail if you know how." From the stairwell a chambermaid approaches. Her name is Mary Major; her son has a *Chronicle* route and he comes at presstime to collect his papers on a Honda 90 that sounds like a bad case of gastro-enteritis. His mother is in her early thirties; Linden House may in fact be the scene of the event that resulted in a carrierboy for the *Chronicle*. Scann is glad gossip is always inexact. Mary Major is not beautiful but at this moment she is mysterious. She passes beneath him and goes west along the corridor on an unhurried errand. Perhaps she is a messenger, or a harbinger, or it may be simply a tawdry little liason she is off to, a piece *sans resistance* that she will become at the end of the long hallway.

Writer Scann waits at the opened transom. No one else appears. For the first time he feels lonely. He stands straight on his chair, breathes deeply of the air that by right belongs to the corridor. No movement. No sound. He whistles softly: a marching tune. He begins to march lightly on the uneven ground of the chair's seat. He drums with his pencil on the lintel of the door, trekking along his own *Via Dolorosa*: he goes willingly but with pain and sweat. Betrayed. Head high. One eye watching. The other still at the hole in the closet. He whistles well and the sound travels easily through the jaws of the opened transom and out into the dimness of the hallway. But there is no one to hear. He marches hard, a happy madness that releases him, his feet solid on the rutted ground and now he conducts with the copypencil, growling out a ground bass in his throat to help swell the brass at his lips and he pounds the wall with his clenched fist fortissimo. Below him, suddenly, a face. Silence. He steps back involuntarily into space at march tempo. The frame of the bed meets with his head. He lies splayed on the eight by nine carpet. Distantly he hears a key in the lock, the chair being pushed aside by the door, firm quick footfalls. Soon, he opens his eyes. Mary Major is looking down at him from a kneeling position. Her red-brown hair hangs in front of her shoulders. Her freckled skin surrounds blue concerned and puzzled eyes. She leans forward, sniffing and he lets her cradle his head on her arm. "Well, you aren't drunk, Mr. Scann," she says. "What's it all about?" He holds her other arm to raise himself up nearer to the source of her perfume. "Mr. Scann is not here," he says. "He's next door." She pulls back, astonished, and looks at him. "It's true," he tells her. She looks over her shoulder: "How?" "An aperture." He sees her watching him. "Did you know there was no death until nature invented the aperture? Living things simply divided and each half went on as before. No death, no beginning, no end, no sneaking through holes to try to beat the system or be born again."

She pulls away and gets up. He sees that she wears no stockings. "Perhaps," he says, "we wouldn't die if in the end we didn't want to escape." She smiles down at him, touchingly and without malice. Her chambermaid's eyes have perhaps seen even him before. "That's great, got any other news?" Scann is glad to see her. He could not have written a better diversion. "Did you know," he asks, "that a very high Vietnamese official's name is Fun Fun Dong?" He lies back disheartened. His sex life passes before his eyes: it has not been memorable. He waits while watching her. She stands erect and holds the deep vee of her smock across her chest. "Your paper," she says, "gypped Billy out of five dollars last week. Short-changed him when he was buying." Editor Scann sits up and stops looking at her. Both subtlety and blatancy have been wasted. She lives in Billy's wallet. He reaches for his own and holds out five dollars, a splendidly rare gesture, he knows, for an editor to make, but it is designed to wipe the memory of the last few minutes from her mind. She leans down behind her outstretched hand and takes the bill. "What are you doing here?" Her forehead frowns and her eyes look serious. "Does your wife know where you are?" Scann shakes his head, holds onto the bedstead and rises slowly. There may be blood. He goes to the mirror over the basin and feels the back of his head but finds no dampness there. He runs water for a drink. "It's a secret," he says to her image in front of him. "That's a funny way to keep a secret, pounding on the door like you were locked in." She tucks away the five-dollar bill. He fills his glass and drinks. "It's only a secret if you share it." He turns. "Somehow you've been chosen." She looks as if she suspects a trap. "What're you doing?" "Writing." She looks down at the papers on the desk. After a moment: "You cross out a lot." He nods. "I thought you knew how, being editor." It is not a remark. She is somehow serious. He puts the glass down and goes to the desk. Odd. Now that he's in room

322 doing what he wants he doesn't think he's being interrupted. He looks at her again, and feels diffident but eager. She watches him, not giving herself away. She isn't George, Marion, Shirley. "Writing's not a straight line," he says. She sees his hand covering the pages. Maybe she thinks he is protecting them. "A story?" she asks. He picks up the manuscript, but his mind is remembering his notes about the Mortons. He doesn't know how to begin talking to her. This is not a private kind of madness, like marching at the transom. He suspects its motives are sentimental — and her arrival too. "Sit down," he says uncertain. "I'll read you some." A story for her. He does not judge the moment now. It might even contain all of his honesty. Her eyes blink against this new light he is shedding. "We're not allowed to stay in guest's rooms — when they're in them too." She stands awkward.

He ignores her, calculating that by this time she is through for the day at the hotel, and he takes up his notebook in his left hand and a sheaf of manuscript in the other. "It's a story that's a little different," he says, struggling for a way into it. He paces, looking at the pages of his opened book. Wedding guest Mary Major holds her own lapels and watches him. She begins to look wary. Scann's movement is random and she can see his face better from another angle, and then from in front of the bureau. Soon, Quarterhorse Scann has cut off her escape and she is coralled between the bed and the outside wall. Slowly she sits, listening, because what she will hear may be good gossip. Scann's eyes focus inward and give her his view of Thrain years away from the cabin at Water Lake. His aircraft has been designed, built, crashed, built again and has been flying now for more than ten years. David and Ro are grown up and up to their hams in the waters of Marble Creek, fifty miles to the northwest, shovelling gravel into sluiceboxes and making wages from the gold dust that gathers on the mat at the bottom of the run. 1935. Their fate is not unusual, except that they are luckier than most. In winter they stay at Linden House and play hockey on Saturday nights and on Sunday afternoons they ski from the trestle on top of Sugar Hill and jump for a ten dollar prize, longest jump takes all. Thrain sees them seldom. He is away looking for precious metals. Mary knows the aircraft: it is more famous here than the Spirit of St. Louis. Ginger Cootes and Sheldon Luck and Grant McConachie are the pilots she has heard of, but it is Thrain's aircraft rather than pilot Thrain she thinks she remembers, although it stopped flying shortly after she was born, the year Thrain flew away north and west and disappeared for the second time in his life.

It looks like a discarded lifeboat, with a high slab of a wing, a square tail and a motor that pushes rather than pulls the whole construction about the sky. The cabin is small, the rudder and stick rudimentary, the one instrument a weighted nail and a string with a ballbearing attached which measures turn and slip as closely as Thrain feels necessary. Airspeed he knows by the sound of a thrumming strut. There is no compass. Thrain does not believe in navigation as such; he has learned the country he flies over mile by mile, and he is never in so much of a hurry that he can't put down for a day or two on a lake and wait out a storm. What he does have are spare parts. He trims the aircraft by shifting the weight of them and his supplies and prospecting tools. Like Trapper Linden and Grandmother Wallenstein, Thrain re-creates the land beneath the leading edge of the glass cabin in which he sits: the earth rolls out ahead of him in pocks and slashes, in white water and blue-green, and there is a fine intimacy in his detachment from it.

"This," Scann tells Mary, "is the story of Philippa Morton. Do you know about her?" Mary pushes her hair back over her shoulders. "I don't think so. Is it a long one?"

"Only long enough. Canadians are a documentary people. The facts, the facts. It's like this: Americans say, I came, I saw, I suffered and what they write is a literature of keening nostalgia. Canadians say I came, I saw and produce languishing statistics. The Europeans say only I came, and all else follows from that simple arrogant fact. . . It's not hard, you see, to be a critic."

Critic Scann goes to the window and looks down into the April street whose detail dissolves in his delight at having an audience. "Maybe I better go," Mary says. Scann begins quickly, his voice loud against the pane in front of him and his notebook and sheaf of blank pages fallen to his sides. Audiences won't wait. The trappings of composition bore them. He tells Mary the story Gauguin quotes in his *Journal* about Catherine the Great, who told one of her bedroom courtiers that she wished sometimes a common brute of a man would break into her quarters and rape her. The perfumed dallier passed the request on to a private soldier, giving him a key to the royal apartments and the understanding that he would be publicly whipped if he did not do as he was instructed. The soldier appeared, ravished her and disappeared back into the ranks of his regiment. Catherine was pleased. The courtier, greedy for more favours than he was already used to, finally told the Empress that it was he who had made the arrangements. He was immediately taken out and killed — horribly.

Mary stirs uneasily on her bed.

"It is Gauguin's opinion that by this act alone she could be judged Great." Scann stands now against the foot of the bed. "Well, I guess there were lots more where he came from," Mary says. "You don't think she was Catherine the Great? Just Catherine the practical or maybe Catherine the petulant?" "Catherine the lucky. She could do what she wanted." She stands up and private soldier Scann pushes her back onto the edge of the bed and holds her there by the shoulders. He is already in the middle of things. "Listen," he says into her eyes, "most women are Catherine but she was great because she understood." He stands back. "She understood. I tell you about her to *remind* you, to give you an example against which to measure Philippa Morton." Mary wipes her mouth with the back of her wrist, as if he had been kissing her badly, and stares up at him. But he feels the tidy winds of communion blowing between them, and he begins with Thrain in his aircraft flying west and south from Linden, on no fixed course because he wants only to find a new lake where he can relax and fish. "You can guess what happens now," he tells her, but she doesn't want to speculate. Just to sit with the noise of flying in her ears and the promise of good things to come. The motor cuts; bursts of power return for seconds, once for half a minute, which gives Thrain counterfeit security. He looks to choose a place to put down, a smooth deep patch of water big enough to serve his crippled approach and, if possible, lying west into the prevailing wind. He sees it to his left and banks, turns left, banks again, turns right, lines up a thousand feet above, and a half-mile east, of the lake. There is time to look beyond and around the place where he will be marooned. South, still to his left, there are buildings sheltered by trees, which thin out to natural rolling pastureland. He knows where he is, even though he has not flown this precise course before. He slips the aircraft closer to the lake's southern shore and lets its white hull touch and settle when it will. His approach is quiet; perhaps a flight of ducks water-walking to launch themselves would make more noise than his settling, planing, stopping, drifting.

He reaches for his paddle and goes out onto the hull between the pusher-prop and the tail assembly. This has all been done before. The craft swings out of the dainty westerly and heads toward land where a dock lies perpendicular to the water's edge. He drifts like civilisation toward the under-developed shore and is met by dogs with grey, black and tawny fur and the tipped-up square mad eyes of their grandfather wolf. Pilot Thrain throws out the anchor and lets it snub on bottom a few yards out. The dogs bay up and down the wharf, craning their necks toward the water as if they hoped it might become suddenly solid so they could run across it and attack the stranger in the winged boat. Odysseus Thrain sits waiting. With his long paddle in his hand the aircraft steadies itself in the eastbound wind and the chorus of dogs make strophe and antistrophe on the dock and along the shoreline. Beyond, pines border a broad pathway to corral, barns, bunkhouses and the tall whitewashed Morton home. He has flown farther south than he intended. He is puzzled by the quiet. This is not his country. It seems benign, dressed in light greens and browns and with the June sun closer, warmer than above the divide where he usually flies. Except for the dogs it could be deserted; they are tiring now and some are only yapping and others whining. He turns his back on them and searches among his tools for the proper wrench that will help him begin repairs, but he knows that he would rather be ashore. He suspects only a fouled gasline.

A screendoor slams and Thrain watches a man approach the wharf, heel the dogs and stand with his hands at the sides of his mouth to direct his voice toward the aircraft. It is a soft voice, a negro voice from out of a negro throat. "They say for you to come on in now. Say you must be hungry." Thrain hauls anchor, paddles to the dock, ties up the aircraft and follows the old man who talks only to the dogs until he chains them to the side of the bunkhouse, then he mumbles quietly to himself as they go toward the screendoor through which he had emerged. But before he enters he stops and points in the direction of the front of the house. "You go in there. Miss Cecilia'll be down now, and maybe Miss Amantha too." Thrain, with helmet and goggles in hand, climbs the three steps to the wide veranda. He knocks on the door and waits.

Narrator Scann stops. His story rises in his throat, sick with the heavy cookery of description. Mary waits too. She adjusts the split ends of her chambermaid's smock above her crossed-over kneecap while she looks up at him. "Does he fall in love with Philippa?" she asks, her eyes wanting it to happen and to hell with the preliminaries. "Thrain is forty-eight years old and Philippa is fifty-five," Scann says. "Does that make a love story?" "Well, how about Cecilia," she says practically. "Cecilia is thirty. But she's ugly, wears trousers, has her hair in a crew-cut." He pauses, pinching his lower lip between thumb and forefinger. "But she probably has big breasts." Small Mary looks around corners: "Then maybe she isn't all ugly. If he could just make her start growing her hair and get into a skirt and sweater maybe he could help her see she is quite beautiful — you know, to him anyway. After all he's forty-eight."

Scann quivers, winces. "I'm forty-eight," he says without much thought or dignity.

Mary sits straight on the bed suddenly and her face softens: "Please, you don't look it." She gets up and puts her hand on his arm. After a moment she says, "You're a funny man. What're you doing sitting here trying to make up stories about real people?" She goes to the door and puts her fingers on the knob, ready to go. "Thanks anyway: for the five dollars, Billy'll be glad to have it back." And she goes, not so much out as off like a light. Stunned, Scann blinks into the darkness she has left behind. His brain goes angry and fumbles for something to hurl after her. "You don't deserve me," he shouts, his voice tearing at its edges. He finds he means it and pushes the chair to the transom again. He climbs onto it and the rose-festooned hallway erupts from the gloom below him. "I won't forget this." Heat burns at the blackness. Points of light appear: flowers of shame. His audience is gone. He launches himself from the chair onto the eight by nine carpet and stands stiff with his back to the door. A funny man, he begins consciously to recite: "Blunt, round head. Quills mixed with long soft hair. Trappers hate them because they, too, wreck cabins. But they die easily." He puts the chair back at his writing desk. Light, bright, white snow starts to drift. He follows Woodsman Linden off the blazed trail and along the tracks of the porcupine. The drifts are deeper here. Downed timber stops them. The footprints in the pristine white pull Linden's eyes along their trail, but the strength of his anger ebbs.

Scann gathers calm about him and selects, programs the days ahead, leaves the porcupine, as he has left Thrain, in poised limbo. "And don't come back," he tells Mary as he plunges beyond the chaos of mere life to where the absolute energies of the universe command. Thrain remains sick at the cabin and also before the

61

Morton's front door; Linden moves to his cabin at Mosquito Lake. He eats, sleeps in front of a snapping spruce fire, gathers more traps and goes west with them to his number three cabin on Cariboo Lake, which sits on the top of the divide and whose waters flow both north and south. Here, he fishes through the ice and hooks a twelve pound char. It is a small but necessary victory. Now the lake is a trap and the big silver and black fish is the bait. He lies at the door of the cabin and watches as the light rises and glares and then begins to fade. Nothing. He is cold. His rifle is long and heavy. The clouds parade east until finally the sky is clear. The moon rides up over his left shoulder and discovers movement on the snow-covered ice. He fires. The cold pain of rising and running forces sounds from his throat but he fires twice more before he comes to the fish. The dead shadow beside it is the char's own. He looks right, down the length of his own black shape lying on the snow and thinks he sees eyes reflect the moon. The gun flashes muzzle-flame and its sound rips and echoes. Nothing. No scream or grunt or even feet whispering through the snow. A final echo arrives and he is alone with the frozen fish. Trapper Linden finally moves, bends to pick up the char by its splayed tail, and his own warm stench bellows out from beneath his clothes. Under the clear sky he feels the temperature drop past zero and he knows that in this cold he is a beacon odour, unnatural in an almost scentless world.

He carries the brittle char to the cabin and chops it into small pieces with his axe. Together with snow, he puts them in his large cooking pot and sets it at the back of the fire. The snow melts, the fish softens, becomes gumbo and its guts gurgle and work one last time. In the morning he puts the pot near the door to cool and he goes to the edge of the lake where he cuts stiff willow wands and brings them to the cabin. The sun is up and bright. The cold remains. Before noon he has made a pile of frozen fishballs laced with sharp bent willow sticks. Swallow one and when the ball melts in the wolverine's stomach the pointed sticks will spring straight. Death comes slowly, horribly.

Scytheman Linden snowshoes back to the Mosquito Lake cabin, sowing death as he walks. He even finds a fisher unmolested in one of yesterday's sets. He sleeps well on a full stomach and remembers where each death-ball has been placed. If tomorrow just one is gone.

But when he goes back over the trail they are all gone, and so are all but the heads of two marten lured to Linden's spiked vees. He looks for the balls. They have been wedged into the forks of trees as if carcajou knows that the spring sun will melt them safe. The work, the wasted fish and cunning, the thirty miles of snowshoeing presses against Linden's ribs. He counts balls and begins to see his traps overturned, sprung, and the bait gone. He hears, sees, smells his breath as he crouches for a long time holding a closed trap in his mittened hands. He begins again to talk to the trees. In the cold, they snap back. He stops speaking and begins to dream, filling the blanks and the voids of his mind with it. The wolverine runs, jumps, plays with him, is taught to kill, to fetch and carry, to make the territory safe from other carcajous. They sleep together in warm cabins, the wildness gone or harnessed. He will go a little north in the spring, hunt a female, kill her, take her young and make them weapons against any others that might come this way. It is a pleasant dream he dreams, and a gentle warmth spreads through him and makes him unwary. He doesn't want to move from this good place where he does not hunt nor is he hunted. Gardens and apocalypses melt together. He smiles as the warmth rises in him, bearing upward with it a small suspicion which worries at the edge of his mind. Across his trail a porcupine moves, humping along in the direction of the lake and his unlocked cabin. He starts but doesn't move. The gun remains still. His hands have dropped the trap. The porcupine disappears into the forest. Downed Linden's mouth, eyes, nose, and brain behind his fur-covered forehead are dry. From a distance he sees his hands trying to reach out. Suddenly he knows he is dying, and he falls with open mouth against the snow, swallows more and more and more until the moisture sucked out of him by the cold is replaced and he is able now to move. He rises to his knees, takes a further handful of snow and stuffs it in his mouth. On his feet, he looks at the fallen closed trap and begins to reach down for it. As if a fault in his guts suddenly shifts he begins to quake and his skin shrinks so that he groans with the pain of it. His mind closes down tight around the urge to motion, to a momentum that can force him toward the Cariboo Lake cabin. A marionette dangling from the strings of his will he goes spindly forward. He sees sprung traps, blazes on trees. He forces himself toward trotting, for balance, for speed. Finally, his mind leaves off conducting motion and begins to understand the cold insanity of the dream it had dreamed. Carcajou. Carcajou. Carcajou. Carcajou. He smells himself again and knows with triumph that he is living once more, and moving, and that this is not part of the freezing-dream. And then the luxury of rage. He shakes a hand he knows is frozen at the marching trees and shouts at them. "Watch, you green bastards, watch. Hide him if you want. He's going to need friends. Yes he is." The talk is stronger than his smell, and it leads even to laughter.

And later, a mile from the Cariboo Lake cabin, he feels the heat of his body begin to thaw at the frozen hand and he takes his mitt off to keep the frost in it until he can nurse it properly. The lake appears, then the cabin. The porcupine is not there. He pushes the door open and fills his cooking-pot with snow. He sits on his bunk and looks at the hand. The fingers are ivory white and the knuckles are without colour. He packs the snow around his hand and moves it gently, still breathing hard and grunting out sounds of wonder at his stupidity. The snow softens, begins to melt and he rubs it over his knuckles and fingers. "We've been playing and hoping," he says out loud. "He'll play until — " He sits and watches while the snow melts and the white shrinks to spots and then disappears. The skin is tender but it will not blister or go too proud. He spreads grease on it and puts his mitt back on. When the fire is lit and the birch logs are throwing heat he lies on the bunk and sleeps. He wakes, builds the fire, eats. The hand is sore. He is gone from his trapline. Carcajou has it now. He grins. He has stopped working for the wolverine. He sits quietly, waiting. Eats again. The soreness in the knuckles diminishes. He takes the mitt off and breaks and cleans the rifle. Loads it. Nothing moves outside. There is no wind. Even the trees don't creak. At sundown he sleeps again, the effects of exposure clinging to him. He wakes late with the sun and listens for the wolverine who must be curious by now. Nothing. The silence is both friend and enemy. He is well. The hand is only tender. It works. It wants to work. He makes up the fire, cooks bannock and brews old dusty tea. He sits again and waits with his rifle across his knees. Soon, he hopes, soon. He repairs stretchers for skins. Carcajou will try the door. There will be a squeak of paws on the packed snow out front and then he will try the door. It will be one trap that he can't put his paw under and turn over so that it will spring and give up its bait. But at sundown Bait Linden is tired, more exhausted than he can remember. Yet he stays awake and listens. He thinks about going to the door but he doesn't want to give himself away. And then he doesn't go because it would be bad luck. He has set his trap and he must not look to see if his prey is circling it. And finally he is afraid to go. He no longer knows what is out there. He sits with his gun and stares at the door. His heart squelches in his chest like a running foot in a waterfilled boot. The small flames in the fireplace throw sudden shadows. If he were to move, the sound of it would reach — no, not the sound, the smell of him, his essence would be pushed out under the door into the iced moonlight, and carcajou, carcajou. There was once no evil in this trapdom, and now there seems no antidote.

H. A. W. Linden knows now that his grandmother Wallenstein had observed well how the land folds up if it is not walked over by the feet of him who would live on it. But she had been only a self-appointed stand-in, a priestess at an old altar guessing how it once must have been. She could only have lost the land by leaving it. Her feet had the whole weight of Truro, Hants, Colchester and Pictou in them. Here, at this moment, Linden has no weight at all, and it is the footpad of the wolverine that presses the land down to keep its horizon in place. He sits without traplines or traps, without courage or resort, a simple consciousness revolving slowly over something new he has not been able to stop from happening. Hunter, hunted, huntless. Tracker, tracked, trackless. The unsaid declensions he has lived rot his mind. Dreamer, dreamed, dreamless. Timer, timed, timeless. Huntless, trackless, dreamless, timeless: he sits motionless, mindless. Less. Less. Writer Scann watches his ballpoint define total war, where hunt, track, dream, time, motion and mind drop like masks and the face of survival appears, freed, and final. And then he looks away toward his witness in the cabin at Water Lake. Thrain sleeps. Thrain sleeps without fever now, moving slowly under the cougar and wolf hides. The movement is strong and the face above the furs dreams. The fire, a bed of coals, ticks out its warmth like a clock. Yesterday Thrain was out and walking. Tomorrow he plans to find Linden's path and to begin to build muscle and confidence enough to find the man who left him to die. He may kill him. The luxury of the decision is happiness. He dreams.

The Great Beast, Judgment, the Stopping of Time: only bad writers go in for endings. Apocalyptician Scann sits worried among the silences of Good Friday night at Linden House. He hears his own thin breathing, watches it fog against the cold edges of his vision, hears it become only wretched history echoing emptily in the tiny airbubble of his room. He puts his head down onto the yellow pad and sleeps, dreams the dreamer (Thrain) dreaming a dream of Trapper Linden small within a stand of thick-butted spruce. Closer. He lies on a crust of snow. The darkness beside him is not his shadow. It spreads from tattered flesh. Parts, blue and frozen, rest in the arms of trees. The wolverine stands humped over in strong moonlight, tearing. The witness fails; Thrain has wrecked his fever, and now the momentum of his new strength floods toward confrontation. Dreamer Scann wakes, no longer afraid of apocalypses where divine retribution orders an ending. He leaves Thrain, as God might any man, to pray for absolutes before he goes out to face the world the way it really is. We dream and are dreamed, but the world isn't. Grey-faced, Scann the man, looks in the mirror above the basin and repeats: the world isn't. He holds his reflection in the beam of his eye and looks at it again. The world isn't dreamed: once upon a time. That's arbitrary. The rest is absolute. And into this world some Mischief dreamed forever-discretionary man. "Think of it, Scann," he says into the mirror, "a *thing* to whom once-upon-a-time happens every moment of its life." And all it produces are thumbs to put against the perfectly spinning top of time to make chaos. He gestures as largely as the small mirror will allow the yells into the silence. He must answer himself, as must Linden, but not Thrain or the wolverine. Those two will become one, and then the real battle will begin.

He takes his small awareness back to the desk and the ballpoint and the yellow pages with his own absolute system upon them. He turns pages and reads Thrain and Linden back into his mind again, abandons Thrain and watches Linden whose eyes are open; there is a small unfocused light in them, a steady light as when the sun is still below the horizon. Then, as if thinking were not enough, he moves. He rests the rifle butt on the floor and the barrel against the side of the bunk. Carefully. He listens and then he rises to his feet. Deeper breaths make clouds against his mouth and the tip of his nose. He goes to the fire and stirs its embers with a stick, puts birch bark against them and watches it curl, blacken, flame. He lays small chips against the flames and then some kindling and finally split logs until the flames are stretching up the chimney. He stands before it, not for heat but for light. It jumps against his eyes, an extra thing that carcajou cannot command. He takes his pot to the door. Stops. Reaches and opens it. The black shape there

66

is the porcupine. The rifle is loaded. He holds it, aims at the loping outline and pulls the trigger. Snow powders, rises, drifts against the windless dawn. The short scream of the bullet matches his own and he runs after the rattling beast until it disappears into the trees. He is laughing. It breaks out of him as he has just broken out of the cabin, and he begins to undress, dancing on one foot and then another to remove mocassins, stockings, pants, everything. He goes in circles and throws what he takes off up onto the low roof of the cabin. Naked he runs, picks up the pot and fills it with snow. Inside, he closes the door, puts the pot on the fire and crouches, waiting. The snow hisses and then melts. He takes balsam needles from the boughs on his bunk and boils them in the water. With this he washes his hair, face, neck, body, limbs and feet and then stands away from the fire to dry. He brings in his clothes. They still smell a little. Too much. He puts them on and takes his axe outside. He cuts and gathers piles of balsam boughs and stacks them outside the cabin. He builds a fire, a big one, six feet long and three feet wide. He pokes and breaks it until it is a bed of coals onto which he piles the green boughs. And now he lies on top of them. He is making once upon a time happen to him. He does not consider whether this is control or the beginning of the end of his fate.

He lies behind a curtain of smoke and rising heat, unfocused, unfocusing; he sweats, sings songs he learned fifty years ago, sweats, turns when the heat becomes unbearable, sings again in his balsam bath a lyric of his own: "We'll smell no more, smell no more. By all the gentle gods of war, the ruby lips of fire, the blue-winged jay sits down the way and calls to carcajou, but they'll never know, they'll never know, the balsam smell is me."

Rising hot out of the flames as the green branches finally take fire, he gathers bait, nails, traps, his axe and rifle, puts his snowshoes on backwards and goes at a steady six miles an hour into the forest north of the cabin. Random Linden walks across his land again, lets directions choose him, allows whim to govern all he does. Below a nailed vee he sets a trap and covers it as if by accident with snow shaken from branches above it. He covers his trail and leaves in another direction. He drops bait and surrounds it with buried traps. He plans nothing. He kills a rabbit, holds it up as if it were a jug of wine to look at it, then he takes a char hook out of his vest and secures it, with the rabbit on it, by a chain to a dead log. He is delighted with his inspiration. He kills more rabbits, listening to the holler of his rifle reclaim his land. And then at Mosquito Lake he finds he still has a little light left and his momentum is not yet spent. He goes beyond the cabin, down the trail toward Water Lake. There is a gorge where the small waters of the creek rattle down an incline before meandering and feeding beaver swamps below. The earth folds here, making valleys ten or twenty feet deep that lead to the gorge and the creek. Over one hangs a fallen spruce. Balsam Linden stands at its butt and sees below old tracks that go in the direction of the swift unfrozen water of the gorge. The sun is suddenly gone but night is not yet here. He takes out his watch. It has not been wound and it has stopped. The hands point to some anonymous moment of darkness that had occurred during his sleep. It seems right that it ceased to tick then, but now he needs it. He winds it, puts it back in its leather pouch and pulls the strings tight. Its tick is loud in the present silence as it begins again to live the moments of Linden's sleep. He edges out and down the slant of the fallen spruce, over the outcroppings of windbare rocks to the middle of the small valley. On fishline, he lowers the watch. It buries itself beneath the surface of the snow. Now, leaning far down, he manages to swing an open trap upside down above it, and then he secures it by rope to the trunk of the tree. He holds his breath and listens. The dollar watch ticks. The trap lies falsely, ready for the paw that will turn it over. There are no tracks, no human spoor, just the tick intriguing. He goes back to the cabin, skins and guts the rabbits, eats a pair along with rice and tea, and goes to bed as tired as he has ever been.

When he wakes the sun is nearly as far above the horizon as it will climb that day. He builds another balsam bath and when he rises once more out of it he stands by the frozen lake listening to it heave and grind, crack and complain. He stays for a while and hears it out. In the still cold it works until at a moment of extreme tension it splits from shore to centre in one long whiplash of relief and is suddenly silent. He leaves on showshoes and walks in yesterday's footfalls back toward the Cariboo Lake cabin. Nothing is touched, sniffed, turned over, disturbed. No paw marks. He walks carefully in his own steps, surrounded by the smell of balsam, without the tick of his watch and with only his white breath to remind him that it is the wolverine who has disappeared and not himself.

In the cabin he sits again on the bunk, still more insubstantial among familiar odours. Carcajou knows the game now and will not play it. Lone Linden leans against the cabin wall, his mind void and drifting. Then it begins to picture Thrain. He must be dead by now. He sees him stripped and frozen lying in an open field belly up, and Linden is watching from a tree up wind, just another balsam smell no matter from which direction the wolverine happens by. This will be too much temptation for carcajou. Let him eat. Let him eat more. And when he is full and slow and unwary, put a bullet below the hump of his shoulders. Linden can hear the scream and cough, the grunt, the thump of muscles in the snow. He can see the twitch of nerves, the descent of predictable wolves, the smell of *clean* and a view of the trapline clear and free. Linden dreams and hunts again.

A final bath in the early morning, and then he moves off on his snowshoes, sure there will be no evidence of carcajou. He sets his traps as he has always done, making a day of it, practising for normality. The weather is milder by ten degrees, as if now, having settled for the winter, it can afford some benevolence. He is half-way to Mosquito Lake before it occurs to him why carcajou is not here with him: he is at Water Lake feeding off Thrain and the supplies there. Linden begins to run.

His pace settles so that he knows he can cover the distance by afternoon. At a windfall he caches his remaining traps. At the Mosquito Lake Cabin he leaves his pack, his axe, nails, bait, the tools of his trade. With only his rifle to swing at his side like a rockerarm as he goes, he makes time down the trail, sweat beginning under his arms and between his thighs, and the smell of himself breaking through the overlay of balsam. He approaches his ticking time-trap, passes it. Then he doubles back, pauses at the sharp edge of the ravine, unstraps one showshoe and bends to remove the other. The movement is too quick. He falls forward and down, his rifle going on before him as he bounces off one snowbare rock and lands in a wind drift with his right thigh broken. Not knowing where he is, he moves and the upsidedown trap twists in the snow, shuts against the loose fur of his parka just below his shoulder blades and holds him immobile. His ear is against the soft surface of the snow and beneath it his watch ticks. Loudly. There is no other sound. He is held by trap and pain.

He begins to push at the snow around him and then beneath his legs so that finally he is hanging nearly upright buried to his armpits in the drift. His weight is held by the trap anchored to the spruce above him and he leans his good leg against the supporting snow. In a new silence he hears the ticking once more, and by digging where it sounds he retrieves his timepiece. He doesn't know whether it is thirteen hours slow or eleven fast. But it is later than the sum of all his time on earth.

Then he sees the rifle again. Its barrel rises blue-black six inches above the snow almost a yard beyond his right hand. He hangs against the trap's rope and reaches for the gun. The ends of the broken bone in his thigh shift, grind, pinch, and pain hammers through his leg and spine to his brain. He does not remember retrieving the rifle, but when he comes to consciousness once more he is holding it before him and his chin is resting on its butt as if he is in water and the gun is a piece of driftwood. The rifle, the watch, the broken bone in his leg, the trap; he is his own bait. Carcajou will come but the rifle will kill him. He pushes the watch deep into the snow and covers it well. Its ticking is hypnotic and he thinks now he must refuse sleep. He yells the wolverine's name and listens for an echo. And then he is silent. There is something wrong. The sun is too high. Carcajou will not come till dark. He blows his breath out into the ravine's still air. It smokes, rises. He relaxes down into the snow and packs it around him for warmth. Perhaps a little sleep. Dangerous. Dangerous.

Author Scann leans back in his chair, conscious of himself seeing Linden having become the object of all the moments and movements of his own trapdom. One does not invent a beginning for a creator, or an ending, but only records his confrontations with the possibilities his creation has revealed; and where all things are possible then there must be evil as well as good, the spectacle of the creation itself growing a mind of its own, and even the actual death, one way or another, of the creator himself. Possibilities. They are inherent and infinite. They force questions, not answers, and to consider beginnings and endings is simply to rope off a little space for Armageddon. Linden hangs from one culminating possibility. This uniqueness may be the key to the house of the immortals. And there is a paradox: he is freed now to be at once a number of things. Scann is humble but proud. Linden is poised at the edge of becoming eternal. But his author's hand is cramped, his mind is nagged by small pain: he drifts a little, pictures Marion at her TV watching David Frost, his childrens' faces, Shirley in bed and perhaps lonely, Mary Major considering the Mortons, his empty office at the unedited *Chronicle*, the hole in his closet wall, himself being interrupted by a sore molar. He puts his pen down on the desk, and tries to think calmly about his dentist, to be understanding, compassionate about his troubles. George, you let me down by impinging, as if you were real life instead of a disinterested expert. Dentists aren't supposed to be part of the system, any more than economists or sociologists. Lindens are, Thrains, wolverines, porcupines. Their acts are contingent. That means conditional on something uncertain, George. Accidental. They create life. You are supposed to guard against it or help head it off. That's why sea captains, soldiers, gentlemen, drug addicts, criminals and trappers are asked to carry the weight of the great questions of the ages. Never dentists, George, dentists are for answers. When you bring Johnny to your office with you, savage at a distance some robed monks, go hang-dog looking for my advice and then hammer my tooth with the butt of your pick and say it has to be pulled, George, that's getting out of line, really presuming. Did the goddamned tooth need to come out, or did *you* need to pull a tooth? That's the question. Life poses similar ones. And now I sit here with your tooth in my head, George. *Your* tooth. That's what happens when an expert becomes contingent. You don't accidentally pull or fill teeth. You're not a creator, George, you've got a beginning, middle and end. You do not become. You are. You have a certificate that says so. Go beyond that and you live in my mouth and choke me with the very life I hired you to help me avoid. This is a world-wide complaint, George, from hippies to pensioners: experts living all over us like viruses manufacturing new life when all they're supposed to do is make the old one bearable. You've had your beginning and middle. My cheque at the end of the mouth will settle your account. It's you or me. Scann rises and goes to the basin to run water into the glass so he can take two aspirin. He looks in the mirror and watches himself swallow the medicine. No biographer, no serious critic, can escape concluding that there is more to Scann than his works and, in fact, he himself may be the more interesting of the two. At four, when his sister was born, he stole a doll from an infant neighbour to have for himself. It was cold, but he transformed it into a baby and when it was live enough he took it out back of the prairie farmhouse where he had been born, placed it on his father's choppingblock and hammered at it with a hatchet. It's composition-head retained its likeness and its blue eyes stared up at him out of a faceful of dents and cuts. It did not cry or bleed. It did not die. Each time he hit it, his mind saw it more clearly. It entered into him. He buried it behind the woodpile in soft unused earth. He carried with him from then on a vision of his own making: a dented face and blank blue eyes. He lived with it, never sure when it would appear. He became anxious. He had tried to kill but he couldn't. He couldn't tell anyone. There was no one to tell. He tried to construct other visions to blot out the doll. One day, years later, he managed another. He took some matches from the kitchen and went across the road and into their neighbour's August field. It was a tranquil moment. The matches flared, burned black and went out. He lit a stalk of brown stubble. The wind caught it. He watched the flame run and then jump. He stamped on it but it escaped out from under his foot. That was the picture he kept afterwards in his mind. Not crawling fast along the ditch, running back from tractor, to car, to barn fence to hayloft, nor his need to return to the field to watch with his father and mother and the neighbours. No one had found the doll, and now they suspected only a cigarette butt. He thought about it: the dented face, the widening circle of black escaping out from under his foot. There was something funny, but he didn't know what the joke was. He couldn't laugh and reveal himself. That was also a picture that lodged in his mind: himself needing to laugh for some reason or another. He made jokes of his own after that, but it was other people who laughed. At him. Which excluded him. And that was also a joke. He still does not understand. But he has come to know that there are two systems of natural law in the world: one for him and one for everybody else. And that may be the big joke among all the small ones. "You're a funny man," the chambermaid had said. "What are you doing sitting here trying to make up stories about real people?" "Because," he says, looking up into the jaws of the door's transom, "I want to see how they make out under the rules the world made for me." He stands stiff and unprotected in the middle of his eight by nine carpet. Then he laughs as if it is necessary that someone do so. He is not unaware. There are clues. He suspects time, he always has, that his time became somehow anchored at the beginning of his life. The tension between where he is and where he must be is immense. Distortions occur everywhere. He picks up his pen and goes to the window. He pushes aside the green shade with his index finger, the pain in his tooth gone, and ponders again the moment he has come upon in the snow at the bottom of Linden's ravine. Once upon a time there was no time. Things existed for measured moments at God's own pleasure. Man was carried by a gentle force through all the space of his days until he ceased by God's will to have any more measures of his own added to the grand and unnoticed continuum that enveloped him. Now time is all there is: fragments of the old continuum. Each gets a handful when he is born, and it is usually gone, used up, by thirty. Then, one must borrow, or steal. Even Linden may have spent his own last moment. Editor Scann worries, stares out through the window into darkness and feels exhaustion eat holes in his mind.

But Thrain crouches at the edge of Linden's ravine and sees a half-century of action stuffed into a moment that dilates, swells and bursts toward the instant of death. Scann listens and sees: Thrain is shouting silently, axe in hand. And below, Linden wakes, coughs phlegm from his throat and spits. There is an echo, and then another. Softly. It is a drier sound than the one Linden remembers making. He tries again. The other cough is repeated. He lifts his head higher, feeling the cold around him burst along his spine and sees that the light is beginning to fade. At the top of the gully and coming toward him is the wolverine. Fifty yards. He lifts the rifle. The pain starts again and he shifts against his good leg. This new comfort brings with it the picture he had had of Thrain half-eaten in the snow, the wolverine surfacing with bloody snout and grey breath. When his rifle speaks now the land will be clean of both of them again. He pushes the barrel forward, pointing it at carcajou who comes slowly, steadily toward him in an insane straight line. He aims, his cheek against the stock, sighting the animal clearly. It coughs again, hacks: there is blood in the snow. Blood.

The snow is red with blood. There is pink too. Polka-dots of pink spray out when the glutton sneezes. He lowers the rifle and stares. At thirty yards he can see the quills. They ring his snout. Carcajou pauses, stares back and snarls with open mouth. Quills hang from his lip, from his tongue. They are around his eyes, perhaps in them. Dangling from his rope, Linden snickers. He can't stop, even when the pain in him cranks up its volume. "Die," he shouts above it. "Die." His own dying escapes him. "Die." Carcajou rears, sits like a bearcub in the snow, and his paws grab at his mouth and his eyes. He coughs, and Linden can hear the rattle of quills in his throat. He can see them even, feel them. He laughs. Carcajou has heard him.

He puts his front feet back in the snow. Coughs. Hacks. Sneezes. He moves forward. He must pass close to get to the gorge's water. Trapped Linden will be able to reach out and touch him.

"Die." He can feel the pain in carcajou. It is not enough. The quills are threading its lungs, needling toward its heart. It is not nearly enough. "Die *slow*," he says to carcajou. The wolverine stops: he turns away as if to hide the sight of himself vomiting. Then he begins again to go forward, his hind feet dragging troughs in the snow. Ten yards. Linden sights along the barrel again. "No," he says. His voice is almost gentle. "Hold it. I want to see." He puts the rifle out in front of carcajou to bar his path. The glutton's paws are also full of quills. He stops walking and sits hunched, looking out from swollen quill-rimmed eyes across the twenty feet between them. Blood bubbles at the bottom of its breathing. "Die," Linden says. "Die, die." He calls softly, sweetly: "Die."

The wolverine closes his eyes slowly, opens them again and begins to move toward the sound of running water. "Stay," Linden says. He shifts the rifle so that beast and barrel are muzzle-to-muzzle. He is not aiming with his cheek on the stock. The gun rests on the snow and his finger can just reach the trigger. Carcajou continues. Linden will not see him go. He fires. The gun jumps, explodes. The heat of his holding hand has melted the snow in the barrel; the cold has frozen it solid with ice. Metal splits, shatters. Bolt, cartridge and magazine shoot back and tear at the flesh that pulled the trigger. Linden's hand feels its own tissue and blood. Carcajou jumps not away but toward him.

Thrain, at the lip of the ravine, is watching: the rope and chained trap at Linden's back, the shards of man and gun, the weakly charging wolverine, the blood of both of them on the snow. He crouches with only his small axe in his hand, ready to leap, but whether it is to help Linden or the wolverine is uncertain. In his head are Linden's best words: "Hold it, I want to see." He waves his arms and gives body-english to help the wolverine's erratic charge. Then he shouts, "Kill. The neck, go for the neck." He slides, still directing, over the edge of the bank and holds a branch of the fallen spruce. He stands poised on the snow-clear rock that shattered Linden's thigh and then jumps, sinking beyond his waist in the snow a yard away from the man who brought him here. The wolverine has ceased his attack and sniffs the gunpowder, metal and blood, and hears in the distance the broken tinkle of the gorge's waterfall.

As if just now noticing Thrain, Linden turns his head and looks through excited eyes. "I've got him," he says. "See?" They watch the wolverine vomiting up a gout of blood onto the snow. Linden and carcajou are within touching distance. Thrain moves too, pushing through the snow until each of the three can reach the others. Linden begins to talk: "He didn't have me, Thrain, no more you did. I was ahead of him all the way." His wretched grin stains his face. "I had him figured, there wasn't no help needed. Look at him, tenderfoot, you won't see another this close." His hand goes out in honour and in pride. Thrain watches it, a jungle of flesh and bone and cold-congealing blood. It leaks pale red onto the animal's furred skull, a gesture both religious and vengeful which overtakes Linden's ability to stand pain. He suddenly hangs slack against the taut rope that holds his trap. Thrain only wonders if he is dead, puts his axe down in the snow, takes off his mitts and holds Linden close to listen for his breath. The wolverine begins to leap; it is a rush as quick as a transfer of affection. Perhaps he is protecting Linden. Thrain raises his hands to ward off the crippled gambado being executed by the bloody carcajou: it is a crazy ball of blackness in this bowlful of dusk where, Thrain understands, as he watches the slow-motion scramble of his attacker approach, that all three of them are dying. One trapper trapped and broken, one hunter hunted and pierced, and one seducer seduced and about to be ravaged by teeth, claws and quills. His right hand lowers, feels for the axe; his left hand stays high and grapples with the wolverine's open mouth as it arrives. Carcajou's leap forces it against the outstretched hand and arm. Thrain's bare hand slides down past the quilled jaws and tongue to the narrow canyon of the throat. He holds to the base of the tongue and sinks back into the snow, all of his strength in his arm and hand. Thrain feels his flesh gathering points of pain. Carcajou tries to retreat. The quills sink like fishhooks into his hand and wrist; carcajou undulates, its eyes wide and red with anger and with foreign terror. Quills from cheek, jaw and tongue hold deeper. Thrain pulls back. The hand does not move. Carcajou screams as loud as a horse, and Thrain's heart rises and plugs his throat; he feels his eyes bulging with effort and his right hand races to find the axe. He raises it and hacks past Linden's bloody unction into carcajou's brain. The writhing continues, and Thrain sinks lower into the snow to try to escape the pain. The axe is flung in a convulsion from the animal's skull and is suddenly beyond his reach. Thrain sees himself attached to the wolverine, holding the blood-greased tongue and hooked by the porcupine's quills. Linden's voice makes him conscious again: "Fall on him, he's hopping like a trout and I can't see a thing."

Carcajou dies. The current of its energy ceases. A gurgle is its last anger, and Thrain receives it lying in the snow face up and between axe and animal and man. He lies alone, staring up into the new blackness of night descending upon him. Then Linden speaks, strong and practical: "Get some poles and drag me out of here." "Why?" "Because I'm hurt. You'll have to fix my leg before you move me." Thrain lies still looking up at the sky. "Never make it," he murmurs, and feels content for the moment to believe he will shortly die. "It's less than a mile to the cabin." "Your leg?" "Broken." "And your hand?" "Leave it, it's freezing good." Thrain turns his head and looks back at the dangling man's frost-rimmed eyes. "There wouldn't be much of you left in the spring." Linden says nothing. He seems to be waiting. His eyes close slowly, then open again, and there is around them a vacuum through which no time passes. Then he stirs, leans far toward Thrain, hangs from the jaws of his trap, elbows out and head down like a great bird in pain. He shouts: "Make up your mind, Thrain, or the rest of the world'll be telling you what to do for all of your goddam life." The vacuum belongs now to Thrain alone; his arm and carcajou hang outside it and are awash with fast tides of stunning hurt. Inside, he holds his breath against suffocation. Then he moves, rolls suddenly out, dragging the glutton at his hand with him and finds his axe. "You would've seen me die," he says to Linden. The old man laughs. "I thought you'd be good bait to catch carcajou. By God, I was right." The laughter and the axe in Thrain's hand help him make a decision. He holds the dead wolverine and the axe close to his chest and ploughs his way up the trail carcajou made when he came down from the top of the gully. Gradually he finds the snow receding below his waist and then his knees. Behind him there is no sound. Lot's wife or Persephone would have wanted to turn, but then Thrain is a man: he goes forward, opts for progress, and holds carcajou as gently as he can against the pain it is causing; and finally he finds in the darkness a windfall where he can put down his burden and begin to hack at it with the axe. The blade fails to cut. The head bounces, holding tighter to the arm and hand. It occurs to Thrain that he doesn't know exactly where his hand is.

He could cut it off along with the head and miss it only because the pain was gone. With his other hand he pries the jaw. It is tight around his wrist and lower arm and seems to be getting tighter. The pain is receding. He suspects freezing. Carefully, he begins to chop with the axe just in front of the shoulders. It is a blind enterprise, but the crunch of vertebrae reassures him and when the gullet finally sucks air he gives one last full swing. The body falls away, and the head feels light as Packer Thrain lifts it against his chest to carry it further away from the gully and Linden and even away from the Thrain he was, toward the cabin on Mosquito Lake and beyond to the divide and down its slope to the confluence of the Linden and the Swifter. The pain is nearly gone; all feeling diminishes. For a while he expects to hear Trapped Trapper Linden shouting after him. But there is only the soft struggle of his feet through the snow. It is dark; there is a black silence all around him.

And now Writer Scann must sleep. He gets up, staggers as he puts out the light so that he stands in a darkness and a silence of his own. It is here that time is finally destroyed, he thinks. It is after furious work that it is denied in all its forms and meanings by a sleep deep enough to efface both man and his element. He goes to the only light available — from the transom — and shuts it off. He looks directly into the closet, and on the back wall a star is pinned. It glows. His exhaustion dies of curiosity. He goes to his knees, crawls toward the yellow spark. His eye fits the hole and he looks into the great room beyond. His eye waters immediately and he sees nothing. The guest has the window open and there is a draught. He wipes his eye and puts it back more prudently to the hole. On the bed is . . . a . . . body . . . brown . . . a brown suit. The back of a salt-and-pepper head . . . just a tired travelling saleman. He presses closer. A portable TV at the other end of the room. (Does he sell them?) Not on. A suitcase unopened. Not even booze on the table. Alone. Forty dollar shoes. He rises up from his peephole disappointed but refreshed and lies down in the dark thinking that an hour's rest will allow him to go back to write some more.

The roil in his head will not be diverted. Thrain is safe now, doing his walk. Thrain at the Morton's front door still stands waiting for his knock to be answered. The chambermaid named Mary is at home asleep and may not be back to ask what happened. She will come to work at David Thrain's hotel tomorrow, but that may be all. He drifts through the war: there is much to say about it. In

77

the well of his mind it keeps coming to the surface. Twenty-five years ago it drew him into the rip of the Thrain tide. Wing Commander David Thrain. All of his life Scann has been a Lindenite; he stopped travelling and began living here only at the war's end. And now his view of himself as an ancillary Thrain grows stronger. He feels he knew Erica, Thrain's first wife, even though he wasn't born until her part in the story finished. The long rope of her hair, a solid braid across her head, has texture for him. The smell of her bread, the shiny cooking grease on her hands, the sweat on her forehead, her long low heavy breasts, the muscles in her calves, the greatness of her feet are all more real for him than the skin-and-bones surrogate-female mother who raised him. The pillows behind his head have flexibility but no softness. Scann throws one to the floor and lies flat. He works to clear his mind. Breathe in for a slow count of three; hold for six; blank out mind; exhale for a count of three; relax body and mind again. Three, six, three, six. Mind empty. A high curve of blackness. Three, six. Light freckles the dark. Hard electric tensions flow out of him and he feels his guts lie easy on top of his spine. Peristalsis. The constant shifts of his visceral parts please him: sound without intellect. He listens with no particular intent. These are not simple noises. Subtle pressures occur here and there which are preludes to small wet implosions that suck at vital areas as if they were limp probes withdrawing. Bursts of activity run the length of a tube, or across a cavity. For a moment there is confusion; then an almost silent detonation, the soft exhalation of what Shirley calls with probity and assurance, profane gas. Bile and urine, acid, blood, saliva, air. A marvellous energy devoted to cell farming. Millions of cells being fed, exercised, used, serviced, their wastes carried away. No pauses. The God that never sleeps, who continues to create, is physical — not even able to be intellectual — and he lives in the gut. Gut bless us everyone, and praise *us* his noble savage, his house, his strength, his refuge, and He creates there a physical madness that somehow results in spiritual obsessions. Being a man for instance: intestinal fortitude. Politics: Gut Issues. Poetry: peristalsis of the mind. Motherhood: the whole visceral thing is there. He has seen it in his wife. She is quite different now that the children are nearly grown. A kind of false release has occurred. Her *smile* looks at you; her eyes grin. God's promise has been fulfilled. She has farmed new cells. It is frightening. She is all through. Like the decent salmon, she should give up. But technology, over which

God has no control, does not now allow that possibility. She has been reduced to walking the streets, doing something she calls shopping, but an insanity inside of herself is driving her in search of another obsession. Horrible. And Scann hordes his male advantage, and demented by history locks himself up to write fictions that deny it. He is no longer relaxing his tensions. He is lying stiff on his bed and thoughts leap up like northern lights in the clear black behind his closed eyes: his perambulating wife walks on; Linden hangs dipped in his own last minutes; Thrain stumbles on, misses the Mosquito Lake cabin, lives off the land, perhaps, or off the flesh of the neck and head he carries attached to his hand, until he crosses the ice of the Swifter and uses the towering chimney of his own hotel as a directional aid. Finally, he arrives with the land tamed (the wolverine dead by his own hand) to begin to civilize the Indian (he takes Ro as a son) and preside over a newly won colony dependent upon man's (his) kingship. Erica waits, of course; even now Erica waits, willing the days over with. The relief of having Thrain away and out of her kitchen and her time and her bed has been lived through. On the other side of it is a vacuum. Without Thrain there is nothing. The magnitude of her decision to marry him gradually occurs to her. When her mother had asked her if she was sure she wanted to give herself to this man, she had thought they were talking about her virginity. She goes now from wall to wall in her bedroom when even in the darkness the day refuses to die and each night she tries to hold herself deaf against answers to questions she mumbles louder and louder to make herself hear. He should be back by now. Where is he? What is to become of us? She goes to the children sleeping. Ro no longer keeps his knife in his hand when he sleeps. David is at the wall, a blanket wrapped completely around his head. Ro is out from under the blankets. Even on the coldest mornings he doesn't shiver. She goes from them and out into the hotel.

Ballpoint penholder Scann is up and sitting on his chair again, following closely the rise and fall, loop and dot of his Erasall Stickpen (medium). At this moment the connection between brain and ink is either electric or magic. Erica stands in the vast innards of Thrain's lobby and contemplates the chimney rising stiff and fieldstone grey through the roof. It is difficult not to admire it. She has always taken chimneys for granted, even though no chimney no fire, no heat, no comfort. But this chimney is special; she has helped it rise up. In very real measure it is as much hers as it is Thrain's. Three times it toppled and the fourth time it rose up to stay, with its fireplaces at its base, and now there are fires in them to warm the air around her. Thrain would notice a difference since he's been away. Much is done. Ole and she have made progress. The bathrooms are finished. Ole whittles and paints door numbers by the light of the big fire in the evenings. She feels better about the hotel now that she has worked for so long at building it and now that it is so nearly complete.

There is movement at the other end of the lobby. Erica holds still in the shadows by her door. It is Ole. He comes into the firelight with only his boots and heavy underwear on. She knows which suit it is. She washed it three days ago. It is the one with the buttoned flap at the back whose knees are worn thin from his kneeling at carpentry. Now Ole is stoking the fireplaces and the logs he throws on make sparks and high birch noises. Ole contemplates the blazes and then resets the screens in front of them. He has been very good to the boys. They have a sleigh with birch runners he made for them. It works well and doesn't go too fast for David. Ole is making skis now. He tells them that in the old country both boys would be able to come down hills by themselves at this age. She watches him leave the fire and walk his hunched carpenter's walk to the side door. For a moment he fumbles and then she realises that she is watching him relieve himself. She looks down and away; but in the silent crispness she can hear. The sound catches her unwary and she is angry. She turns to find the latch to let herself back into the apartment. The click and the squeak of the hinges make her pause and she knows he turns at the sounds. She waits. Perhaps he doesn't see her. The outside door closes and the shuffle of his feet decays; the noise the fire makes takes over. Erica raises her head and looks at the long grain in the wood of her door, listens once more and, hearing nothing, goes back into her bedroom. She is exhausted. Ole gets up to stoke fires. Thrain would freeze before he would do that. She has always kept the kitchen and parlour fires going in winter. "I'll cut it and bring it in, you burn it." But he never cut it, either. Ole did, and before that there was always an Indian.

She sleeps, and wakes with Ro standing quietly beside her bed. Often this happens. He never wakens her. His tough little face gives her no evidence. This morning she reaches out and holds his arm in her hand. "When you grow up you're going to be a fine handsome man." She smiles at him. "If you don't freeze to death standing by my bed these mornings." He draws away and she watches him a moment before she makes him go and get dressed. She lies still for a while and then feels tears on her cheeks; suddenly her nose will not draw the cold air. The little bronze man worships her. Thrain does too, and David. And perhaps Ole. So much is she needed to fetch and carry, draw, comfort, cuddle, cook that worship comes easily: so long, she thinks, as she continues to serve. But Ro is special, as anything young and strange is special. And he is a distraction from the routine of being Thrain's woman, as tramping off into the high bush with Trapper Linden is a tonic for Thrain. She sits on the cold polished wood of the commode beside her bed and remembers, before she remembered not to, Ole going to the side door of the hotel, holding himself and looking up into the stars. Over the first toilet they had installed upstairs, she had seen where he had stood before it and had spoken on the wall with his carpenter's pencil, had lightly written as if talking to himself: Fool, why are you looking up here. The joke is in your hand. She moves to pin her hair up out of her face. Yes Ole, at least you can hold the joke. She blushes into the mirror. It is uncomfortable to know that there is more to Ole than his hammer and those slow blue eyes that watch more pointedly because they try to watch not at all. But who can say it is simple lust when he can think about the joke of it. She begins to dress and lets her mind move timidly over new ground. She deliberately thinks of Thrain, and is grateful to have him to focus unexpected sensitivities upon. If Thrain knew, he would be home. Yes. In the other bedroom, David and Ro are laughing, struggling and wrestling to make new muscles strong. Quickly she sits at her desk and writes for a cold minute in her book: If you don't have anyone to talk to pretty soon you lose who you are. We are beings who have to *say*. What we think and dream and believe and are afraid of can fill us up and take us over. Like hot air does a balloon. It makes the balloon bigger, yes, but it also floats it away or bursts it. Thrain, he goes out and finds people to talk to and leaves me behind with Ole. He will be lucky if we don't talk to each other — especially when Ole is time after time *saying* in other ways. Ole is good for the boys and he helps them make things: If it wasn't for Thrain I could do his job, he is saying. And I am accepting his help with the boys, which Thrain would never give anyway, and I keep saying *no*. I think that is easy. But I must now try to say no to him when he tries to do Thrain's job. I must or I will lose Thrain inside myself. Maybe we are both, Ole and I, losing who we are. It was easy when he just wanted my body. But he has gone beyond that now and he is another person with the boys and he is dreaming that Thrain is not coming back.

The pen is leading her to where she doesn't want to go. She dresses warmly, feeling her body become ordered and controlled under the comfortable constraints of clothes. In the kitchen, she shakes down the ashes in the range and lights the fire. The pot-belly in the parlour still has live coals and small flames in it. She builds it up, and then she answers Ole's knock on the door. He wears a hat which he touches but doesn't remove, and in his hand is a bundle of boards he is making into skis. The sight of him reminds her where she is; the distance from civilization grows greater every day. The boys run from the bedroom to see how much Ole has done since suppertime. The boards are hand polished on both sides and a groove has been burned from end-to-end. He probably used the big fireplace poker to do it. He stands in her kitchen and holds the pointed sticks for David and Ro to see. His white-flecked blue eyes are dazzled by their admiration. "We turns up the ends," he says, "and we are pretty near through." He laughs with them. "We got to have leather to make the straps but I bet the mother's got that." They want to know how he is going to turn up the ends. She makes breakfast while he shows them. Steam the boards. Put them between the rollers of her laundry wringer. Nice big round rollers. "They will make the wood curve just right. We put weights on the back ends to make the points stay up, and then we leave them for a couple of days." He is crouching in the middle of the room and the boys are feeling the smoothness he has made for them. She watches while the porridge bubbles. Ro looks up at her. His eyes tell her who she is: just a woman. "I skied when I was your age," she tells him. "We were all taught when we could just only walk." "Ya," says Ole, "it's like snowshoes here." "But the mother can't make them," Ro says, and David laughs, rolling on the floor at the joke. She shakes her head, and Ole punches Ro's arm gently. "Anyway, we need her pot to steam them and then the wringer, eh? And after that do you know what we do?" David sits up and looks anxious: he was always the anxious one. "We take her candles and drip wax on them, and after that we take her flatirons and some paper — see, we put the paper on the ski and then we hot iron the wax smooth under the paper." Ole nods his head. "Ya, without the mother we'd be stuck for skis I'm telling you." She turns to the porridge and dishes it out. The milk on the table has ice in it. They each put brown sugar on the mush, and she begins to put some on David's. He shouts at her, grabbing the spoon and slamming it on the table. "I'm *sorry*," she says. "Take it away," he yells. She cleans up the sugar, putting it on her own breakfast. "Here, you can do it yourself," she tells him. Ole and Ro watch. David pushes the spoon back. "No, take it away I want a new bowl from the stove. You bring me some more." She turns from David with the new spoonful in her hand. "Who wants it?" Ole lifts his bowl to the spoon. "It's good to be helped sometimes," he says, without looking at David. "He is such a goose about doing for himself," she says and stands: "Now he will have to go to his room and maybe he can eat when we are through." David holds to his chair and looks up at her. "I want new porridge without sugar on it," he shouts. "Come," she says and holds out her hand, "you are making breakfast just one big noise." "Goddam woman," he yells. Ole's hand flicks out and cuffs his head, maybe his ear. David jumps to be near her and Ole says loudly, "I guess you don't want your skis."

Erica (Scann sits upstairs in Room 322 and feels a terrible and eternal seriousness in her, of a kind that makes the wolverine head on Thrain's arm or the cold trap suspending Linden, matters only of immediate life and death) holds David's head tight to her tall thigh. She doesn't know how to break the silence. She can see that Ole thinks he has done right; his eyes look at his porridge and then at David but never at her. She would laugh if she could; he agrees with David: he thinks she is a goddam woman too. "Is this how you make a man?" she says. "All he wanted to do was tell his mother he was like you and Ro. I would have not thought to hit him and take his skis away for that." Ole's hand shakes a little when he spoons his porridge to his mouth. He chews it as if it were tobacco and stares past her and David to the window and the six feet of snow beyond. Then his eyes and his face begin to reflect his understanding of her words. He stands up and lets himself see her again. "Ya," he says softly, "let's make the skis some other time. Maybe I'll finish the work today." Ro goes for his mitts and jacket and leaves with him. David is quiet against her and she hopes that she is left alone to bring up this only cub in her own way, and then she sits suddenly in fear that it might come true. "Where is my dad?"

David whines, and for a moment she wonders if it is her own voice she is hearing. "Thrain?" she says. She kisses his forehead. "He will be back like he said, any time now."

The day is too cold for him to play outside for long. She takes the skis and steams them while David plays with a bagful of tagends from Ole's carpentry. Ole and Ro come back for lunch. Breakfast is not remembered by the boys, but she looks at Ole and puzzles about why she talked to him as she did. Why teach him as she would Thrain? David shows him the skis steaming. Ole's eyes laugh. "By God, I told you we couldn't finish the job without the mother." After lunch they take the skis and clamp and weight them in the wringer. "Two or three days of steam and the wringer and it'll be done. We can have a try on them before I go." "Are you going too?" David asks. "Too? Too?" Ole says playfully. "I think," Erica says almost as if she is interrupting, "I think we will ask Mr. Johnson to stay until your father gets back." "You will be safe," he says. "There's lots of people here to take care of you." "Don't speak of this now," she says.

Ole does something then that he has never done before. He picks both boys up and turns with them in a kind of dance. "You'll be safe," he says, and his Swedish face finally laughs outright. "This place is like a castle." He puts them both down. "What you gonna do?" Ro asks. "Take my hammer and saw and go another place. That's what's good about my trade." She has not seen him like this. "Ole, sit down and eat. You're making more noise than the other two put together."

Writer Scann hears a new sound. Someone is knocking softly at his hotel room door. He puts down his ballpoint and slides his chair to the transom. It is Mary Major. From above she looks slim and demure in a green suit and brown shoes. She looks up and sees him. With one finger to her lips, she motions with her other hand for him to let her in. He stands down. There are no beginnings or endings, but there are conclusions. He comes to one. His breath chokes him. He sweats. He opens the door, thinking she is thinking the same thing he is thinking. He sees her standing in the dim hall light among the blue roses and reaches automatically toward her. She ducks beneath his arm and is behind him in the room before she can turn around. "Close it," she says. He does, and looks at her. She is agitated too. He stands near her.

"I know it's getting late," she says, and sits at the bottom of the bed and holds onto it with a gloved hand. "But I was going home and I thought — " He moves to be closer to her, and she looks up at him, her expression annoyed. "Now, see here, if you think I came to play — " She moves down the bed and stares into her lap. "I mean, what's so wrong with him falling in love with Cecilia? I've been thinking about it ever since I left, like some damned tune I can't get out of my head." He sits on his chair with his back to his ballpoint. His mind says, Well, she's here, isn't she? "No matter. No matter at all. I mean, there he is, fresh off his private aircraft — " He tries to swallow. What he is is frightened. Maybe she has come to — "A kind of 1935 jet-setter downed by a clogged oil or petrol line in the most fortunate of places. He could have landed on a lake without so much as a footprint on the shore. But there he is at the Morton Ranch and old Zed Morton is dead, has been for years. Only his two girls are there and Philippa, protected by some dogs and an old negro." He breathes better now, and he can swallow. "What would you like to have happen?"

She looks across at him and her eyes narrow as if she had rehearsed a speech and was trying to remember it perfectly and with gestures. "I asked John Lowry about the Mortons tonight and he said that there wasn't any around now. I said a guy had tried to tell me this afternoon they had a ranch and it was protected by wolf-dogs and a negro keeper, John looked at me as if I was queer and says you know there aren't any blacks around here, and I do. So, I figure if you'd lie about that, you'd lie about Cecilia having her hair all chopped off and having, you know, that kind of figure, too."

Scann feels sad. Lowry is very old. Past sixty. He looks at Mary. Her green skirt is short. Almost as short as the ones his own daughter wears. He glances across town at Shirley. Like the Queen, she wears them just *at* the knee. He sees himself sitting before Mary. Forty-eight is an awkward age: too old to be a threat and too young to offer himself up and cry. "So tell me," she says, "were there even any Mortons at all?" He sees her looking at him, all of him. Her red-brown hair hangs along one side of her cheek. Her freckles are healthy. There is a slight buck to her teeth. He does not know who she is. He tries to compare her with a dozen other women he has known. It occurs to him that he never knew who they were either. This one excites, listens. Wants to listen. Is a miracle that has arrived and is interested. Even that can lead to the edge of depravity. It probably has happened before. "All right," he says. "Right. The Mortons." He begins to pace in short arcs as if he is making a place to lie down in the midst of jungle grass. "Who was Zed?" she asks. "He was husband of Philippa, father to Cecilia and Amantha. Zed was Zed Morton. Zed was obsessed." Big cellos and french horns tearing aside frilly curtains of chintzy violins: written, produced, directed, composed and edited personally by Amory Scann. 140mm Cosmovision with colour by God Himself. He sees her sitting stiff. He throws the pillows in a pile on her side of the bed. "Lean back, this might take a moment or two." Thirty words and already she is betrayed. She lies back, comfortable, linear. Screw you McLuhan: the *word* is the basic unit of consciousness and to understand is to write metaphors with the mind. "Listen," he says. "Zed was mad, as Linden after whom this hotel is named was mad, and Thrain who visited Zed's ranch in 1935 was and is mad. Insane. Why? Men are made unique by obsessions and insane through the experience of them. We feel the winds caused by their goings and comings, assume changes are taking place and call that history. But there is no history except that it is metaphor. Assume," he says fiercely, "assume consciousness, the smallest amount of it, the real history stops until the expansion of that consciousness to include all there is in the universe, at that moment, is complete. The first and last principle of consciousness is that somehow one *is*. Its active phase is that one *does*, as the passive phase is to *be*. If the highest level of being is Nirvana, say, then the highest level of doing is Zed's, Linden's, Thrain's kind of obsession. Both states can be perverted, are perverted by what we call reality, and when these obsessions become unacceptable to us petty Normalities, we either build jails and prosecute or construct asylums and commit. Insanity, however, is allowed at the boundaries of our civilization, both physical and intellectual. Given that there are far more people who are physical than intellectual and that our physical frontiers are confined to Russia and Canada and two or three other unlikely places, we will soon see the incarceration of all our Thrains, Lindens and Mortons and it will be the end of doing in the world. Eh? Soon we will sit and think — or pretend to think lest we be committed — and because not all of us can think for ourselves we will be given rosaries of thought which will make our eyes grow bright and may encourage us to bang our folded knees with pulpy fists while we insist that soon we will *do* something."

"I just asked who Zed was," Mary says, sitting up. Scann says aloud and fast: "And I'm telling you. It was because they were capable of obsession, and because they might have been locked up, that Morton, Linden and Thrain came to the end of the world, which sixty years ago was right here." He stops pacing, goes to where she sits on the edge of the bed and gently helps her lie down again. He is away from her once more before he realises that he has been near. He looks back and licks the salt from his lips. "So, remember, there is no such thing as history. There is only individual consciousness expanding. Therefore, it doesn't matter at all where or when people are. I mean, Thrain could be in two or three places at once. Who cares? We all are. You are, via newspaper, magazine, radio, TV, train, bus, aircraft, car and other kinds of transport such as sex, religion, love, sex, spectator sports, sex." The edges of her mouth twitch a little. She likes the old jokes. She watches him again and he tells her: "The only person who must stay in one place, in one time, is God's own writer. He must be isolated for his moment of obsession. Quarantined. You have violated that silence. When you came in here you reduced me to a slavering male with only one hope and one awareness. How do you like that?" She looks almost angry. "I don't, and I have it said better to me all the time. 'Come to my room for a drink,' they say, 'no one'll miss you.' Now if that isn't an invitation to be in two places at once, I don't know what is. And if I did go with them they'd crawl all over me and keep asking if I was coming." She sits up. "I guess that's one up on you, Mr. Scann, eh? Here there and on my way. What's this all about? Are you trying to insult me?"

His performance withers. Experience will put down the intellectual every time. He turns and sees himself in the mirror. The flesh under his eyes is weak. It looks like the surface of a tossed bed. He is very tired. So tired that he begins to laugh. It is the right thing to do. Over his shoulder he can see her expression relax and it encourages him to face her. "There is much to say." He feels abject suddenly. "You ask about Zed, about Cecilia and Thrain and Philippa. Listen." He lies on the bed, his head on the last of the pillows. "Zed came to the country a long time ago. He came in a caravan. Himself, Philippa and Amantha in her belly, Cecilia toddling. And he picked up an entourage along the way. Isaiah Jones was a negro, George and the others were Indians. He came north. He *edged* north — God knows how a man like Zed does what he does. Up the valleys and around lakes and across deserts, I suppose, and through the mountains and down old Indian and pack trails until he arrived here, or near here. He didn't come to ranch or farm or homestead. He came to colonize and to build a settlement around what he believed. I told you about consciousness expanding because I wanted to tell you about Zed and his struggle to keep his own from expanding. He wasn't like Linden who made a whole universe out of his trapline and spent his time understanding it wrongly so that he wound up a child unable to share what and where he was and what he knew; and Zed wasn't like Thrain who was sure that everything here was new and clean and gift-wrapped and who couldn't settle it or walk it or live quietly in it for fear he'd be missing something new. Zed was a tyrant, which is what happens to anyone who tries to live with a fixed idea he's borrowed from somebody else. But he was a tyrant unconsciously. He thought the house and the quarters for the 30 or 40 slaves he'd made, looked and felt just fine. He refused the six month winters. He went without a hat close to home until it was thirty below. Every week he'd go down to the place where his people lived and teach them. He'd sing with them and play with them. He believed they were childlike, and they were, but they learned his ways because they thought they must. He'd take his whip down to their quarters and after everyone was drunk on potato liquor and they'd done some singing he'd tie up one of the women and whip her. This was to help them learn how to moan. Our history is full of men who've tried to teach us their music. And then he'd be full of remorse. He'd cut her down from the harness rack and hold her in his arms and tell his moaning and isolated people that they were his jewels. And then he'd take the girl back home through the cold to tend to her hurts. This was the religious side of his life, the thing that brought him here. It wasn't an original part of him, or even part of his father, but there had been his grandfather for whom his father grieved until his own death, and no matter where he lived in the world he always whipped a slave before he made love to her, or perhaps it was what he did so he *could* make love to her. 'When they hurt they don't smell,' he told his peers, putting the observation in an innocent context, and because he was white and it was a long time ago he could believe anything he wanted and act upon it. But with Zed it was a ritual thing. He had come to believe in the institution of the slave and he worshipped it and the slaves too. At the same time, not far away, men who would lock up Zed if they'd known about him had Chinese chained together to do the hard work of building a railroad, but those whites hadn't brought in any Chinese women so they missed out on the deliciousness of sexual guilt, which until now has been the chief perversion of the orthodox. In any event, Zed was forty when he burst out of civilisation and built his dream on the edge of the grasslands south and west of here, and he was only fifty-three when he passed away. Nothing spectacular about it. A little rain fell on the unjust is all, and he died — cancer perhaps.

"Which brings us to Philippa who, of course, immediately Zed died left for the south. She returned the same day. The reason, although she never told anyone, was quite simple: she had forgotten where south was. Her private needle pointed north now. She wasn't more than five miles down the trail, with Cecilia and Amantha and three pack horses strung out behind her, before she understood what it was that Zed had left her. Institutions accumulate just as living things defecate. It is proof that their anti-digestive systems support perfectly their anti-lives. (It is only when they die that they reverse the process for a moment and live: people all over the world are beginning to understand this and are busy now killing them off, which is causing a lot of bad smell.) Zed had left her an institution. She turned her horse and, dragging her children and packtrain behind her, went back to the ranch to kill that institution so that she might live."

Speaker Scann rolls up on his elbow so that he is very close to Mary Major. "Listen," he says urgently into her ear. "What happens now isn't complicated, but it may be difficult to understand. It was for Philippa Morton. She didn't know she was going to kill it; all she knew in the beginning was that the new direction of her life was north as Zed's had been south and that what he had left her was an instrument for measuring the long history of their differences. She had tended north since her arrival: when Zed built the big house, she demanded and got a place of her own in it. At first the third floor was unfinished, but the more she grew to fear Zed the more she made it a fortress. In time she gradually left south and began on her own, as one must, to turn toward north. The truth about north is that it is not so much a state of being as it is a long moment of transition. Or, perhaps it is a high white pure balance between two seasons of fruitfulness that tend southward toward decay."

"You mean a kind of New Year's day," Mary says. Scann sits up. "Yes, I think so." Mary smiles faintly, with the corners of her mouth down. "She's going to turn into Queen Catherine now." "No," Scann says, "not quite yet, if at all. You see, she came back to the ranch not just because she had forgotten, literally, where south was, but because it was important for her to change, to be responsible for the change that was to take place now that Zed had died. She might not have known where south was, but she remembered it. It was decay. Perversion of primary instincts and original views. It was living the metaphysics and acting out the symbology and ritualizing the metaphors that are left behind when an era and its seminal idea dies. There are whole literatures devoted to telling how it is inside the South: *The Satyricon, Don Quixote, La Recherche du Temps Perdu, Light in August*. It is a temptation always to write of Zed rather than Thrain. You don't understand, do you?" "Well, I think you're pretty funny. You talk and make up words as you go along for all I know. Jesus, all I wanted to hear was what happened to Cecilia and old man Thrain. Does there have to be the whole history of the place? In the Bible they just say somebody begat somebody else and when they come to a couple of people who did something more than begat then they tell the story and that's called the History of the Jews. So Zed and Philippa begat Cecilia and Amantha, and Thrain came down in his airplane, now what happens?" "But what did he land among? *Who* is he about to see when the door opens?" Mary shifts down on her pillows. "How should I know, except there's a couple of girls and their mother and they haven't seen a white man for a long time." "But we have to get there," Scann says. "It's going to be fifteen years before someone answers the door, so let me tell it. When she got back, came riding over the rolling green and brown of the bushland and fields, Zed's people were sitting confused along the fencerails on the sunny side of the big house. Philippa walked her roan along in front of them as if she were Elizabeth inspecting a rank of guards. She carried Zed's whip in her hand, and after she'd been down the line she turned and came back up the length of the fence again. She paused before Isaiah Jones and looked at him full in the face. I.J. (they called him I.J.) didn't even blink. Then she passed on and stood her horse before George and after a while she gave him the whip, handle first, as if she were surrendering a sword. She let the length of it slip through her hand. 'Bring it and show it to me every sundown,' she said so all of them could hear, 'and let me see that it has not been ill-used. This is our treaty, that we will own the whip together as a sign that we both have power and that we will never again crack it in anger.' The female slaves moaned; why, it is not known: Zed taught them well, and perhaps they were moaning for a way of life Philippa had just obliterated in one short clear-eyed ceremony. They were free. More: the whip was theirs. Philippa rode on out of their presence and went to the house. Cecilia was on her bay, and Amantha rode her black. Cecilia sat plump and competent, like a deputy sheriff in a western movie. She was fifteen. Amantha rode like a dude and looked the part. She had grace, but she didn't belong. She was the only Morton born here and the only one who had not lost her way. Her heredity prevailed over environment. Nothing could persuade her that she wasn't a Morton, and nothing could make her believe that she was one of *these* Mortons. She waited without tension for her release, and she lived the ranch's deprived life without ill-will. She was thirteen and loved her horse, the pups I.J. bred and all of Arabella's kittens by whatever father. Philippa watched these two being watched by her people. They rode up out of the pasture toward the fence and then Cecilia saw George with the whip, stopped in front of him and with a sudden movement of her hand took it from him. George grabbed it back. 'Goddam,' she heard Cecilia shout at him, 'give it to me, it's my dad's.' George spoke. Cecilia and Amantha looked up toward her at the house. Philippa nodded her head in agreement with what she knew George was saying. Cecilia reined her horse sharp along the curve of the corral fence and galloped to the house. Amantha came more slowly after her. It was easy to explain it to Cecilia, but hard to make her understand. 'That's my dad's whip,' she kept saying. And when George didn't bring it to the house at sunset, it was even more difficult to try to explain to her the whip's meaning to the people in the ranch hands' houses, that it was perhaps part toy and part symbol of authority and that they would bring it to her soon. But whatever happened, between them all at the Morton ranch, it would be easily worked out. Philippa was confident. She cooked the girls' evening meal herself and brought it to the dining room. Darkness isolated them from what was going on beyond the corral."

Writer Scann pauses. Mary says, "I'd like to believe it, but I don't." "You should," he says seriously, "this is a real ranch, and these are real people: the mother, Zed's daughters, the ranch hands and their women of whatever colour or creed. Zed simply isolated them by talking to them of his ideals and at the same time kept them away from any real process of law. This is the most honoured aspect of the frontier — its lawlessness. It's not true that there was no law. It was just slower at the periphery. Except for parking tickets it still is. Zed's people came here for freedom's sake. He told them so. For a new life. But what it really meant was a new and free life for Zed, and in order to free one man a lot of other people have to become slaves. But Zed died without thinking he was going to do it so soon and he left no son or heir or instructions about what to do with the whip. Philippa gave it to George as a sign that Zed's kind of tyranny was over. She didn't understand that you don't share whips. It's a useful sentimentality to proclaim if you happen to own one, but any good establishmentarian or committed radical or three year old at a playschool will tell you only to speak of the joys of sharing, never share. But she did try to share, and it caused chaos. What Philippa and the girls thought might be revelry was riot. No one was killed but nearly everyone was hurt. Then there were factions formed. This seemed necessary because George fought hard to keep the whip for himself and in the end, when the fighting was over, he still had it. Almost everyone said that it belonged to no one. George said that as long as he had it he was leader over everyone including the Mortons. Some believed him. Others said they just felt free anyway, got out the potato liquor and began to roam around restless, shouting and fighting. Some of the women were used rather more roughly and more often than they wanted to be, cattle and horses were turned loose, and George didn't seem to want to interfere. He was a natural leader and his instinct told him to wait until he could be sure the whip would work to prove his primacy. He got a little smashed himself and so he wasn't around to protect the Morton girls when they came outside to order the men to round up the livestock again.

"It was suddenly a strange scene. One of the men, laughing hard to cover his anxiety and temerity, reached out and touched Cecilia. She stood motionless by the corral and didn't react. The man touched her again. The gang of men wasn't restless or bored anymore. Someone held her, and someone else did the same to Amantha. There was a silence. Then the shock of both sides wore off and Cecilia swore and kicked at the man holding her, and Amantha began to scream. The few strands of fear and respect that had been holding the men back disintegrated. One of them ripped off Cecilia's clothes from neck to waist. The men held back for a moment while they made those kind of noises you might hear at a circus when the aerialist plunges whitely through a spotlight and manages to complete his triple somersault. It was a kind of awkward, breathless applause, half vocal, half physical, the sudden worship of an outsized perfection. Nearly all of them raped her and only a few the smaller Amantha, which may have saved both her life and her sanity. Cecilia had fallen silent to the ground when the first man attacked her; Amantha never stopped screaming until she heard men beginning to shout, 'Get the lady, get the missus,' and then she saw Cecilia lying near her, a fat grey doll in the moonlight. She was cut and bleeding, a catalogue of horrors that made her own violation seem only a discomfort. Yet when the men left them to go up to the house to find Philippa, Cecilia got up, took the torn clothes she had been wearing almost prettily just fifteen minutes ago and walked away, down moon to the east, as if she were going to the ranch hands' compound on a special mission. The men didn't find Philippa. The door to the third floor was hidden. George had built it in for her when Zed was away. The third floor was her sanctuary, but it contained also all of her helpless rage. The men pounded through the house, broke and wrecked, but they found nothing they wanted. Cecilia came home the next morning. Her cuts had stopped leaking, she had on a workshirt and pants, and she'd slashed her hair with a knife she'd found in the trousers when she stole them. She was dirty from her ordeal but she didn't wash. She stood in the doorway of Amantha's room and looked at her sister and her mother with reflectionless eyes. And when she spoke it was as if she were thinking out loud. 'You go upstairs and don't come down,' she told her mother. To Amantha she said, 'Lie there and get well, and don't worry.' Then she went to the kitchen and ate bread and blueberry jam without sitting down. Maybe she couldn't, perhaps she just didn't dare. Her mother went past her and up the back stairs to the second floor and beyond. She said nothing. Amantha was quiet too. She'd seen her sister angry before. Then, in a while, Cecilia went out to the compound and rang the head wrangler's triangle until everybody was up and out and standing in front of her. She was in their territory. She watched them assemble, and when she spoke to them it was to a quiet crowd, half of whom had raped her, half of whom last night had wished they'd been there too, and all of whom

93

were anxious about this moment she was creating among them now. 'I have a message from my mother. It's this: return the whip by sundown or there will be a disaster by morning.' That was all to the message. She waited perhaps for the count of ten and said it again to them. Then she stood staring at one and another of them until they all were dispersed. She whistled up her loose horse that was grazing by the lake and rode off, perhaps to round up cattle. George told everyone that the whip should stay with the people. He didn't return it. That night Cecilia came back quietly and burned a house in the compound. Three children and two adults died, and it took a bucket brigade from the lake to save the rest of the buildings. George said anyone could set a fire and to pay no attention. He rang the wrangler's bell, and with his whip in his right hand, declared that he must lead. He chose guards and set watches. At noon the gusty wind dropped, the sky became black, what light there was turned a sulphurous green. One long bolt of lightning struck the Douglas fir at the north side of the compound and it split, fell and set fire to an empty horsebarn. A cloudburst followed and put out the fire. Nature is often more merciful than man. Cecilia appeared on the porch — the same place where Thrain is waiting, goggles and helmet in hand, for the door to open — and stood silent until the rain was over, until the sun came out again and the people were gathered before her. 'Enough,' she said, and wiped her nose with the back of her hand. 'You can have the whip, but if you want it to work for you, listen to what mother says: Let George lead you, send I.J. to look after her now that she's moved to the third floor for good, and today clean up the mess and put the stock back where it belongs. George should meet me here every morning to hear what mother wants.' She knew they'd obey. And then Cecilia went inside. She lay by her sister on the bed. After a while, she began to talk in a way Amantha hadn't heard before. 'They cut me and hurt me, somebody bit off my nipples and I'm all swollen like there's sand up inside me. I don't give a damn if I get well or not except neither of you ladies could fend for yourselves alone. Now I made this place mine I don't want it. Maybe you or I.J. can speak for momma when George comes in the mornings.' Amantha sat up and found she wasn't as stiff and as sore as she'd thought. 'Then what are you going to do?' Cecilia got up again, moving as if it were a substitute for thinking. 'I'll be in my room a while. I don't know. Haven't slept much lately.' 'What about the dead?' Amantha asked. Cecilia paused near the door. 'What about them? It's for George to make arrangements down there now. I guess when you start burying the dead you know the war's over.' It was. New graves appeared in the burying ground. George got the hands working the ranch again, just like old times. I.J. came to the house. He brought his stud-dog, Master, whose sons and some of his grandchildren met Thrain's aircraft. Amantha took I.J. and the dog upstairs. She ran ahead of them across the room and when she reached her mother lying on the great bed, she began to weep. Philippa cradled her daughter's head in her lap and waited. I.J. stood and Master sat at the end of the bed. She looked at them. 'I made a mistake,' she said. 'If I'd given you the whip, you'd have brought it to me like I asked.' 'No ma'am,' I.J. said. She turned her head from him and looked out at the sky through the small high window. It was difficult to think with Amantha crying, but after a moment she said, 'Then what are you going to do here?' 'Stay safe and see what happens. I got more grievances than George.' 'No you haven't,' she snapped. 'Yes,' he said and his voice didn't change, 'but he's in charge down there now.' I.J. sat on the bed and rubbed behind Master's ear. 'One time there last night I thought I was going to be leader.' He turned to look at Philippa. 'Maybe somehow I'll get him yet.' 'Yes,' Philippa said, 'I suppose you will.' She petted Amantha, stroked her hair and helped her stop crying. 'Surely, you will be greater than George,' she said to I.J. He sat down on the foot of the bed, scratched his dog's belly and smiled.''

Scann the story-teller gets up and drinks from the tap at the sink. Mary watches him and says nothing. He turns again. "She was right, you know," he says. "George was a natural leader, but Philippa knew how to hold power. She knew how to stay safe and how to be properly represented. I.J. was what the people of the United States call a house nigger, and it is always, wherever you go, the house niggers who do the ruling for the powerful. Historiographers call them prime ministers and presidents, assign them greatness even, read their memoirs as serious pieces of literature and use their comments and chest-pounding as if they were the real tools of research into the truth of the times. So be it. The real truth is that they are always neutered. I.J.'s elevation to prime ministership came about in the following amusing way. It may even be a most typical way if you think below the surface. Philippa stayed on the third floor. I.J. became her representative, Amantha her servant, and she let Cecilia do as she pleased (a third power on the ranch and perhaps a mistake). George took I.J.'s orders, because he and his people were afraid of Philippa's lightning and fire, and he made the ranch feed, clothe and house them all. The rituals and ceremonies of government grew naturally. I.J., Amantha, even Master participated. You see, they had very little else to do on the third floor except eat, sleep, exercise their prerogatives and protect the mysteries of their dominion over fire and lightning. Philippa came out mostly at night to exercise, but they found that she could make an occasion for everyone by appearing during the day, especially in winter when she was able to wear her furs and the beaver hat she'd made for herself. Master, the dog, was impressive on these occasions. Philippa walked with him on a leash, and he would strain at it and raise his lips like curtains to reveal his teeth. But he was especially good at times when he was called upon to breed. He'd be led by Philippa to the pen where he held court and a bitch in heat would be brought to him. He needed no help. He was polished, ceremonious, consummate and in the end thoroughly vicious. Afterward the bitch would be taken away, summarily impregnated, and then Philippa would return with the dog as if they were a parade to the third floor. She was past her middle forties now, the memory of Zed had faded, she had killed his institution and built one of her own and thought, as institutionalists usually do, that hers was ultimately good. Her picture of herself was also excellent; it made her secure, relaxed. She found nothing to be surprised at, therefore, when she discovered herself contemplating Isaiah Jones both as her own self and as his sovereign. Master's performance had been stimulating. 'Undress,' she said to I.J. He took it as an order. 'Now,' she said, playing, 'see if you can undress me.' While he was doing it, she explored with a dreaming hand and looked at Master who sat point-eared at the foot of the bed, his eyes questioning this new thing. He didn't know he was the final catalyst in a long process that carried I.J. from simple servant, to messenger, to ruler and to high priest, during which time I.J. had kept himself pure and ravenous (which is the priestly mode) until now in a moment he would change again, become something new when he mounted Philippa as Master himself had mounted his bitch in the pen below. He watched eagerly, wanting to share. He could smell her odours as they were released when I.J. took off her clothes. He could see they were playing. He bounced back and forth from one front foot to the other, bobbed his head and smiled, looking for a way to join in. He was young then, capable of breaking his training and being delighted by anything new. When I.J.'s black butt began to swing above Philippa's slim white form, he danced to the music of the praises she was crooning into I.J.'s ear. Closer he came and closer. He put his front paws on the bed and gave little yelps of his own in concert with their duet. Then something happened that switched Master from intelligence to instinct. Philippa was suddenly in pain. 'Oh my God, oh my God,' she cried out, and I.J.'s great black butt rose like a threat before him. He snapped. Master's teeth and I.J.'s testicles met at the moment of Philippa's climax. She always looked on this gelding, this elevation of I.J. from envoy-priest to Prime Minister as having been accomplished as part of a plan that she saw, through the splendid narrow lens of hindsight, as divine. From that moment on she became consciously religious as well as Absolute."

Author Scann gestures, touches Mary and is reminded that she is there beside him. He rolls so that the whole length of him is contingent upon her clothed flesh. He kisses her and is surprised that she lets him. Then she draws back. "Why are you doing this?" Her voice is soft and inflectionless. He likes her, and he shakes his head and lies: "No, you were just too pretty not to kiss." It works. She smiles. "And I am lying beside you on a hotel room bed." "Well yes." After a while, she says, "I can see how a man who writes bullshine stories like you've been telling me could get pretty mixed up about, you know, what's really going on." "Well, you *are* lying beside me on a hotel room bed." "I was thinking about that. I'm like Philippa Morton. Here I am alone with a man in a room on the third floor. A secret room because no one knows I'm here. It's like being free, eh? So why not? God knows I'm normal. So why not? Maybe it's like buying clothes, it should be as exclusive as you can make it. Now in Queen Catherine's case she was looking, just like any woman does, for an exclusive model, and she could snap her fingers and have it sent up. How many queens get made love to by buck privates? And in the story about Philippa Morton, that dog made it very exclusive: no one else ever had a loving like that. But me, I just lie here and if I'm lucky I get a little pleasure, but then it isn't the end of the story. Not for me. I don't just go away until the next nice thing happens. You know, right now there are thousands and thousands of girls being laid in hotel rooms, and it isn't exclusive for them either. They're just like me: another name on a list and the guy's snoring already and they have to get up and go home sometime. Frankly, Mr. Scann, it makes me mad to think about it that way, because I want to think about it any other way there is. I mean, if you can make it happen like Catherine or Philippa Morton, then I guess I can be talked into something."

Scann does not reply. He lies on his back and faces the ceiling; it is a long way away. She is accepting this silence as his refusal to meet her challenge. And it hurts. His gut sucks away at the vacuum she has created there. He wants to be angry, perhaps violent. But she would scream, other guests would come, the night clerk, the police, his own newspaper would report him and his family would disintegrate. Then he understands that by not answering her he is putting her on the defensive. She gets up and he doesn't stop her. She looks down at him and he sees her through half-drawn lids. Her eyes are busy not seeing; they search for something on which to focus. "If you hadn't, you know, tried," she says finally, "then that would have been exclusive." He opens his eyes wide to see her better. She likes games. He is not ready to forgive or understand her. He settles himself into the softness of the bed. "Philippa liked games," he tells her. The *non sequitur* forces her attention. He wants to finish with Philippa and go to sleep. "Games played without rules often result in discoveries no one expected to make." He can feel her begin to listen to him, as if he were the teacup reader at the Redbird Cafe. "Philippa discovered that she had freed I.J., in a way, in a very real way. What is it that enslaves a man? Any old poet will tell you: his passions. And who had nipped off I.J.'s seed pods? His own animal, the dog Master. One's own animal serves life in its youth and at its extremities, but when it's cooped up to play the games and take part in the ceremonies of civilisation (ceremonies are always about obedience) then it will certainly and ironically chew man down to mere male. And out of such observed violences to our persons come the rituals by which we have lived. Someone will rule us whether we resist it or not, so: the ceremonies of the ballot box and the dainty ballets of palace coups; or the ritual herding of the oppressed by the oppressed; or the press (the *media* we are now) making the bark called Free as it does its own pee against the four fences (good business, good thinking, good taste and good for us) which surround it and keep it civilized and safe. Enough. Philippa, bless her, sensed how far she had gone beyond Zed. Almost before her delicious pangs and her sensual plunder had ceased, she was able to see her dead husband as her precursor and she forgave him everything. This was her auto-beatification. Her sainthood followed shortly when she realised suddenly one day that everything she had touched since Zed's death had turned to significance and might, at any moment she decided, turn to magic. But apocalyptic saints are given to great silences after the magnificent energies of their visions have been brought to ground. Philippa, having seen some of the meanings of her actions and having lived through their culmination, retired to Godhead. Her last human act was to send I.J. on a mission worthy of his new prime ministry. 'Go for the whip,' she told him. 'It's time it was here again.' And I.J. did, and proved himself by bringing George to the 3rd floor and having him sentenced as he stood by Philippa's bed. She stretched out her hand for the whip. George made a quick movement to save it. Later outside, again on signal, Master leapt once more and was allowed to kill George. I.J. picked up the whip, rang the bell and carried George to the wrangler's platform. He made a speech to the assembly while he held their leader's body in his arms and their whip in his hand. 'The dog will die,' he said, finally. 'Would you like me to do it for you?' There was no dissent. He handed George's corpse to one of them and borrowed a knife from another. He whistled for Master. The dog came. He sat on command. People jostled one another to be near. The crowd breathed short and heavy. They knew it was his favourite of all the dogs he had bred. They knew he loved it. Someone giggled with happiness."

Scann pauses, looks up at Mary Major: she is quiet, waiting too for I.J. to kill his dog. "Stories," he says, "are always stopping off to make little points, moral and otherwise. The point here, Mary-Mary, good and therefore innocently ignorant citizen (the world will never be a paradise until everyone is a bad citizen and dangerous), is that thrilling acts of inspired leadership are always two-headed counterfeit coins. Nothing significant is ever done by him who plays the power game except that his potency has teethmarks on it, and nothing of significance is done that does not, without exception, kill two birds with one stone. Thus, I.J. looked down at Master, the dog, and saw both his own election and his revenge ready to leap from the point of the knife he had hidden in his fist. He held the scruff of the beast's neck and cried real tears; the crowd moaned; Master raised his snout and howled. Everyone understood.

It was a beautiful moment, marred only slightly by Cecilia at the back of the gathering who raised a firearm and shot the dog dead in I.J.'s hand. She didn't do anything else. She didn't want to rule. But she waited and the crowd waited. Isaiah Jones pushed his knife under Master's throat, through the base of his tongue and into the brain, and he raised the hundred-weight dog as if it were suspended on a meathook and as if no shot had been fired from Cecilia's gun. He looked out across the crowd at her. 'This whip will revenge you now, Miss Cecilia,' he told them all. 'We know what it reminds us of.' The people cheered, even the ones on whom the revenge was going to fall. Two more birds were killed with a single stone. Cecilia rode out of the compound. I.J. lowered the dog, threw it to the crowd. He left the stage and went back to the house. Amantha, feeling safe for the first time since her father died, met him on the porch and kissed his black leather cheeks. Inside of him the great angry memory of his dead manhood twitched — a noisy corpse on a mortician's slab — and he held her by the arms and said, 'We're going to revenge everybody now and keep the ranch safe for the good life we can have here. You'll be helping me, Miss Amantha.' He was expansive. Who better than a slave knows that everyone wants to be a slave? Amantha served Philippa and I.J. and her rewards were these: she was no longer fearful and she did not anymore have to try to think. I.J. bred more dogs and eventually achieved what he thought was another Master, and he began the ceremonies that kept Philippa interested in life; but never again did that wonderful moment occur as it had the evening of I.J.'s promotion. Master's grandson was merely vicious where Master had been civil or playful or unpredictable and always contingent but in the end a positive force who helped create that truly significant miracle on which religion at the Morton ranch was based. You can smile if you want at the picture this conjures. But for I.J. and Philippa it was serious business to try to recreate the wonder of the moment of their own epiphany. They worked and planned. Oddly, during training sessions when I.J., acting as Philippa's worshipper manque, mounted and went through the motions, the dry run would result in good, even perfect timing. Not so when the real ceremonies were held in soft candlelight and atop wolf and cougar skins, the whip and knife in evidence and the ritual bath by Amantha done perfectly. Often Master would sulk. Once he sneezed and yawned. Amantha suggested painting the sacrificial lambs' butt-ends black, and they made that part of the ceremony, yet it improved nothing but the length of the proceedings. Philippa often experienced great moments during her part in the ceremonies. She would feel the miracle close at hand and would then stay I.J.'s knife so that the man might return to try again. One cowhand came back thirty-six times (a veritable Scheherazade) before I.J. balked and made him a full citizen. Cecilia was exluded. She often stayed away from the house for weeks at a time. Still, she seemed to be the only one blessed with second sight. She never missed being home when religious observances were being conducted. She had her own ceremony. When the three on the third floor were through with their man, she put him and what he owned on horses and rode them off the ranch and into the wilderness. It was a bloody ride to freedom and not all survived it, but those who did. . . ."

Taleteller Scann begins to peer into the blackness of sleep. He hears Mary's voice, windy and reedy in the distance: "What?" He doesn't remember what. "If they lived what did they do?" He thought for a moment. "Do? Do? They were made free. Isn't that enough?" "What're you telling me?" "You don't understand it?" "No." "I'm sorry, it seems understandable to me." She doesn't move or say anything for a while. The silence almost makes him watchful. Then she says, "It just makes me feel bad." "Is that all?" But she doesn't answer the question. "What about Cecilia and old man Thrain?" "Someone's going to answer that door soon." He feels her put a blanket over him. An envelope of warmth. He feels triumphant, even though exhaustion has neutered him.

THE SECOND DAY OF CREATION: EASTER SATURDAY. Light gathers, leavens under his eyelids and forces them open. There is no colour. The space before him is neutral, grey, empty. The lenses of his eyes focus, and a picture achieves definition but he recognizes nothing. He reaches out and finds the bed empty. Marion is gone. No, he remembers, it is he who is gone. This is Linden House. Easter. Easter Saturday. Easter Saturday? What happens on Easter Saturday? He reaches for the Gideon in the drawer beside the bed. Who tells? Matthew, Mark, Luke, John, it makes no real difference. They were only fallible chroniclers, but they agree that nothing happens on Easter Saturday. It is just one more Jewish Sabbath. The whole of western civilisation is held up for twenty-four hours for this soundless Holy Day. The trouble with history is that it demands that the holes in it be believed in too. And that it may repeat itself. But the Jews have been given a country of their own and now they will be too busy with the claims made on them by territory to manufacture culture for export, let alone produce another Messiah. He puts the Gideon closed on his stomach and watches it rise and fall with the tides of his breathing. He thinks of last night, of Mary, of Philippa and I.J. Focus decays. He dreams lightly and without significance. Small fragments attract his attention, like hummingbirds at the flower of his pre-consciousness. He wakes, his mind is working, and goes with the Bible to his desk. On copypaper he writes: "Like hummingbirds at the flower of his pre-consciousness." He laughs out loud and shouts quietly: "Yes. Yes. Yes." He picks up the phone and orders breakfast, goes to the basin, washes, hesitates, opens the door to the hallway and looks out. The blue flowers there are still blooming. The corridor is long. He feels exposed and in danger. He closes the door and completes his ablutions at the sink. He waits tense for the food to arrive. He eats and plays with the Gideon, opening it at random. Begat, begat. Tries again. A boring letter from Paul. Again. "The soul of the sluggard desireth, and hath nothing; but the soul of the diligent shall be made fat."

Yes.

He puts down the Bible and takes up his pen. With it he traces the last words on the page: "Ole, sit down and eat. You're making more noise than the other two put together." But now Ole isn't making any noise at all. The sound that finally wakens Scann fully is the repeated monosyllable made by feet pushing through deep snow; the soft struggle, Writer Scann has said, of Thrain's feet moving through snow toward the cabin on Mosquito Lake. It is black dark. The arm and hand with the wolverine head on it drags beside him making a blunt unseen line in the impeding crystals. Snow. The axe hangs impotent over it. There is a sharp sliver of moon resting in the quick of the sky. Thrain sees it through the tops of the trees and keeps it on his shoulder as he goes. It may be getting warmer. He tells himself he is in good shape, well-dressed, hungry but fed not many hours ago. There are no sounds in the forest to worry him. He follows his feet, feeling sure of them, and doesn't worry when the moon glides down behind the thick of the trees. He has been walking longer than he expected to. The cabin on the lake was close, Linden had told him. The name in his memory stops his walking. Linden is dead. Thrain has let him die. He lives comfortable with the fact. He begins to walk again and the land beneath his feet falls away. He will see the flat of the lake soon. He steps again and there is nothing at all beneath his foot. He tumbles, lands awkward, and when he surfaces from beneath the snow he hears laughter. It rises to a cry like a coyote. Then: "I've been hearing you make your circles. Now d'you want to see the cabin at the lake, or do I have to send you around again?"

Thrain lies hurting in the snow. His chin has hit his chest and has driven a tooth through his lower lip. His body is both twisted and bruised. The axe and the head of carcajou have hurt him. His legs have done the splits and muscles and tendons burn. He listens to dead Linden's words and sucks his own blood back into his mouth and swallows. He lies out the truth, "I've come back for you." He has, he has. His aloneness is gone. Carcajou feels warm around his hand. And Linden says quickly, "Then cut some poles and drag me out." "Where?" "To your left." Caged Thrain moves. There is scrub pine near the base of the little ravine. He feels for a trunk and onehandedly swings the axe at it. It is so cold that the top vibrates, breaks off, falls on his head. Where once he had no sense of direction, he now has no purpose. He lies holding the axehandle close to him without knowing why. "Did it come down?" Linden's voice has changed its pitch and Thrain is pleased. He feels again for the tree and remembers he is making a sleigh to haul Linden out. He makes the axe chew at frozen wood. He chops away at all of the impossibilities between here and a fire and food at the cabin on Mosquito Lake. He cuts at the branches on the trees when they are fallen and drags the trunks to Linden. He stops, almost shy, and is glad of the dark. "The trap," Linden says almost softly. "Get the goddam trap." Close up he can see the man's face. It is luminous. The fact that he was left to die has got to him. Righteous Thrain tells him: "You know now you son of a bitch, you know now don't you?" And then he adds because he has thought it of him before: "You can think God if you want, but you can't *be* God." "Thrain, get the trap away from me." "I'm not going to leave you, stop whining." He doesn't see Linden's fist until it hits him just below his right eye. "Stop talking, we're in a hurry. Put the poles together and use the trap-rope to bind me. Do as I tell you or there isn't more'n an hour for you to live through. You don't know where the cabin is no better than walking to the moon."

Thrain swings one of the poles across Trapper Linden and lets it bounce on the top of his head. Anger and fear drain out of him; the old man lies anesthetised and physician Thrain, who has healed himself, works fast, binds untrapped Linden to the poles and manages a quick maneuver with his one free hand that allows him to knot the rope round his own body so that he can haul the unconscious trapper out of the deep snow in the gully. Drayhorse Thrain goes forward up the trail he made when he left Linden to die. And now he has carcajou holding with teeth and quills to his arm and Trapper Linden is tied to his waist. He dares not think. The axe is useless, except that it is carried high and in front of him at the end of an extended and straining arm as if it is a counterbalance to the load behind. He makes headway a foot at a time. His lungs burn from sucking frigid air. Behind him Linden groans awake. Thrain turns in the darkness and sees that the old man is twitching. Finally he screams: it is not pain. Thrain listens and thinks comfortably that it might be despair. The sound dies and the echoes stop. Then Linden's voice says hoarsely: "Thrain. Thrain? Come here."

Thrain wades through the snow to Linden's side. "Friend, I want you to know I deserve all of this. Since I come here I never talked to a man I didn't have to. I come here so's I could shoot any son of a bitch that got in my way. You know what I mean?" Thrain feels himself nodding, affirming his understanding. "But in the end I never shot no one but myself, and I talked to you just for the hell of it. Fact is, all I had to do was one little thing and I might as well've done them all. I should've shot you on sight. Come here, Thrain, come close. I want to whisper something so no one'll hear it but you." Thrain bent toward the luminous face supported by shadowed snow. Linden stretched his neck up. "Maybe when we get out of here I won't be in great shape. Thrain, listen careful. I'm going to live with Mrs. Thrain and the boys in that hotel of yours and in exchange I'm giving you my trapline, traps and cabins, the whole bloody country." Linden falls back against the snow. He is suddenly capable of gesture. "Now," he says, "haul me out of here." Thrain, because he is Thrain, takes the gesture as an insult. He stands the axe beside them in the snow and begins to undo the rope around his body. His hand is numb and the knot is tight. Linden is lying bound by hands, body and legs to the bed of poles. He laughs. "Pull," he shouts. "How else can you save us?" Thrain raises the axe. The laughing, ruined face knows something: they each can kill the other only if he is willing to die. Linden with his laughing face is a great man, a great teacher, a great enemy. Thrain lowers the axe through shame and humiliation, through blind anger, frustration, hunger, cold, exhaustion, until it impinges on his kneecap and produces pain. Animal Thrain savagely pulls.

"Go straight on, beyond the windfall, then only bear right," Linden says. "You'll see a clearing on your left. Keep in the lee of the trees on the right of it where the snow won't be so deep. Ahead's a hill. Now we can go right where the slope's not so steep and the trail should still be broken from when I come down this way earlier on today. It's flat at the top for a while but if you feel down good with your feet you'll sense the land falling off to the lake ahead. See? Now that will take you straight to the cabin. Bear a little left between those two trees."

"Shut up," Thrain says. "Shut up, I can see it." "Just haul me in and leave me while you make a fire so we can see what we're up to."

The door is ajar; rather, it leans out and pivots on the leather strap that is its upper hinge. In the grey light that is beginning to dawn on the edge of the lake Voyageur Thrain sits exhausted on his heels and stares at the half-opened door. Linden is behind him, bound to his poles and now in too much pain to twist around to see. "Take me in," he says. "Build a fire and bring in some snow for water." "It took nearly dying to make you talk," Thrain tells him. "Now shut up and listen. The door is off its bottom hinge and there's something in there." They hear together a scratchy rustle, and before Thrain can see what's coming out, Linden says, "It's the porcupine, tenderfoot." Thrain stands and raises his axe. Linden's head comes around. "Don't you kill him, Thrain. He got carcajou. He got him and nobody else could. Share with him, Thrain, remember to do that when you come back to trap this line. He'll mess up a cabin for you, but he's the one who'll get carcajou to make a mistake. I never knew. I been a sinner in that, Thrain." The porcupine appears as if he is interested in Linden's words, comes toward them over the doorsill and down the one big step to the packed snow in front of the cabin. It pauses, raises its nose to them and then waddles in the direction of the trees at the edge of the lake. It is wounded and dying. "It won't make it," Thrain says. He looks down at the quilled head on his arm and then behind him at Linden. "He's got a hole in his back the size of a fist. It must be the blood freezing around the wound that's keeping him alive." "You never know," Linden says, "he may live . . . Thrain. Listen Thrain, you leave me out here while you clean up inside and put the fire on. The porcupine's bent on saving me. He come by to say it's important for me to stay outside."

Thrain tries again to undo the knot that ties him to Linden but he is too weak. Near him is a chunk of firewood. He lays the rope across it and a blow with the axe frees him. Linden is mumbling as if he is telling beads. Physician Thrain crouches beside him and looks at the shattered hand in the new light. Mitt and blood and bone are frozen together. He looks at it closely and then pinches the arm above the wrist. "Feel that?" Linden nods. Lower, nearly to the mess of blood and bone: "There?" Linden almost smiles. He is no more mad than he ever was. "Just a little, Thrain. It hardly hurts at all." Thrain looks and sees the reason Linden's face has seemed luminous in the dark: it is frozen. "Rub your cheeks with snow. Start to unfreeze." He stands up and feels again the weight of carcajou's head. He holds it out to Linden's good hand. "Pull," he says and jerks at the quilled jaws. They struggle. There is pain. He leans down to relieve it. Linden thinks he is to push now and the wolverine's head moves up his arm. His whole hand shows beneath the frozen neck and the teeth and quills are holding now from elbow to wrist. The new hurt makes him dance away but there is a new balance too. The freed hand works: his muscles hold and swing the arm; the pain dulls. The fingers of his hand are tipped with white and feel stiff with frost. He crouches again and rubs them gently with snow.

"Thrain, we got things to do. Go see what mischief's been done." He looks at the wolverine's head. "It'll rot off once we're in near the fire all the time. I guess you'll have a few quills worked into you. You can cut them out easy enough with a knife."

Thrain shivers, stands up again and goes into the cabin. It is still quite dark but there is enough light coming in through the door to let him see that the room has been disturbed. The porcupine, not able to climb well or grub for food outside, has sampled everything he could knock from the shelves inside. Thrain's arm throbs now. He can feel it swelling. He sits abruptly on the doorstep and grabs the head with knees and hand and rips at it suddenly. Pain makes him feel faint and frightened. "Linden," he calls out of the darkness in front of his vision, "I've got to have this thing off." "You got to make splints for my leg. You got to make a fire and get some food. I don't think you got it straight, Thrain, carcajou's yours now and don't think the less of him for that. Time goes by slowly here. There ain't no starting or stopping. The good Lord didn't create this place. It's just materials he didn't use yet to make something from." "If I held it and you took the axe and split the skull we could crack it open and then it would come off." "Food, Thrain, get some food, it's yesterday since I ate." Thrain rubs his frozen fingers and looks around him. The lake is an expanded circle of snow, a disc growing brighter as day comes on. "It's forty below." "No, not more'n ten or twelve. Can you set my leg?" "Not with frozen fingers." "It hurts again." "Maybe it's thawing out by itself." "Thrain, do you have a gun?" "We're out of guns." "What'll persuade you to feed us?" "I pulled you out of the ravine." Thrain yawns tightly. "I dragged you the rest of the night to get here. I saved you, Henry. It's not like it was when we got here, or like it was last week and it sure as hell's not like it was last night." "You still don't know which way's home." Thrain lets himself smile. "I can make the river quicker than you." "And drown between heaved-up ice. You're crazy. When I go, you can go. Jesus man, ain't you cold and hungry?"

Thrain is beginning to feel blood in the fingers of the hand below carcajou's head. "What've you got for unfrozen fingers?" "Bear grease in a can." Thrain goes inside. It seems warmer there, but it's still too dark to see more than the porcupine's scattered ravaging. Thrain gives in and lights some chips and adds kindling and then split pine. The new heat hurts his hand but the light from the fire lets him rummage through the cabin and find the grease. He shoves his bunched fingers into it and then goes outside to get a pot of snow to boil for tea. Linden's eyes are closed. His cheeks and nose are solid now. If they moved they would crack like old porcelain. He reaches out with his foot in anger and revenge and shoves at Linden's chest. The body jerks with pain and the eyes open. "Got to do the leg now," Linden says with finality. Thrain ignores the words and thinks of him dead. Carefully he crouches and works the rope free of the poles. Linden settles, groans, faints. He breaks saplings and cuts them to length with the axe. Carcajou stares up his arm and its teeth and eyes grin peacefully in the early light. Thrain does not know what he is doing. He gets up and goes back into the cabin and puts the pot of snow on the fire. It hisses. Why is fire always the villain? He goes outside and sits at the feet of Linden. He holds the twisted foot in his hands and puts his own foot where he must, in the unconscious Linden's crotch. Doctor Thrain, M.D. C.M. takes a detached view. The ends of the broken bone must meet. Certain things must occur if this is to happen. Certain discomforts, disturbances. In this case, out in the wilds, a foot on the genitals is necessary to gain purchase so that the muscles of the leg may be stretched, the broken bone set. Thrain heaves, the leg lengthens. He twists the foot. Linden groans even in his deep faint. Thrain's fingers burn and slip. The ends of the severed bone make contact but grind off again and the sharp ends stab the flesh once more. Thrain pulls again, fits the ends more carefully, gradually increases the pressure to test the fit and finally reaches for the saplings. He binds the splints tight and drags Linden toward the cabin. The experiment is a success.

At the step he pauses and looks carefully at the old man. His shattered hand lies pinkly frozen by his side and his nose and cheeks shine with crystals of frost. Thrain lays him down on the packed snow parallel with the step. Inside, the water is steaming in its pan, and among the rubble on the floor are cans in which are tea and sugar. Thrain takes the pan from the fire and dumps tea into it. It steeps, infuses. While he waits and tries to think, he puts what the porcupine has left undamaged back onto the shelves. The place stinks of human even in the cold and with the door open.

"Thrain?" He stops working. "It's bloody cold out here." Thrain walks to the door and sets on the step, his legs arching over the prone Linden." Look," he says, "have you thought what that hand's going to be like when it thaws out?" Linden holds it up to see it better. He says nothing. "It looks like half a pound of tripe," Doctor Thrain says. He stands up. "It's frozen now. Maybe we better do something about it before we take you in." He kneels again suddenly as if he were giving in to a bad habit, takes the hand and breaks off what is left of the shattered thumb. It make a small sound, like an icicle snapping. Patient Linden looks at it. "You son of a bitch," he says. Thrain smiles, feeling alive and warm. "You didn't feel anything, did you?" "I felt it even if it didn't hurt. That's my thumb. Give it to me, goddam you." Thrain lets him have it. "Think," he says, "how bad it's going to hurt when it thaws. Who's going to fix it way out here? We don't even have anything to bind it up with, and which way would you wrap it?" "What," asks Linden, "are you saying?" His voice sounds every word distinctly, despite his frozen face. "It's up to you. It's your decision. I'm just offering to do it." "Snap it off?" H. A. W. Linden sits up. "No, I don't think it would snap." The thumb in Linden's hand is turning soft and a blue-grey. He looks at it with a certain solemnity. "Chop it?" he says quietly. "If you want. Or there's a bucksaw behind the door." He remembers that surgeons have saws. Patient Linden's tongue appears briefly at his lips. "That's a hell of a choice." "Quick, painless," Thrain says. He puts the axe on the step and goes for the bucksaw. The noise behind him angers him. It is a chopping sound. He turns. The axe blade is buried deep into the chopping-block step. On the right of it lies the tattered hand. Impatient Linden is sitting on the snow holding tightly to a wrist that is dripping between his legs. Thrain shouts: "We weren't ready. Nothing was ready." He stoops down, looking at the stump. "Did you do it in the right place? How do you know you cut it. . . ?" "Shut up." Linden voice is bright and vital. "Back away. Get me a pan of live coals. Move: and take the discard with you. Burn it." "Does it hurt?" Thrain is touched by sentiment. "No. Pick my — that thing up and go." Linden's eyes are points of light illuminating fear and disbelief. Thrain rises and goes inside holding the cold amputated hand carefully out of sight at his side. The fire is bright with coals. With a frying pan he scoops out a hole and hides the shattered hand among them. Outside again, he hands the pan to Linden. He doesn't see what happens. Almost listlessly he leans against the doorjamb and watches, at the water's edge, the porcupine fall out of a tree and lie struggling beneath it. At his feet, Thrain hears the hiss of blood and flesh on live coals (he remembers David standing by him when he was eating steak and asking, "Do you like cow's body?"). The porcupine lies still, dead, and already beginning to be preserved by the cold. And now Thrain finds he has focused again on the old man. His frozen face has cracked beneath eyes that are staring at his smoking stump. A black crust seals off the blood. He holds his arm and lies down quickly as if he is saving himself from an expected fall or as if he wants to faint but can't. He looks straight up into the diffused light above the trees, and his watering eyes overflow and tears run down crevices in the broken flesh. A tremour shakes him gently. No more than a shiver. Thrain squats above him, watching. Then there is a groan and a rush of breath, a howl and a convulsive quaking. Thrain puts his hands on the old man's shoulders to hold him away from smashing his head against the step. Then he shifts his position, lifts under the arms and drags the shuddering body into the cabin and across the dirt floor to near the fire. He fixes the door shut and throws furs over Linden's heaving frame. The tea Thrain has made still steams in the yellow light. He pours a tin cup full, dumps in sugar and lifts Linden's head to it. "Come on, Henry, drink up. Tea will cure anything. It doesn't hurt now, does it?" Linden shakes his head. "And the leg's all right?" Linden sucks on the tea. "More," he says. Thrain pours another cupful. "This is more service than I got." Linden jerks down the tea. "Not much you can do for a head cold," he says, and lies still for a moment before more shuddering begins. Thrain sits beside him drinking the pan's last cup. "The porcupine's dead," he says. "Fell out of a tree by the lake." Linden tries to talk but all he can produce is a hiss of breath as if he has just been kicked in the stomach. Then there is a small time of quiet. Thrain wishes for more light so that he might see Linden's face better. He leans closer. The eyes are not now roving and wild. By some extreme effort they are again focused. "Get him," the old man says. "I'll tell you how to cook it." Thrain rises, and the convulsions at his feet begin again. But at the door Linden's voice stops him. "Thrain, you son of a bitch, I'm going to make it." "Sure you are, Henry." "You know how to pick up a porcupine? Under the tail. Turn him over and slit the hide on his belly. He skins easy." Thrain goes outside into the light of day and does what he is told as best he can. His wolverine arm impinges again. It is a paining hinderance and his greased fingers are sore and nearly useless. He looks closely at the black and cream quills left on the porcupine's chewed-out back. They hang loose and innocent among the animal's winter fur. But where his mitt brushes by them a half-dozen cling firm, like logic to an unanswerable question. Each one has to be pulled out singly and each tears a little leather from the mitt. His arm stings in sympathy. But his stomach sucks and rolls around the cup of tea he has just drunk. He slits, skins, cut, hacks. They will eat soon. He returns to the cabin with the meat. Inside it is warm, almost hot. Linden is asleep, or seems to be. In this new climate carcajou begins again to assert himself. His smell rises above the stench of Linden's cabin. Thrain sits on the bunk with the head of the animal resting in his lap. Hurt subsides. With his knife he traces the axe-wound in its skull that finally killed it. He slits off pieces of furred skin, gradually exposing the bone beneath. His stomach goes quiet and the dry burning behind his eyes subsides. He has the left ear hanging now and the wet shine of raw bone dominates his work. He pierces an eye and pries it out. As it comes it makes the biblical sound: pluck. He leaves it to hang beside the animal's bared teeth by its own optical-umbilical cord. He takes out the other eye. Carcajou stares deeper into him. He works harder with the knife to deface the wolverine's empty regard, but the clean uncovered sockets only look dour and mystic. If it could talk it would speak Gaelic. The head nods gently as it is cut and sliced, working the quills into his arm more firmly.

Linden shifts his stump, waves it in the dusty air and groans softly. "If you're a good lad and treat me right, I'll tell you where the gold is." Thrain stops knifing the wolverine and kneels beside the old man. Linden's eyes shift above the frozen nose and cheeks. Thrain feels watched. "I give you what's here, but maybe you want to know more about it. Get the pan and put it on the fire. We'll make ourselves a bit of stew." "You don't know where any gold is." "You don't know I don't know. You don't know nothing, Thrain." Linden is frozen solemn, but his eyes lighten a little now. Thrain says, "Talk, just talk. Tell me and then we'll eat." "I want to see my cabin on the river again. I guess I'll tell you when we're there in the yard looking down on the water." He shifts as if searching for comfort. "Thrain, just thinking about it makes me want to talk." Thrain leans closer and then pulls away. He stands with carcajou at his side still eating his arm. "You aren't going to give me anything, Henry, and you know it and I know it. You lie or tell the truth or mix them up, whatever's easiest, or make a bad joke because you're holding back something you know that I don't." "There's no joke but you, Thrain." Thrain sits on the bunk again. He sees Henry Linden lying looking at the ceiling. His good hand trembles as he raises it to feel his nose and cheek. "If I was you I'd go," he says. "And I think I'd like that even in the shape I'm in now. What you do is follow the south edge of the lake and then keep the slope of the land on your right hand. Easy. In fifty miles you'll be able to shout across the river for help. You'll be a hell of a hero. And I'll meet you here in the spring." "Spring's pretty far off, Henry. You'll starve. I thought you said you were giving this up and going to live at the hotel." "I got mixed up, Thrain. I didn't remember you'd be there too. What'd you say her name was?" "Who?" "Your wife." "Erica." "Funny name." "Scandinavian." "Big feet." "Well, she was wearing my boots when you came by with Ro." "My grandma had big ones and she could go from Truro to the end of Colchester County and only breathe hard a little. Does she make good bread, this one?" "I'd rather eat hers than cake."

Thrain drifts past the lake, keeps the slope of the land on his right and crosses the ice on the river to home. A great comfort. He holds his arm out to Erica and she knows how to remove the quilled head. Together they bury it behind the hotel. The arm feels light and cool and lively. It bears only slight marks from the quills. He thinks of Henry Linden and is unhappy that he didn't stay to see him die.

"I'm going to teach you to make bannock."

Thrain comes back hungry. He smiles at Linden. "All right. We'll eat your saviour." He goes outside and picks up the frying pan from the step. The coals are dead. He scours it and brings it in.

Scann hears a key slide into the lock of his door and guesses it is Mary. She knocks. He sits at his desk without changing his position. The door opens a quarter of the way and he sees her eyes looking at him for a moment. Then she comes in quietly, as if he might be sleeping. She leans her mop and carpet-sweeper against the wall and goes to the bed. It needs only to be smoothed and the spread drawn over the pillows. He had slept all night as she had left him, with his clothes on and the extra blanket over him. He turns to watch her. She hesitates and then takes cover among her routines, but her movements are stiff. He is suddenly tense. The moisture at the back of his mouth dries into scales that cause him pain when he swallows. She comes around the bed, dusting as she goes, and then she mops and finally uses the sweeper on the 8 x 9 carpet. He tries to see her eyes. She sweeps nearer and nearer. He gets up and sits on the bed. He has gone too long without talking now and there is nothing to say. He feels he may be disappearing. She holds his empty chair up with one hand and cleans beneath it. When he opens his mouth he has to shout to be heard from a great distance. "You're not speaking." He is embarrassingly here again. He rises up off the bed and finds himself standing in front of her. She looks up at him. "I'm thinking," she says, and turns to find a mop. "And I'm busy." She opens the door. "Thinking? Why? What about?" "About me. Us." She closes the door again. He leans against the desk and his face shrinks shut. "On the one hand you treat me like a human being and on the other — " she brushes hair back with a curled wrist " — like I'm easy. You tell me a story."

She stops, looking very seriously at him, and he finds he can work his mouth again. "I don't tell everybody stories," he says. He thinks he might touch her now, but she shakes her head as if she knows his intention. "I don't know. I've seen you around since I was about ten or twelve." She opens the door a crack. "Well, you're different than what I thought." "And so you're thinking about us," he says quickly. She doesn't smile. She might be angry. "I got up this morning and it hit me: I never been so intimate with a man, ever." "And," but he doesn't know and what. "That's what I'm thinking about." She goes out into the corridor and closes the door behind her. Scann reaches, misses the knob. He is too far away. He looks up at the open transom. Then he moves, reaches again and opens the door. But already she has disappeared through another door, and someone is coming up the stairs toward him. He steps back and closes his door quietly.

The room is different. He sniffs. There is her cologne in the air and her tidiness around him and in him. Cleaned out by deeds, and a word. "The word," he says, "is intimate. In tim ate." His mouth and throat are still brittle but the moist syllables relieve the condition. He feels his specific gravity reduced. No traction. Intimacy is to the male-female relationship what grace is to religion. He has never been granted it before. It is a peculiar transfiguration, because he has no idea what he has done to deserve it: but it is not a word a woman uses loosely. She knows it almost from birth. She may be cursed with puny intelligence, small vocabulary, little morality and no physical charm, but even then she knows the moment and how to name it. No man can say he was intimate with a woman. "George, last night I was intimate with Mary Major in room 322 at Linden House." Even having been told, he cannot report it. It is not a word with gender: it is perhaps the one utterance in the language that is purely, even mystically, heterosexual and yet can be articulated only by a woman. "We can't be intimate, George, you and I, and you can't be intimate with my teeth. Overfamiliar, yes." Think of Thrain and Linden buried in snow beyond their waists and with carcajou swallowing Thrain's arm. A moment of unalloyed balance, of intermingling of fates, of terrible togetherness, but not intimate. Think of himself and Mary. She sat on the bed. Then she lay back on it propped against pillows. He paced, talked, lay beside her, told her about the Mortons, rolled over, kissed her and encountered no resistance, only a distance out of which came her other word:

exclusive. He had not granted her exclusiveness, but she had understood that they had been intimate. Not then. This morning when she woke. During the night their time together had borne fruit, real or otherwise. No matter which. This is a realm where fantasy can generate fact. Scann, too, believes he has been intimate. He sees her in the room again, returned to the scene, perhaps enjoying once more their meeting's criminality, silent as she works to neaten and smooth the edges. At the door, her eyes a little outraged that he doesn't understand because few men ever do. And then the statement, the pronouncement, the flight from her sudden knowledge of lifelong privation. Scann is forced by emotion to move. He walks around the room and disturbs her work. Then he wants to see her. He feels battered by warm breasts and soft thighs, which has nothing to do with intimacy and he knows it. He refuses not to be confused. He needs her to explain what happened, which might make it happen again. He needs to understand. Last night he had not thought he had travelled in straight lines. But he has been trapped. Not his animal. Him. The male component in intimacy is responsibility. He opens the door. The blue roses have grown larger overnight. He wades through them down the corridor and listens at doors. Out here in the long narrow dimness he feels exposed, perhaps hunted. His own quarry is nowhere that he can hear. He looks back toward his room. From outside, his door is as anonymous as all the others, and he may not be able to identify it now. He walks slow toward where it should be. Then he hears her carpet-sweeper, and he raises his hand to knock. But he doesn't. Once his knuckles hit wood, the interruption will be complete. Easter Saturday will be Mary's. He will have to explain, tell her about lust, talk about the urge to depravity as catalyst in the process that ends in sainthood. He stares at the door and the vision of Mary returns to normal, his mind gains traction. Seeking her out may shatter her artlessness and prevent her from returning to him again. She might even send another chambermaid. Women return to intimacy. It may be one of their natural habitats. Scann stands free of her door, and then moves again toward his, down her hallway, a kind of inheritance, it occurs to him, from Erica, whose imprint is gone from the ceiling, walls and floor but whose time is still ticking quiet among the blue roses. He stands at his opened door and watches her go along the chill bare boards of Thrain's unfinished hotel and down the stairs to her own quarters. He shivers, shuts himself in, calm and intentional again, and sits with his ballpoint in his hand. Erica works. In time, that solvent in which she lives, she makes either wine or vinegar. These may be the only alternatives in her nature. She lives watching the children, listening for Thrain and feeling the presence of Ole.

He hasn't gone. Maybe it's too cold. The train has brought, unexpectedly, radiators to heat the hotel. C.O.D. She pays for them out of her own money, and they take buckets of ashes mixed with coals from the fireplace to the rooms where they work connecting heating units to the pipes that run from Thrain's boiler room. She does not want to be near him all of the time, but it would be hard for him to work alone. The hotel is empty and unfurnished and frigid. She sees them moving about it at its mercy, and once more she hates the place. They hardly speak. There is no need. Ole has taught her the job they are doing. The ashes and coals, the blow-torch, the heat from their bodies make the work possible, and they do it as if it is necessary. One radiator after another in blind rooms where the ice is an inch thick on the windowpanes and the light coming through preserves the memory of the sun, like an egg in waterglass. Her mind goes stiff in this bitterness and she is glad. Away from the rooms she cooks and cleans and looks after the children, and Ole packs wood, builds fires, hauls ashes. At some noons it is warm enough to teach Ro and David to ski. The view outside is better. The hills, the mountains beyond. The sun occasionally slides out from behind a lard cloud and draws up the landscape into surprising light. Her eyes dazzle and pain, but there is hope in that crispness, even at the turn of the year. The boys stay up late on New Year's Eve, but she finally is able to persuade them it is midnight and makes a hot drink so they can toast the birth of 1919. Erica drinks also to the end of the war. Even this reminds her of Thrain who didn't have to go because of his slightly clubbed foot that hasn't stopped him from going where he wants when he wants. Into the bush to die like an animal. She hugs the boys, leans over to kiss them and wonders what she will do if Linden somehow comes back to take Ro away. She undresses and puts her nightgown on. There is a dumbness in her. It seems now always to have been there like wax sealing off the preserve of herself beneath it. And what is there may be only a kind of misery she has carried with her all of her life, a kind that Ole understands because he carries it with him too. She goes out of her bedroom to be near the warmth of the stove. This is another special night. She had managed Christmas. She turns and turns again soaking up the heat and trying to make an honest prayer for Thrain's return. She feels hot on her skin but what is inside of her begins to churn as if it is broken river ice. She tries to think that it is better than nothing, that something of her is coming alive. Then she spits on the stove. The white ball rages across the hot iron, jumping and hissing. She watches, surprised at what she has done, and it distracts her, makes her unwary. "Thrain," she says, almost a shout. She does not want to cry. She thinks words and says them. They are for Thrain. She has never heard them before in her mouth, but she knows she has felt them. She sweats and talks to the stove, harsh and loud, and then it is real midnight. The railway whistles blow, a puny noise for a minute or two and afterward not even an echo. Nothing. She begins to laugh, struggling to empty herself, to make her pressures equal inside and out. It seems she may have done it. She wipes her eyes with her wrists and breathes deep. She might after all have been crying.

Ole's knock on the door sounds no different than the one he uses when he arrives for breakfast. She turns, and he comes in unasked. His slow eyes have bloomed in his face, but they are uncertain flowers. In his hand there is a lump of coal. He doesn't even know that it is bad luck for someone blond to be the first to come in the door at the New Year. The coal in his hand is another joke. She knows he has been waiting outside, and hearing. She wishes he hadn't heard. Her words are still with him. They are making his face grave: he is that from head to foot. He doesn't speak, not even to say "first foot" as you're supposed to when you come in with a lump of New Year coal. His mouth twitches and he takes his breath in sharp and then lets it out again like a man waking up. Neither of them is moving but she has the sensation of travelling fast. She must begin to make some control if there is to be any. "Ole," she says and goes toward him, "I think you brought me a present." His eyes shift. They look down at himself and then at the coal. "Yah," he says and hands her the lump. Then he touches her. His hands become very quick when they begin to touch. They are not gentle. What they are doing is wounding him. Erica lets go of the coal. She knows she drops it because it makes a thud on the floor. They stop, close; and maybe he is afraid too. "Thrain will kill us," she tells him. "Thrain?" There are tears in his eyes, and she thinks that now she herself may be able to weep.

Behind her, she hears bare feet on the floor. They come a little way from the bedroom and halt. She knows it is David by the sounds he has made, by the way he now breathes whimpers into the silence. Ole's face is stiff and there is a big pulse beneath his jaw. But he is the one who moves. She watches him stoop for the coal, go to the boy and take him in his arms to the bedroom. David doesn't call for her. She waits. Thrain would never do a thing like that. He would say, "Take your child back to bed." Ole returns wearing the face he works with. "He asked me what we were doing." His voice is thin. "I said we were praying for the New Year." "A little lie," she tells him. "He says you were doing something and it was hurting me." He doesn't have the coal in his hand. It seems better only to wonder about that. Ole says, "It is a lucky thing for him to have for the rest of the year." He might be away in his room and she is just hearing him in her mind. "We didn't do anything," he says. She sees him again, and when she speaks her voice is too loud. "You should say you're sorry." She watches him look at his hands. "Not for." She stops. He is on David's side, and Thrain's. It is his protection. It is better to be just hurt so the mind is taken up with only that. Her breasts pain a little but that is all. She touches him on the arm. "Ole, we got regular things to do in the morning." He nods his head, and she tells him, "Goddam, Ole, goddam, isn't that what you say?" "Sure," he says, "but I don't think it's what you say."

Scann watches, feels them being reduced to further incompleteness and without being able to do anything about it. For the rest of their lives there may be moments when each will try to make different endings to the story they have begun there near Erica's stove. Feelings were shot off like lightning with no ground, creating the static imagery of temptations. He gets up and walks the passages around the obstructions in his room. Love stories threaten him. His own happened at fourteen. He touches the edges of it again. They are sharp, a measure of the durability of unique cruelties. She was wearing a white blouse cut like a boy's shirt, blue shorts, white ankle socks and runners. Her hair was a live colour that turned light brown in the summer. Her eyes were grey and her face, he knows now, was unfinished, as perhaps her bones were. She lay wrapped up in him on the boards of her grandmother's porch in the sun. Scann halts in front of the green windowblind. Her mouth is puffed from kissing. There has been almost a year of this. The top three buttons of her shirt are undone. He puts his lips against the soft hollow below her throat. They have no separate lives. Their names are run together as one by friends, perhaps even their families. He feels her body pressing beneath the palms of his hands. She has grown up beneath his touch. She depends on him. He goes to see her every day. She is quiet. They have never talked much. He makes love to her every night in his bed and the next day he tells her a little about it and says it was a dream. The secret of what they are doing he doesn't share with himself. He draws houses for her. He still doodles houses. Scann's lips are moving. He is reciting as if she is in the room with him: You must understand that an emotion shared by two people that comes before its time is a monster. He lets his mouth slide across the tops of her small plump breasts. There is no sensation: Maybe you knew, he says. She puts her arms around his head and lies very still. He is caught there awkward, and she begins to smell. It is raw and strong. He pulls his head out from under her arms; the garden they have been living in is set about with the toadstools of reality and he feels disgust. The odour is her first heat, involuntary final proof of love, but it is years before he knows. And gardens he has reason to deny. He stops seeing her. Her older sister phones and says, "You're killing her, you know. She doesn't understand what she's done." He doesn't know, or can't or won't give the answer. That way you're only allowed one love. Cruelty is a debt. It accrues interest, grows and is not payable. Moratoriums only seem possible. Other debtors say so.

There are other sentimentalities too. He moves the windowblind to one side so that he can see the heads of Linden's Easter Saturday shoppers. He may go down and walk with them. He stares. His mind refuses the act. "Gardens," he says quietly, "and apocalypses, are for the unconscious." He turns voluntarily back into the room. When the emotions are blocked, one becomes an intellectual and makes theories which beg decisions. Already he knows what is going to happen to Erica and Ole. Their monster will seem natural enough. Most people's do. Are. Adam and Eve didn't leave the Garden, they. Scann stops himself. Love stories are about boundaries. Yes. He sits at his desk again and hopes for a vision of Erica at her's. But what he senses he cannot see. He feels only the warmth of her kitchen, Thrain's presence. Outside the door, nailed to the wall, is a ten-foot kite built from a network of thin cedar ribs and laminated paper. Someday he will build an aircraft. But nothing is happening now. Scann sits tense as if he might be in danger. He looks north to the Mosquito Lake cabin. The door is closed. He watches himself watching the yellow green-lined page in front of him. What happens when the mind is also blocked? He leaves his desk again and walks the dimensions of his room. He sees the aperture in the back of the closet. It pulls at him like habit, or hope. He kneels before it. Kneels. He knows what he is doing. He thrusts his head forward and puts his eye to the plaster hole. Ro is lying on the bed facing him. Scann is reluctant to see. He takes his eye away from its escape route and sits on his heels. He sees anyway. He has always lived like this, in a shambles whose origins are only partly known and not entirely innocent. He looks again. It is Ro, older than the picture of him in the *Chronicle*'s files: nearly sixty, but when he yawns his own teeth show. It is a benign face where Trapper Linden survives only in the eyes. His skin is high copper and his grey hair is short. Scann goes back to his writing table and flips through a notebook. After the war, Ro had come back for a brief moment to tell the truth the whole truth before a court of law. Then he had gone again, one of those the war had liberated. There were some, there were some. Ro had a pool cue, and he became snooker champion in 1954, 1955 and again in 1958. He still gives exhibitions. Perhaps he is only home again to do another. Yet, whatever else there is significant about his presence in the next room, Ro is news.

Editor Scann lifts the phone, dials nine to get a line out and then his own number at the *Chronicle*. The ring of the phone is a return to duty. He listens to Shirley answer and knows he has made a wrong decision. Quietly he hangs up. He has been a long time away from what he is supposed to be doing. He sits on the bed, abject. His animal whines uncertainly. "Pitch-catch." He holds his head higher: "There is no such thing as history." He stands: "Only bad writers go in for beginnings and endings." He paces and intones again: "Gardens and apocalypses are for the unconscious." He takes his chair from the desk and places it at the door. The open transom calms him, but still he says: "No contact. No connections. No quarter given." And then he begins to laugh. He wishes he didn't know why. The sound of it is bringing Mary. Her anxious face is peering up in his direction as she strides toward his door. He climbs down off his chair, puts it back at the desk and waits. Her keys jangle, one is inserted in the lock, her knuckle raps twice perfunctorily and then she is in the room. Her eyes are capable of rebuking God. She dismisses the tears on his cheeks as she closes the door. "I don't know what you're doing here," she says and stands very close to him. "Maybe it's a free country and you can do what you want, but not in the hallway. If you stand on that chair and shout over that transom once again." Their intimacy has been thought through. They may be strangers again. Or enemies. She begins to walk around him as if he is a tree and she is judging the best way to cut him down. "Philippa Morton," she says and stands in front of him again. "Freeing slaves. Liar." "She did." "She didn't." "She did, with the help of I.J. and the two girls." Mary hits him hard on the chest with both fists. She is surprised and perhaps delighted with herself. "How come no one ever reported her? Answer me that." He holds her wrists. "Slaves who are freed never report. The price of freedom is very high. Everyone knows that. They accepted the bargain and rode on out with Cecilia's blessing. Free. Goodness me, who's going to report someone for giving him freedom? She stops her struggle and moves to the door. "I'm fed up with you." Scann doesn't want her to go. He wills her to turn around. She does. "I have to work this floor. It's mine. You understand? It's what I do for a living." "Yes," Scann says, "and how rotten it'd be if I had to put up with one of the others." She looks at him. "I've hardly been home since you got here. Just to sleep. It's like you're something I have to keep hidden. I keep coming back and listening at the door, or I hear you starting to make a fool of yourself, shouting over the transom like you're in pain or something. I don't give a damn about old Thrain or Cecilia, not the way you tell it. Besides, if I want the truth I can go out to Dorothy Carmoddy's place and talk to Thrain." She moves closer to him again. "I can, can't I, Amory Scann? and he'd tell me what kind of a liar you are." "No," Scann shouts at her, "of course not. He doesn't know what happened out there, he just knows the facts." She shouts too: "What the hell else is there but the facts. In one little sentence, did he and Cecilia — or didn't they?" "It's come to that, has it? You mean screw, don't you? What happened to love? What happened to Making Love?" "Well, screw's what people in stories like you tell do, isn't it?" She stops shouting. "You won't tell me? Okay, I'll go and see him." "He won't tell you either. You ask him and he'll see you to the door." "I wouldn't ask him right out." "Then how do you expect to hear about it? Do you think he's going to sit in his rocker with a rug over his knees and give you the scurrilous and salacious run-down?" Scann sits on the bed and points to his chair at the desk. She looks as if she might cry. She blinks quickly, trying to re-focus her eyes and then she pleads: "You won't say you're lying?" "No." Mary sits too and stares out across the space between them. Finally she says, "I'll be fired for being here." "That's your story," Scann says. She gets up. "It's true," she says and begins to walk. He sits silent and lets her fend for herself out in the wilds of the room. She looks frightened, a little out of control. Her eyes switch back and forth as if she has lost her way to the door. "What if I screamed?" she says abruptly. "I have a very loud voice." He rises and puts one hand on her shoulder and the other under her chin. He hears the audience begin to laugh. He explains to them that this is the kind of girl she is. She believes only well-known gestures. She can only be touched, gentled like this. He begins: "You will remember," he says, feeling free again, "how when Thrain arrived at the front door of the big house he still had his helmet and goggles hanging loosely around his neck in that negligent 1930's imitation Lindberg manner." "He is forty-eight," Mary says, "and Philippa is fifty-six. She has been fifteen years in the secret room on the third floor, only it isn't secret anymore because there's no one left who doesn't know how to get there." He smiles down at her. "You've been listening to me. There's even an echo of my style." He squeezes her shoulder a little harder than he knew he was going to. "Go on, what happened next?" She ducks her head. "I don't know. It's that knife — " "Purely for show. It's the ceremonial dog that should fascinate you." "I guess I'm not that kind of girl." "Don't you think so?" He drops his hands and her body shifts before him after the release of weight. "What happens next is this. His knock is answered. He is brought in. He meets Cecilia and Amantha and is properly introduced to Isaiah Jones. Thrain knows nothing of these people. He is an innocent thrown up on this farther shore through the failure of his engine. He has swooped down quietly on the Morton ranch, and all of them there, including the dogs who barked and bayed at his arrival, feel a fault beneath the crust of their lives here shift. For Cecilia especially the ground trembles. She seems to Thrain always to be standing in front of Amantha and looking up at him like a belligerent." Already Mary is sitting on the edge of the bed. Scann moves around the room. "Thrown up on this farther shore," she says, "that's nice."

He goes to the basin and looks down the sink hole. He turns. "Hardly original. It's been used before." She looks at him surprised. "Maybe that's why it feels good. Does everything have to be new?" He goes toward her. "It made you feel safe?" "Yes." "Then it hasn't anything to do with life," he tells her. "If you feel safe you're dreaming." He leans over her and stares down. "Catherine the Great's boudoir rabbit felt safe. Do you come back and back to this room because you feel safe?" She is beginning to laugh. She has her hand to her mouth as she once did before when he had Thrain on the threshold of the Morton's life. He grabs away her hand and lifts her to her feet. "Thrain did not feel safe. In his whole life he never felt that way, but especially not now when he has walked in on the moment of the final disintegration of the Morton Empire, a moment in which he is to be both catalyst and observer. Are you listening?" She nods, he releases his grip on her wrist and stands clear. "He came ashore out of curiosity. He could have fixed his gas line and flown away without visiting. But the dogs, I.J., and the largeness of the house, the sudden smell of all that decadence shimmering in the sun made him want to see it close up. He was not disappointed. He had a meal with the two women. They ate in the kitchen, an enormous room with a ten-foot table placed near a bay window out through which could be seen hundreds of acres of neglected beige ground. Cecilia whistled through her teeth when her mouth wasn't full of food. It was a furious tune and as melodic as a safety valve. She plunged her fork into the beef on the platter in the middle of the table and sliced it with a huntingknife. As she chewed, her eyebrows went up and down in an effort to camouflage her staring at him. She spoke like an angry folksong: a statement or maybe a question and then a refrain: "We don't feed strangers here often." Thrain, himself, made an effort not to stare at her. He found himself roused and his throat went dry. He couldn't help himself; the innocent immodesty of her began to obsess him. He had to force himself to look up to remember what her face looked like. It wasn't fat and it wasn't altogether ugly, but there was something porcine about it and her very short straight hair did nothing to relieve that notion. He looked up and then down at his plate and put more beef and potatoes in his mouth. He seemed not able to swallow it past the upper reaches of his esophagus. It cemented there in a block. Her eyebrows went up and down. He saw her watching and shovelled with his fork. The pain in his gullet spread to his chest without really distracting him. He was worried that he might have to stand up. There was dirt beneath her fingernails. It excited him. His breathing became difficult and he realized that he was in distress. He leaned back and looked up at the ceiling, trying to stretch the muscles in his throat and give them leverage. "Gas line you say?" she asked for perhaps the fifth time. She had been reduced to this because he did not answer and she was becoming angry. She pointed the tip of the knife at him and sighted along it. "Mister, we don't hardly ever feed strangers." He tried to smile. There was no water on the table, only a pitcher of cream. The pain was beginning to make his throat rebel and he couldn't understand how he'd managed this predicament. "Is something the matter?" Amantha inquired as if they were playing dolls but he was only peripheral to the game. He looked at her and she leaned forward a little toward him, but Cecilia was up and had come around the table. He knew his face was red and gawping. Cecilia, too, leaned forward. She swung down over him. He saw nothing except the knife still in her hand. He waved it away and his hand came to rest softly against the causes of his distress. She twitched as if she'd been touched by a live wire and he gulped involuntarily. The meal in his throat shifted and scraped down. The pain made him rise up out of his chair. "Now what made you do that?" Cecilia asked. He wanted to tell her. Amantha was there but his consciousness had not broken all the way through to her. He was only aware that he was caught between conventional politeness and Cecilia's body and knife. Through tears he watched the knife, and without thinking he reached out to take it from her. She flicked her wrist and cut off the tip of his little finger. His vision cleared. She stood, still pointing the knife, delighted with herself. Her face was flat and immobile but her eyes were pleased with her aim and the eloquent statement the knife had just made. Blood scattered on the wooden floor when he moved his hand to look at the finger. Amantha was going past him. I.J rose and stood near the stove. His smoky eyes stared, his lips moved. He looked eager. The power game is always played with blood markers. Thrain began to know where he was. Cecilia had her feet apart and her knife-hand seemed to be the centre of her equilibrium. Thrain watched her for a moment and came, without emotion, to a conclusion: she was not insane. She simply lived this way. He bled on the floor and looked at her more closely. There were small scars on her face and neck and forearms. How they got there was not easy to say. She may have fought with her knife often, or they might have come from riding fast through the bush. He thought of taking out his own knife. He would lose the draw. He held his finger to stop the bleeding and as a sign of his unwillingness to argue with her knife. She seemed excited too; he wanted to reach out for her. She turned suddenly away from him and tossed the knife in the air. It stuck into the ceiling. The dog at I.J.'s feet stood up, launched himself and took the knife down in his teeth. He presented it to Cecilia, she took it, patted his head and ruffled an ear. Still she said nothing; her eyes looked at him and searched for his understanding of the knife, the gesture, the dog. He gave it, and she sat again at her place at the table. Then Amantha returned. She had a piece of torn-up rag in her hand. She sat by him on a chair and took his hand to wrap the finger. He stood close over her and saw that she was Cecilia's sister, but with none of her excesses. She bandaged the finger tightly, looking up at him occasionally, saying nothing until she had finished. Then she smiled and told him, 'You must meet my mother.'

"The knife clattered onto Cecilia's plate. Amputee Thrain clenched his fists, more to protect his fingers than to fight. I.J. stepped forward from the region of the stove. 'Isaiah Jones will conduct you,' he said, but Cecilia was standing again. 'I.J.,' she said, 'you do no such thing. Mr. Thrain's welcome around here just until his airplane is fixed.' I.J. stood straight and looked as if he were trying to shrug years off his shoulders. 'Our Philippa already said she'd like to have the man taken up.' Cecilia took her knife and flipped it toward him; it stuck into the floor at the tip of his mocassin. 'Do as I say.' I.J. picked up the knife and held it in his hand. He looked at it and then at her. 'You're stupid. Now I got the knife and my whip's like usual beside the stove. You might get some teaching.' Cecilia didn't move. Beside him, Thrain felt Amantha still holding his injured finger. He glanced down. She was silently sliding to her knees on the floor. He moved in front of her and held her hand firm. I.J., his whip in one hand and the knife in the other, circled, the dog at his feet. Cecilia stood still. The whip snapped near her. His voice was loud and bass and it cracked with power at its edges: 'She's going to come back down here if you don't watch out. You don't want that.' The whip drew blood on her arm. She looked at it, trembling and biting her lip. Then she raised her head and began to walk toward I.J. while the whip cut her again and then again. It didn't stop her. The dog snarled and leapt. I.J. drew the whip back. Cecilia paused and slammed the dog hard with her fist. He dropped back stiffly onto his legs and began to moan. The whip came around, aiming for her legs. She danced up like a small girl skipping and reached for the knife in his left hand. He held it away and she went for the whip. Now both hands were above him and his back was against the door to the servant's stairway. She was touching him, reaching him, and in that moment there was no movement. They simply stood as if the next command had not gone from their brains to their muscles. Thrain held Amantha's hand more tightly and felt her head against his leg. At the doorway, Cecilia broke her stance, punched I.J. in the stomach, and when he doubled over she slapped his face twice, as hard as she could. Then she took both the whip and the knife from him. Thrain knew this had happened before. Slowly, I.J. straightened and those two looked at each other. It was as if something more should happen now, but there was no anger, hate or passion, just unassigned emotion that rose between them like a confusion of dust after a collision. In a moment she gave him back his whip and turned to Thrain, ignoring Amantha and speaking up into his face as if what she had to say were important: 'It was just berries and cream for dessert.' But her eyes were struggling for control. Thrain nodded. With her there, turned toward him, the violence of what had happened caught him like an updraft, confusing him too, and when she continued to speak he found himself looking at her as a woman and not a collection of outsized spare parts. 'Maybe we can eat them down at the machine.' He looked down at Amantha. Cecilia put the point of the knife against the softness of his stomach. 'You're going to have to bring him back,' I.J. said. 'Our Philippa, she wants to see him.' The knife pressed harder. It felt good to turn and walk out into the heat again. Once more the decay in the kitchen was rousing him."

"I don't know what you mean by decay," Mary says. She is at the window now, dusting the sill, keeping safe by continuing to be a chambermaid. "We're talking about rot," Scann says, "and about old gods and new ones, and about made up dances and real rituals, of beasts and humans, of governments and their subjects, of churches and religions, of hunting knives and plugged gas lines and man's urge to climb mountains because they're there."

She stops dusting. "I can see it now. I know what's going to happen and it's not fair. Cecilia's the only one there who's not nuts.

She's alone and I know how she feels. Everyone looks at you as you go by and smiles and puts you out there on the edge of everything, and then when you blow it — big deal, they knew it would happen. She must've felt good putting that knife in Thrain's stomach."

"Very good, and virtuous. Most do, you know. Violence, except in very small children is never done for its own sake. Yours against Thrain is really against all men." He leans on the desk where his manuscript lies inert and folds his arms across his chest. "The same as the violence you do against me." Mary turns from the window. "You?" "Yes." "I never did a thing to you yet." Scann goes close to her, lifts her off the floor, a hand under each elbow. He imagines he smells her clean pink flesh beneath her smock. "Put me down, Amory Scann." He walks with her to the bed and does as he's told. She slips away and stands looking down at him. "See?" he says. She stares back. "You start it every time. I'm not going to let you, you know." She straightens her smock and smoothes her hair. He tells her: "That's just the way you get your kicks, is all." She laughs. "Wouldn't you like to know the truth, Mr. Author Scann." She looks at her watch and Old Fighter Scann, knowing he's made a bad mistake, rolls over on the bed and stares at the wall. He waits for the kill. You can run toward something only for about as long as you can run from something and then you must give up. When she closes the door it will be the last of Mary and Amory, of Cecilia, Amantha, I.J., Philippa. His mind waits painfully for this new vacuum. He is fond of them all, no matter how it is he's treating them. Morton Lake, too, Morton Ranch and Creek. The Morton name lives in them, but he feels the death of his own name approaching: Mary Major would rather comb her hair than listen to his story. Her finger taps his shoulder. "I should have all my rooms done by now." He turns over. "You want me to go on?" He sees her face, nearly friendly but impatient. "How much time have I got?" She looks at her watch again. "Maybe ten minutes?"

He leaps up, goes to the window; there are people milling below. It is Easter Saturday. He goes to the sink and sees himself in the mirror. It is a pale handsome face, sensitive, but the kind of countenance one often sees on a man who is not afraid of a challenge. "Ten minutes," he says, "to tell the story of Cecilia and Thrain. Ten minutes. Right. I will speak quickly, so listen. They go out the door, down past the ruined corral." "It wasn't ruined when he came in," she says. He turns from the mirror. "Believe me or leave."

He points. She shrugs. "Everything is in ruin. The compound is filled with piles of rotting logs that once were buildings. The barn sags. Didn't I tell you that? The animals are all bushwackers and roundup is more like a big game hunt than anything else. I.J. spends his time making flags. When they go neither Amantha nor I.J. follows. Cecilia marches Thrain in front of her knife. It was a gesture, not really necessary, but Cecilia was happy with the knife in his back. It was as if she had been waiting for her own victim all these years and now here he is, a wiry leather-faced man who, she senses, has not yet begun to think of fighting back. She doesn't know or understand that he is different from any other man she's ever met. His is a madness different from her father's. No rituals have ever tainted his life. His rules are private. His view of the world is distinct from convention. Almost two decades ago he inherited the country, and his belief in the gift and his acceptance of it is profound. But right now he is thinking of Philippa. He would like to meet her. He felt the knife in his back and wondered how he was going to do it. His decision was to go along with the knife to the aircraft and let it force him to fix the fuel line. They approached the dock. The gentle noon waves were lambent curls against the shore. The flying boat undulated and moaned as it touched the wharf. The water was black-green flecked with pollen. The heat raised odours that in another time would have assailed the senses, but now that tender rot only angered the knife. It forced him forward quickly to the aircraft. Without speaking he got out his tools and began the job of disconnecting and cleaning and blowing out the lines and filters and screens from gas tank to carburetor. He had done this so often that his mind and eyes could be freed to other concentrations. He saw that Cecilia was in trouble. Perhaps the excitements of the kitchen were still with her. The hand that grasped the knife was tight and bloodless. Her skin was shiny with sweat. Her face was a defiant blush. And her eyes were outraged, as if she were unexpectedly losing control of her bladder in public. 'I'm going to go up and see your mother,' he said. She shook her head. 'No, you're going to fix this thing and fly out.' 'I don't want to leave.' 'You better or I'll slit you.' She seemed in better control now. He reached out with clenched fists and put his knuckles against the hang of her breasts. She didn't move. His fists searched and his fingers opened to help. He had expected to hold her, to guide her by tumescent flesh toward him. She pulled back an inch. He dropped his hands, not thinking at all about her or her knife, but wondering at the inaccuracy of his aim. "Why do I have to go?" he said without hearing the words. "Because we were happy when you didn't come and we'll be happy when you go away again.' "

Scann has been standing in the middle of the room. He breaks his pose. "Sex is the most innocent of man's exploits. Thrain's wanting to see Philippa is a far greater violation than anything he could or did do to Cecilia." Mary is sitting on his desk near the manuscript. She is not listening. She looks distressed. "Was there something wrong with her — I mean so they couldn't. . . ." "You mean, did they make love? Strictly speaking, the answer to that is no." Mary gets down from the table, making negative gestures. "None of those perversions please. I'm not going to listen to that stuff." Her hands scrub out the direction she thinks he's going and her eyes are concerned. "Whose story is this?" Scann smiles tiredly. "You're telling it to me and I don't want to hear garbage about them." "And you want — " "The truth, goddamn it."

The truth, Old Sweat Scann thinks, is that Mary is sentimental. A chocolate with a cherry centre. The truth is that she is right and what happens between a man and a woman, even between Cecilia and Thrain, is vague, perhaps holy, certainly a mystery. It's a country that has no absolute borders, and trying to map it is always a perversion. "Let me ask you," he says, "let me ask you to change perspective for a moment and think again about this thing that's going on in the aircraft. Think of Amantha and I.J. at a second story window looking down at Cecilia and Thrain. Amantha stands quietly with her clenched fists supporting her on the windowsill so that she is leaning forward. I.J. stands behind her. Neither of them wears any discernibly abnormal expression. But they watch. Below and beyond them at the edge of the lake is Thrain's aircraft — a hull, a wing, struts, a pusher motor. He is no longer working on the plugged gasline. He may, in fact, have it fixed. Her knife glitters occasionally in the sun." Scann moves to stand near Mary and feels a pressure striking against the smooth rhythm of his diaphragm. "Amantha and I.J. watch. Is it less innocent to watch? Or to be watched?"

"I don't think they feel anybody's watching," Mary says, "and that's all they need to know." She looks at the time once more. Writer Scann continues: "Amantha's lips are moving. I.J.'s aren't. Amantha's corn-coloured hair is in a braid and it hangs down over the windowsill toward the ground that leads to the shore of the lake on which Thrain sits like a Viking in his winged boat. Amantha still doesn't move." "What's she doing?" "What would you be doing?" "I don't know. Praying? Praying he won't be hurt with that knife." "You wouldn't pray that she not be hurt?" "Not for Cecilia — she wouldn't get hurt." Scann pinches his lower lip between his thumb and index finger and turns away from her: "They have been sitting facing each other across the knife. The scene is quiet, but it's like tension on glass. Nothing happens. No intimation. Movement becomes necessary. Suddenly there is an intense sound and the surface of the glass disintegrates without shattering so that neither depth nor perspective remain. Thrain has shouted out a single curse, a lone syllable, and he rises, and Amantha echoes the sound, holding I.J.'s wrist in the same way that Thrain holds Cecilia's. I.J. is talking again. He gestures but neither of them moves from the window. At the flying boat Cecilia is up and fighting. Thrain holds her knife hand and uses only his left to do battle, a handicap he assumes with over-weaning pride. Cecilia punches him and he has to hang on to keep from falling into the water. Cecilia yells like an angry mare, forgets her knife and drops it. She slugs him happily, teaching him with every blow better manners. He falls and feels the knife beneath him. Thrain, excited now, laughing, rises with the knife in his hand. Amantha shouts and gestures hugely out of the window toward the aircraft. Her cry is not partisan. She is simply horrified to see a knife in a man's hand. She drops I.J.'s wrist and tells him: 'Get her out of that airplane.' He only looks back at her. There is no difficulty in telling whose side he is on. 'Give her a cut, a cut, a cut,' he is saying as he watches again the scene below. 'A little blood'll teach her.' He is very angry. Very angry indeed. Every prime minister is caught between religions and the sweaty people. He hears Amantha's order, but only as a kind of harmonic to the tonic note of his revenge being played below. He does want to be nearer. Thrain has the knife. As Amantha begins to watch again, and just as I.J. emerges from the house, he uses it. He presses the point to Cecilia's belly and rakes it up toward her throat. She flings herself backward and upwards onto the broad slab of the wing, losing only shirt buttons to the slash of Thrain's blade.

"Mammaries loll."

Scann stops and then says, "Under a golden sun in a blue sky, as Cecilia lies across the yellow fabric of Thrain's wing, tipless mammaries loll." Scann looks down into Mary's face. "Language is beautiful," he says. "The precise phrase is always without uncalled for implication, always takes the side of natural vision. It leaves the reader free. Even you who are female and whose pointy little breasts will never under any circumstances loll — efficient as they may have been to suckle Billy — you whose interest might be minimal in whatever attitude to Cecilia's various and abused parts might assume as she escapes the knife in Thrain's hand, *you* were struck by the aptness and clarity of the phrase just as I who invented it am. But, you might say, I'm a man and might therefore have a certain salacious interest in lolling mammaries. Wrong. Wrong. I am, you may be relieved to hear, a bum man. Mammaries I have at home, in abundance, but not a shapely backside. No. None of that. My spouse has what can only be described as an ass, the old-fashioned kind that used to be measured in axe-handles." Scann reaches around her until his palms are cupping her buttocks and he says in an unrehearsed whisper: "You *are* relieved to hear of my proclivities, aren't you?" Mary's lips sound the unknown word as she pushes her fists against his chest. "Amory, please, you don't know how many times I've had men expose themselves to me in this hotel and I still get embarrassed." He moves a little away from her, looking down at himself involuntarily. She says loudly: "You aren't going to, are you?" "I have, I have," he says. "I already have. Weren't you listening? I'm naked before you. Stark." "I don't know about that," she says and turns away, "but anyone can see what's happening to Cecilia is being made up by a man." "No, it's true." "It isn't." "So what happened?" "There she is with her, you know; well, it's how they got that way that's all wrong." Mary goes to the door and Scann stops her. "How? Come on, lets hear it." She turns again, as sometimes real poets will upon mere writers, and says quietly: "She let him. That's how. She let him and it's the end of something not the beginning. She would be attracted from first seeing him. And the knife, she would hold the knife or play with it all the time because she was nervous and trying not to be too interested. I mean after all how many men has she seen up close since her daddy died, and except for being able to, well loll a bit, she was pretty ugly. It would take days, all this. Thrain would have to be there for a long while and she would have to see that he was attracted to her sister. Then, you see, she would order him to fix his plane so she could follow him to the shore and be alone with him. She'd be *so* ashamed when she let him, and feel *so* rotten that she knew all along that he was paying her attention just because she was there and he was lustful. But she wouldn't care. And then I guess she'd give him the knife to show she was going to trust him. That's the way it is with a woman and that's why they have to be careful about following guys to their planes and whatnot. I mean, whether she knows it or not a girl's held together by only a few little things that make her decent and once they're gone she doesn't care for shame or being used. She just gives it all away at once and believes, you know, really believes that what he wants is love and this thing she is doing now is building a bridge to it by showing him she can sacrifice best and love best and be goddamnit violated best. You see? That's how it would really happen for Cecilia, and as soon as Thrain's gasline was fixed, well, Thrain'd fly away and Cecilia might do something desperate, but I don't think so. I think she'd just go on being the one who's really running the ranch. And like I said, it's the end of something, not the stupid beginning of something else." Scann has listened carefully. He points a finger. "You admit the knife?" "Yes." "It is essential?" "Well, it's there, it makes it interesting a bit." "It is the sign of violence between them." "The way I see it, it gets to be a sign that there isn't going to be any fight between them. I mean, for me it's a thing that makes them have to trust each other." "But before she gives it away to him, it's violent then, isn't it?" "No. It's a steak knife." "It's a knife. She could use it like we think her mother before her did." "Yes." "And so the essentials of our stories are the same." "All right." "Yes or no, please." "Yes." "She does it herself? She undoes her own shirtfront?" "No. I said she let him." "She sits there and he reaches across, looking into her eyes, and his shaking fingers fumble the ying buttons through her yang buttonholes?" "He undoes the buttons, she lets him." "And *then* she gives him the knife." "Well — " Mary's face breaks and she smiles. "Maybe she lolls a bit first." "You are not being serious." He faces her straight-on. "No. I'm sorry." "In your story, then, they make love." "Yes, but not right there. They have to go somewhere. You can't make love on the wing of a plane." "Do you know what?" "No. What?" "You are a crypto-pornographer." "What's that? My God, you should call me names with all your dirty sex. I'm talking about unrequited love." "I think not; you're talking about giving people their jollies." "And what are you talking about?" "You would give people their jollies by completing their

131

attacks on each other, by letting there be an ending. There are no beginnings or endings. There are just plugged gaslines and knives and black widows upstairs and high priests become prime ministers — "

"And endings. We die!" Writer Scann wonders, in fact, if he doesn't love fighting with this stupid girl. "That's different. We've been talking about life. Crappy sentimentalists have always said life imitates nature and put a mirror up to it and it's art, and they mean it imitates dying. Rotten stinking nature dying. It's because they watch for death. It's easier than seeing life. Death we know about. Death is a category. Life isn't: it's botch and disarray, and simply extends by any means its own urges. It has no beginning. Can you remember it beginning? Does anyone know where else it began or when? No. Life is I got the knife and then you got the knife and Amantha is watching and Isaiah Jones is on his way and Philippa is up there on the third floor with Master the Second and in the middle of all this Thrain has the temerity to remember the erection he's had all his life and he goes after Cecilia with her own knife and cuts her buttons as if she is a candidate for dishonourable discharge. And when she is up on the wing and exposed (Scann's voice slacks its pace) to the nooner breeze and the rockerarm of the flying boat's motion he puts the knife to her throat and in the presence of the great black Governor of the Land of Morton, Isaiah Jones, something occurs that Amantha can't quite see but can only feel. She is suddenly terrified that what she is trying to watch and understand is an unexpected capitulation by Cecilia, an act of violent devotion by Thrain and a ritual blessing by I.J. It may have been, of course, it may have been all of those things, because every now and then events willingly construct a sentimental configuration. Amantha in her window with her hair hanging down like a rope from her cell, has a vision. She sees Cecilia and Thrain rise up as one flesh and fly away, taking I.J. with them and leaving the ranch to two incompetent women. The vision loses intensity and through it she sees the figures down at the aircraft again. She turns from the window, runs down the stairs and out of the door. She is sure she is running to catch the first plane in and the last one out of the Morton Ranch. Indeed, the sudden increased motion of the aircraft would force even a less agitated runner to suspect an imminent take-off. It has been a bad day for Amantha: Thrain with the knife in his hand, the vision of Cecilia going away with him and I.J. and — now, dear girl, the world turns over."

Scann sits by Mary Major on the bed. His mind is easy. He knows what it is he has said, but Mary is restless and tense. "The world can't turn over, not even in one of your stories." "Yes, it can. When Amantha made her run to that aircraft it was a run from isolation to alienation, as sure as Columbus sailed from flat to round, or as inevitably as Nietzsche wrote himself from God to man. Amantha's run, of course, has not been recorded before, but I wonder how many Columbuses there were before we were able to believe the world round, or how many Nietzsches before God and Church became dead and false?" "I go to my church," Mary says. "I sing in the choir. Without that, God knows where I'd be." "Yes, I'm sure," Scann says, rising again, "but don't worry about losing it. There are many institutions that advertise themselves more falsely: Parliament, the free press, the university, charity, justice, community, nationality, and other cosmetics which are used to arrange the outward appearances of our times in accordance with the necessities of whatever social fashion most easily leaves the spoils to the powerful." Mary looks at him in a way she hasn't done before, as if he is young and not able to tell the truth. "You're impossible. It gets worse every time I come here. Imagine what it'd be like if we had — well, another kind of relationship." He sees her peering toward her watch again. He tells her, "Amantha has run over the edge of her faith. The disintegration of her belief in the ranch, its rituals, and Philippa has been going on for a long time, but now she has broken with all that. As she runs, she pulls at the strands of her braid and lets her hair fall loose, she kicks off her awkward shoes and tears her blouse a little at the neck. When the gods are weak even the most rigid bourgeois finds art becomes important."

She looks at him now with a little triumph in her eyes. "That's why you're here then?"

"I'd be here no matter what," he says, laughing down at her from the funeral cart he rides through his own freedom. "We are talking about Amantha. All through her maturing years, since her father had died and his serfs had raped her, she had never been able to rise above faith. She may have — they all might have — if Philippa had not established her religion and her church and her government to enshrine and use it. Listen, you were born here. You came naked and unadorned. When others arrived though, full grown and pioneers, they brought with them the things that were precious to them, and those things were the trappings of their reasons for coming:

Zed's whip and the very architecture of his house, the ways he thought a man should live; Linden's rifle and his madness; Thrain's wife's money, although she never complained or even mentioned it. Many brought silverware and evening dress down the rivers in canoes. In another country all these might have become part of the folk tales by which a people understands itself. There have not been such prodigious humans for a long time as the ones who came to Linden. But they came too late, when the rest of the world was already living by machine, and they were from the beginning out of fashion. Who can live out his version of the dethronement of the gods with telephone and telegraph and radio and wire services reporting the rise and fall of glamourous Romes every day? Because the old immigrant gods must fade to inconsequence at the frontier if a new civilization is to mature. If they don't, they bring in relatives and even new acquaintances and keep their subjects colonial forever, always with a sense that this place may not be home or perhaps, at any rate, not one worthwhile defending. Think of Zed. He recognized his culture as portable, came thousands of miles and never left home. The price of his freedom was physical exile, nothing more. He hardly noticed. Very inexpensive indeed. But when he died he left no home for his family, Philippa couldn't find her old direction and she knew it wasn't where it had once been for her. She had changed, and so perhaps had all directions. Hers, she knew was opposed to Zed's, but that was all she understood when she returned. She came back to the house and became Zed's people's prophet. When you're a prophet, a redeemer, the one who pledges to take life out of pawn, you have to deliver the goods. There are four miracles at least which have to be performed: the first must be to get the people's undivided attention, the second is to show the way, the third is to go that way yourself, and the fourth is to take your followers with you. Philippa performed the first two by circumstance and her natural proclivities, which is not unusual. The third was accomplished by illusion through retreat, mystery and ritual. Then, since she couldn't go herself, she compromised on the fourth miracle: with Cecilia's anticlerical help she sent her followers on ahead. Everyone believed. The people in the compound had their own rituals which celebrated the possibility of freedom now, and at sunrise, before the rest of the day began they stood in a circle around the head wrangler's triangle and antiphonally (male and female) shouted out ten Our Philippas. Amantha believed too.

She believed in the whole process from the snapping canine and the substitute knife to the horse of another dogma that took the newly free off into the wilderness. She believed that she would some day be free too, and even though she wasn't when the ranch was empty of all but its practising priesthood she still had the habit of devotion. It was a fine faith. She had spent all of Philippa's great periods of activity longing for all men to be free. For her, the gods were strong and her own arts were simple and without depth. In the end she only waited quietly and hopefully for her mother to take them to South, that wonderful place Philippa finally began to talk about in her moments of greatest clarity after the compound was empty. But now, as Amantha ran toward the aircraft, the membrane of their ritual waiting, inside of which Philippa had kept some sort of order, was punctured — or perhaps she simply understood that it was broken and that it was Thrain who had done it. She fears Thrain. We always do our uncertain deliverers. They offer a way out, but we must change our ways and ourselves if we're going to ride on their flying boats. It's terrifying to shift and break inside yourself, even if you think you're heading for safety. Emotions make Amantha strong. She leaps from the wharf to the aircraft. Neither man is conscious; each points like a dog; and each holds a mound of Cecilia's flesh as if it is claimed territory. But their eyes watch each other. Imagine what is going on in their heads. Each holds a great ragged, nippleless and useless breast. I.J. has come to help mutilate Cecilia, to bring punishment down on her atheist and anarchist head. He had always thought she was whole. He feels at once akin and betrayed and can't force a sequence of conclusions in his mind that will allow him action. He doesn't know, suddenly, enough about himself, and certainly not enough about the man holding Cecilia's other breast. And Thrain has retreated to innocence through the arrogance of logic. All the facts had, a moment ago, pointed to their violence as being love play. Thrain had fought with Cecilia and had been elated, immersed in nostalgia for Katerina who in 1922 had come to Linden House and had taught him Greco-Roman wrestling. At their very first encounter she had stood in front of him, hair ragged, face torn with emotion and had cried out: 'I must relieve first my anger that you are man and I am only woman' (She was five feet eleven inches tall) 'and find my female gentle suffering once again.' She never did. They had always fought to a standstill and had begun their other performances from there.

An American philosopher once pointed out that if you fail to learn from history you will have to live through it again. If this is true we should make sure not to learn from pleasant events so we may count on having happy circumstances repeat themselves. Thrain must have learned a lot from Katerina because there was no replay with Cecilia, just I.J.'s eyes watching him and then Amantha running, coming down the length of the wharf and jumping. She lands and the aircraft rocks. She falls against the outboard gunwale. The wing dips and the tableau, already tilting the boat, collapses and slides into the water. Amantha holds to a strut and stays on board. When she can look again a monster has been born. A chimera — three heads attached to one body rising out of the disturbed waters of the lake.

"Amantha-Bellerophon sits on Thrain's Pegasus and watches. Almost at once she can see that the three-headed beast is fighting itself. She looks at it thrashing and sinking, rising and moving away from her. The bottle-green water is deep around it. This is a lake that has filled a long fault in the land and there are no shallows. The mutilated trinity maims and mangles at itself bloodlessly, impeded by the foreign element it finds itself challenging. I.J. is fighting Cecilia, Cecilia Thrain, Thrain I.J., Celicia is naked and flashing like the underbelly of a trout, a white-silver movement quick beneath the water. I.J. rises, holds her trousers like a split black flag above his head and pitches them toward the shore. He grabs for Cecilia's short hair to pull her toward land and he keeps shouting, 'Who done it' and when there is no reply, 'I didn't know.' He receives Thrain's fist on the side of his face and drowns a moment, surfaces and keeps talking. Cecilia puts her hand on Thrain's head and pushes him under the water. Amantha slips the knots on the ropes that hold the aircraft to the dock. The small wind drifts her east. She finds Thrain's paddle and it helps her keep a course that brings her finally close to the dying monster. Thrain holds to Cecilia now and I.J. pulls them both by her head and hair, rescuing them without meaning to. Amantha has seen her sister helpless only once before. She sits in the flying boat and watches, holds the paddle across her knee for a long moment and then reaches out with it toward them, offering to help. They don't want help. The paddle is heavy. She begins to raise it to bring it back on board but it slips and falls hard on Thrain's head. He drifts face-down. She leans far out over the side and hooks the collar of his shirt with her forefinger. Thrain

136

bobs unconscious and weightless. Amantha lies over the gunwale and feels comfortable, almost, once might say, at peace. There is very real relief in touching and controlling him at the same time. She allows him to sink a little into the deep green water. Small bubbles rise. She lets him float again, and on the shore not far away Cecilia is beached. I.J. staggers upright on the coarse sand, and Amantha watches. In the pretty sunlight, water glints on her sister's pale torso. I.J. breathes a deep groan. He has discovered her. She rolls and rises. Each is naked. They stare. Thrain still bobs beneath Amantha's hand; in the utter silence she considers what to say across the water to them. Her mind can only retrieve the word Don't. But they do. Cecilia seems to fall forward, yet it is a movement that contains all the cunning of randomness. Her head becomes a battering ram and hits I.J. between the stub of his withered sex and his umbilical dimple. Slow motion. I.J. makes a noise like a mechanical airhorn and then they fight in silence. It's a strange battle, without reason and with everything ultimately at stake. The place where they have finally and nakedly met is common but vacant ground. When one conquers one rapes. The arsenal of rapine has been lost to I.J. Cecilia cannot be further ravaged. They see, understand, but refuse to believe. Amantha watches a while and feels nothing. They only dry-fondle each other with hopeful violence. She struggles with Thrain, maneuvering him up over the gunwale and finally onto the narrow flat surface beneath the tailplane. The aircraft drifts slowly away from the ranch. The air is redolent of denouement. She crawls up out of the long shallow dream of the acolyte and straddles Thrain's prone body. The weight of her on his chest forces water out of him. She rides him as Cecilia might a horse and watches him choke and cough to life. She talks to him, urges him on. Suddenly he breathes once more. She tries to find her gentleness again but it is gone, buried under the rubble of new emotions. She doesn't care that he lives except to fly her out of here. She has no understanding of the mechanics of the enterprise. Thrain came through the air and he can go back that way. She sits across him, holding him firm beneath her thighs. The aircraft is drifting west again before light airs. Thrain turns his head to look at Cecilia and I.J. and he grins but he doesn't speak because there is no need. She sees them too, standing side by side staring out at the aircraft, naked. It is essential that we return to Eden at every moment of truth, and always we are kicked out again by our continual rebellion against the pain of not being able to understand."

Scann goes close to his chambermaid and takes her hand, covering the watch on her wrist lest she look at it again. "Mary," he says quietly, almost choked by the grandeur of what he has pinched up out of his own inventiveness, "surely you must understand that conscience must be immaculately conceived and borne. Isn't that the one message, the truly new testament of our civilisation, even if its content is buried in a pretty but awkward myth concerning your namesake and her Jesus son? Perhaps now you can see that Cecilia — heartwarming as it would be — and Thrain could never play out the story you wanted me to tell. Forces always gather forcefully, never haphazard. Amantha's run to alienation, her rising above faith, even if it is to lead to tragedy some day, is the miracle that unscrambles the eggs in Philippa's omelette. Cecilia and I.J. are separated out. Out. They stand on the shore together and feel themselves threatened, the priest-governor and his violent consort fear the act of love they think they are watching. And it is Amantha who understands. She rises beside Thrain, who sneezes. She watches the aircraft drift closer to the dock and knows what must now happen. She looks back down at the rusty Thrain whose breath still squeaks in his throat. On the shore Cecilia and I.J. are moving black and white against her grey thought. They run, and she follows their separate progresses. They have gone sane with the necessity of citizenship. Had they flags they'd banner them in the breezes of their running. She looks down into the cockpit and discovers Thrain's toolbox. From it she takes a heavy wrench and hands it to him. Kneeling, she makes almost a ceremony of putting it into his hands. She doesn't have to speak, he too can hear the dogs. He props himself on his elbow and touches her for balance and she understands in that moment that she also has been *seen*. On shore the citizen's army of dogs charge them. Thrain moves to the edge of the flying boat and waits. She stands beside him, and the breeze blows them against the dock. Thrain fends with his foot. A dog leaps. Thrain pushes the aircraft away from the rest of them while the dog scrambles and then cuts him down with the wrench. Amantha, who knows the dog's name, has seen it grow and be trained all of its life for this moment, throws the body overboard. Thrain is smiling now, but she works beside him without either hope or fear. The breeze blows, Thrain entices, another and then another and then another dog leaps and the ceremony of the wrench repeats itself. I.J. stands dumb at the shore end of the dock, and behind him Cecilia, dressed again in shirt and pants, comes from the house with her rifle. The final dog is dead or drowning. The heavy work is done. There remains now, Amantha guesses, only the ceremony of the gun.

"Every story," Scann tells Mary, "that hopes for greatness should have a pilgrim's march. There are few of us left who understand this device. The pilgrims, yes; but the march, no. Via Dolorosas always lead away from the romance and the melodrama of life and toward the ironies and the instruction without which authors and readers alike are lost. The danger, of course, is that the procession will stop short, at sentimentality, for instance. So many do. Authors are only human. They wish sometimes to shore up the unthinking hopes of themselves and their audiences. But the only march of consequence is the one whose internal force (thus Cecilia's gun) brings each pilgrim flush against the central ikon of his ignorance, whose wretchedly unyielding surfaces supposedly guard the substances of the mysteries of their faiths.

"Of the four in our procession, only Amantha marches without trepidation. Thrain goes alert inside his own awareness: he thinks he is his own God and Saint. I.J. holds to the barrel of the rifle, clings to its power and hopes for Grace. Cecilia goes in a caul of bravado to see her mother, to rescue her ceremonies from oblivion and right the world again. She has her finger on the trigger and the knife familiar in her other hand. They go slowly, Thrain in the lead and walking deliberately to gain time. Amantha speaks into their shuffling silence: 'You look a lot better with your clothes back on, Cecilia.' She takes Thrain's arm as if they were leaving the dock and going in for dinner. They walk for a moment and then she says to him, 'Were you going to rape her?' When he does reply, it is finally encouraging. 'You might get raped, but not her.' He looks up into the mackeral sky but not at Amantha. She keeps watching the side of his face and thinks that he's only really seen her once and hasn't bothered even to glance at her since. But then he speaks again: 'Whatever the other thing is, that's what'd happen to her.' She measures the distance to his ear with her voice. 'Fucked,' she says. Thrain's head jerks and his eyes look quick like a bird's. 'It's what animals do,' she comforts him. He walks on with the gun in his back, prodding a little now. She continues: 'She's not very lovable.'

His back might as well have been turned to her. 'You want me to say the word again?' He slows almost to a stop, facing her: 'It's not your word,' he says. But it is: and it gives her a peculiar thrill to know it. 'I want you to look at me and keep looking at me so I can say something. Who fixed your finger after she cut it? Who saved you from the lake? Undressed I'm better looking than she is. That's a fact. And I'm readier to fly out of here than she is.' 'You're not going anywhere,' Cecilia says. 'Move.' The rifle pushes them on. Isaiah Jones begins to sing. He has lost his dogs but he believes the balance of power remains securely enclosed in the clutch of his hand. Amantha turns her head and sees the flying boat steady at the jetty and Cecilia's face hovering like a stone balloon above the butt of her gun. Amantha says close to Thrain's ear: 'I know what happens now and I'll help.' She holds his arm more firmly and laughs to cheer him. 'Just one more dog and then we can go.' They walk more quickly now along the pathway beside the dead corral and to the house that Zed built where Philippa waits for them."

Scann is still half-holding Mary's hand and is looking down into her face. She shakes her head as if she is about to begin keening. Her eyes are hardly dry. "Poor Cecilia," she says. "Poor Thrain. Poor everybody." "Yes," Scann says, "That's always one of the truths: poor everybody." "You like Amantha. Why?" "Unlucky Amantha," he tells her. "She can't really cope." There is a knock at the door and Mary Major dives under the bed. Scann is delighted with the movement. It is so desperately skilled. Without thinking of consequences and only wanting to play the scene out, he picks up some manuscript pages and calls out for the knocker to come in. The door is locked. Scann makes loud noises that indicate he has forgotten. He rises from his desk and opens the door. It is the resident manager. His name is J. B. C. Burke (a sign on the front desk delineates this identity). He is dark, youngish but of no particular age and looks not at all as a manager should. He says stiffly: "I'm looking for chambermaid Major." He speaks with a slight British accent. "I'm sorry, sir, but I thought I heard her in here." He looks at Scann as if his recent correspondence course in management had given him complete details on how to handle artists in temporary residence in small hotels. "I read a lot out loud," Scann says, smiling sanely. Mr. Burke wheels toward the closet. It is both doorless and nearly empty. Less certainly, he eyes Scann who feels sorry for him, watches his animal climb slowly up into the chair. He looks down on the manager. Burke's face doesn't change expression. "You know what this means, Burke? One more insinuation and you're a candidate for oblivion." He puts a foot on the desk, a threat to escalate. "Did you know I fought the war with the owner of this hotel? I can assure you, my having his whole staff of chambermaids in here and I *in flagrante delicto* with all of them would only bring cheers and applause and shouts of well played from my old and dear friend." Burke steps forward and takes hold of Scann's elbow. "Down we get, sir," he says briskly. "Feet off the furniture. What you wouldn't do at home don't do here." Scann is swung down. Burke steps back a respectful few feet and then sniffs. "Urinating in the sink. My, my, you really do feel away from home." "Out." Scann points. "Out, I know my rights. You can visit my domicile but only by appointment. I do not give you an appointment now. Come back after lunch. Perhaps I can arrange for a chambermaid to be here by then." Mr. Burke doesn't seem impressed, yet he begins to go, but as he passes the bed he crouches and sweeps aside the spread. Scann finds himself staring into a slow-motion half-second, and then Burke stands and moves to the door. Scann sits carefully back onto his chair. Burke says to the door: "She *is* missing, you know. I didn't make it up." Scann rises again, relieved. "Not that pretty redhaired one I see occasionally in the hall?" Burke turns as he opens the door. Scann sees something in his face that is more than simply managerial. "Ah," says Scann. "Ah so, you are looking for someone who is only incidentally a chambermaid. You couldn't care less if I had all the others here at once. But not her. Not her. Territory. Burke's territory. If I see her I'll tell her. You are Burke's girl, I'll say, and don't you forget it." J. B. C. Burke's cool face is only a little sad as he closes the door. Scann falls to his knees, and under the bed there is a quiet thump as Mary lowers herself to the floor. Slowly she rolls out; her face is pale; her hands are stiff bloodless claws which have held tight too long to the bedsprings; her breathing rattles with residual anxiety and her eyes look at Scann and then fill with tears. He bundles her up in his arms, moved by her performance. A real professional spirit has been revealed and old reporter Scann feels suddenly proud to know her. He draws a breath to speak but she puts a hand over his mouth and whispers in his ear. "Do busy things. Open the window and then the transom." He puts her down carefully on the bed and begins to sing A Hundred Pipers and 'a and 'a. He opens the window. Easter Saturday pours in over the sill. He goes to the other side of the room and opens the transom. A breeze scatters some of his manuscripts. Muttering normally, he collects them and makes them safe again. She is up on one elbow pointing for him to take the chair and look into the corridor, but he shakes his head and continues to putter. He runs water into the sink, singing again. Then gradually he subsides, as a writer would, and he is at her side again, lying quietly and looking at her. She meets his gaze and then her eyes go merry. She hunches over a silent giggle and gradually collapses against him and puts her lips to his ear. His heart rams his chestcage hard enough to make the bed move. "No," she says to his hands and mouth, but she is still almost laughing. "Amory, I've got to get out of here. He'll be watching. He's been chasing me ever since he got here. Now please, walk out that door and see where he is." "If I don't, then you're trapped. You'd have to stay," he says. "It'd be rotten to let you out into the clutches of a swine like that." "Look, I don't want to be fired. I've had the job for fifteen years and David pays me good wages." Scann finds himself sitting up. "David, David is it? I figured you were being faithful to someone. David Thrain of the shadow cabinet and the chambermaid at his hotel." Muckraker Scann is on his feet and almost pacing. Then he remembers where he is and who is next door. He thinks of having hung up on Shirley. Newsman Scann faces Mary across the foot of the bed. The starch in her smock holds the material in such a way. "When you go," he says, pretending to concentrate his eyes on a far point whose clear focus is beyond the grail, "you'll have to go somewhere, not just downstairs. Ro is next door." She sits up. "Ro?" He leans close to her. "Go next door and do up his room. Find out about him. Why is he back? What's in his luggage that'll give us clues? Where has he been and where has he just come from? Who is he now?" She looks confused. "I'll pay you space rates," he says. She rises slowly from the bed. "Amory," she says, "we don't spy on guests." "This isn't spying." "What do you want to know about him for?" "I think you'll find his room the closest safe place." "He may be still asleep. When did he get in?" And then the right question occurs to her. "How do you know he's here?" "I see through walls." "No, you can't, you've got some scheme going. What is it?" "I just want to know about him. An interview with that one isn't any good — 'I'm in town to visit Thrain. No, I don't play snooker for money, that's being a hustler. I'm no hustler.'" He points next door. "There's a story breaking there. I want to know what it is." She shakes her head. "I got to do his room up, but I'm not saying I'll see anything and if I do I'm not saying I'll tell you." "Good girl." He takes her hand and leads her to the door. She leans against it and looks up at him. "You sure got a lot of energy. I don't know how you keep it cooped up in here." Then she looks over her shoulder at the open transom. "If he's out there he'll fire me." "No he won't. We've got a friend in court." She breaks out of seriousness and tries to contain a laugh. "I could use Cecilia right now to put a gun in his back." More serious: "Did she really do that?" "Now, how else could she keep Thrain under control?" Trying not to laugh again: "Well, she could've tried lolling a bit." Scann is suddenly sad that she must go now. "She isn't her mother," he says quietly. "She understands violence but not the finer points of revenge." "That's Philippa's thing?" "Well, yes, revenge usually becomes a mad ritual: Jack the Ripper, blood feuds or eating ham at Easter. It's Easter Saturday, did you know? Think about that ham you bought for tomorrow." "You're not a writer, you're a preacher." "Name one who isn't." He takes her arm and helps her pass through the door. "Good morning, Mr. Burke," he says. But Burke isn't in the hallway either right or left. Mary Major runs to Ro's room. Scann closes the door.

A review seems necessary. He walks toward the window. On the desk is a stack of yellow paper placed neatly parallel to the wall against which the writing table is pushed, and otherwise there has been a leak in the security arrangements — Mary, Ro, Burke. It would be quieter at home. His testicles rise up in his scrotum, a protective maneuver. That's where fat Marion lives, who has almost religious convictions about marriage: ritual love that dances over his quivering guilt. It is tragic that a man must spend his life with what he managed, emotionally drunk and panic-stricken, to bring home from the mating dance. One expects better luck even from a system based on nothing more substantial than nearer-my-genitals-to-thee. Poor Marion really had very little to do with it. She had been only plumply proprinquitous, and he supposes now that her plumpness and nearness had produced certain automatic reactions, and when she had tried to resist both of their temptations out of a sense of self-preservation, it had made him mad. And that kind of madness thinks it can be cured only by giving it both the object and the subject of its insanity: unlimited access, the possibility of license and all of those attendant, lazy libertating fantasies that make the theory so attractive. But there were virtues that had accrued on the periphery. One of them he sees while he stands at the window. She passes below, wearing her weekend clothes — bellbottomed atrocities that serve as jeans, shoes that look as if they had been designed for a foot both large and clubbed, Rasputin's old greatcoat and an uncovered guitar bar sinister across her back. Her friend also wears the dress uniform of protest. He is thin, dark and not much taller than she. His hat is tall, however, and black and religious. The Puritan is abroad in the land once more. Scann watches them cross the avenue and disappear beyond the bank building, and he wishes he could say that he didn't understand them, but he does, however dimly, and it annoys his daughter to have him remain untouched when she happily induces near hysteria in her mother by threatening her with attitudes.

Scann goes to the phone, dials out and then rings his own number. Marion, his wife, his Marion, answers. He listens, not to her voice but for background noises which might tell him about the climate at his house. There is nothing to be heard from the two younger girls. Marion says Hello again, questioning the silence at his end of the phone. He puts his handkerchief over the mouthpiece and tells her softly: "Lady, this is an obscene phone call. You will want to listen carefully." "Amory? Amory Scann, where are you?" "Where did he say he was?" "Banff. Banff in Alberta. Is he safe?" "Safe but not sane." After a pause and a sigh, Marion says, "Then this is an obscene phone call. What's he doing?" "He's locked in his room." "Who with?" Scann holds the phone at some distance from his face and shouts: "The four whores of the apocalypse!" "Scann? It is you, Amory and you're drunk." He hears her girl's voice fade as he lowers the phone gently to sleep in its cradle.

The inventory is sparse: himself, a pecular pile of manuscript in this peculiar room with a hole in it. And, not far enough away, duties that until now have prevented insanity: the machinery of his life which, godlike, grants him daily surcease from license. A lot of energy, Mary has said, cooped up in this little room. But that is how man controls nature: by putting it in narrow confines and directing its natural propensities. Think of the dam, the power line, the retort, the cylinder and valve, the bombcasing. "I have confined myself," prisoner Scann says aloud. Water flows, electricity goes to ground, man manufactures communications. Keep man in crowds and free enough to be insecure and he will remain unconscious.

Secure even the most brutish in isolation and he will make images like a film-maker at least, or words to shout down the corridor to where he thinks the turnkey sleeps. He wants to *say*, whether he knows how or not. And the artist makes his own cell and plots experiments for survival. He becomes conscious of the circuitry of consciousness: the pen in the hand spurts the mind onto the page which excites the eye which makes more active the brain which works the mind that jerks the pen that fills the page that Scann built. He stands stiffly by the desk. It's mere philosophy to shout through empty spaces and listen afterward for the silences of the universe: nostalgic, romantic, pitiful, a call for reasons, directives, rules. It's saying connect, connect. It's saying speak to me of love, belonging, or even of gaining a majority and changing the system. It is saying, ultimately, make me unconscious again. No directed energy. Only the splayed-out measure of man's inability to cope with the way things are. And when the silence is defined, he makes technology and chemistry, both unconscious efforts to manufacture turnkeys which always become monsters.

Scann strides again to the window and calls down to the Saturday farmers below him: "Do not spray for a miracle." One or two of them must hear him through the glass faintly. They glance up and complete his inventory. They are final and all else there is, the other, the real silence. Quietly, he goes back to his desk and takes up his Erasall Medium. Stickpen, it says in larger letters on the barrel. Stickpen. He begins to clear his mind for the ordeal ahead.

Why? Everything has been set in motion. The system is complete. It will revolve according to its laws which he himself has established. The construction will circle around itself until its energy runs down and out. All he has to do is sit behind his ballpoint and watch it go by. Already other systems are occupying him. The Mortons, begun by a fragment thrown off from Thrain, and Mary and Ro and Shirley, and Marilyn his faun daughter and her male friend Paul and fat Marion, and what else? Tell me God, what else? There is a lack of oxygen here, a definite lack. There is a pain across his forehead. Perhaps his brain is rotting and gangrene is setting in. Scann rises to take two aspirins. Without sniffing he can smell that Burke is right. A definite smell of urine. He leaves the water run and goes to the window.

Across the sill flows fresh new spring air. He kneels at the edge of the blind and close to the windowledge. To whom does God pray?

To whom, to whom. The great grammatical owl of the universe swivels its head 180°, even as earthly owls do, and seeing nothing behind it but absolute nil, teeters momentarily, turns again and sits silent and uncertainly surprised. Then he causes a mountain to convulse and when a mouse is given forth he does not marvel at its significance. He catches it with one stabbing claw and eats. On whom, indeed, does God prey? And why? Because the void behind him is only oblivion? Scann the man is used to it. He doesn't even teeter. He gathers spring ozone into his lungs, rises and stands once again before his own work and threatens it with his stickpen. Slowly he sits and then he writes: Thrain. Thrain kneels with his axe in his hand and carcajou's skull choking his arm. He swings. The head cracks. Again. The rotting tongue and gums and palate stink even above the stench of Linden's excrement and all of the new and old smells they have manufactured and resurrected in the time they have existed here in the cabin at Mosquito Lake. Pieces of bone come away from Thrain's arm. Each time he hits with the blunt of the axe he becomes more free. But his arm swells, and it pains so that he rises with it and kneels upright but weak in front of the fireplace. His breath is a tongue of fog in the cold air. There is no fire. He has not been outside since the burial, since just after the tourniquet, the bucksaw, the blood from the sawn leg and finally the searing. It had been heavy — a full length of leg from hip to toe; he had staggered, the knee folding unexpectedly, the greasy rot mixing with congealing blood, stinking and staining; as he had held it and his axe with his right hand and with the skull of the wolverine still watching, spitted on his right arm, he had waded uncertainly through the snow until he had found a wind-cleared circle of blue-black ice a hundred yards from the shore of the lake; then he had chopped a hole through the bleak gelidity to water that had lapped with spring or even summer alacrity (the sun had been shining), perhaps fifty or even sixty degrees warmer than the air above it. Gravedigger Thrain had contemplated that unseasonable sight, and had been delivered to lethargy from the tense pleasure and pain of sawing Linden half legless. But soon, very soon, the hole he had chopped had begun to narrow and had shown signs of healing over. He had held what he carried of Linden by the purple-green foot and had shoved it stiff into the lake's cold white aperture: and had felt the world shift and roll. He had put his own clubbed foot on Linden's dead and naked one and had levered this much of the trapper and as much more of himself toward the bottom of the lake. He had heard the leg rise again and bump against the ice. The small, echoless sound had pounded like a padded hammer on the door of the newly turn-over world and he had walked through it and back to the cabin where Henry Linden was alive. He had stood over him and had listened carefully to the shallow wind of his breathing haunt the near corners of the old man's lungs. He had stooped to feel his forehead. It had been warm. He had rocked him with his foot, and had felt a quill leave carcajou's head for the flesh of his arm or the flesh of his arm leave for carcajou's head, so that suddenly, quite suddenly, the skull had shifted to a new position: its dogteeth had gleamed in the narrow spectrum of light coming from the fireplace. Gently he had begun again the work of loosening the jaws and releasing his arm. There had been pain, swelling, tenderness. But there was also the madness of hope. And now it is climactic, this work. He can stand the hurt of each blow the axe sends through the swollen arm. He kneels, hauling the glutton's head once more into a position on the hearth, against the stones of the fireplace where the hard angle will double the efficiency of the axe. The split bone folds like a concertina against the softness of the rotting palate, tongue and throat. New pain assembles and riots in the streets of his arm and his heart strains to supply troops of blood to put it down. Once more Thrain runs away into blackness.

He sleeps, wakes, sleeps and wakes to cold numbness. Linden still breathes. Holding carcajou, the glutton wolverine, close to his chest, he starts a fire and after a while, still infected with the delirium of faith he begins to tear broken pieces of the skull from his arm. They fall away. It is almost a simple pasttime. Each piece of bone releases stench and rot. He peels it off. He can feel helpless Linden watching when he can: a brave man, surviving for all those years, patching his own hurts, building his own empire out here in the woods and opening up the country. Thrain is pleased he is here to help him now. Occasionally, the purple swollen stumped arm swings up over the mound of furs and once (perhaps yesterday) he had called out: "What're you going to do with it, Thrain?" And a few moments later. "Maybe you done it already." "I put it in the lake," Thrain had told him. But there had been no reply.

Scann watches Saint Thrain at work and doesn't question his change of heart. It is not really a cleansing. It's a sudden indifference brought on by having Linden's threat impotent and by having punished him sufficiently for his transgressions on Thrain's person. Who else is a saint but someone mad enough or revenged enough to think his enemies neutered (in whatever way) and who is thus freed to bring wreck and ruin to the world through faith and good works.

Shards of bone lie in a pile near the mouth of the fireplace, a miniature charnel dedicated, it would seem, to the quick fulfillment of surgeon Thrain's sanguine expectations. Soon he is able to reach inside and scoop out decomposed brain and then more bone until at last the tongue is ready to be cut. Thrain takes his knife and severs connections with the head. It is a delicate operation. His own blood drips down on the hearth-stones from cuts the knife makes in his arm. He crouches, a muscle in his thigh suddenly cramps. He rises quick. The head gyrates wetly on the floor and his arm springs up weightless, even though the tongue and its neighbouring flesh lie along it like a leech. He looks through tears at it and laughs. A moment ago insane with hope, the hope is now achieved: he is willing to make a deal with the new age now dawned. He moves up and down on stiff legs to the rhythm of his laughter and then his walking becomes a dance, a shifting of gears from exercise to bacchinal. The tongue is simple rot. He picks his arm clean, pitching the wads of corruption from the circle of light before the fireplace and into the dimness of the wild garden of the room beyond.

Then, at last, he sits once more in the red and yellow light of the fire and looks at his naked arm. It is round and thick, the same diameter from wrist to shoulder, and it is a dark smoked blue. The fingers on his hand articulate but they refuse real work. When he touches his forearm, pain glows and makes sheet lightning in his mind. The skin is not smooth: there are quills, hard dry sticks that are gripping and piercing through his flesh. He touches one; pain makes it impossible for him to hold and pull at it. As if he is reading by braille he runs his fingers from elbow to wrist and around his arm. Twenty-one quills. He checks the figure as if it is important. One has worked its way through his arm further than the others. He takes his knife and cuts around its point. For a moment even pain recedes. He grabs at the quill and pulls. It slips and slips again in his fingers, but it comes out. Some of the meat of his arm clings to it and more blood leaks down onto the fieldstone hearth. Twenty. He leaves the knife and the twenty-first quill by the fire and goes to Linden. He is a pile of stinking furs in the middle of the room. His handless arm is visible; it is swollen to twice its size along its cold

148

length. Except for the missing hand it might be the twin to Thrain's quilled one. Henry's face is there too: it is a pile of proud flesh. Where the skin has been frozen and cracked there are now long and suppurating sores. "I've got my arm back, Henry. The head is gone." But Henry is not listening. His breath is shallow, lame. There is spruce tea by the fire. It is warm. Thrain forces some between Linden's lips. He chokes and wakes briefly. "I got my hand back," Thrain shouts at him. "We're going to make it." Linden's eyes peer. His swollen lips draw back a little from his birch-bark teeth. Thrain is not certain what the movement means. "I've got the fire on and . . ." It comes clear to him what is next. "Henry, I'm going to clean up the place." The idea of order supports him to his feet. He is not tired now, but his stomach fires off a salvo to remind him that he has been starving for too long. But first harmony between them and what is around them. His own miracle must be celebrated. Thrain opens the door and kneels again, but this time it is to play Hercules. He throws everything out into the cold brittle blue daylight beyond the stoop. Pots, pans, sacks, tin plates, traps, hides, ropes and leather laces. Axe, saw, shovel, hammer, clothing, tarps, stretchers, all of the accumulated shards of Linden's civilization. He takes the pile of furs from the old man and throws them too, leaving him cooling dangerously on the floor. Rising he turns slowly on his heel and stares into corners and then under the bed: one more thing that he hadn't known he was looking for appears. He retrieves a pair of pliers that had fallen near the foot of the bunk. He builds up the fire with the last of the wood piled inside the cabin.

He turns Linden over and then over again until he is beside the bunk. One careful, exhausting lift has him prone on the bed with his one foot toward the fire. He smells so rank that Thrain can't face the task before him. He goes outside and fills his lungs with clean air and moves quickly back in and strips foul Linden of his clothes and pitches them as far as he can beyond the doorstep. He regrets his revenge, melts snow, warms the water, washes his victim and again goes outside to build a fire on which to heat water so he can boil the old man's clothes. While the fire begins to burn he goes to the lake and chops out the fishline he had set there after they had arrived from the ravine. The lake is trying to feed them well. There are three fish on it. The first took the bait, the second ate the first and the third had eaten the second and the first only a short time ago. Thrain separates the first from the others and leaves its head on the hook for bait and lowers it back into the water. The trout weighs three or four pounds. Now, he has cleaned the cabin, built two fires, put Linden on the bunk and there is a double fish stiffening in his good hand. Thrain looks around him and sees that what he has done is good.

And these are the acts of the re-born Thrain. He causes the fire in the cabin to burn low and hot with knots of wood so that shocked and legless Linden may be warm and both of them fed.

He manages bannock to go with the fish, and it is greatly giving of strength.

He listens to the man Linden struggling and tends to his seared leg and still-swollen arm. He also shakes clean his furs and brings them back in to warm before the fire. Then he covers his old enemy and sees that he is comforted in ways he has not been before. He thinks he sees tears of gratitude in the old man's eyes.

He makes water boil on the outside fire and in a bucket boils and cleans the shitted garments of Linden on whom he has revenged himself. Then he dries them before the inside fire. Outside, the feeble sun has gone.

He sleeps.

He wakes and they feed.

He goes out into the great white quiet with snares and sets them. He moves across the face of the land confident and without plan.

On long evenings he sits before the fire and pulls ripe quills from his arm with the pliers that he had made appear as his reward for cleaning out the cabin, and his arm begins to heal around the holes of eight and then thirteen and finally nineteen quills. One escapes him. One escapes him and he expects to feel it elsewhere in time.

During the daylight hours he cleans and repairs the artifacts he has thrown out from the cabin and takes them back in, creating order around the walls and in the room.

He causes trees, small ones, to be felled and chopped and split for the fire; he fishes and gathers white-furred rabbits from his forest, and everything is good.

Linden, the pioneer, lives on in suppurating silence and Thrain's will to preserve him grows. Who, after all, dragged him from the canyon into which he had fallen? Who doctored him? Cared for him? Fed him? Took a bucksaw to his gangrenous leg? All of these things has he done, and the change in Linden is great. Soon he may be a voice again in the land, remembering events, but more especially directions.

A warm wind, a chinook, blows through the valley and the temperature rises forty degrees in the space of an hour or two. The sun shines, the surface of the snow begins to melt and sparkle. Loads of snow on the branches of evergreens grow heavy and fall. And he makes a promise to the old man: "Listen, I will transport us out of here and we will be home in time for the April naming of the town." But Linden's face doesn't change expression; it shows neither hope nor interest. Thrain is disappointed. His care, his love have made no impression on the old man. Linden puts up two fingers and Thrain goes for the pot quickly. It is the old man's habit to foul himself if the service is not good.

And after the thaw comes again the cold. The land splits and cracks under the sheen of ice. At fifty below there is a haze across the face of the sun, and at night the fire in the fireplace needs wood often.

He has hoped for Linden's company, but the old man remains silent, and Thrain directs himself to begin building, in the quiet and with some small bitterness, a means of transport for the trapper: a sledge with runners of smoothed pale birch and lines fashioned from braided rawhide. The crust beneath the snow is thick now and good to run on. He goes to the creek where it flows fastest and searches out a rock of fine sandstone and with a probe loosens it and brings it to the surface. He sits in front of the fireplace and hones his knife and the axe to finer and finer edges. In the shadows Linden sleeps. His arm seems healed; the short stump of his leg is black and swollen with trapped blood, but soon perhaps this oddly symmetrical form may be moved. But there is time. The grip of winter is still white-knuckled.

He stays indoors. The cold is arctic and there is a wind, small but lethal that prowls across the open lake and pounces every minute on the cabin. The place is clean, swept. Time is a heavy liquid that flows a little every now and then. Linden sleeps often, eats, holds up one or two fingers. That is all. Thrain, one day, moves out for more wood, closes the door when he comes in, stuffs the cracks with strips of fur and sits again. After a while he gets up and pushes a slim piece of spruce into the coals and watches it light. He holds it before him and then up over his head. The shadows fade. He rises and goes to Linden who is in constant twilight. He gazes down at the ruined immobile face. Still it rots where it was frozen hardest. The visage offends. He opens the door to let in the natural light and the cold. He takes the sharpened knife and leans down over Linden and with quick firm slices takes off the ears and the nose. It is an act of love and of order. And he feels, he feels as strong as Linden's bellow. There is blood, but not as much as he had thought. He turns to throw the greasy hunks of flesh into the fire, and Linden pulls himself up and tries to roll off the bunk. As he ties him down with rawhide strips, he tells him that soon the cold will break and the sledge will be finished. Then, he promises, he will haul him from here to the Water Lake cabin to wait for the proper moment to descend the Toebroke to the Bear and then take the canoe back down the river to home.

And he does. Observing the canon of his promise he does, even though matins with lauds are not sung by Linden whose anguish and pain during the ride is inimical to praise and grace. The land falls away fast from Mosquito Lake and in one long dark above-zero day he moves the earless, noseless and handless, legless Linden and what belongings and food he can to the cabin on Water Lake where Tenderfoot Thrain had once been left to die. And Linden, despite himself, points the way. It is as Thrain had planned.

These, then, are the acts of the new Thrain. He holds himself confident as he imposes his will on their new home. And now he begins to think of Erica and their hotel, and he imagines her sitting at the table in their kitchen, secure and strong, waiting with only enough trepidation to add real beauty to his homecoming in the first days of spring. He is in command of all he sees in these first days at the other cabin. He sees; he provides; winter is about to crack when he gives the order; time itself is under his ordinance and he can let it drift or live it by his own rules as he chooses. By his acts and by his control of them he feels himself defined: his own portrait is clear and satisfying. But sometimes his face becomes incandescent with a kind of dumbness. He wanders to the edge of the lake, the stupidity of his expression not apparent to him. In winter there are few reflective surfaces. Nor are there many moments when the voice will reverberate across the land. In winter loudness and surreal definition are substituted for the echoes of beniger seasons. He stands erect, a rack of antlers on his head, his greatness rigidly concentrated and he calls through the dead air to Erica. Momentary affluence has come to Water Lake. But Erica doesn't hear. She has not been listening since the turn of the year and now, perhaps because she cannot break away for a moment to be with herself, she hears nothing. The hotel is open. Bodies lie on beds, mattresses, homemade stretchers, on piles of blankets in the great lobby around the hot mouths of Thrain's stone fireplaces. Ole feeds the fires with four-foot logs and together Erica and Ole supervise this biggest room in town which Dr. Currie has taken over for his sick. They help nurse too, and arrange for the disposal of the dead in boxes Ole makes up at a steady rate of four or five a day in three sizes. With six feet of frost in the ground, the graveyard Royal Murdoch has donated to the villagers out behind Sugar Hill resists pick and shovel and holes are hard to dig. And there are fewer and fewer who are not too sick to dig. On the coffins the names of the occupants are written in black carpenter's pencil, and the boxes are stacked against the north side of the hotel so that the bodies freeze quickly and those who can dig may do so without panic. Even so, there is a terrible delay. The well are uneasy; bodies above ground, even frozen ones, are unclean and uncivilized, perhaps even unlucky. Then, too, Father Berceau and Mr. MacNee, self-appointed from the Church of Scotland, regret also the delay. Mr. MacNee is beside himself. Never has his unordained presence been assailed with such conclusive evidence that God is galvanizing the attention of the whole world by sending this plague of influenza. Mr. MacNee insists on evening prayer. He always prays for a long time and his gladness drives him to temptation. Erica directs, nurses, hears him through ripples of disturbance in her mind. "Don't ye see, ye inhabitors of Sodom," he shouts, "the Lord God of Hosts has come for us. We have not been forgotten. Armageddon is here. The prophesies are *true*, and the Pope will at last be revealed as the anti-Christ. The moving finger writes and the Elect read it. We know the time has come to face the judgment seat. Too long have the swords of evil been sheathing and unsheathing from the scabbards of rot and sin." "MacNee," Ole hollers, a different man here among the sick. "That's enough for you tonight." Erica watches him stand beneath MacNee on the first landing of the stairs. "Help Pardonny with the buckets or go home." Ole is big. MacNee is quiet and he goes. He is easy, and even Father Berceau knows it. He walks now among the sick, smiling, nodding and with medals for the relatives of those who are most ill. Death is an arduous trip home. He smiles while MacNee shouts. That one, she thinks, dances; in his long black robe he moves away as if he is before an altar. There is no question for him. He has not been able to imagine one.

Erica is kneeling beside a pallet mattress on which an Indian girl, nine months pregnant, is nearly dead. It is the middle of the fifth week of the plague. It has been a noise getting louder, until now the decibels have forced her beyond mere hearing to where she is part of the thing making the noise. *She* is influenza too, a wild thing working, it seems, for Death. She touches Father Berceau as he passes. "Regardez," she hisses. "Regardez votre fille." She leans toward him so his attention will be caught. "Tu," she says, "tu es . . ." "Tu? Tu?" He draws back from her, his loaded hands festooning his chest with silver. "Chère Madame. . . ." she shouts at him: "J'ai besoin de l'eau. Ecoutez!" He does not take orders. The young woman dies. Erica sees it out of the corner of her eye — a swift passing thing. Her small, struggling, ramshackle movements stop. Erica sees Father Berceau see what she has seen. They kneel together. Through the thin grey blanket over her taut belly they both notice movement — a knee or maybe an elbow pushes upward. The priest acts first, beginning to walk quickly toward the stairs MacNee has just left. As he goes he begins to run, his head down and cocked slightly to one side and his legs unusually stiff like a bird's.

Erica shouts toward the doctor, "Currie! Currie!" Straying a little from the body as she does so. Dr. Currie is near the fireplace, dressed in tweeds. His red face sweats as he bends to listen to a rattle in a chest or a drowning lung or a weakening heart or a voice rising above the noise of fever. Royal Murdoch is beside him, talking. Erica sees them face each other and exclude the rest of the room, and she moves swiftly on sore feet toward them, arriving at a moment when Murdoch is pleading: "A name is of permanent importance. The committee has no time left. We can't call it after a dead poet." "Royal, this place will probably live on no matter what. Even if the 'flu gets us all. Go. Get the hell out or I'll have you escorted to the street." "You'll be at the meeting tonight, then." "No." "Yes, damn it, I need my votes." "Your votes?" Currie laughs. Murdoch is serious. "My votes." "Royal, I'll try. I think Linden is a good name. I do. I do. A fit memorial for the old coot." Erica takes his arm and watches him turn and grow redder in the face. "And what memorial have you for Thrain?" She looks at Murdoch. "You great shame. Go and do your little voting." And to Currie: "A girl has just been brought in and now has died. She has a live baby inside of her ready to come. You will take it out for me now, please." Currie stoops for his bag and she says to Murdoch, "You are not welcome in my hotel. Go away and tell your wife — and even your mistress — we need help." But Murdoch is not listening. "This 'flu is sudden," he says to Currie. "Maybe we'll be in the driver's seat by tonight." Currie begins to walk away, leaving Royal with his hands in his pockets and his head down. "He's got to win," Currie says to comfort her. "It's his life, and I believe that's a good kind of man to lead us." "To lead us? We are nothing to lead. A few hundred nobodies and a bunch of poor Indians who think we've got a miracle here for them. At least Thrain didn't wait for the country to serve him. He did not play Murdoch's little games." She looks towards where they are going and sees the priest beside the girl. He is kneeling between her legs with his head down, and his lips are moving. He lifts her skirt as if it is an altar cloth and regards the portals through which all mortal flesh must emerge. He lets the fingers of his right hand trail a moment in his bowlful of water before he spreads those paradoxical lips.

Erica stands outside herself watching herself watching Father Berceau. She sees Dr. Currie watching too. His young face is slack and blank. Father Berceau's smile is beatific.

The girl twitches a dead twitch, shudders. Erica moves. She is released against weeks of pain and now this violence. Her fingers close down on Father Berceau's coat collar and she drags him to his feet. She feels excited and regrets that he is too small to fight back. He doesn't move. He seems only to be waiting.

He stands before her, and she hits him and yells in his face: "Forgive me, Father, for I have sinned, yes?" The priest seems not able to understand why retribution has not already arrived.

She pushes and kicks Father Berceau across the lobby and out the door; then returning, she kneels beside Dr. Currie whose refuge has been the girl and whose diligence has become mechanical. He turns as if he must now protect himself from her. She puts her hand on his arm and looks down into the red body he is excavating. "Will it live? I do so want it to live." And she knows she has calmed him. He leaves off looking at her and reaches for the infant. He does last things to free it and then he rises and almost runs to the kitchen. She follows, stepping over the indifferent sick and when she is inside her own sanctuary she gives him a basin and some warm water, clean towels and then she goes to David's room for his baby blanket and a flannel sheet. She puts them by the stove to warm them. The baby is crying.

Dr. Currie cleans and oils and wraps without speaking. Finally she says, "What do you want me to say, that I'm sorry? I'm not. In this man's world there is not even a moment for a woman, not even when she's dead." Currie shakes and then nods his head. He is too young. She takes the baby from him. "Maybe you'd be good enough to tell me when you last slept," he says. She looks down at the tiny mottled red copper face. "Every night I sleep a little. I feel wonderful. Please now go and clean up that mess out there. Our Ole has not much of a stomach for that sort of thing." Currie nods more certainly this time and turns to wash his hands once more. She sits with the baby near the heat of the stove. Her fingers unbutton her dress and she holds it close to her breast. A new kind of ferocity rises in her. She looks up and sees Currie watching her. "It is all right now," she says. "I will see to her." He gives no answer. There is no knock, but the door opens and Father Berceau comes into the room. He stands in the kitchen, pale and newly touched by life. His face is without its usual smile; instead, he looks by turns puzzled, outraged and righteous: he might be a newly-ordained Presbyterian. She turns toward him so that he can see the baby warm and protected, but he is handing Currie his medical bag. "She," he gestures over his shoulder, "is with a blanket over her." Erica watches. Currie bows: it spans a distance between them. Father Berceau returns the compliment. "I have come for our baby, the baby of the Church," he says to Currie. Erica listens carefully but there is no reply. "Release it please from your hands," the priest says. "There is no father?" Currie sounds distant still, and formal. "No."

Erica rises up from her chair, careful not to disturb the baby. Father Berceau is looking at Dr. Currie. "Take the child to give to me," he says. "Take it." Incredibly, Currie is moving toward her. "He's right, you know. He can find a family to look after it. You're working beyond yourself here as it is." "It is the baby of the Church," Father Berceau says loudly. "God, through the church, through I the priest who have baptised demand what is ours." He comes close. They form a little triangle against the door to the back yard. Erica puts out her free hand and he jumps back. "The police. They will be sent for when all is well once again. Two of them." He holds up two fingers to show her how many and then begins to snap them and motions for her to give the baby up to him. She is shoved toward him by the door opening behind her.

Ro has David over his shoulders as one would carry a buck deer. David is comatose and Ro looks up at her with questions in his eyes about David and the baby at her breast and the others in the room. She releases the baby to Currie and kneels down to take David from across Ro's shoulders. He is heavy after the infant. His eyes flicker, small blue flames from a damped-down fire. She looks at Ro, questioning him only so he can talk if he wants. She knows what has happened. Behind them Father Berceau is triumphant. "Merci, thank you, and who is that?" "His name is Ro," Currie says. "He's old Linden's son." "But Linden is missing dead. We shall have that one too. All native people are the children of the church." Erica watches Father Berceau come forward with the new baby still wrapped in David's blanket on one arm and his other hand extended towards Ro. He does not see the knife appear, nor does he for an instant feel that it has cut his palm, but he does see it slashing a second time towards his arm and he withdraws, bleeding. "He is mine," Erica shouts to Currie. "Linden gave him to me." She rises because Currie is not hearing her. "To me." Father Berceau retreats farther but he is not ready for the doctor to tend his bleeding hand. "We will see, we will see, lady." Doctor Currie shakes his head. "Enough," he says loudly. "Take the little one and come with me." He turns to Ro. "Put that away." Ro, surprisingly, does, and Erica holds him by the hand to show she will also protect him but she cannot get sense from her head to her hands or her lungs or her eyes or her heart. She rises and sits again: holds David to look at him but sees only Ro standing looking into her eyes. "How are you?" she asks him as if they are just now meeting. "We were sliding on the pond. I didn't see him stop. I thought he was maybe playing dead." She looks down, trying to breath, listening to her heart go silent and then rummage in her chest for another beat. But she knows it is David and not she who is sick. "Get his mattress and cot from the other room," she says to Ro. "By the stove, where it's warm." She finds she can stand. She holds him and begins to walk with him. Her son: she holds that thought too. It calms her. The face of the priest has been floating like a patch of broken sunlight on the rough waters of her mind. Now it flickers, gutters, goes out. She puts her son on his bed and sits in a chair beside it. Ro comes uncertain to her and she lets him put his head where the baby was. He goes tranquil, and in a while he says, "The priest. They got a school. My father said he'd take me there." "That's how he made you be good?" she asks. "Yes, but I wouldn't have gone."

She needs to talk now, and she tells him: "When a woman died with a baby in her, the priest did something to her. I hauled him away. You know, I hurt him. I kicked him out of my hotel."

He smiles a rare smile and then gurgles tightly in his throat. He runs to the door, a miniature man, and stands looking into heaven's fetid waitingroom. "No," she says. "He's gone, I'm sure." "Priest," he shouts. "Priest." And then he is silent but perhaps he is saying to himself what he might have shouted to Father Berceau. She calls him to David's side. "He will not get you," she says. He nods without concern. It isn't even a joke anymore. "Play outside as much as you can. Keep warm and don't get tired. Be by yourself. Be by yourself, it's the only way." But he knows this. She tends to David without being able to push out beyond the shock of what she has done and seen and been in this last hour. She is in jeopardy. The priest's way will force him to keep his promise about the police. There is a turning inside her. She stands up beside David and looks down at him. Soon he will be very sick: he will need her every moment. And now she wants sleep. She leaves him unconscious and walks among the sick, feeling nothing for them. Her madness with the priest has blown away her citizenship. Those are sick people. They will die or get better. She must return to her own.

She climbs the stairs to Ole's room and goes in with only a tap of her knuckles to announce her arrival. Ole is there. And someone else. In the dimness of the lamplight she cannot see for a moment whether she knows her. There is a little hat without style, down from which hang wisps of brownish hair. The face is: she looks. Stupid. And below that a thin body that hardly pushes against a white blouse and black skirt. Ole is there, yes, his face a bookful of confessions under a dustcover smile. "We are married," he says. "This morning when I should have been making boxes. Her name is Maria."

"And," Erica says, both Norwegian and Canadian failing her. But she does not want to see more: "And I shouldn't be here." Ole's face goes silly; Maria's colour changes in her cheeks. Then she is not a doll he maybe ordered from Eaton's catalogue that is wound up and made to go. Erica begins to see her. She is a shock: it is almost one too many. She turns convulsively from them, and then turns again, seeing them once more. His face is stupid. It always has been. "Ole," she says, feeling a final confession coming like a new shock upon her, "I have. . . ." Then a moment of clarity visits her mind as it had when she had the priest in her hands. "Ole, have a good life." Ole grunts. He is not listening. Maria suddenly shivers as if she has come awake. She tugs at his arm. "Who is she? Ole?" It is enough done, Erica thinks, and she says, "David is sick. I had thought you would want to know. I must go back to him." Ole is freed. Only disaster could have done it. "We will help," he says with eagerness. He is even able to go to the door and open it. To Maria, she says, "I am Mrs. Thrain. This is my hotel," and going down the back stairs she listens to the words and then sees them before her, chiseled into the granite from which she must carve out the rest of her life.

Seeing them together, Erica writes in her book to stay awake for David, is like seeing a great hope and wish turn into a narrow escape. It is also like seeing myself more naked than before. Thrain saved me from ever having to do that. He came when I was not fully awake and put me back to sleep again about myself. This is true. Look who I turned out to be. What a surprise. Who was it my mother raised? A little girl with long hair and some prettiness who was made to feel good because she had parlour manners and would not so much as show an ankle in public after she was twelve. A young girl they tried to teach to paint and play the fiddle and who could make pastry. A grown girl who could marry Thrain and come here and know nothing about herself until he was gone away forever. My mind is beginning to wander. I am becoming foolish too. Like Ole. The priest. The doctor who upholds the church. Like skinny Maria who will, yes, because of all this, win. If it matters at all that anyone wins. We are none of us great prizes, not even Ole. Or Maria. Or Thrain. Or me. I am Mrs. Thrain. This is my hotel. I said that. It is not true. Mrs. Thrain would have a husband, wouldn't she? And if she owned a hotel, it would have paying guests. Those out there are paying only with their lives. How many of Ole's boxes are along the north side of the building?

Mrs. Thrain puts down her pen to go and answer a knock on the door. MacNee is there. "Doctor Currie is down with it," he says, his voice still preaching as always. "Murdoch has taken him home this minute." "And the priest?" "He's gone hours ago with his new prize." MacNee looks a little pale himself and she puts the back of her hand against his forehead. He ducks away, shaking his head. "No fever," she says. "But you need sleep. Lie down in here." He walks backward out of the door. He knows, she thinks, still with herself. She follows him a little way. "The doctor's sick," he says. "We've none but us to do the job." "You've done nothing but pray," she says and yawns. He looks earnestly at her. "Very few out there understand the Lord's retribution, or know his grand plan." "MacNee," she says, "you're scared, that's all." But he has turned and is fading off into the dimness, still talking. Erica looks behind her to where David lies quiet on his cot, and then out upon the sick, the dying and the dead. The town has never encroached before. It has lain at a distance under the shadow of Murdoch's Sugar Hill. She had hardly been asked for her lobby. Currie had simply taken up residence and if people wanted attention they must come here. She sees that they are still coming, assuming Currie is well. The sick know he is gone. He doesn't come when they call. But they are served still. Water, heat, broth in the black kettle on the hearth. The men have built a wooden tank on the back of a sleigh and excrement is taken every day to the bridge and pumped over the side onto the iced-in river below. O'Sullivan drives and Loney Pardonny, who even sings with a drawl, sits on the edge of the tank and stirs so it won't freeze. He is very solemn and takes his job seriously. He is also given to making speeches about what he calls safeguards, and what is to happen to the town if there is not more co-operation. He has written up a pageful of what he calls points for discussion and adoption, designed to ensure safe passage through the perilous days ahead. He used to be lazy and happy and the last to volunteer for anything that looked like service. It was a way of life for him, a kind of merry aloofness. But not long ago, Ole had told Currie: "It gives him something to be important about, this being chief shit disturber, but it's made a terrible talker out of him."

It is night now. Everyone is sickest at this time. She does not move from the doorway. More cry out. More need help. More sink toward pneumonia, their lungs fill with fluid and they somehow turn black. It is not a 'flu, it is a plague. One of the smells in the air is fear. No one sleeps, they beg for sleep. There is great faith in liquor. Some who have never taken a drink before are drunk now and perhaps unafraid for the first time since this Spanish sickness blew across from Europe. Even drunk they do not sleep. They sing, some of them. Currie is gone. She has helped him organise this hospital. But he was the one who had done the most. Found aspirin powders enough, water, soups, O'Sullivan and Pardonny and people to try to sponge down fevers. The priest is still away. MacNee beyond being useful. A log is thrown on one of the fires and flames stretch up, revealing Ole at work again. She watches him and knows that she is smiling. She looks around for Maria but she isn't there. In this new light from the fire a decision is made. She calls to Ole. He comes, walking his curious walk across the room to her. "Ole, I am in a bad position. The priest is after me and David has this sickness. I need a place to hide away until he is well again. Can you get me a horse and sleigh, just between you and me?" "This is your place, you shouldn't go," he says and doesn't look at her. "I have to nurse my child. Help me go." "Where?" "Not even you will know." He nods. "I will know." She shakes her head. "Tell me Ole, how is your marriage?" It is another violence she can't help. His blue plate eyes watch her for a moment and then answer her without his speaking. It's as if there is a sudden step down in the dark. She is afraid without knowing why and it makes her only vulgar. She puts her hand on his arm and goes closer, but he laughs. "It's none of your business, is it? Where do you want the horse, out back?" "Yes, and a sleigh, Ole, a good-sized one, I want to take stuff with me. Where will you get it?" "The livery stable. They're there for the taking. Some of us feed the horses when we can." "Magdan's sick?" "Dead." "And you brought Maria to this." "When I first wrote we were fine." "Is it bad where she comes from?" "She's happy to be here." "And you too? You feel you got a good. . . ." "What, Erica? Fit was what you damned near said, hey?" She holds his arm tighter. "Ole, no." She tries to think what she nearly said, but she has been taught too well not to say. She looks up into his face again. If she could tell him by pounding nails he might understand. He might. She goes from him into the kitchen to be with David again. And Ole doesn't follow. Yes, she thinks, a widow with two children had better know how to live alone except she wind up taking advantage of herself. When he comes back with the sleigh she lets him in to warm himself by the stove. He holds his hands out and doesn't look at David, and after they are warm he turns and holds her and takes her into her room. They drown and surface. "This is what Maria has done for you," she tells him. He is silent for a while, and then he says, "You don't know Thrain is dead either, damn you." And he laughs, and she laughs too. Between them everything strange has disappeared and now they are free. It is the best feeling of her life.

In the sleigh with David and a wakened complaining Ro, and pots and pans and blankets and food in the back, she is still indelibly conscious. And after she arrives at Linden's cabin north of the bridge, has unloaded and whipped the horse and sleigh in the direction of the town, she does not go to bed. The cabin stinks. She heats water on the fire and cleans by dim lamplight. When she comes upon the packrat's nests she sets one of Linden's traps and sits and waits for the snap of its jaws. Editor Scann sits behind his pen, and waits too. Everything has come to rest. He wonders if this is what has happened to Erica and Ole. Ole is free. Erica is perhaps too patly lucky to be free also. Some women can stay sick with a disease like Ole. Never get better. He rises to answer a knock on the door as if it is normal, expected. She is inside and removing her gloves before he finds it odd that she is here, and she is speaking before he can question her.

"Amory, do we have a new stringer filing copy with us?" From her purse Shirley takes Linden House stationary. "A new friend, perhaps?" Her eyes remind him she is real. He holds the paper and looks at the neat penmanship that runs not quite evenly across the page. Shirley's smile has been seen often on television. It is the smile of the mistress on an afternoon soap, who has suffered for love, only to be finally treated Like This. The old queen of Reading Goal was wrong: life does not imitate art, only the garbage peripheral to it. Which doesn't make Scann feel any better. After all, he has created Shirley. "Don't," he says, holding the copy between thumb and forefinger. "This is a very public place." "Not public enough, Amory." Her eyes mist over and a hurt glows brighter beneath their surfaces. "Read it." She sits in his straight-back chair. Her uncrossed knees are together and the points of her black shoes are pigeon-toed. Her back is stiff and the little hat on the back of her head must be pinned on or it would fall off. Scann looks away. "You were at the office and found this shoved through the door?" She nods unhappily. He finds that he is enjoying himself. The one barrier he has never broken through is the one behind which she keeps her confidence. He feels a great strength in him, and a sudden compassion for her. "Read it," she says. He looks again at the single page.

Amory, he doesn't talk a lot, but he's fine, really fine, who would think he's nearly sixty? The reason he is here is to see David, but he wouldn't tell me more. This is David's constituency (did I spell it right?) and so maybe he has something he wants done, I don't know. So David's coming home too (just in case it's news) he may be here already, except my friend at the desk who came today to rescue me (he didn't fire me) didn't say anything about it, and I'm the one that has to do out his rooms special when he is here. Mary.

He feels his scalp contract and a coldness in the small of his back. She may be laughing, making a fool of him. "Mary," he says out loud, and walks to the closet and puts his eye to the hole. The bed is rumpled the bed is rumpled the bed is rumpled but no chambermaid would leave a bed rumpled or would she?

"Amory, come out here." He rises and turns. "What," she says, rising too, "does that note or whatever really say?" He crumples it in his hand and pitches it into the wastebasket stacked nearly full of discarded manuscript pages. "It says Ro Linden is here and that David Thrain is coming or may be here already and they are meeting for some reason." "Mary who?" Her voice is rising. "Mary Major." "Mary Major is a chambermaid." "Yes." "And you've been spending time with her here?" Foreign Service Officer Scann stands with his back to the Embassy door and issues a statement on behalf of his government. "Miss Major has been here three times on hotel business. Because of the idiosyncracies of my schedule she has been able to talk with me, and now she has supplied me with certain information of some importance."

"My friend who came to rescue me," Shirley says as if reading from Mary's notes. "Rescue her? Amory. Rescue her?" She is close to him. He may change mistresses now. This one does not know her place, nor does she know that he cannot right now tell the truth. "Go," he says, his teeth aching with the effort, "and check out both of them. Get to David. Get to Ro. The story may be a good one." He holds her loosely for a moment. "A big one: bigger than both of us." It is hell to have stopped thinking; even Shirley shudders. His arms go limp to his sides. She backs off a pace to look up into his face. "For God's sake, Amory, buck up. It's not that bad. She wouldn't lie down. That's the long and the short of it, isn't it? And you had to trot out Scann's Trojan Horse: give her a job and sneak through her defences. But she's a better girl than I was. She saw you coming, Amory Scann." He feels a comforting glimmer of hate. "You fight dirty and are ungrateful. Who has expended so much time and energy on you? Who has invited you to his own wife's house for Christmas so you could share it with kids instead of a bunch of drunks elsewhere? Who?"

"You are sick, Amory. Unreal and sick. Go and get your own story why don't you? You'll only tear up what I bring you anyway. And re-write it never mind the facts." "I'm composing," he says softly so she will listen. "This is my time. The long long Easter weekend, the longest stretch of days I've stolen in my whole life. I want to write, to finish what I am writing, to write what I'm finishing. To this end I locked myself in here, lied to my wife, lied to my publisher, and what's happened? I am invaded from all sides. Yes, Mary Major with her auburn hair and slightly bucked teeth and lovely legs that rise like pillars to heaven — " "You said that about me! It was original for me!" "Like hell. A minor Irish poet wrote it. There's nothing original anywhere, ever." "But it was for me." Her eyes are watering. He is beginning to feel traction again and he lays rubber right across her heart's familiar pavements. "Sometimes trophies change hands, Shirley. Were I to extol any of your physical attributes now it would be your mouth. A bowlful of roses for your mouth. A rosebowl suitably engraved celebrating your precious yapper. I am your editor and not your lover. I will let you know when I'm your lover and not your editor. Go. Go now and research the beginning, middle and end of this story: Ro, David, Ottawa, Linden and any new angles, as you would call them, that arise out of your sleuthing."

She is not going; she is leaving. She has left. Even the blue roses that bloom plushly in the hallway cannot deaden the intended staccato of her heels. He goes to the window, and kneeling before the crack between the sill and the blind, watches. She does not appear, even though he can see her car parked across the street. The shudder of her heels going down the hall begins to pain behind his eyes. For a moment he thinks she may be coming back, but even this cannot be true. Nothing is true. Below on the sidewalk everything is still. Not even a spring dust-devil. It is an odd hour on the tiny clock of his passing. He wonders if Shirley has actually been here. He has had his fantasies before that have turned into nightmares. Or have been premonitions.

There is a knock on the door. He goes across the room, from the window to near the bed, over the pattern in the carpet, around the corner of the desk. He places his hand upon the doorknob and opens the door a fraction of an inch. He has control. Shirley is there. He stares with one eye at her. She stands yellow against the beige walls: her new spring suit is a sunburst. He remembers the ad in the paper. A sunburst of spring yellow. She smiles mousily. "Amory, I know you didn't want me to." Her eyes are moist and her lips. Her heavy warm odourless breath insinuates. If the light were brighter, he knows he would see a patina of sweat on the skin of her upper lip. It is Easter Saturday. He counts. It is twelve days since the start of her last period and she is in heat. Poor woman. She will come in and rub herself against him with open mouth wallowing: a tight little dance to serve as legal tender in her passion market. And he: through the crannies of her clothes she will feel him approaching and will shudder at the intimacies of this delight until, rigid, she will, as if experimenting with ecstasy, implode. Once he had said, you take off your clothes and I'll take off mine. But Shirley likes to arrive from a little distance, to imagine herself becoming unveiled, to arrive at the ready, tangled in her own skimpy metaphors of desire. She is incapable of objectivity, of seeing them making themselves make each other nude. What pair of inspired comedians will some day recognise this kinesthetic romp as found comedy?

He holds the door against the toe of his shoe to keep it open a steady half-inch. She is very close now, saying nothing, just looking and breathing. Then beyond her there is the sound of an obsequious voice muffled for a moment by the angle of the corridor and the bad acoustics of the stairway. He feels Shirley press against the door, but Worker Scann tries to think of the voice as reinforcement arriving, and he holds shakily firm long enough to force her retreat. She turns quickly and walks away, head down and her hand searching in her bag in order to manufacture some disguising fiction. Burke arrives first, carrying a suitcase, smiling, talking over his shoulder and oblivious to all but David, who is following him, walking along without style, his black overcoat open, his homburg held in one hand and his dispatch case in the other. Editor Scann watches. Parliament has recessed for Easter. It is sometimes normal for David to be home. And this is his hotel. He looks tired, but capable, grey at the edges but handsome. He has never married. The perfect career M.P., dedicated. His complexities left behind in another time, and forgiven. The pole-star of his constituency for the 15 years he has sat in the House, he began with a seat so close to the back of the chamber that he might as well have been beyond the green curtains that hang at its entrances. But he won his seat back often, and old reporter Scann remembers when he arrived at the extreme end of the opposition's front bench. There is a note in his files from David: "At fifty-five I'm in line for a command once more. Too late for the leadership, but Linden might yet have its first cabinet minister."

The sound of Burke's voice attenuates. Scann closes the door and goes to lie on the bed. He believes he has been interrupted completely. He tries to direct his thinking, but his mind won't return to Erica. It touches first Shirley, and then Mary: sharp hisses of memory. He gets up again and, like an unwell horse, stallwalks. Seriously, quite seriously, he wants a drink. His body sucks at its own liquids, searching, testing, rejecting. Then his olfactory memory stumbles on the smell of English beer. He tastes it, an image fills his mind and calms him. He lies upon the bed once more. He may never see Shirley again. She may leave the paper, sell her house, move away from Linden. The ashes of sacrifice dry the good taste in his mouth. He sees her looking at him through the crack of the door. Her eyes gathering hurt, and her face disintegrating around him. He sits up against the pillows. "You presume," he says. "You've set up housekeeping inside every moment of our time together. *Who* is re-writing the story never mind the facts? Let me tell you about a mistress. She is not a wife *manqué*. She is the decent's man's perversion. Domesticated pornography, and no begging questions asked, no rules laid down: pasteurised depravity. An attempt at the ultimate dream of healthy corruption. A delicate operation. Art." He rises again from his bed and faces the telephone on the wall beside the door and beneath the transom. "You do not understand the possibilities of the anarchy of the five senses. You are still fighting for your virtue and you have forced me to know at every second what it is that I've been doing. Real porno." He lifts the phone to his ear and dials his office. The signal rattles like dice in a box. He listens, counting. At fifteen, she answers: her voice is controlled. "*Chronicle*, may I help you?" A small discomfort is wedged under the periphery of his project. His mind haggles with different directions, but he is carried forward by his initial momentum. "Listen," he says, "you presume. You've set up housekeeping inside all our moments. You talk about me re-writing never mind

166

the facts. It's you. You're not a substitute wife. A mistress is a decent man's pornography." He stops, and understands that he is trying to listen. "Perversion," he says, "it's a delicate operation. An art. It's true. You don't understand the anarchy of the five senses. You're still fighting for your virtue."

"Listen," she says, "you've set up housekeeping inside all our moments. You talk about me re-writing never mind the facts. It's you. You're not a substitute wife. A mistress is a decent man's pornography. Perversion, it's a delicate operation. An art. It's true. You don't understand the anarchy of the five senses. You're still fighting for your virtue. Fifty-eight words. That'll be $3.50 or $10.00 for three days. Who do you want it addressed to — mom?" "Screw you, Shirley Carstairs." "You are my boss," she says. "When you are my lover I'll let you know." "No one can be your lover. I was never your lover." "Right. You are something else, really something else." He can feel her rising from her desk, phone in hand. "Perversion, Amory, is lying there being poked and pried at by a sniggerer. "Sniggerer. *I* am?" "Yes." "Everything that implies?" "Yes." She is trying not to cry now, but her nose is plugged with tears. "A sniggerer?" "Yes, Goddamnyou, yes." "But you always said." "Said said said. I said, yes I said. I'm not fighting for my virtue, I'm looking for it. In you, you bastard. I gave it to you and you were supposed to give it back." "Sniggerers don't run newspapers. They don't write books." "For God's sake, you're not talking to yourself. I'm trying to tell you something. Me. Shirley. A person. Can you hear?" "You call a man a sniggerer and you expect him to have a heart-to-heart about your virtue?" There is a long pause. Then she says, "This isn't going to work for you, Amory. I'm not going to quit. I'll be here outside your office every day." Already he knows he won't fire her. "Why?" "Because I want to keep reminding us, me especially." "About what?" "Not just about what, Amory; about why. You're listening now, aren't you? I'm making it sound as if you might be in for a little discomfort." "I may fire you." "You wouldn't dare." He begins to put the phone down, but it's a gesture whose time hasn't yet come. He holds it to his head again. "Look," he says, "You're interrupting me." He sees her at her desk, him in his office. George's tooth hurts. "Then hang up," she says. "No. You hang up." "Do something *real* for once in your life, Amory." She speaks with more breath than voice. "I came here," he shouts, and she says, "Who got you the room?" "Without bath."

"Who told the lie to Marion? Who's keeping up the fiction around here that you're at Banff? And who's going to have to type up whatever you've done when you get back?" She really isn't moving out. It occurs to him that she is not fighting with him but is only struggling with what she thinks he is. The rest of the world is happily alienated, and he is standing here with a phone in his mouth, *engagé*. "I can hire a typist." "Or a lover. I've done it and paid for it with fifty hours a week slave labour." He fights abjection. "What do you want me to do about it?" He needs to know. "Hang up and do whatever it is you went there to do. I have a meeting to attend." He puts the phone down as if he is following orders and grabs it up again: "Who the hell do you think you are? Sniggerer. You weren't even shaving your legs when I found you. It wasn't a case of making you, I had to *invent* you." The buzz in his ear interrupts him. He dials again. It is a wrong number. His dentist answers. George's voice is as distinctive as Shirley's. They are both professional phoneusers. "George," he says, involuntarily starting something he can't think how to finish. "It's Amory." "Is it?" "I didn't call you." "Well, somebody did, the phone rang and when I said hello you answered." "Some mistake, I guess. I was calling my office." "I'm at home. Where are you? I thought you were away at a meeting." "I am. Sorry to bother you, I'll just ring off." "But you made a connection, Amory. You'll be charged for it. I'd better call the phone people and let them know it was a mistake." "I can do that, George, from my end." "Don't mind doing it at all. If we both tell them they might get it straight." Scann imagines George conferring with the long-distance operator, gathering facts, coming up with a diagnosis: Amory is sick, drunk, or lying. George phones home. Marion answers. "Look, George. It's a very simple matter to handle it from this end." "The least a friend can do." "What did you say, George?" "I said it's the least a friend can do." Scann needs a friend. "Yes, you are, George." "Glad to do it. How's your tooth?" "You hit it pretty hard. It still hurts every now and then." "Sorry about that. I was just trying to show you how far gone it is." "It seemed alright before." "Rotten, Amory, dying and rotten." "It hurts now." "Take codeine and see me when you get back." "I will, George. Thanks." He doesn't want to hang up. It's a relief to talk to a man. "You've known me a while, George." "Hard to think about how long." "Would you say I was a sniggerer?" "A sniggerer. What's that? Someone has been calling you names?" "Well, yes, a sniggerer. You know, in matters of sex." "No, I don't think I'd say that, Amory. It's a pretty serious charge." "I don't strike you that way." "No. But you tell a fair run of jokes. Before Rotary a while back you told one I'll always remember. It had real point, about the squirrel on the railway track and the train came along and chopped off its tail and when it turned around to see what happened it had its head cut off. The moral is, don't lose your head over a piece of tail. And then you said, I remember it very well, that losing our heads that way was our most ubiquitious folk-tragedy and the cause of ninety per cent of the pity and terror in the world today." A good review: Scann feels warm and grateful. "Not a great joke, but the tag saves it." "I'd say that, Amory." George's voice is concerned. For him. Scann tries to think of a way to reciprocate. "What about Johnny, any word?" "He's back, Amory. Yesterday, Good Friday." "I'm glad. Then everything's all right?" "Fine. A couple of weeks on the road showed him he wasn't quite up to it. All this affluence makes them a little soft, you know, but we'll snap him out of it." "He went the long way around for a haircut." Scann is unhappy to have said that. "Amory, it's what's in the head that counts. Styles change." "Sounds good, George. Helen must be happy." "She's been a brick through it all." "Give her my best." "I will." This run-down is boring, but it's good to know he has a dentist again. The tooth no longer pains. "Look, George, I'm going to pay for this call. I got advice about my tooth, and I can put it on my expense account." George chuckles. "I guess worse things have been put on those." "It's been good talking to you, George. I'll see you when I get back." "Fine, Amory. Just give me a ring before you do." "I will. And thanks."

Scann breaks the connection with a finger and then dials again. He rehearses for a dozen rings before he hangs up, the possibilities for revenge drained from him. She was an invention that had worked. He tries to think what it was that he had done wrong. Nothing occurs to him, but culmination surrounds him. He goes and lies down on the bed again. His nerves make perforations in his skin. A drink seems more imperative than it had before. He may go downstairs to the bar, even though it doesn't stock English draught beer. What the hell's Shirley going to do now? The possibilities for her are infinite. He is condemned, but is not yet sentenced. She could be meeting with Ro. Or Mary. Even David. There is a fire ladder down from the exit at the end of the hall. A taxi is easy to find, and a plane to connect with a jet to go with another one hundred and nineteen passengers to England. Nine hours into

THE THIRD DAY OF HIS CREATION: There may be no Christmas for the Scanns this year. All of his savings are gone and so is the total amount of the credit printed on the back of his Chargex card. His removal is complete. He is in Graydon village again, sitting at the bar of The Rooster And Juggler, and in front of him, blended as before is a pint of mild and bitter. The bar is small, ancient, the contemporary pumps that serve this precious liquid are a desecration, but his long thirst for this return makes the draught sparkle. Its odour is made up of all the scents of the English countryside. Its taste is a harvest, sweet-tempered, sapid. Its secret is shared without being told. Scann drinks and drinks again, orders a third and slows his pace. He contemplates the barmaid as she bends to rinse a glass. Doves stir, tremble semi-privately in the vee of her decolletage. She has smiled at him and they have agreed about the weather. He considers her age and suspects her of being old enough to have been here during the war, even though her plumpness has kept the wrinkles from her face. He wonders if he remembers her, someone like her, and decides he does. "Did you," he asks, "say about the winter of '43-'44, have a dress, a red, a bright mandarin red, made out of corduroy perhaps? It had a big full skirt and the top fitted tight." She raises her head to look at him and then stands straight. Her eyes compute the ponderables in his question. In a moment she smiles, even laughs. "The little lady in red." She holds castanets above her head. She was famous. He laughs with her. "You could give a girl a start with a memory like that." She looks down at herself and breaks away to get her cigarettes from beside the cashbox. "You were here at Graydon?" He nods. "Then you're a Canadian. I thought you was a Yank when you came in. Must be losing my touch." She leans forward, peering at him. "You really remember me?" She wipes the bar near his glass. "What was I like?" "Very pretty," he says, "and lots of fun." "Lively, you might say. That was me. We all were. And why not. There wasn't any tomorrow. No food, no petrol, no coal." "No decisions," Scann says. She goes silent except she taps the old wood in front of her with a red fingernail that might be a quarter-century preserved. "Well, we never missed them either, did we? Especially you lot. No flipping sense at all. You might not've been here at the beginning when they were billeted at her Ladyship's. Left a grand piano there, she did, and one night when it got cold, they took a fire axe to it and had a fine old blaze. Made a waterfall down the grand staircase with the fire hose another time, and her poor ancestors on the walls, they were boarded up, but not for long. No proper respect. Wild they were, those Canadians." Her smile has become a glare. Scann drains his beer and regrets his citizenship.

"I was here at Graydon a very short time." He pushes his glass toward her. "How long?" "Only days." "And you remember me? Nah, what'er you, some joker? Or maybe a tax man. What'd you say your name was?" "Scann, Amory Scann. Thrain was here when we met." "Who?" "Wing Commander Thrain." "Oo that one." She takes his glass to fill it. "Whatever happened to him?" "Member of parliament now." "That's right. It figures, it figures." She puts the glass in front of him again and empties her ashtray in a garbage bucket. When she comes back to stand across the bar from him they are friends once more. "My old dad was in the first one," she says, and looks at him across the flame of the match she is using to light another cigarette. "Did what he was told and got a leg shot off. Nobody asked him to run for parliament that I know of." He blows out her match for her. "It's like going to church. You have to believe in it." "My dad was only ignorant. Now, with us we knew a bit more, but we had innocence. What'd you say, when we was here before didn't we have a lovely innocence?" "I think it's called naîveté," Scann says. She looks mysterious. "Anyway, I never got cured of it. I'm an innocent, that's what I am. A throwback. I had my own fish and chips shop in Leicester for a long while after the war, and then went to London like everybody else. It's not a town any more. It's world war three and all the innocence is gone. It's souls they're after now." She takes a glass and draws herself a half-pint of mild. "I watched it for ten years. Nobody owns themself anymore. The suffering. I never seen anything like it. If you're going to have a war then have it, I say. So I left. I got a soul of my own and I wasn't going to stick around down there and offer it up like those poor skinnies who think their war's only been a revolution. It's a freehold this pub is, and you're looking at the lady what owns it." Scann watches her face flush a little and she begins to laugh before she drowns it by drinking her beer. "I guess you think I'm the one, eh? Well I feel safe. When I was here before I never gave up a thing, not a thing. I had my one red dress and even if I was in the Land Army, I still got to wear it when I wanted, and I always slept in my own bed." She drinks to that, draining her glass. "Finish up now, will you? I'm going to close."

Scann says. "Is it time?" She nods. He looks around the empty room. He can think of nothing to detain her. He does what he is told and puts his glass down beside her waiting hand. "Little red," he says remembering suddenly what he'd called her, "I think you made a good decision." He lets her know he is looking at as much of her as he can see. "And you still know how to dress." She can laugh easy again. "Dressing's the only pleasure I got here. It's like living in the bloody colonies, Graydon." She comes out from behind the bar and he climbs down from his stool. "I forget now just exactly how to get to the squadron from here." "*Think* now," she says. Mocking him. "You know." "It was a mile or so, but it was dark when I came. Take me there, have you a car?" She shakes her head. "I never did learn to drive." "Then we'll walk." She begins to laugh again; it springs up through and around her words, protecting them from fragility. "Two old sods looking for where they used to be. You've got to be joking." He looks straight at her. "The place is there. You're saying it is." She shakes her head. "No, of course not, it's a farm now, just an open space." She looks up at him. "Were you really here?" He nods, and she asks lightly, "Can you prove it?" He closes his eyes and sees. "There is a strawberry birth mark somewhere up your thigh, on your right leg, I think." Her lips draw back from her teeth, a gesture, and it brings her completely into focus for him again. "It is shaped like a drawbridge," he tells her. "Yes it is, and it's as far as I let you go." He doesn't disagree. "It's pretty near as far as I let anyone go," she says. "Ever." He buttons his foreign correspondent's coat. "Where do you live?" "Upstairs." She flips a switch and the light dims down to the light of one small bulb above the door. The oak beams loom blackly. "So I'll just point the way. Come back to tea if you want. Ring the bell at the side door." She goes before him, hunching a little as if she is protecting something. Outside, he leans against her signpost. Perhaps she doesn't want him to go. In the twilight he wonders if he sees her shrug as she begins to talk again: "Look it's right and then right again and up the rise at the sign that says Woodhebrington three miles. Can you make it?" "Oh, yes, I expect so," Scann says, imitating the cadence of her speech. "Thanks so much." And she begins to leave, going at her own solid pace toward her door. "Lady in red," he says after her, but she doesn't turn, "you tell a great war story." She is gone around the side of the pub and through a small evergreen jungle of a garden that must have been young when they were here before. Her door shuts and the village is before him, a single row of buildings facing a secondary roadway that is distinguished only by the gentleness of its curve as it passes by. His bag leans easy against his leg and he watches where she has disappeared. "I remember you, Red, and you were battlewise," he says in tribute. In your magic red dress, Little Red Hiding Dress who never gave away a thing. You sang and danced. Never a serious moment. It was all for laughs. You would hold anything in your hand until it was empty — a plate, a glass, a man. A tactician of rare disarmament, who somehow understood that war is only life pursued by other means toward the same ends, and all's fair signifies all's unfair too. And it still is, isn't it, Red? Because the laughs have yet to be justified, or even understood. How serious war becomes once it's over. Scann sees her shadow move across her lighted window and he wonders that he was able to unearth a memory of her at all.

The lorry pulls up beside him in the fog and Pilot Officer Scann lets the young driver with the Chinese red cheeks push his baggage in back while he himself climbs into the cab. He looks out through the windscreen at the nothing there seems beyond it. The driver slides behind his wheel and they move off from beneath the sign of the Rooster And Juggler toward the airbase. "Sorry I kept you waiting, sir. I had to put petrol in this thing and then the fog." "No bother at all," Drinker Reporter Scann says, feeling the warmth of the pub still against his skin. He rides listening to the wheels pounding on the concrete paving beneath the lorry; he looks at the young man driving and smiles, hearing Hopkins' words sound through his mind: "Yes. Why do we all, seeing a soldier, bless him? Bless our redcoats, our tars? Both these being, the greater part, but frail clay, nay but foul clay." The rhythm of the wheels is sprung open and his pride that he possesses the priest poet in the file of his reporter's brain excludes for a moment the driver's voice. "The station." "What?" "We'll pass a drem light at the corner, I said, and then we're almost there." "Drem light?" Scann, with too much to drink in him, feels his newness and inexperience gather about him like a second fog. "Part of the drem system. Don't you know?" "I'm afraid not." "Roughly speaking," the voice becomes precise, "a drem system is a circle of lights around an airdrome that they use to help guide aircraft down at night." Scann closes his eyes and sees a circle of lights around an airfield. "Like a boundary line," he says. "Once you're inside, you're safe." "Sure," the driver laughs. He points up through the windscreen. "There's the light." "So we're safe," Scann says. Above them there is the sound of motors, an aircraft flying low. "Someone coming home?" The driver nods and peers harder into the fog. The sound fades quickly. At the gate, he stops the lorry to check in. The engines come around again. On the runningboard the driver stands and stares up into the thick overcast. The motors cut power and there is only the quiet hiss of the aircraft passing overhead. Then there is a fog-muffled crunch. "Christ," the driver says, "he missed." The truck grinds and howls into motion and almost immediately, it seems to Scann, it goes from the rough macadam of a roadway onto the smooth concrete of the airfield's apron. A sandra light behind them laterals a white beam toward the crash somewhere in the fog. It is like driving into pure dazzle. Other trucks, other vehicles, are running with them. The explosion is another crunch. Pieces of aircraft make shadows down the path of the light. Scann's camera is in his luggage at the back of the truck. He opens the door and stands on the runningboard. Fire appears, a tall contained flame rising out the centre of a spread of wreckage. The truck is slowing as if the driver is becoming more and more fascinated with the reality emerging from the fog and less sure of his interest in the lorry. "Stop," Scann shouts, and the driver does: he is used to orders. He waits. Scann goes to the rear of the vehicle and finds his camera equipment in the dark: his Graphlex, his new synchronised flash gun, the bag full of number 22 flash bulbs. He goes to work. The liquor in him calms his movements. He mounts the truck, stands on the cab and pictures the scene. He is lucky. A flame geysers up as he pushes the cable release. A firetruck crew, dressed in asbestos, hoses white foam over the shattered remains. Ambulance men wait behind the foam. In a moment they will go in and find the bodies. Scann sits down on top of the cab. "Move in," he shouts to the driver, and when there is no response he bangs his fist on the roof. The truck moves. He thumps again to stop it and take another picture. They are the closest vehicle to the flames. A voice below says, "What the hell are you doing? Get down." Photographer Scann feels for his magic press card. He has none. He is at war. He gets down. A stretcher goes by with a charred body on it. The liquor in him rises up against his diaphragm. His reflexes aim the camera, and it is taken from him. He takes it back and stands close to his antagonist. There are three bands of blue on his epaulets, a Wing Commander. He doesn't bother to salute. The face in front of him is the one he has come up from London to see. Thrain: twenty-eight, pale, blue-eyed, sharp nose with narrow nostrils, flat planes from temple to jawline, rigid mouth, Viking ancestry visible, six feet and a bit, looks better in his pictures. "Scann, Airforce News, sir." Another stretcher goes by and Wing Commander Thrain shouts at it: "Use this truck here, let the ambulance go." The body is still smouldering. It is better to look at it through a view-finder. "Take another picture and I'll have you arrested. Get off this field, you are unauthorised." The voice is calm. Shot down over Berlin, just three days to walk back, killed three men on the way, high-jacked a fishing boat at Stettin to take him to Sweden, and then phoned London (phoned!) for an aircraft to come and pick him up. Wing Commander Thrain D.S.O., D.F.C. Yes. "Sir, I just came in on this truck. We were at the gate when the crash happened." "Get back in the cab and stay there." Pilot Office Scann, ace, hotshot, flash, twenty-three, commissioned, six years on the *Star, Globe, Times, Sun, Citizen*, name-it, salutes and sits again in the cab. He points the Graphlex through the windscreen and takes a time exposure of the light and dark and occasional flame from the wreck. Men kneel beside a stretcher at the rear of the aircraft. They move, swift, lift it and walk toward the truck. Thrain walks with it. The body's arms writhe above its head. The noise it is making is neither a scream nor a shout; it is simply a very very loud, terrifying noise. Beside Scann, the door opens and the driver vomits out onto the runway. Reporter Scann takes out his notebook and pencil and begins to write: "The war came back to Graydon-on-Moor at seven twenty-seven p.m. on a foggy night, February 5th, 1944. The aircraft was flying against its other enemy, the weather, and it didn't have a chance. Boneweary after a successful raid on (where? Ask them.) Pilot (who?) and his six crew members (names, addresses later) tried to penetrate the winter fog here at Graydon airbase, but their numbers were all on a weather map and not on bullets or ack-ack shells. They crashed and burned."

The writhing man is on the back of the truck now. He is a closer sound, almost intimate, a thick noise that cloys like blood. The stench of the driver's vomit floats up into the cab. He is being helped in by Thrain. "Snap out of it, Billy," he says. "Drive to the hospital."

"By chance the first on the scene was driver Billy (?) and his lorry which was to become part of the mission to try to save the men. But there was nothing he could do. The flames from the burning aircraft leapt like dragons. Petrol, and what ammunition there was left from the hazardous raid exploded. Billy ducked behind his wheel and waited. In moments the fire-fighters were there spraying foam on the flames. Then the ambulance men waded into the wreckage and appeared with one, two, three ... six men who would not fly against Hitler again. But wait a minute: there is a seventh. He is alive. Hurt. Desperately hurt, but not dead. They place him gently on the bed of Billy's truck, along with four of those not so lucky. And now it is Billy's war. For this moment, no one is more important. He drives by sure instinct out of the hellish light and smell around the burning bomber and into the pitch-black fog. Billy is young, barely eighteen. His stomach rebels and he is sick out of the window, but he presses on, driving fast but with the positive reflexes of youth pelting him along. The terribly hurt flyer on the back of his truck is perhaps only moments from death. Aircraftsman Billy drives the 1,000 yards to the hospital with the skill and elan we've come to expect from Canada's air force: man-for-man the most implacable enemy the Luftwaffe and German heavy industry has today." The truck bumps against the wall of what writer Scann assumes is the hospital. It is camouflage-green in the light of the lorry's capped orange headlights. Billy backs off: he may be laughing or crying or preparing to vomit again. The man on the back screams as he is unloaded and taken in through the building's double doors. The stretcher is met by a Flight Lieutenant Medical Officer who gestures left, waves the bearers on. He lifts the blanket on the next and then the next and the next, pointing always right now. It is as if he is looking for some kind of perfection under the covers of dishes just sent from Escoffier's kitchen. The dropped blankets are taken off stage right and the Medical Officer walks left, removing his jacket as he goes. Scann leans back against the cushions of his seat again. The various stinks have gone. "Do you suppose we could go to the Mess now?" Billy is pale. His hands still grip the wheel. "Yes, sir," he says and leans out the window to see where he is backing. The lorry circles. "Billy who?" Scann asks. "Dolan." After a moment, Scann tells him. "You are tonight's

hero." "Bullshit." "I could have you arrested for sassing an officer."
Billy slows the truck and looks across the cab. "Bullshit, sir, bullshit,
sir newspaperman, get some time in." There is no reply but violence
and Scann is relieved to see that they are stopping again. Billy slides
out and civilian-in-uniform Scann climbs down and goes through
the door of the Mess into the lobby. He is alone in a square, empty
space until Dolan joins him with his luggage. He puts the pieces
down on the floor near the wall and stands waiting; for a moment
Scann thinks it might be for a tip. "It's okay, Dolan,, you can go,"
but he stops him at the door. "Where're you from?" "Hongkong."
Scann gets out his notebook. "I'm here to do a story, Dolan. How is it?
Is this the best squadron we have?" "I just drive, sir. Why don't you
ask one of the skippers?" "I asked you." "It's great," he says looking
out into the dark. "How did you get here from Hongkong?" "My
dad came out from there when I was fifteen. We went to Canada."
"You joined as soon as you could?" "Yes, aircrew." "Not just
another irk? But you washed out." "Yes, sir." "Why?" After a
moment's silence — "I hit a man." "Mid-air crash?" "No, in the
chops. He called me names and pulled rank." "You're pretty
bitter?" "No." "You'd like to be like Wing Commander Thrain?"
"Who wouldn't?" "He doesn't call you names?" "Sure, every time
I do something he doesn't like." Billy looks away again. "I guess
I'd better get back to the duty room." "All right. Where's the bar?"
"Straight ahead."

A corridor runs the length of the building. Scann crosses it and
finds a door marked BAR. But it only opens onto another corridor.
Down it, on the right, are two more doors: MEN, WOMEN. Of
course, there are women. On the left is a double door that opens
onto a room that is small for a bar. He climbs onto a stool and puts
his notebook in front of him. The barman is tall and looks as if he
might be dead and beautifully embalmed. He has a phone to his
ear and puts it down beside its cradle when he glimpses Scann. He
looks sad, but perhaps that is usual. He is cheered a little when he
finds that Scann will have a mild and bitter. "The real liquor's
scarce," he says. "Eleven pence." Scann gives him a coin. He has
flown over from Gander with the ferry service only a couple of
weeks ago and he still makes mistakes with English money. The
barman is British. He works in a dress shirt and apron. Very correct.
"My name is Charles," he says. He goes back to the phone and
listens a moment before he hangs up. "But some of the younger ones

calls me Charlie. They're good lads all. What a shock about Flying Officer Windham." Scann puts Windham's name in his book. "Are you visiting us or joining us, sir?" Scann looks closely at the wax nose and smooth face. "Is this the best squadron in the group, Charlie?" "I've no complaints, sir." "You go out at night when there's a raid and wave them off?" "Well, no sir, not always. There's good business in here at that time. The Intelligence Officer, the M.O., the Met Officer and one or two others from Pay and Accounts. Even the padre drops in from time to time. It's a different crowd, sir, but interesting in their way." "You find everything interesting, I take it?" "My, my, sir," Charlie says, "you sound almost as if you was making some kind of investigation. I'm sure you'll find I'm just an ordinary bloke doing my best, even if I can't fly." "Where are you from?" "Down Hants way. I was — you'll never believe it — the village blacksmith, and my shop was under a chestnut tree. Flight Lieutenant Esterby quoted me the poem about it. He's the one with the books in his head, if you want that sort of thing." "And you'd like to go back to your smithy as soon as possible?" "Me? Oh dear me no. I'm off to London as soon as this lot's through. A whole new trade I've been given here. Smithing's done. Finished." He leans forward on his elbows: the face at this new angle has more blood in it. "Mind you, I've other reasons too. You might say I've been given my independence. And then there's the added attraction of the younger scenery here." He begins to wipe the bar which is already dry and shiny. "Over the years you begin to get a taste, you know, an educated taste. Now, Squadron Leader Brannan tells me our WAAF girls are like climbing into bed with one of the boys but *deegoostibus* as Flight Lieutenant Esterby says." "You match scores with Squadron Leader Brannan?" "No, sir." Charlie becomes Charles. "He's second in command here and a fine flier with just three more trips to do to finish his second tour. Of course, I see the more human side, you might say, of the men when they're at my bar. I won't deny that. And Squadron Leader Brannan is a most human chap. I've had extraordinary talks with him on occasion." "I like your beer, Charlie. Draw me another." "It's not like peacetime, but we do the best we can. Warrant Officer Cleary was our buyer but he's been posted. Rather sad, that. Cleary was a good all-round provider." Charlie smiles. Who's to say the teeth are not his own? They even have a neat little gold filling here and there among them. "So Cleary did have a steel box of fivers bolted to the bottom of his bed. Who's to say he didn't bring it with him when he joined up? And, it's been a long war. He was judged guilty to begin with and that's hardly what you'd call British Justice." "Wing Commander Thrain found him guilty, Charlie?" "Wing Commander Thrain is one of the great fliers of our time. You won't find him a prophet without honour in his own country. Might I have your name?" "Scann, Airforce News." "And how long will you be with us, sir?" "I'm not sure." Charlie's face brightens. "You're going to do our story. Bless you, it needs doing. These are brave lads and they deserve recognition in the press. I know this isn't Biggen Hill or Hornchurch at the Battle of Britain but there are stories, Mr. Scann, wonderful tales, and you've come just at the right time. This fog has laid in here longer than it should and the men are restless. Windham's crash won't make sitting here without action any easier either. Maybe you can take our minds off it." "Charlie, you've made the press most welcome indeed. I know my job here is going to be much easier with you around. Tell me, have you been here since the beginning?" "Since the beginning of this here station in 1941, January 1941. Hampdens we flew then and dropped sea and land mines on the most unlikely places. And we had a Wimpy Squadron after that. Mind you, those old Wellingtons were a great aircraft, but they needed another couple of engines so they could carry a bomb or two more and make better odds for coming back. Then we got some Halifaxes and after that what we have now, the Lancaster Two. Now they are a unique aircraft. They combine the litheness and the ability of the Lanc air frame to float nicely with the guts and indestructibility of the Hercules engine, if you follow me. You can shoot three pots out of those engines and they'll keep running, whereas the Rolls Royce engine you've heard so much about needs only a hole the size of a pea in it and it loses its glycol and packs it up for good. Now, we've got a kite right here, H-Horse, that's been over Germany 123 times. The frame's twisted and the fabric's all been patched and she won't go above twenty-thousand feet all out. It's famous. The National War Gallery sent out an artist to do an oil painting of her. It's Thrain's kite now. He changed her letter to T for his own name. Seems a pity when she's done 123 ops as H. But that's the Wingco for you." "A bit of a grandstander," Scann says. "No, just made it his own." Charlie says this quickly as he rises from his elbows and smiles a greeting across the room.

alone, foolish, scared and in the middle of the war, "What if I won't?" "Maybe we'll see that you're missing in action." "What the hell do you mean?" "Or worse. Hand over your camera. Everything." Two knocks on the door and they are joined. Ace Scann looks again into Thrain's face. It is smiling. "You've found Geddings. Fine. Giving you good service?" "No. He wants my camera and my pictures. I've got authorisation." Thrain leans back against the door. "Yes, I suppose you have. To take pictures of pretty WAAFs at the Valentine's Day dance." He looks at Geddings, concerned. "We should leave him his camera though, don't you think?" Geddings doesn't answer. He puts his hands in his pockets. Thrain says to Scann, "We have a very good film man here. Holt. He'll do your developing and send the pictures to me." "We have official censors at Headquarters," Scann says, finding himself at attention. "We have one here too. Me." "Under no circumstances will I let this camera or my film out of my hands." Scann hears himself saying the words, one by one as if he hardly knew the language. Thrain's hand, his large hand, reaches out and tugs very hard and the camera's strap breaks. He is holding the Graphlex. Geddings' expression lightens, and the colour seeps back gradually into Thrain's face. Finally, he says: "Scann, you are officially welcome. And while you are here you are under my orders. I'm not going to hinder you in any way I don't have to. I'm even going to overlook this little scene because I understand your view. You think we are running a newspaper and only reporting a war. Not so." He looks at the camera, not knowing its mechanics and hands it to Geddings who expertly removes one plate from the camera and the rest from its dark-bag. Scann receives his camera back and watches Geddings take a manila envelope from his top drawer. "Plates to Holt," he says and writes the name without waiting for a reply from Thrain. Naked Scann runs for cover; there is no precedent for this attack on him in either his life or his training. "I'd like transport back to the village so I can get a train to London tonight," he says in a rushed voice. "No transport at this hour," Geddings says. Scann breathes deep. "Then I'll walk."

Wing Commander Thrain is standing in the at-ease position and still leaning his shoulderblades against the door. "Why don't you do what you were sent to do? Or have you done it already?" "Sir?" "Go down to the bar and have a drink, Scann," Thrain says mildly. "We'll send your pictures on to London for you." Scann senses a bargaining. "Not good enough, sir." Thrain stands away from the door and Geddings opens it. The room is small and there is an awkward moment while he forces his luggage and equipment out into the corridor. Scann turns to threaten Thrain and Geddings with high justice, but the door is closing and already their tiny consciousness of him has been occluded. Reporter Scann stands bag, baggage and camera in the hallway and hears Wing Commander Thrain's voice come through the door: "Funeral for six, possibly seven, at 14.00 hours tomorrow, Harold. Bring the Padre and tomorrow's Duty Officer to my room now, will you?" And Geddings says: "Tomorrow? That's a bit soon, isn't it?" "I'd do it tonight, if I could." "Too soon, David." "The quicker the better. Get it over with while the fog's with us. Anyway, I'm cleared to go ahead." "I'm going to speak frankly." Geddings sounds as if he is at attention. "There needs to be a little time elapse. Let it sink in a bit. I know it's stupid but there's a ceremony to these things." Geddings pauses. "And you haven't been here long enough to pull it off this way." "What?" "They don't know you. David, efficiency isn't everything. The Cleary thing was unfortunate. We didn't get a chance to look as if we were defending him." "He was just a thieving NCO. There's one on every station." "It was too quick." Thrain's voice rises. "What's your point, Harold?" "Ordering Windham back isn't sitting well, and Christ, if you bury him tomorrow it'll look like you, like you planned it." "I didn't know he couldn't fly. All he had to do was bring his kite home for servicing. I need it for Simms when the fog clears. My old man could have done it in his homemade plane." "I know, I know, but with Cleary and now this you can't afford another wrong decision." "What the hell are you saying, Geddings?" "Whose side are you on?" And the doorknob turns and the door begins to open. Holding his bag, suitcase and camera away from his body, Scann runs in stiff silence down the hall and the stairs and to a side door he finds at the bottom. He stumbles through it, out into the fog. He moves as quickly as he can away from the building and he is beginning to talk to himself, the disease of young children and old men. It is the first time he has ever walked out on a story. But he was not sent for a story. He is a feature writer. Bomber squadron. A feature about how the boys are fighting the war. Red white and blue journalism. Yes. He turns a sharp angle with the roadway. A free press cranks out bullshit for the provincials in Toronto and the cosmopolites in Lethbridge, in return for which

183

there should be a relationship with the officials of war, a policy of trust, a camaraderie, a shared conspiracy against the yellow and the tattletale grey in newspapering, for the moment. "I write," he says, "out of another consciousness, just as you fly out of a new conscience." He walks backward through the fog and shouts: "That's my excuse, what's yours, Thrain?" But neither of them needs an excuse. He walks again, his arms filling with the acid and lead of fatigue. The yellow lights are behind him and he follows the texture of the pavement with his feet, occasionally wandering off it. He thinks of Cleary, of Windham, of himself. And then of Thrain. Why should he be privileged and the rest posted to oblivion? Wing Commander Thrain D.S.O., D.F.C., should be attacked, and — what? Scann puts his gear down on the road and feels alone. This is not peacetime. He sits on the upended duffle and holds his hand out in front of his face without being able to see it distinctly. It is only a paler black suspended in total darkness. Why, yes, of course you can take my films, Flight Lieutenant Geddings. Perhaps you'll let me have prints. I understand, I understand completely. Listen to how bright I am on the subject: in war there is a double conflict that makes the experience unique. Two egos are already involved; one is the nation's and the other the individual's. Mister Adjutant, you are right to want my films. I was playing by the wrong rules. I sit here on my duffle and I have understanding and even compassion. Men are not able to be responsible for themselves under the ordinances of war and therefore are not whole men. A part of them is defenceless. But we are not pawns, Harold, that's old fashioned. Listen: war is new, different, improved. Where once it was two professional armies drawing old blood and new boundaries, it is now a catastrophic breakdown of the complete national structure to which man is normally loyal. It is one of the ironies of war, Geddings, that it's just this loyalty to the nation as law and administration that withers first when the conflict begins. It produced me, Geddings, and Charlie selling bodies in his bar and Cleary procuring. Maybe this is why the jingoistic hoo-haw that suddenly appears at a war's outbreak: it's an attempt to reconcile by emotional means the strange animal the nation has suddenly become with the cripples in uniform she has quickly produced. That's my view, Thrain-Geddings. And yours is simply to try to find out how to preserve your half-men selves and at the same time serve the instant monster that says it's going to save your philosophies at whatever cost in bodies. Yes, I think so. He

184

has begun to walk again, a reaction to stringing words. But his mind fills with the pain of physical effort. He stops thinking and only feels the duffle heavy in the curve of his arm, the suitcase hanging heavy at the ends of his fingers, and the camera disintegrating against his chest. The fog settles in the back of his throat. Acrid cotton that dries his epiglottis and shrivels his soft palate. The friendly lights of Graydon village should be welcoming him soon. He is sure there are shapes in the dark around him. He puts his burden down once more and changes them from hand to hand. This going is a double defeat: he is not riding and he is running away. His feet burn with cold and unaccustomed use. His nose developes an itch and then a sneeze which clears his nasal passages. Along with the wet acidity of the fog, he smells a new odour. It is as if guns had gone off recently, and perhaps there is smoke. His right foot strikes a solid object and he stumbles around it. The impact drives him in a new direction over another object. He begins to curse out of fear. He has no way of knowing where he is. He stops and waits, then shuffles forward. A light, small and close, shines suddenly in his face. "Don't move, not one more step." It is a female voice. Scann, in shock, says, "I'm harmless." Her voice comes back out of the dark behind her light, "Who are you?" "Scann, Pilot Officer." "Never heard of you." "I'm from H.Q., London, Airforce News." The light looks down at his duffle and suitcase and he can see that she's in blue and not more than a couple of inches over five feet. He grabs her arms hard and pins them to her sides. The light points straight down at her shoes. They are officer's. "Get your hands off me." "When I hear your gun drop," Scann says, feeling there is very little strength in her. "I haven't got a gun, stupid, let me go. What made you think I had a gun, for God's sake?" Relieved, Scann has another thought. "Where am I?" "On runway 240 and ten yards from the wreck of an aircraft." "Windham?" Her breathing catches, stops. "How do you know?" "The lorry I came in with was first on the scene." After a pause, she says, "Why did *you* come back?" "Got lost in the fog." He is holding her gently now and she can move if she pleases. "And you?" "You're new here. Let me introduce myself before somebody else tries it. I'm Marie, Windham's good friend." He releases her, and everything he is feeling, alone in the fog, is somehow gone. "Let me see now," he says, "you're trying to tell me something." "I was also Gerry Murphy's and Freddie Greenslade's and Roy Newland's. All my menfolk are good and die young." Reporter Scann takes the light from her hand and shines it in her face. She is weeping, and she is not very young. "Now I know," he says, "you want someone to feel sorry for you." She is not unattractive. "I *do*," he says, "but let me tell you my story before you go any farther. It may change your tactics." He takes a deep enjoyable breath. "I'm Amory Scann, a man of the forties. I collect histories and spread rumours of apocalypses for which I manufacture happy endings." She turns from him and begins to walk. "You're too young to be that corrupted." Her shape fades quickly: he picks up his load and follows the sound of her strolling footsteps. She doesn't vary her pace, nor does the fog ever trick her sense of direction. After a while she says, "You're another fool, Scann. Do you belong to King Thrain or are you with the rest of us?" "I'm my very own fool, and I think you don't like Thrain." "Who does?" "I asked someone earlier if he wanted to be like Thrain and he said: who doesn't?" Her voice sounds disappointed. "There are those too." "Why?" "Why indeed? Because he lives and goes on living, and he thinks for us all and gives hope to us all, and fear and example." "And you've been been standing out there at the crash thinking up a speech and now you're giving it to me for practice." "You're right about me, Scann, you should be hostile. But I'll tell you anyway what I was doing at the crash: I was trying to feel something. Then, just before you came along, I thought, why the hell should I? There's a great strength in not feeling anything. It's why I've said what I've said and it's why I was crying. It's a kind of relief, you know, to understand that from now on at least part of what I live is going to have to be the truth." Loser Scann is suddenly affected. Has he not just finished running, too? After a moment, he says, "It's the only way to operate, Marie. Feelings lead to emotions and emotions make witlings of us all." He cannot speak it light enough. His voice trembles. It has been a very long evening. "Where are we?" he asks, to divert her from himself. She doesn't answer. There have been lights around them in the fog. Occasional voices. She is beside him now, and she holds his arm. "Watch your step." She opens a door and the lobby of the Officers Mess is before him again, dimly lit and deserted. Scann puts his suitcase and duffle in the corner furthest from the door and turns to face Marie. She is as old as he had thought. Her hair is short and reddish. Her skin is dry beneath large pale-blue eyes. When she walks with him toward the bar she moves with strength. He imagines her having been a swimmer, a skater, perhaps a tennis player. She is not talking now, nor has she more than glanced at him since they came in from the dark outside. He thinks she doesn't really want to go down this short corridor to the bar. "Full circle," he says, to break the silence. She stops at the door and looks up at him. "That's for me to say, not you." "I meant only that I began my evening here." It occurs to him that she has large breasts. Beneath her athlete's slouch, in the hollow of her chest are surprises. She is opening the door into a roomful of people. Oddly, Charlie's barroom looks larger now that it is filled with battle dress. He has help at the pumps: a young WAAF, tall and pretty. Charlie's face glows a little. He touches her as he moves to get change. The only other woman in the room is near the piano singing with some men: Does your mother know you're out, Cecilia? They finish lightly, almost quietly, with two high cracked-glass chords from the piano.

The silence the singers make spreads through the bar. It is fitting, because one by one they see Marie, and Scann knows she has not lied to him: she is looked at uncomfortably as bereaved people sometime are in uncertain surroundings. At the bar, a squadron leader does not see her and does not stop talking. His voice is at last the only sound in the room. He speaks through phlegm. "I think she's a jinx, Esterby, I really do." A chuckle. "There *are* such things. I told Windham but he wasn't listening." The quiet is concrete. It is cracked by the small flower of the female voice from near the piano. "Marie, darling." The rest of the audience is engulfed by the action, as if it is at a cinema. Marie is just inside the door. She shouts as if the Squadron Leader is a long way away. "Brannan, you're a lying bastard." He rises from his barstool as she crosses the room and stops in front of him. He stands looking down. She looks back into his eyes a moment and then kicks him hard on the left shin. Brannan winces and lifts that foot off the floor, and she kicks the other with her stout airforce shoe. Brannan sways and his mouth opens, but he doesn't say anything. There is a lot of beer in him. He looks for a moment as if he might win the struggle to discover something positive or vengeful to do, but his face crumples with pain and frustration. Marie reaches out her hand and he looks with real terror at it. She pulls him away from the bar and says quietly, "Now you can go and find Thrain and report me." And he goes as if it might have been an order. Observer Scann wonders if he will do as he's told, but it seems unimportant to speculate about it. Marie climbs onto the stool Brannan has just vacated. The Flight Lieutenant who had been listening to Brannan watches her a moment. "If you wanted a seat I'd have given you mine," he says. Marie ducks her head forward and she bites her lip. "Now I feel something," she says, and Scann doesn't know whether she is relieved or simply reporting. Geddings comes over to her. "Your manners are atrocious, Marie." She looks around at him and grins through tears. "You're not my conscience, Harold." The girl from the piano comes near. "Leave her alone. She's upset, can't you see?" She turns to the piano player. "Play something, Roger. Roll Me Over, anything."

Into the rising level of noise, Marie says, "I went back to the crash, Steph." She looks up at her friend. Geddings reaches round Marie and puts his glass on the bar. His face is suddenly tired. He turns and Scann feels his voice impinging: "So you've decided not to leave." "Maybe in the morning." "There'll be no transport, then, either. We're holding a funeral at 14.00 hours and the station's parading, no exceptions." Marie says, "Funeral tomorrow?" She stands up on the bottom rung of her stool, a head higher than Geddings. "This isn't the bloody tropics." She steps down on to the floor in front of him. Geddings smiles at her. He speaks as if he is choosing maximum velocity words to stop her attack for ever. "The arrangements will be simple. Just the bodies in boxes, a large grave, Padre Sweet in good voice and everybody there." "Harold," Marie's friend says. Esterby stands. "You're way out of line, Geddings." And now there is another silence. Participant Scann reaches out his hand, but Marie is gone from the place she had been. He sees the door open, and then the one across the hall marked Women. Marie disappears beyond it. The room is full of eyes and ears. "Stephanie," Esterby says, "bring Marie back when she's ready so Mr. Geddings can apologise to her." Geddings' lips are all of him that move. "That won't be possible. I'm meeting with the C.O. now about tomorrow." Esterby sits carefully on his stool. "You don't feel an apology necessary?" "No, she's been in mourning ever since I've known her. Meaningless. Just a way to attract attention." Among the crowd tentative smiles appear. They want to smile at something. Geddings sets his gloves under his arm as if they are a swagger stick. "The funeral's a good thing." "No it's not. It's much too quick to be good. Tell David I think it's a bad idea." Stephanie leaves the bar to be with Marie. Geddings sees her go. "Without those two," he says, stopping. Then: "Give Thrain a chance. He's right. What's worse than flying? Not flying. And what's worse than not flying? Half a dozen bodies lying around dead reminding you of what the war's all about, so let's have the funeral and get back to normal." "Let's have some preparation, let's have some dignity," Esterby says. "Let's bloody-well hope we can be civilised, Geddings. Let's hope we can remember who they are. Not garbage. Those aren't bodies, they're Windham and his crew: our friends." "They were my friends too," Geddings says, "but they're dead now and they should-n't be left to lie around and stink up the place." He slams the door behind him, and Esterby, after a moment, says after him, "Nice try, Geddings. YEA team." He turns on his stool and faces the bar and says to Charlie, "So we parade. You're the oldest member of the squadron, Charles. What are the precedents? Are there any outs?" "No, sir, there never was a night like this in my time and I've been here since January first, 1941. A cold nasty day it was too."

Scann sits on the stool vacated by both Brannan and Marie. Charlie is looking his way and points at the gin. Scann nods, and glances down the bar. Simms is on the final stool; he leans against the wall, white-faced, his mouth ajar. His hand is attached to the handle of a beermug. His eyes open and he begins to talk. "Esterby. Esterby, I'm not going to go. I don't like funerals." Esterby doesn't answer. "Know why?" His head rises from the wall and it wobbles. "They smell. They smell of the smells they make to cover up the smell of corpses." Simms looks around as best he can. "If I get it . . . if I get it." Fear surfaces in his eyes. Esterby says kindly, "Have another beer, Simms, you're still conscious." "Fuck you Esterby, watch who you're talking to. Just a navigator is all you are, take your pencil and shove it Esterby. Don't tell me I need another beer." He pauses. His face is blank with concentration. He might be having a bowel movement, or a thought. "Go screw Marie," he says, and leans along the bar toward Esterby. "How'd you like that, hey, Clifford? *Clifford*, for Chrissakes." He stands, picks up his beermug and lifts it to his face. Then he looks around the foam-stained glass and grins. "Sure, Clifford, whyn't you try it? Maybe she just puts the hex on pilots. Ever thought of that?" Esterby stands up too and says loud and fast, "You want a fight, Simms? Step outside." Simms smiles almost happily and walks his private acclivity to the door. Outside of it he crashes. Others are leaving. They pick him up and bear him away. Esterby sighs and sits down once more. Scann says to him, "Smiling, the boy fell dead." "With help, with help," Esterby says. "I can't think what you young are coming to. No respect at all. Who are you?" "Scann. I'm up from London." "Welcome. Who have you met here?" "Don't bother, I'm going back tomorrow." "But you must meet a few of us. We like it known at HQ that we're names and not just numbers." "I know Geddings and the C.O.," Scann says. "I talked to Simms and walked in the fog with Marie." He signals Charlie. "I know a driver named Dolan, but my first friend is Charles. What will you have?" "Nothing, thank you, must go study the manual, eh Scann? Do they parade a lot at Headquarters?" "No." They both rise, shake hands, and Stranger Scann remembers without much emotion that he has nowhere to sleep. "I think I'll stay and have one more if you don't mind." "Not at all, we're hospitable folk." As he speaks he is walking toward the door doing, Scann thinks, something that seems quite natural to him, a slow fade.

He decides on a second drink. The torn edges of his day are repaired. He is neither righteous nor embarrassed. He feels freed. He has this moment for his own, and he thinks how long it has been since this has been true. His has been a durable obsession. There is no god in newspapering, only self-evident faiths that copyboy Scann had learned at sixteen, and still believes, as anyone does who is blinded by the light of reason rather than stunned by awe of the everlasting. It is a faith and a belief still stronger than Thrain-Geddings, and the sentimentality of that knowledge pleases him. He drinks lazily. There are few people left in the room, although there are sounds from elsewhere. It occurs to him that he has had nothing to eat all day since the sausage roll at noon in the pub at Graydon village. The decision about whether or not to go find where they serve supper breaks his moment, and Steph enters the room. She is taller than he remembers, yellow-blonde, and with round brown eyes quick with emotion. Her neat blue hat rests on rolled-up hair. She walks toward him and sits on the vacant stool beside him. "Poor Marie's going to sleep now. Such a curious scene. One wonders if Brannan will press charges. No, don't stand up and be a gentleman. The shock. I'm Stephanie." Scann begins to offer her a drink, but Charlie puts a gin down in front of her. There is a moment of real contact between them, and she drinks. "Thank you Charlie Fox always among my chickens." "I deny that, my Lady."

He smiles as if at someone beloved who is acting a little addled. To Scann he says, "Miss Braithewaite's people have always been the principal landlords in my village." Stephanie laughs. "Miss Braithewaite. Do you want the whole handle? Stephanie Martin-Hellingsford-Braithewaite. I won't spell it. My family worked very hard at marriage contracts, to consolidate fortunes. Charles understands. We should be filthy rich, and we are, I think. In any case, I'm the only direct heir, so you see I'll have to marry someone also rich who'll want to have his name tacked on then I'll wind up something-something-something-something. Silly, isn't it? One wonders how much longer it can go on. Perhaps, instead, I shall just emigrate to Canada and buy one of your lovely provinces and marry a lumberjack who'll call me Steph and love me for the nice girl I am." Listening, Scann wonders if she's babbling drunk. She finishes her drink in one swallow and stands up, pointing. "I do not exonerate you, Charles Fox whose strange powers are already legend." Charlie's face is flushed and he seems to be standing at attention. "Please m'am, a joke is a joke." "You're a Scarlet Pimpernel or something among those poor dears." She turns abruptly: "And who are you?" "Scann, Amory Scann, innocent bystander." "I'm going to supper, are you coming?"

They walk together out of the bar, past the doors marked Men and Women and the place where Simms crashed, and on down the corridor to the foyer. There, speaking on the phone at the foyer desk, is Wing Commander Thrain. As they pass, he holds Scann by the arm and stops him. He is listening and nodding. Stephanie pauses too. Thrain looks at her, shakes his head and motions for her to carry on. "Berrigan, let me say it once more: you should not have diverted the training aircraft." Stephanie doesn't move; she watches him listen and then speak. "I know. I'm aware of what happened to Windham, but that shouldn't have influenced. What? Listen, Berrigan (a) don't interrupt me and (b) I'm tired of your arguing. Pack it in down there. Leave it to Stubbs." He hangs up and turns to them. Stephanie says, "I will go, but first I want to say just this: Berrigan is right, and Marie and Esterby and I and everybody." "Is that all?" "No." Her face stiffens and looks as if a dangerous wind is blowing against it. "Geddings is a monster for what he said about Marie. She was right, this isn't the tropics, there's no hurry." Thrain smiles. "She say that?" "Yes." "And you agree?" "Yes." "How about you, Scann?" "You wanted to see me?" Scann says, but he is ignored. "Anything else, Miss Braithewaite?" "They need to be buried well, David. I haven't called you David before. You aren't David are you? You're a fist. I'm sorry, I shouldn't have said that just because it's true. They need to be put away from us in peace." Her eyes go steady again. "In the middle of this dreadful dreadful war, real remembrance in a moment of peace. Not just shuffled off in a hurry. Don't you see? And if you don't allow that then they'll be feared as dead things, as ghosts, and you will be hated." Thrain takes one step toward her. Scann thinks: he *is* a fist. "You seem to want an explanation," he says. "It's this: when Group phones and says to go bomb the Germans, we go. You can't fly and go to funerals at the same time, and this fog isn't going to last forever. You're upset, everybody's upset. It can't be helped." "But where's the honour is being hurried off to the graveyard like this?" "The honour is when you win and you're better than the odds against you. You parade tomorrow with your girls, all of them, and Marie too. 13.45 hours." Stephanie only keeps looking at him, and Scann is afraid for her. "You're wrong, Wing Commander, you're very wrong." He goes close to her. "Will you do as I say?" "Yes sir." "Then go." "Very well." And she does go. Scann wants to call after her to wait, but her retreat is swift and his arm is held again. "Scann, why are you here?"

It's as if nothing had happened. Scann turns to Thrain and feels weightless. He is neither reporter nor subject to this man. If he has a small concern, it is to go with Stephanie. "Why?" He feels older, definitely British: "Why indeed. I did try to walk out, you know. Lost my way in the fog." "Why are you here, Scann? They've got all the copy on me they need to write a book if they want. So why are you here?" Scann focuses his attention. "Look, sir, I came here to do a feature on a squadron led by Wing Commander David Thrain D.S.O., D.F.C., fifty trips to Germany, and all the rest. I've read the copy. Small town boy makes good. The true north strong and free. It's part of the business of the world to make stars out of the successful and then use them to make the whole system we live with look good. But I'm not doing that story any more. I'm on my way back to HQ. If it worries you that I'm here, forget it, sir." Thrain leans on the desk. "A Pilot Officer newspaperman. Who the hell's commissioning writers?" "We have officers," Scann says, "in fact we don't have any troops. Everyone has a title and a little empire. Just like here." Scann holds his gaze steady and wonders at the concern in Thrain's eyes. He feels his pocket for his notebook. And then the padre is beside them. He smiles an official smile. He is slim, and looks older than Scann had imagined a battlestation padre to be. Thrain glances at him and then back at Scann. "Right," he says, "That'll be all. We'll see you get out of here sometime after the funeral tomorrow." The padre's face remains calm. "The funeral?" Or perhaps it isn't a face, only a mask for the Wing Commander to look at. Scann goes slowly to his bags to remove them from the foyer. "You'd have known earlier if you'd come to my room when you were asked." "I was with Miller." "Was he conscious?" "Not all the time." The padre takes off his gloves finger by finger. "In any event, I'm here now." "How is Miller?" "Burton took him to the operating room, so it'll be a while before we know." "The funeral's tomorrow at 1400 hours." David is herding the padre from Scann's presence. "David, I really don't know how I can do it by then." They go around the corner. "It's all laid on." Scann carries his bags and equipment across the room. "The next of kin will have to be notified." The padre's official voice is beginning to break up. Scann goes quietly from the room, trying to keep comment from rising to the surface of his mind. He has never written editorials. He goes through the doors into the lounge and quickly puts his luggage in another corner and shoves an overstuffed chair in front of it. The noise at the moment is one great yell. Scann senses having arrived at the beginning of his assignment. He stares down the long narrow room with its high ceiling at a crowd of bottled-beer drinkers who are watching a young man climb a pile of furniture towards the smoky limits of the room. A piano is playing and some are singing a ritual song. The gamesman mounts a chesterfield and goes on up to a table resting on a stack of hardback chairs. He balances with a bottle of beer in one hand and a pencil in the other. There are more chairs and another table. He goes carefully to the top. The encouragement he has been getting fades. The piano and a few singers sing. At the peak of the pile he must stop. Words are flung up at him. He sways on the utmost chair. There is almost silence. He reaches for the ceiling with his pencil to write his name among others that are already there. His balance goes out from under him. He falls down over tumbling tables and chairs to the floor. The beer in his bottle spills and he lies perhaps unconscious. Friends pull him away. The game is an RAF import, one invented by gentlemen away from home and school and club. "Many are maimed, but few are killed," Stephanie says over the new noise and into Scann's ear. She sits on the arm of his chair and they watch another failure, and then as if by signal everyone grabs furniture, beer crates, tables, chairs and benches and pitches them in a great pile. The mountain grows. It becomes easy to climb, and it is a new, perhaps Canadian, game. Brannan storms the peak and holds off anyone who wants to go to the ceiling to write his name. Chairs crumble, tables crack. Gradually the pile becomes rubble and Brannan, with each assault, sinks farther and farther away from the ceiling until he is fighting at ground level and three men have to pin his arms and lift him, legs and shoulders, away from Simms whose arms are still feebly windmilling in front of his grinning and bloody face. Brannan is borne away, perhaps to his room. Simms finally stops fighting and begins to hiccough. Two men shout a warning and, laughing, they grab him and pitch him out through the window onto the ground outside. Almost immediately, the fog begins to insinuate itself into the room. Scann and Stephanie get up. The crowd is delighted with everything. They hold each other up, shout laughter, stagger around the room and out into the hallway. The piano is silent. The barman is taking wooden cases of beer away. The bones of the evening have been broken and lie crazily about them. "They don't do this every evening," Scann says. It is a question. "David beware," she says, and takes his hand to lead him to the window. Simms is not dead. His breath can be seen white against the black ground. Shards of glass and a pool of vomit lie around and beneath him. Stephanie pulls out the broken glass from the frame of the window, hitches up her skirt and climbs out. Scann follows the whites of her legs and the blonde roll of her hair.

Simms is not even cut. There is glass in his hair and his clothes, but they can't see a scratch. Stephanie crouches beside him and tells him how lucky he is. They roll him away from his vomit and Scann contributes his handkerchief to her ministrations. "Christ, he's suicidal." She doesn't answer him. She is still talking to Simms, talking and talking and encouraging him to wake up and see how fortunate things turned out. It is damp and cold. They each take an arm and lift him up. Scann thinks they are going back to the mess but she pulls him away from it. "Not far," she says, "we don't all live at the palace." Like Marie, she has the face of the station committed to memory. "Old habit," she says. "You'd never guess but I was a stretcher-bearer in the blitz, and then when I'd nearly bought it they made me a driver. Had to be able to deliver a message to anywhere in London, blind. Now, here we are. Let's not bother to knock. We've all seen the young in bed, eh Scann? Four to a room. Yes, here we are, just open the door and we'll see if we can find the little skipper's downy. In we go, tiny Simms. Let's give him plenty of blankets because I think his resistance is down right now. There." At the door, Scann turns right, thinking he's got the direction he wants to go in his head. She takes his hand again and they go in the opposite direction. "Will the bar be open?" "Not really. There's a kind of ritual, you know. Brannan orders Charles to keep the place open until he's given permission to close it. It's all very gamesy and I'm surprised Charles hasn't grown bored with it by now. But I suspect he and Brannan are a bit in cahoots, as you people say. In the end, he closes up anyway. Just left here, and watch your step." They go in a door. "And I think we should be quiet for a moment." She whispers. "The stairs creak a bit so let's do it in unison. There, that's very good. I'll just open up and you can relax until you can see better in the gloom." She goes to the window and Scann closes the door. She lets the blind up and there is a kind of light that seems to be part of the fog behind her, giving her an outline, and the room some definition. "The bed's just there, Amory, I had it brought from home. After London, where I was able to keep on daddy's flat, this all seemed very bivouac. Gladstone, who was here before David, exacted a terrible toll to turn a blind eye. I was glad when he went back to Canada. It's nice, isn't it? I left the chintz and the gewgaws behind." She walks past him naked onto the bed, and his fingers, understanding, begin to pull and tear at the buttons and laces and sleeves. "But it's a big old thing and every now and then it feels very empty. Amory, your hands are quite cold. And mine too? Now, love, we've got lots of time, don't hurry. We're groundlings, and no one is going to stop us and send us off into the wild blue yonder to get shot up. The fog's right inside me tonight and I need warming up. Let's be close for a while, and you won't mind if I cry a little? It's possible, you know. I want everything to have a place and be in its place. But these are very sad and out-of-joint times too. You were with Marie tonight: some girls are virgins all their lives, do you know? We're too young to know that, both of us. How old are you, Amory?" Scann tries to remember. "Going on twenty-four." "The same, the very same. Do you know I'm the youngest Section Officer in this command? Have you some french letters with you?" This omission is a sin Scann can't forgive. "Well, never mind, there are one or two in the drawer of the night table." Fumbler Scann fumbles. "You're an odd sort, Amory Scann, but you're gentle, which is more than I hoped. No, Amory, your hands are lovely and warm but don't feel me there. It's not pretty. It's my little red badge of courage except it's mostly purple and it's on my backside so I look a coward instead of a heroine. The plastic surgeons are away at war too, so you'll just have to put up with me in the dark. Maybe sometime after the war you can come back and we'll have mirrors if you want. I've heard that's fun. Oh, Amory, I am going to cry. Because it can't happen. I'll be somewhere else, and the surgeon will have done something with my scars and I'll be being normal with three kids and a husband who goes up to the city for business, Amory I do like your mouth and your hands and I'm warm now. Amory, let me tell you, I wasn't quite twenty. Come to me darling and let me say it instead of crying. Do I talk too much? It's just tonight, I think. It hasn't been a wonderful evening till now. I was almost nineteen and Cissy and I had come out and we went on the grand tour. Amory, you feel very good. Slow and good, keep it slow. France, Italy, Geneva: nobody ever went to Geneva then, Amory, but that was where Robbie was, and he was in London when we got back. Amory, darling, I'm sharing with you. You see, I can do things too, can't I? Robbie was like you, your size, a big man. He had a Fox Moth and we flew to Paris for weekends and parties with lovely people. We loved and made love. Loved and loved and loved, darling. Robbie. Amory, I want to tell you something, but you're going to come, aren't you. I am too. I am too. Amory, we'll get together. It's not far now. Just a little way and you're so good at it. But not yet. Let me. I let you. Robbie flew those little bombers we had at first. Let me say when, Amory. Listen. He took mines and flew them across the North Sea. Everything's so beautifully tight. Just get me past this part. Amory, once a mine blew up in his aircraft before takeoff. Everyone was killed but him. I love you for this, Amory, I love you. Robbie wasn't even scratched. But he's still in hospital. In a soundproof room. And now, Amory, now, the slightest noise gives him hysterics. There are worse things than burying your dead. Yes. Yes yes yes. *Make* me." Scann is as big and as strong and as necessary as she has told him. The long, live mania in him explodes along all of his passages, up all of his blind and visceral alleys and then down the one swollen corridor of their connection, and he feels her body shudder and leap beyond her tongue and mind. The sound she makes is the one he gives her: "Jesus," she says back, "oh Jesus." And because there is then silence and everything is new and he understands that this may be love he begins again without ever finishing and goes on until she says, let me, and he does. Then the insanity is his and she has to talk to him again, telling him lies about greatness in him, in her and in them and he knows then that they are only accidents, right moments that already he is fearful will never occur again. It is the beginning of Writer Scann. And they both insist once more, and he wonders if his heart will stop, if it *has* stopped, but he wakes and there is daylight at the window. She is washing him with a warm, wet towel. Her skin is roses beneath an open kimono. She takes another towel and begins to dry him. "The service is complete here at Graydon," she says, kneeling on the bed beside him. She is fresh and bathed. He puts up a hand and brings her down beside him on the bed. The light in the room distracts him. He is used to hearing and feeling her, not seeing her. "I'm going back to London today," he says. Last night is elusive; he wants to go back and live it again. What she was then jams his sensibilities. He tries to think clearly about it. "He's in a hospital near here, isn't he?" She pulls away a little so she can see. "Yes, and you see, I must keep myself from dying. I mustn't let myself die. I must keep myself alive." She smiles and ducks her head as if in shame. "Do you understand?" she says into his shoulder. "It doesn't seem to make sense, does it?" "Perhaps," he says. "I've only been over here a little while. At the war." He can feel some wet from her tears on his shoulder. "And how do you like it?" "It's melodramatic." She sniffs and rises again to smile at him. "Yes; and all soft and mushy and sentimental." She sounds as she did when he first met her. She is back now, returned, as if from shock treatment and with an aberration relieved. "I guess you do this often." He doesn't want to say it because it makes him just another one night stand. She takes herself away from him and begins to dress. "I shan't forget, Amory," she says after a moment. "No matter what you say now to try to spoil it so you won't mind leaving." She looks up at him from putting on a stocking. "You shouldn't you know: life's not exclusive. Wait until you have to live as if it is. I pray God you won't, but I suppose life might touch even a journalist sometime." He rolls over and sits shrivelled on the edge of the bed. She is combing her hair at the mirror. "Look. What I said is no good.

You're not just another woman." He comes fully awake, and how she has brought him here and why explodes in his mind. "Where is he?" he asks. She turns on him. "No, you're not to see him. You know enough now and he's." "But he's." "He's the whole bloody war, yes, would you like me to explain?" "No, I don't think that would do any good. He's your war, not anybody else's." He gets up and begins to dress too. "You know why I'm angry, don't you?" She shakes her head but looks reassured because he smiles. "That's the best lover I ever was last night, and it had nothing to do with me." She goes back to combing her hair. "Other than that, how do you feel?" Her eyes in the mirror are composed. "I don't know — far away?" "Do you have strength enough to use the fire-escape? It's out the window and three feet to your left." She looks at her watch. "I think you'll have to go quite quickly before the girls down below hear you." He is being dismissed. But she puts her comb down and comes to him and kisses him. "Amory; believe in it." There isn't anything left to do but go. He opens the window and climbs down to ground level. He stands in the fog again and realises that he hasn't asked directions. He can't shout or climb back. He finds the road and stands with his hands in his pockets shivering. A greatcoat goes by with epaulets. He follows as close as he dare without having to speak. He passes a flagpole and then he recognizes the door to the mess. His guide holds it open for him and he goes in. He shaves behind the door marked Men across from the bar. The toilet and basin are clean, the water is hot and he is undisturbed. It is a pleasant moment he spends there, and he thinks that today might turn out better than yesterday. He goes back to the lounge to repack his kit. He tries to draw himself away from Stephanie, but the edges of ecstasy still nudge at his guts. He sits in the over-stuffed chair that has protected his gear all night, and looks over the debris of the evening before. A couple of irks are slowly sorting it out. They do their work as if it is a familiar chore. He takes out his notebook and turns it over so that its last page is now its first. He writes in it. I have never before had an experience whose outlines I couldn't set down in four sentences. By God, I feel small, I feel foolish, I feel apologetic, I feel frightened, and most of all I feel — when I think of these people here and who and what they are — most of all I feel cheated. And embarrassed. I always wanted to report the big time. Welcome Amory Ace Scoop Scann. Put your press card in your hat and see if you can last the day. *NB*: Drop fuck from your vocabulary. The prevalence of its use may come from its comfortable inaccuracy: the act itself may not even exist. Of course, it could be that I'm in love. Or, worse, I may be all atremble because I've been forced to some sort of consciousness. He turns the notebook over again. "War came back to Graydon-on-Moor at 7.27 on a foggy night. . . ." He reverses the notebook once more: Don't laugh, Amory, you wrote that. The time is the same, Scann; it is new space you're seeing. You darling romantic: "Here it is: The heart/ Since proud, it calls the calling manly, gives a guess/ That, hopes that, makes believe, the men must be no less. . . ." And what of the women, Gerard Manley? What of the virgin, Marie, for instance, who cannot, so the story goes, lose it? A strange doom. And, finally, before breakfast, what do you think now of Wing Commander Thrain who has to preside over this all?

At the junction of the corridor and the diningroom door, there is Geddings. "Where did you sleep last night?" Scann wants to tell him: Geddings, last night I slept in the middle of things, among rockets and guns and landmines exploding. "Left to my own devices, I found a corner." "Damned sorry about that. You should have banged on my door." "I had officially left." "But you checked back. I saw you." His office-manager's mind struggles with this untidiness. "Well, never mind, you'll be on your way before tonight." He gestures toward the diningroom. "Marie had her girls find an egg for us this morning."

He lets Geddings leave and goes in slowly, taking a tray and moving through the line past the serving counters. The egg is poached and lies pale in its dregs, like a sea-creature dead on a white plate. He puts toast around it and accepts a cup of coffee. He sits alone, not far from Thrain and Esterby. They don't talk until the doctor comes. His face is another of this morning's eggs. He has only a cup of coffee in his hand. Thrain looks up at him, and Burton says, "He's dead." They are joined by the padre, who has neither breakfast nor a cup of coffee with him. His official face is gone. It's as if he's been told he has six hours to live and is trying to cope with all of his life at once. He sits on the edge of a chair. Thrain says, "When?" "A few minutes ago. I was lucky to keep him alive as long as I did." "Funny he should have bought it out there in the tail," Thrain says. "Gunners usually are safe from fire." "He wasn't burned. When we took his helmet off the top of his head nearly came with it." "And you couldn't just let him go," the padre says, "you must operate, and without anesthetic, I'm told." "Padre," Burton says, "neither the skull nor the brain need anesthetic. I used a local on his scalp. A general would have been just one more thing for his system to cope with." "He was hopeless." "It seems that way now, but do you ever diagnose your cases as hopeless when they come to you?" "God," the padre says, "is not medical science." "Maybe God isn't here and you're on your own just like I am. But I'll tell you something, if those parishioners of yours would give me something besides hangovers and the Manchester clap to practise on I'd be as big an expert as you. All my hands are good for now is playing bridge." "Death, God, clap," Esterby says, "hardly fit topics for this time of day." "Miller's dead," Thrain says. "Let's leave it at "that." "And it makes seven," the padre says. "I must have the files on them all, Wing Commander. Will you tell Geddings?" "What do you need their files for?" "To find out who they are, something more personal about them. I don't see all the men, you know. It's a large." "Look, padre, all I want is the short service, the one from the book. I hope you won't take off on happy boyhoods and mother's cooking." The padre draws a breath, then: "Yes sir." Thrain doesn't ignore the inference. "Not yes sir, just try to understand what's necessary." Brannan arrives and sits slowly beside the others. "Good God, what happened?" "See what I mean, padre?" Burton says, "you get all the business." "He doesn't need God, only the good die young." He looks surprised at himself but not angry. "Come, come, that's only a rule of thumb," Esterby says. Brannan groans. "I repeat, I say again: what happened?" Esterby tells him, "You know damned well what happened." "Stiff upper, Brannan," Thrain says, "Lots to do today." Brannan looks at the padre. "Man's the only animal that dances at a death in the family." "Well said," Esterby tells him. Brannan pounds his fists without making noise on the tabletop. "Bang the drums slowly." "Here's a list of the funeral party, Brannan," Thrain says. "Warrant Officer Cates will assist. Rehearsal parade at ten hundred hours." Brannan looks at the list. "Do I have to spend the whole goddamn morning doing this? I'm a flier, not a parade jockey and I don't like funerals — " Thrain stands up. "Your personal bitches don't interest me, Brannan, especially in public." Brannan looks down at the table. There is colour in his cheeks. "Yes," he says. Thrain waits a moment. "Yes what?" Brannan's face upturns; he rises awkward: "Yes sir." "Right, now get some food into you and stay sober." He nods to the padre. "Come on, I'll give you those files." Brannan returns to his chair slowly. "Jesus, Esterby, where are we? Where the hell are we suddenly? He walks back from Berlin and takes over here. Walks back. I like flyers better." "He could fly a wheelbarrow better than you can your own kite," Esterby says, "what the hell's eating you?" Brannan doesn't answer. He goes for a cup of coffee and comes back, slopping it. "Maybe that's the trouble. Gladstone couldn't fly a helium balloon but he knew how to run a squadron." "It was a wet fuse when he was here and you know it. David only wants the squadron ready and working. It's all he knows." "That's just it, he wants to win the fucking war." "How the hell did you get to be squadron leader, Brannan?" "Age, pure bloody age. I'm the longest lived man in the RCAF. I lived so long they had to promote me when Tubby Parsons got it at Cologne." Brannan looks around and then leans toward Esterby. "The same night Greenslade got it. Between the Hun and Marie we've had a nice total lately. And we're down to seventeen kites." Esterby smiles. "Well, Marie's had it now, struck a superior officer, she did. That'll be our next entertainment, a stake through her heart." "Know what Thrain said? What'd you do to provoke her, Brannan? I said, Post her or I'll call Group, and *he* says, call Group and you'll get to finish your tour in 1960. Who the hell side's he on?" Esterby gets up and starts to go. Brannan follows him. "There aren't any sides any more," Esterby says, fading again.

Scann's twenty hour fast has made the food taste good. His stomach is full, warm and soporific. He thinks again of Stephanie. He supposes that what he is feeling can only be glut. The beat of his heart is slow and heavy. Each pump might be its last — sweet lethargy even there in the full-flooding valve of existence. He breathes light and shallow, always on the edge of a yawn. He might drown comfortably now, or freeze to death. Surely Stephanie's barrack is empty at this hour, and her bed, the best this side of London, must be vacant. He will go there and sleep away the day. Perhaps I will die, he thinks. When I have to die I want to feel like this. A feeling of having done. Of having done with. And in the city room and the Press Club they will say he died with glory in the kip of Lady Stephanie of Hants: raise their glasses and shout Scann instead of Sköl. He walks slowly out of the diningroom, along the corridor and out through the lobby to the entranceway. Around him are people, some already in their parade blues. He goes outside into the fog and tries to remember the direction he must go to get to Stephanie's. But then Marie goes by him, and he follows her, hoping she lives in the same building with her friend. She walks with her head down. Shapes surround them, other people coming and going. Where they are walking the light is weaker, the fog thick; he lengthens his stride to keep up with Marie. She stops without warning and he has to go by her. Perhaps she has forgotten something. Then he turns and walks back toward her, trying to walk like someone else, but she has disappeared. He comes to a halt and stands as he remembers having done when he was eight and was trying to walk home from school with his eyes shut. But there he knew the route by daylight; here he has been living since quite suddenly a long time ago and no one place is connected with another. His travels, unless accompanied, are random. Where he goes is chance, nor can he be sure of going back to where he started. It is a game with penalties but no assigned rewards. And it's the only game there is to play. He steps off the edge of the road and walks through wet grass to the end of a building. The door has glass in its top panel, and through it he can see a light burning in the hallway. He can't remember if this is where Stephanie lives. A door opens beyond the light and a man appears, buttoning his coat. He goes in the opposite direction. He could, of course, be the janitor, or a lover, or a thief using the fog to cover his retreat. Scann yawns and takes his hand from the doorknob. He moves right along the front of the building and then goes down its side until he finds the fireladder. Here, between the buildings, it is darker and he feels safe. He climbs the ladder silently and leans left at the second story to look in the window. In the gloom, he is sure he can see Stephanie's bed. A great comfort grows in him. He reaches for the window and pries at it with his fingers. It rises a couple of inches. Inside, the light goes on. Its yellowness extends outside into the fog and he is illuminated, caught. He heaves back and clings to the ladder. No one comes to the window. Writer Scann begins to search out a reason for his being here like a blue moth on the side of a woman's barrack in the fog on a battle station in the middle of England and with a war climaxing all around him everywhere in the world. His brain clogs and stops. But he is no longer tired. He is cold, except for his genitals, which burn. Stephanie's voice says, "You just don't know, Marie." He leans closer to the window. "He was drunk enough not to know who he was. They carted him off as usual when he isn't flying. I don't think he saw the C.O. at all." "They were together at breakfast." "Plotting?" "I don't know. I was busy most of the time in the kitchen. It gets worse by the morning. Those girls they send me prattle about men more often than they work. 'There I wuz just standin' takin' the air and he comes and runs his 'and oop me laig as if'e owned it; silly faart. I says'oo the 'ell do you think you are askin a girl of 'ardly any acquaintanceship to do it standin?' They're shocking little tramps. Should have their mouths washed out with soap. Can you imagine what it's going to be *like* when this is over?" "Darling, you're being very grim. That doesn't sound like you. The boys get shot at and the girls get got at. It's war and it's hell. Why don't you just skip the funeral. I'll say you're sick. What can Thrain say? In this fog he may not even notice. Then afterward you can buy Brannan a drink and put things back in their right perspective. He's just a bit jumpy, with only three trips left, and I think maybe a little jealous? This bloody fog makes a mess of my hair." "Maybe, and maybe I'll buy him a razor to slit his throat. Steph, I'm going to the funeral. I've got to, it's the only one those poor boys are going to have." Scann is leaning toward the window, and his muscles are quivering with the strain. He hauls himself back for a moment and then leans out again. Stephanie is fixing her hat onto her hairdo and Marie is at the door. "All right, love, why don't you come to my rehearsal parade and see how it goes? I'll see you at the bottom of the stairs. I want to spend a penny." "How's he going to live with it?" "Who?" "Thrain." The door opens. "Marie, don't hope for him to suffer." "Surely to God he wishes he hadn't ordered them back." "Darling, last night I heard him giving Berrigan hell for diverting the training aircraft. Don't you see, he only wants to get on with the war and let the people fall where they may." The door closes. Scann heaves himself upright and relaxes against the ladder. Somewhere a toilet flushes. He waits, and then the outer door downstairs opens and slams. Marie and Stephanie are laughing. "Well, I only asked if he might change his mind and stay." Fading: "Marie; darling, you're incorrigible." Scann lets the last two sentences move once more through his mind. He struggles not to imagine Marie, the incorrigible, undressed, and then gives up. Before he crawls in the window to lie on Stephanie's bed, he takes a copy-pencil out of his breastpocket and writes on the side of the building: *Inopem me copia fecit.* Which means, Abundance made me poor. Scann, of course, knew no Latin. As with most of his early writing; it is simply borrowed. In this case he retrieved it, as he himself admits in his notebooks, from the Foreign Words and Phrases section of a 1936 Webster's Collegiate, fifth edition. Scann had a rough eight day voyage overseas on the filthy, bug-ridden *Louis Pasteur*. Some of those who served in World War II may remember it. That greyhound of the sea gave a new meaning to "pasteurised" and was for many their introduction to the holy illogic of that necessary war. In any event, Scann found a dictionary on board and because, as he tells us elsewhere, the meals were "inedible variations of the same gangrenous stew" he subsisted on milk chocolate and read it when he should have been eating. This is Scann at his most obvious, and, at the same time, his most appealing literary moment. He was young, true, but if we are to deal with the making and the meaning of that first novella of his, we must see him at many times and in many stances. When he saw an officer of the ship, he might shout at him *Respice finem* (Look to the end) or the Hawaiian motto, *Ua mace ke ea o ka aina i ka pono* (The life of the land is established in righteousness) or continually sick, as were most of the passengers, he would vomit on the deck, with some show of defiance, and yell out, *Hic et ubique* (Here and everywhere). Thus his use of Webster. And yet his circumstances were fortunate. He had by some *usual* wartime slip been commissioned an officer. This miscue must have been a bitter pill for many of our country's best newsmen who languished in "other ranks" while Scann held his narrow bluestriped epaulet throughout the two tepid war years he spent in England. His war novel *But Frail Clay* (the title is from Hopkins' "The Soldiers", and how inaptly!) chronicles those years during which he views himself as a kind of hero-whoremaster, but in truth he is a lecher at play while the real heroes are away winning the war. Indeed, the Canadian Airforce, whose losses ran past 12,000 dead and whose exploits are legend, can hardly be glimpsed at all through the smoke and beer and nylon panties cut from parachutes. Nor can one believe our gallant "Lancs" could have gotten as far as the Channel coast, let alone to Germany, under the command of the neurotics Scann manufactures. Some might complain that we are hard on Amory Scann, and might sigh that a prophet is seldom honoured in his own country. Scann is no prophet. He is a literary cheat and a hack to boot and the sooner we get back to the authors of our post World War II renaissance the sooner we will be able to honour our prophets. Scann's problems with humans and human relationships, which plague his later works, have their roots in the earlier. Neuroses fuel the engines of his characters always, and he drives them helter-skelter across his landscapes in an endless search for technical solutions to his weird narratives. He seems in a panic at every moment. Imagine what escapes and panaceas he must have been driven to at that point in his story when Thrain has dragged what is left of Linden to the cabin at Water Lake, and Erica has left Ole and his wife at the hotel to go to Linden's cabin to escape the last wave of the great influenza epidemic in the early spring of 1919. The whole story is in jeopardy, as is the novella form itself, the very form he is here trying to master. Scann seems hardly conscious of E. K. Bennett's beautifully stated fifteen points that identify forever the novella as a genre. (A History of the German *Novelle* from Goethe to Thomas Mann, E. K. Bennett, Cambridge University Press, 1934, pp 18-19). How our poor authors can embark on the perilous seas of genre and sub-genre without once cocking an eye at the British and American weathermen-critics who have gone before and charted the voyage properly, is beyond comprehension. Most authors these days seem hardly capable of syntax, much less a sophisticated overview of the forms of modern fiction. One gets the distinct impression that Scann read very little. He had a mania for chronicling, and it is very easy to see where his main interests were: in himself. One only has to turn to any page of his notes (he tried recently to sell his notebooks and manuscripts to the university, but it will be some time before he is accorded that honour; however, before sending his stuff back a few pages were copied to see whether in fact they would show up well on the Xerox machine, and they luckily corroborate the main thrust of this present study). Take, for instance, that salacious group of entires which is the basis of the character of Stephanie in the war novel. They give us Scann at his dreamlike most, with his fantasies of superpotency and sexual gymnastics. If these notes do nothing else they give lie to the self-projected image he has of himself as a newsman first and an *inamorato* second. There were, on the original pages, saliva marks. Professor Gilhooley of our Chemistry Department confirms this. That aside, one supposes that were the adventure even half true it would be a diffident man indeed who could assign his memories of it to the trash basket. However, there is startling evidence that Scann lives almost totally in an insecure and ambivalent dreamworld whose inner workings only a psychiatrist could hope to penetrate. Scribbled on the back of one of the pages of this set of notes is the following limerick: "A man with a very small dingus/ was instructed in true cunna lingus./ But when confronted he asked,/ What's the key to the task?/ I'm tongue-tied and only have fingus." We think that here is the true Scann, wallowing in the scurrilous and enjoying it, but still revealing himself as he sounds the note of uncertainty found in that macabre last line. And it is also Scann-like in that it isn't a very good limerick. The *dramatis personae* are vague, the setting absent — who does the student fail with, and at her house or his? — (as they are not, for instance, in the one about the young man from Boston who had the adventure with the Austin, or the classic about the Bishop of Chichester), the tone and texture are rather rough and ready, and the whole production cries out for a more careful rendering. But surely there is pure gold for the critic in this scribbled inadvertence if he can get below its dingy surface and dig hard. Yet, we must not leave this sexual mania of Scann's without remarking on his grasp of the ontology of sex, especially in that portion of its *be*ing which touches on time. Scann has claimed elsewhere that sexual time is the only time that contains the very essence of slow and fast, the going while the coming persists, making a transitional state of infinite extremes. And Scann is a good transitionist. His native technical talent in this area is amazing for a Canadian, and his use of this "sexual time" and allied violences in many of his transitional vehicles, which in effect obliterate time and miraculously move the narrative clock ahead, serve him quite well indeed. He tells us at one point in his notes that while writing his war novel, the ladder and window had struck him as useful and always-fruitful sex-symbols (see Romeo and Juliet and countless tales of sexual intrigue from before Bocaccio to beyond Rapunzel) but in the book itself the exigencies of the story-line forced him to prune away all but the element of gossip in order that he could move with some grace to the noonhour of the book's day when the rehearsals are over and the funeral and what is to follow can begin in earnest. Scann lies on Stephanie's conquistadoreal bed and surfaces from a troubled rest. He is dreaming that he is in a deserted ante-room and when he wakes, he says out loud, "I shouldn't be here." He sees Stephanie and sits up. "But it's the best bed I've ever slept in." "And how, just how do you plan to leave?" "The way I came in, the ladder." She comes from the door and sits on the bed, looking severe. "Any other day of the year my girl would've come to clean and tidy — and then what?" "Is she coming now?" "No, she's been on parade all morning and now she's at lunch." "Then come to bed." She doesn't even smile. "Last night was last night, Amory. Please try to understand we have a funeral today." She gets up. "Really Scann, this is too bad of you." She doesn't speak again, and he lies watching her dress for lunch and the funeral, and then, after a while, he gets up and opens the window. He thinks about saying goodbye to her, but her back doesn't invite it. He swings, with some ease now, out onto the ladder and climbs through the fog to the ground below. The route to the mess is well defined by moving bodies in the murk. He follows along until he is at the flagpole and then goes with some alacrity to the door, holding it for others, some of whose faces register a dim and puzzled recognition. Another day and he might be one of them.

In the lounge, he checks his luggage behind his over-stuffed chair. The room is clean now, falsely decorous, perhaps as if an aging and alcoholic aunt had been picked up from a tumbling fall and set on her way again. She will fall again soon. Seducer Scann sits down and waits. He doesn't know what for. Maybe for Stephanie to come in to fetch and forgive him. He takes out his notebook and looks at it. "War came back to Graydon-on-Moor. . . ." War correspondent *manqué* Scann closes the pages and leans back so that he is staring at the ceiling. He can see the names there. Hundreds of them perhaps. Scann glances around the room. There are not more than a dozen loungers. He stands up and swings the end of a chesterfield out toward the middle of the room. He climbs on its arm and then its back. Some of the names, even at this distance, are legible. Starr, Stamaroff, Hogan, Ripstein, Horseleigh, McDougal, Scott, Kvapilik, Anderson, Willson, Baker, Lawrence, Etheridge, Munroe, Redlin, Mcphee, Odlum, Calabrese, Brannan, Simms, and in with this contemporary cluster, Thrain. Scann squints his eyes, balances, and tries to imagine David Thrain on top of a pile of furniture, a bottle of beer in one hand and reaching with the other to write his name on the ceiling. The picture will not form. He stands down from the leather chesterfield and shoves it back to the wall. Maybe there are two or three Thrains. When the squadron is flying, Thrain no. 1: white silk scarf, sheepskin jacket, high fur-lined boots, walking commandingly to his aircraft. And in his office, Thrain no. 2: angular, a little pale, rigid and meeting crises on the ground with efficient decisive action. Thrain no. 3: at a party, drunk, jolly. Not likely. The clock on the opposite wall says it is nearly one. There is time for a drink before the funeral parade. He wants to see, hear, David there. He feels part of the squadron now, a false emotion, but an oddly keen one. He examines it as he walks to Charlie's comfortably crowded bar and stands with Esterby while they signal for a couple of glasses of bitter. Scann can't think of small talk so he asks what he wants to know: "Where does the burial take place?" "I suppose you're writing this all down to slander us with later?" Scann shakes his head. "There is a cemetery just across the perimeter track from the far end of runway 180. The remainder of a twelfth century abbey church is beyond that. A pretty spot. It slopes away from us here. The view — if a graveyard has a view — is south down into a shallow valley where there's a trout stream of some merit. I have a bicycle and poach there occasionally. Are you really interested? The church is chiefly notable as being part of a monastery which was alive and literate when Northumbria was independent and was the keeper of one or two of the embers which burst into flame and helped warm the Renaissance. So, you can see this is going to be a high class burial. Not that our friends are to be laid to rest in the old cemetery, but there's some passable ground free at the periphery and we've been allowed to use it for interments. Not many, really. The last we had was an eighteen year old WAAF who died here in secret childbirth. I wasn't invited along to that one. Many of us, including her suspected seducer, were making ready for a previous appointment inside enemy territory. But I gather from the social notes recited afterward that the young principle's mother journeyed up from her home near Bow Bells and pronounced the ceremony lovely and the burial plot almost pleasant enough to make up for her permanent separation from her daughter." He turns to the padre, who is now standing near them. "You'll remember the strange sequel better than I." The padre has been listening. His eyes are remote, and the lines on his face seem now to be holding it together. "Esterby," he says, "your cynicism has never evoked a positive response in me. The fact is," he says to Scann, "the girl's mother met the girl's suspected seducer, as Esterby calls him, liked him and, despite the fact that she had a husband away fighting in North Africa, she stayed to live with him." "Took over where the daughter left off," Esterby says. "And now the story takes on the dimensions of a saga. A whole community feels itself forced to act in accordance with the dictates of conventional morality, and in doing so changes the face of the world. Melvin, for that is the lad's name, rented a caravan — trailer to you, Scann — on the banks of the river that runs through a town not far from here. Mother and Melvin nest there happily for a number of months, but one day the husband arrives back in England, finds his bird flown, does a little detective work and discovers the lovers. He storms their caravan one morning and is about to kill Melvin, when the neighbours rise up in righteousness to protect a happy, if odd, marriage. They lay unfriendly hands on the intruder and throw him in the river. Melvin and his bride are assured protection, and the husband, no doubt addled by his adventure, or so it seems, goes away as if it is the only gentlemanly thing to do. The latest bulletin from the sergeants' mess is that Melvin was given such a fright by both the appearance of the husband and the townfolk that he now is not always capable of doing the job mother is anxious and insistent that he do often and well. You can't file the story under hard news, Scann, but if you ever want a little lifelike experience as a vehicle for a fiction of real significance — the inappropriateness of always obeying our moral codes, for instance — well, there you are, free, gratis, and witnessed as truth by two impeccable sources."

The padre signals Charlie for another beer. "Wetting your whistle good," Charlie says. There is concern under his banter. "Nothing so simple as that, Charlie. You must know that your padre is a complex man, eh? He wouldn't just wet his whistle before the ceremony, now would he?" He has a good deep voice. Scann can easily imagine him in the pulpit holding an audience. "Esterby, here, would wet his whistle. A simple man full of simple concern and simple delight in the follies and foibles of mankind. Perhaps you just heard his parable of Melvin and the jolly adultress from the parish of Bow Bells. Did you like it? An artless tale about how life goes on despite or perhaps because of the intrusion of tragic events." Charlie smiles. His eyes search the padre's face as if he can't quite place him, and then he moves away down the bar to serve someone else. "Are you putting me up as your replacement?" Esterby asks, "or are you suggesting I already occupy the minor ecclesiastical post of anti-padre?" The padre laughs as if it is a stage direction. "No. You're being obtuse, Clifford. Can't you see how I'm tinged, maybe even tainted, with envy?" Esterby is delighted. The padre looks down at him: he is a tall man. "There seem to be no traps in life that can catch you. It's easy to catch me, a man who walks a straight line, right?" Scann opens his notebook to the first clear page. "Straight lines require commitment," the padre says, "a sense of direction. I am trapped at every moment, it seems. And so sometimes I envy you your dog's hind leg existence." "Dog's hind leg?" "Yes, you run happily beneath life's soft underbelly and carefully raise yourself out of the way of it's excrement while helping to direct it." For the first time the padre begins to smile a little around and in his eyes. "All this," Esterby says, "all this just because I told a true story about our mid-upper gunner?" "No, no, Clifford: because you're unnatural through and through. You're untouched. An eighteen-year-old WAAF who died in childbirth, indeed. You knew her. She was the most beautiful child I've seen. Even in her coffin she looked more alive than most women do in their best moments." "And you want punishment, the wrath of God, to descend on poor Melvin whose only possible sins were demurring in the face of a little uncertainty about his fatherhood and having better than average control of a better than average dong, brought on, no doubt, by insensitivity rather than skill. Why ask more punishment than just being alive is already forcing on him? And whence comes your judgment? Why does it fall on him and me? Not four hours ago Burton admitted his skills were diminishing. Did he botch one? Let's consider his guilt. And how about yours, if you please, before you get to mine?" Esterby stands looking hurt for a moment and sips down the last of his beer. The padre seems disposed to say nothing. Scann puts his notebook away. He has written in it: "Straight Lines Lead to Traps." "I thought my story rather well told," Esterby says. "It was good gossip; which is what a story worth hearing should be. It was about death and life. And the machinery of the gods, which is always public morality. It moved blindly and ironically to render poor Melvin impotent, and at the same time it removed his middle-aged mistress from the lucky heaven of exciting incest with her son, the Saskatchewan bull, and plunged her into the hell of real commitment to a kind of life with Melvin the guilty, the scared and the limp. Padre, the big stick of your retribution is a comic bladder compared with life itself." "You've convinced me, Esterby. No need to go on." He drinks at his beer. "As you always do." "Cheer up, padre, poor rehearsal, good show. This is still your day." Scann thinks that even Esterby thinks he's gone too far. He finishes his beer and moves away to the bar for a re-fill. Scann drinks too. The padre looks at his watch. "Twenty minutes," he says. "He calls that a day." Scann says, "Which way will your parade go?" The padre looks at him as if for the first time. "Down runway 180, right down the flarepath." He takes his gloves from under his arm and begins to put them on, and says to no one, "I can't think why I'm here."

Brannan comes in through the door dressed in his blues. He grins. "Good to see you here, padre. It's raw out there. No offence, but I hope it won't take us long." "No, not long, Squadron Leader." He is still putting his gloves on, as if they might be vestments, one finger at a time. Then Simms is there, standing in the middle of the room, taking a deep breath. "Know what?" he asks loudly. He gets little attention. Brannan turns to him and they look at each other. "It's about the C.O.," he says. Conversation ebbs. Brannan says, "Well?" "Maybe it was a joke." Brannan stands and waits and the padre is finished putting on his gloves. "Who?" Brannan says. "What's it about?" "Sergeant Ferrier, the duty wallah, says the Wingco has ordered transport out to find twenty-five kegs of beer and as many women as they can and." Simms' face flushes; there is silence in the room. "And," Brannan says. Simms looks around. "And roller skates. It must be true. Ferrier could never think that up." There is a very long pause while everyone ponders. Then the padre says, "Ferrier told you?" "Yes, just now, outside." Brannan says, "It sounds like one hell of a party. Where's he planning to hold it?" "In number three hangar, for all ranks." "So, we're to be paraded to look sad for Windham and then lined up to have the ashes washed out of our mouths." "But the roller skates?" Simms says. "No need to speculate, young man," the padre says. He stands alone in the centre of the room. "Your C.O. is consistent if nothing else." Scann watches him walk to the door and exit as if he is forcing himself out. Movement away from the bar becomes general. Brannan lashes back a gin and tells Charlie to close up. Charlie calls out time, and Scann walks out behind Brannan into the corridor. "You're not going on parade, are you?" Scann says, "I thought I'd walk over and see it begin. Where is it?" "On the tarmack in front of number one hangar."

Personnel are blue shadows moving in the fog. The hangar looms. Lone Scann leaves Brannan at the point where the parade is massing and follows blue perimeter lights to where they merge with the yellow sodium lights along the runway. He walks between them for twelve minutes by his watch and then falls into a ditch at the end of the cement. He crawls out and wipes himself as clean as he can. There is a narrow paved road under his feet, and in the muffled distance he can hear sharp orders being shouted. He is careful about the other side of the road. Then, to his right, he finds a broad wooden culvert that allows him to cross onto a dirt roadway that leads through the bomb dump to the cemetery. The gates are open and he goes blindly through them and walks among the dripping yew trees while he listens for the parade. It comes with the marching-drums muffled: the advance guard, the coffins on the shoulders of bearers, the drums, the officers and men of the squadron trying to remember how to slow march. Scann goes to be near them. He listens to the orders: Thrain's voice, Brannan's, even Stephanie's surprisingly brisk and formal. And then silence, followed by uncertain and off-balance shuffling. Orders. Then the small careful scrape of boards on gravel. The coffins, seven of them, in a long ceremony in praise of gravity, darkness and disposal, are lowered. Scann takes out his notebook and turns to a clean page. In it he writes large: "In defiance of the laws of Canada, and in celebration of its vastness, my body is to be spirited away to a place where man has seldom or never been, and it is to be lodged on a platform in the crotch of a tree, Indian style, so that I may return to my elements through the grace of predators and at the pleasure of the climate. Amen. Amory Scann. p.s. I do not intend to die in England."

Scann goes nearer to the parade, skirts it, walks toward the graveside until he may not be more than twenty feet away from the padre, and he imagines his face as split from stone, its planes remarkable and consistent, the eyes, in spite of the fog, seeing whatever they want. His voice carries its own echo. "For if we believe," the padre's voice is saying slowly and with insistence, "for if we believe that Jesus died and rose again, even so them also which sleep in Jesus will God bring with him. For this we say unto you by the word of the Lord, that we which are alive and remain unto the coming of the Lord *that* shall not prevent them which are asleep." Loud: very loud: "For the Lord Himself shall descend from Heaven with a shout, with the voice of the Archangel, and the trump of God; and the dead in Christ shall rise first: then we which are alive and remain shall be caught up together with them in the clouds, to meet the Lord in the air: and we shall ever be with the Lord." Sharp break; and then a new modulation. "Wherefore comfort one another with these words." He allows a moment of silence. From the parade comes shuffling, coughing. The padre begins again. "Man that is born of woman has but a short time to live, and is full of misery. He cometh up, and is cut down, like a flower, he fleeth as it were a shadow, and never continueth in one stay. In the midst of life we are in death: of whom may we seek succor, but Thee oh Lord, who for our sins are justly displeased? Yet, oh Lord God most holy, oh Lord most mighty, oh holy and most merciful Saviour, deliver us not into the bitter pains of eternal death. Thou knowest, Lord, the secret of our hearts; shut not Thy merciful ears to our prayers, but spare us, Lord most holy, oh God most mighty, oh holy and merciful Saviour, Thou most worthy judge eternal, suffer us not, at our last hour, for any pains of death to fall from thee." A curious noise. Scann moves to see. It must now seem to any who notices him that he is assisting the padre. He watches him take a shovel into his hands and slam it hard into the pile of dirt that has come from the grave. He swings the spade out and down. A rock hits a coffin with force; it bounces from lid to lid, each hollow sound distinct, separated by a silence. Then it stops pounding and it becomes clear that the rock is spinning on the smooth surface of a coffin. Someone in the parade, anonymous and sexless, says Oh God and breaks ranks. The rock stops spinning. The padre's voice reverberates; it is almost a shout: "Forasmuch as it hath pleased Almighty God in His great mercy to take unto Himself the souls of our dear brothers here departed, we therefore commit their bodies to the ground; earth to earth, ashes to ashes, dust to dust; in the sure and certain hope of resurrection to eternal life, through our Lord Jesus Christ. Amen. Our Father which art in Heaven. . . ." His voice sings, and the parade takes up the words and the sound is like the muttering of an engine. The padre's voice rises and falls above it as he leads. Scann sees his misted form swaying as he speaks. "Deliver us from evil." His hands rise from his sides and his face is a challenge to Heaven. Scann cannot move away. "For Thine is the Kingdom, the Power and the Glory." The hands are high fists now, and Scann is suddenly embarrassed. He looks around for Thrain, but he is not visible. Surely he will know and will begin to move soon. "Forever and ever. Amen." And solo now, the singing still in his voice. "Lord God, these are our friends. These are our friends. These are our friends of whom our brightest memory is why and how they died. The pity, God. For neither king nor country nor ideal: they died by whim, by the snap of the fingers of brute power." And now Wing Commander Thrain is coming. The padre turns towards him, but Thrain sees Scann first and stops: in his face there is shock, a question, perhaps even fear. Scann wants to say, "David, get him out of here," but there is only Thrain's back suddenly, and the padre is saying, "God forgive. Forgive oh God this power, but strike at the truth revealed of men at war." David's hands hold to the padre's arm but the preacher's voice only becomes great and rolling. "What say you to this, God, what say you to this? Thou turnest man to destruction; again thou sayest, come again ye children of man." David is shaking him, and one of the Padre's feet is dangling near the ground. "Flight Lieutenant Sweet!" "Come again ye children! How?" He points into the grave. "Sweet, goddamn you!" "Is there forgiveness? Is there forgiveness for him who says, These things must be done?" Thrain drops his hands and turns to the parade beyond the grave. He shouts: "Squadron will move to the right in column of route, right turn!" And then Brannan in high relief: "Funeral party, right turn. Quick march!" The orders go on, and then there are only boots marching on bare ground, making way for another silence that the padre will not let happen. "I pray forgiveness, Wing Commander, for you. I pray for you." Thrain turns once more. "Are you sane?" "I pray that there be forgiveness. No. Yes!" "Do you know what you've done?" "Buried seven incompetents, Wing Commander, whom you only just tolerated alive and are treating shamefully when dead. Truck loads of beer and flesh." "You're on leave, padre. Go and pack and get off my station." The padre does not answer. He stoops and picks up his shovel and begins to fill in the grave. Scann watches David watch the padre wade deep into the dirt and fling it down onto the boxes. It is a long moment, full of possibilities, then Wing Commander Thrain turns and walks away toward the road. Scann follows, going three paces for every throw of the padre's shovel. At the culvert he catches up with him. Thrain looks at him and keeps on walking. The parade is far ahead of them, and someone has made the band play. Scann wants to say something kind. "You were right," he says, "leaving him there to do what he thinks he has to in his own way." "You think so?" "Yes. I think you might do the same for me." "He's done all he can, but with you I might have been preventing something, or was I just helping you out? Everytime I turn around there you are. What have you got in those P.O.'s pockets of yours: handcuffs?" Scann tries to think what to say. They march together. "I came to do a feature," he says. "I'd like to pick up where I left off, if I may." It is too polite; but he has to start somewhere. But it is the finish. Thrain doesn't reply. They go together along the cement runway. The lights on either side have burned away a little of the fog at ground level and it seems they are going down a corridor with no beginning and no end. Movement is measured by passing one of the lights. And without Thrain there would be no direction. Ahead of them a tractor motor starts and moves back and forth. It is some time before Scann realises what it is that it's doing. Number three hangar is being cleared for the party. Scattered notes appear in his mind. It is the young who fight wars: they can be aggrieved and frightened, but not for long. His mental reflexes are still flabby. War isn't traffic deaths and hotel fires, but if he'd come when the squadron was flying he might still believe it. Yet even understanding this is only another form of sentimentality. The whole war is sentimental, sentimental violence. He walks with the silent Thrain toward the greater noise of the tractor; then he turns to him and says, "Simms tells us you're giving a party." It is the first time he has noticed that Thrain has a smile: it oscillates electrically across his face. "Not exactly giving." He shrugs. "What the hell, they're being told to attend." "You're afraid they might not come otherwise?" "Some would, some wouldn't. This way I'll know where they all are." He turns away and disappears into the fog. The movement is so abrupt that Scann is disoriented again, and he calls out, "Which way?" Then it occurs to him that Thrain might think he is still being followed. Scann shouts again and listens. Thrain could be twenty feet away, laughing at him. He moves forward, through thick fog now because he is off the runway, trying to remember the direction Thrain has taken. He comes to the wall of a hangar. He chooses another direction along it and finds a door. Inside are the flight rooms. He walks through them, looking. In one is a keg of beer propped on a table with beer mugs around it, and on the wall a poster showing a pilot driving four engines as if he is Ben Hur and they are chariot horses. The caption reads: Are YOU in Shape to Drive 4800 Horses? Scann tests the spigot on the barrel. There is beer. He takes a mug, fills it and walks out into the hangar as he sips it. There are still two aircraft to his right, and to his left the space is empty. Beside him there are stairs up to a mezzanine. Scann goes up them slowly because they are dark. At the top is a landing with a dirty window looking out over the acre of cement below, and beyond it is a short corridor. At its far end is an orange bulb that almost lights it. There is a door, and on the door is a white card on which is typed: "Wing Commander David Thrain." The 'a' of the typewriter that printed it needs cleaning. He has not finished with Thrain. He decides to drink the beer and then knock. But from inside, Marie's voice says, "I didn't know where to go. I hate my room and I didn't want to go back to the mess." Scann kneels and puts his eye to the keyhole. There is no key on the other side. Marie is there, sitting at Thrain's desk, her feet up on the blotter. Her C.O. is out of the picture. Shards of last night's emotion when Stephanie walked past him naked in the dark stir. Voyeur Scann moves to try to see Thrain. He appears at the side of the desk, but Scann can't see his face. Marie is smiling brightly. "I've been playing wing commander." He doesn't question this. "Twice I picked up the phone to order the tower to tell Windham to quit napping down there at Woodbridge and get on home. But I couldn't even pretend." She keeps looking up at him. "How did you do it?" Thrain speaks carefully, as if he doesn't want to disturb her. "He could fly." But she begins to weep anyway. "Not long enough. Not as far as the end of the goddamned runway." "What happened to Windham was an accident, or a mistake. Everything on the ground was working perfectly. I've checked that out. He should have made it." Thrain goes closer to her, moves her feet from his desk and sits where they had been. "When I came over, there was no radar and damned few lights and beams. We flew anyway. The war said we had to. Gerry and I — remember your husband, Marie?" Scann does not see her move. He blinks his eye at the keyhole and she is up. "Do you?" Thrain says. "Do you remember what he looked like?" "Yes." It is tentative. Then she says, "Yes, I do." "He was brave. He had to be, to live the way he did and still fly. Because he talked himself out of staying alive and fought himself out of it, and gradually he went over the line. When he got it, he must have felt like he was going on a holiday." Scann says under his breath, Why are you telling me these things? But she is only silent for a moment, then she says, "I wasn't sure you knew I was his wife." "It's all on your file." "And you never said." He says: "Everyone runs a little. You better stop it now or you'll go over the line too. Quit feeling sorry for yourself." She allows herself a burst of anger. "I do not feel sorry for myself. Why should I? I don't have to die yet. I don't give orders that make other people die. I don't have to feel anything. I don't pretend that if I wear my ring I'll live a charmed life, or if I keep myself pure nothing will happen to me. Maybe I'm trying to make something happen. I'm not crazy, David. When Gerry went missing I knew he wasn't coming back, but I got a posting over here anyway. And then there was no word and no word and then just time itself changed him from missing to presumed dead. It was as if my temperature went down and I lost my sense of really being alive. Have you noticed how England is wet and dark, and above all else it is waiting? I couldn't sit here and wait too. I'd rot. I wanted not to rot. David, all the way back from the graveside I wished I'd loved Windham. He's gone now, and I felt I should be ringing a goddamned bell and shouting unclean." Scann presses his other eye to the keyhole. David doesn't answer. She doesn't expect one. Marie smiles. "I'm glad we talked about Gerry. You're very different than I thought." She puts her hand on David's arm. "You like the war, don't you? And it's been good to you. I used to want to hurt you for it." Viewer Scann wants to yell a warning, but it is too late. She is close to Thrain now, leaning against him, face up and waiting for him to move. Scann holds his breath in the silence, then Thrain laughs and eases her away. "I've got a squadron to run," he says kindly, and in the same voice he adds, "I just haven't got time to help prove someone can sleep with you without going for the chop." She stands before him, gradually stiffening as if rigor mortis is setting in. Scann wants to tell her that he didn't mean it quite that way, and Thrain is standing now too, looking very unlike a commanding officer. Thrain, Scann says silently, they don't change for you just because they confess. Marie comes alive. Her hands float by her sides. She may hit him. Her mouth hardly moves. "I didn't mean that," she says, and runs. For Scann there is no time: he is still on his knees with the beer mug clutched to his chest when she opens the door and slams against him with knees and airforce shoes.

Even before he rises, thinking he might help her up, and before he looks into Wing Commander Thrain's eyes, the pristine Scann knows that he will never be the same again. Lines and cracks of age and experience, and the kind of knowledge God meant in Genesis, appear on the surface of his soul. They are hairline faults, but deep. Marie is lying beside him as if she is about to begin pushups. Her face is a curse, her eyes are screwed closed and Scann is afraid to touch her. He stands and extends his hand down toward her in case she might want to use it to get up. But he is pushed against the wall by Thrain stooping and hauling her to her feet. They stand, the three of them, shoulder to shoulder, in the narrow doorway to Thrain's office. The orange light above them sprays down a dull shower of light. Marie begins to make a noise in her throat. Just a noise. And she stamps her feet and bangs her fists on their chests. "No," she shouts. "No!" Thrain tries to hold her, but she goes free, backs against the wall and kicks at both of them. They dance for a moment and then see her disappear down the stairs. Her feet clatter like iron wheels over a rough track. "I'll get her," Scann shouts, and tries to run. D.S.O. holder Thrain also holds him, and he knows how it was that Thrain walked back from Germany in three days. Scann has none of Marie's conflicting emotions to frustrate the muscles in his throat. He screams in fear and pain and shouts for help as he is hauled through the door and flung hard down onto a daybed against the wall of Thrain's office. The door slams shut. The echo from the hangar below is a definite clang. The dream must soon end or it will become life and he will be in extreme danger. Scann looks up into Thrain's colourless face and tries to come awake. No new consciousness occurs. Slowly, Thrain's head floats away and Scann hears him talking into the telephone. There is no reason not to sit up, slide to the edge of the daybed and then escape. Outside there is plenty of fog. A cover story would certainly come to him on his way to London. He begins to get up, shaking his head as if in pain to distract Thrain from his intention. He holds himself tense and looks to see if his plan is possible. A voice shouts on the other end of the telephone and Thrain holds it away from his ear to prevent damage. It is Curtis Bainbridge speaking. His words are clear. "Scann? Scann is young, stupid and can barely write a letter home. None of them can. The good writers are where they've always been, working for good newspapers. How the hell I got here is a mystery to me. The liquor is lousy too. I sent him to do a feature on you, yes. He's perfectly actual. His problem is to appear even vaguely real." "Thank you," Thrain says politely, and while Bainbridge is beginning to talk again, he hangs up.

Prisoner Scann stands and faces Wing Commander Thrain. With Bainbridge the informed alternative, he chooses to remain here. Thrain, when he speaks, does so in a remarkably calm voice. "You followed me and when you heard us talking you decided to listen." He sits down for the first time in his own chair. "If I'd wanted you here I'd have asked you. I'm going to write Bainbridge a letter, but it won't do much good. I can't beat the shit out of you because you're standing there in the King's uniform. And I can't have you arrested for obvious reasons. How much did you hear?" "I don't remember." Thrain swivels his chair and puts his feet up on the desk. "That isn't the answer. Tell me." "From where she was playing wing commander, I think." "Good. Now tell me, P.O. Scann, what would you do in my place?" "Let me ask you the same question, what would you do if you were in my place and had a feature to write?" "You can't and won't write anything but wild blue yonder crap, and you can't even start doing that until we're flying again." "So, all you can do to me is put me on a truck back to London." "Which is what you want." "Yes." Scann sits in the straight-backed chair across from Thrain, and Thrain says, "You figure we've played to a stalemate, and considering how much rank I have to pull that's as good as a victory." He stands behind his desk. "Get up, Scann." Scann rises. "Now, let's start back at square one. You arrived with Windham. Scrub that. It won't be in your story." He picks up the phone and says a number into it. Scann hears him ask for the Oxford to be made ready to fly. He has to ask twice. Scann has a moment of real feeling for him. Thrain hangs up and comes around the desk to open the door. "I'll lead the way," he says. Scann follows. In the flight room he watches Thrain put on his flying gear and then go to a locker and select another suit and hand it to him. "Put it on and I'll find you a 'chute." "No," Scann says. "Don't be afraid." Thrain looks at him and puts his hand on Scann's shoulder. He seems a different person in his flying suit. There are two Thrains. "If you want to do a good writing job and make Mr. Bainbridge happy you should have the facts." "I've flown," Scann says. "Do you think I'm going to get you killed?" "Maybe." "I'd have to kill me." He leaves the room and comes back with a parachute. Scann looks at it. It is a pilot's seatpack. He feels the exhilaration of being tempted. He may begin to laugh. It occurs to him that Bainbridge might also murder him — with one stroke of his pencil, as one kills copy — by simply putting him behind a desk and leaving him there. *I flew With Wing Commander David Thrain, D.S.O., D.F.C.* At 4.43 on a foggy and chilly February afternoon Wing Commander Thrain shot the throttles open and the huge aircraft trundled forward down the runway toward what looked like an undefined oblivion. Then we were airborne.

But it isn't a huge aircraft. It is a small one, has two engines and it rattles like dice in a box. The groundcrew corporal who has helped start the engines removes the chocks. Out of his window, Scann can see blue lights move by him. At the edge of the runway, Thrain parks and runs through the ritual of his flight check: a priest without wine or wafer, he bends and reaches, flicks, pushes, pulls, guns and listens, watches. Evening is almost here. The fog is growing black. Scann sits on his seatpack beside Thrain, eyes watering, mouth dry, palms sweating, diaphragm tense, sphincters sucking and the God of Nature dead and excluded from this and all other machines. An electric voice sounds in his ears. "If you want to speak to me, just flick the switch on the nose of your oxygen mask. Try it." Scann flicks and says, "This is no good. I'm here against my will. I demand to be let out." Thrain trundles the Oxford onto the runway, straightens out and opens the throttles. Scann is pushed back into his seat.

The small yellow aircraft accelerates between the rows of lights which do not lessen Scann's sense of limbo. The cockpit is a capsule which runs along but does not move; the lights move; they sink, disappear. For a moment, he sees the outer circle of the drem system. The aircraft breaks through it and he is back outside it again. The undercarriage shudders up. Scann thinks the Oxford turns over and flies on its back. He holds on hard to keep from crashing to the ceiling.

Then it banks right. He is careful to remember that upside-down this means they are turning left. His last awareness of place is Thrain's office. He wants to be able to get back there. Left again. His arms are numb from holding himself in his seat. He jams his right shoulder against the window, looks over at Thrain. Why is he seated comfortably, fingers on the wheel and his eyes flicking from instrument to instrument on the panel in front of him? Upside-down doesn't concern him. Scann's hands are sore. He gives up and lets go. He is heels-up but still in his seat. The sensation is foreign but tolerable. Thrain puts his hand on the throttles, signalling a new maneuver. The noise of the engines change pitch and he thinks the aircraft dives. Scann braces his feet hard against the forward wall of the cockpit. The engines seem not to be working, the aircraft is losing height and they are still upside down. Coward Scann screams, but the switch on the nose-piece of his facemask is not flicked and Thrain doesn't hear. The scream embarrasses him. He tries to force himself to be insane, as his pilot is, and to believe they are right-side up and not falling. Slowly he makes his eyes look around and out of the window. In the blackening grey he sees the propeller turning, and behind it the exhaust pipe of the engine glows cherry red. The aircraft is also burning. But as he watches the plane rights itself. Ergo: as long as they are incendiary he is safe from crashing upside-down. He looks away from the flaming engine toward Thrain, and holds on to keep from falling to the ceiling.

The pilot's voice says: "We'll be passing eight thousand feet soon. Turn on your oxygen. The flowvalve is beside you on the wall of the cockpit. Turn it in the direction we are going." Scann feels slowly along the metal surface on his right but finds nothing. His hand comes up to flick his talk-switch and encounters the oxygen hose. The rubber is softly wrinkled as if designed to be tumescent. He lets his hand slide down it and finds the valve. The smell of the gas is metallic. His nostrils cool and feel extra-sensitive and he is more alert. Every motion of the plane is a little exaggerated. The light fades and he turns to Thrain, concerned. The hands on the wheel tighten; the aircraft plunges and pitches. They are going down. His guts pushing physically against his diaphragm tell him that. It is darker. The instruments on the panel glow and none of the needles are steady. Thrain fights the wheel and his hand pushes the throttles forward again and adjusts knobs below those levers so that the engines howl. And then there is a calm where they are suspended. A moment goes by slowly and then the wheel snaps backward and forward, Scann's wing goes down, the nose comes up and he is jammed down into his seat. Thrain turns on the powerful lights that shine out from the edges of the wings. Outside, the cloud they are in becomes white swirls. Scann understands that the cloud is becoming solid and he sees them trapped and suspended for ever like a yellow fly in white crystals. The lights go out. The pitch and yaw ceases. Thrain's shoulders are hunched and his hands still hold the wheel hard. The sensation of rising is strong. Scann's belly distends against his parachute harness. He breaks wind. His vision fades. He begins to talk to himself. And finally he shouts into the dead mask in front of his face, "Goddamn you, Bainbridge." He says it fast and often.

The aircraft rockets out of the top of the cloud into clear twilight-blue sky. The scene is blank. No sun. No stars. No fixed point of reference above, and the overcast below is a rolling white desert. Thrain flies on out of danger, and adjusts his engines and levers that changes the attitude of the aircraft. Then he banks left and turns around. In front of them is a great muscled turret with a flat black crenelated top that rises out of the white dunes five thousand feet below. It is single. Vain. Celibate. Author Scann doesn't reach for his notebook. The cloud is one and whole, and he believes that if the aircraft were to fly against its side it would shatter like a bird against glass. Thrain's voice tells him, "Have a good look. We shouldn't be here." Scann turns his eyes from the cloud to Thrain and flicks his switch. "Let's go home." "Go back? How many reporters have been up the funnel of a cumulus nimbus, Scann? It should have ripped us in little pieces. Where's your notebook? Put it all down while it's hot in your head." The aircraft is almost up against the side of the cloud. Scann would rather not listen. Five miles high, winds of 140 miles an hour circling up and down again. Thrain is an expert, knows the monster in detail. Birth, life, death. Explanation becomes a lecture. Scann understands that he is trying to help him. "Interesting," he says, finally, and it is. He tries him on the German air defences. The discussion is thorough, a recital that combines experience with theory. Heavy flak, accurate to 35,000 feet, light flak to 8500, fighter squadrons and their probable deployment, the German early warning system and ways to fox it, and the searchlights out of whose clutches few aircraft ever escape. It had been a cone of searchlights and a fighter that had finally got Thrain. He chronicles the moments before the final death of his aircraft and tells without emotion of throwing his half-alive bomb-aimer out of the forward hatch and seeing his parachute open before he himself tumbled head-first into the cold dazzling light that was still following them down. And finally the brute burst of gunfire that tattered his bomb-aimer's 'chute so that he fell to his death. "They're getting desperate," he says. "Their machine is breaking down." Below them the cloud and fog breaks. Beneath is a smoother blackness: water. "I think we should go across for a moment, Scann. Give you a taste of the real thing." "We can't," Scann says. "No. They're not expecting us." Thrain does know how to laugh. The coast is below them. Ahead there is a terrible nothing. "Just in and out," Thrain says. "It'll make you an expert for life." Scann can't speak. He is betrayed. He looks down onto the dark land below. The enemy is there, prepared and vicious. Thrain is spiralling gently toward them. What can he say? "Go back?" It is not enough. Just going back is more danger than he's ever been in before. What he wants is to *be* back, and that is impossible. Thrain's voice begins to explain again. Scann listens: it is something to hold on to. "We just passed over their channel defences. Behind them, the secondary defence is mostly aircraft and mobile flak units. The searchlights are nearly all in the Ruhr Valley and the larger German cities. But those units are mobile too and I suppose they could move them here when we finally attack with the army by sea. We're still too high for you to experience light flak, but we might get a burst or two of heavy. You'll see it first. It shows up as a puff of white at night, but in daylight it's jet black. I'm circling around now to head back." There is a flash, a fist hits the aircraft. No sound. But after a moment there is a slight smell of cordite. The plane ducks and dives, evades. Bursts of flak are pale, vicious butterflies in the black around them. Scann holds on and sees out of his window some red marbles accelerating up toward him. They go past the aircraft, very close, and curve off into starred space above them. "If they hit us, it'll just be luck," Thrain says. "We can count ourselves safe, I think, until we reach the English coast." Slowly, Veteran Scann hears what Thrain has said: safe until the English coast. Of course. They are flying illegally without orders. Going out they were the enemy, going back they are also the enemy. The aircraft is down near the water. The atmosphere in the cockpit becomes warm and humid. He looks across at Thrain. He isn't flying by instruments any more. He is leaning forward, watching the water that seems only a few feet below them. In the dark, small glints of light show up on the white peaks of the waves. Scann feels better. Then, suddenly, he wants to know why. Thrain's hand comes up slowly from the wheel and flicks his talk-switch. "Relax, Scann, this is how gerry does it, the other side of the story. It'll give you objectivity. Sit tight, here we go." The land comes at them, dark and quickly rising. Scann watches. His mouth is dry and his hands are damp inside their silk gloves, but he is no longer afraid. Two hours of tension have tranquilized him. A row of trees, buildings, a street: the sound of their motors echoes between pavements and brick walls. Thrain's intercom is still on and he can hear him breathing. From a tall building, perhaps a hotel, tracer bullets fire over them and across their path. The colours are primary. Thrain shifts his ground, puts one wing down and turns with a highway and heads out from the town they have been flying through. They are climbing fast. "We got them by surprise," Thrain says. "Someone down there'll catch hell for that." And after a moment: "Scann, do you see that glass bubble in the roof just behind you? Be a good lad and stick your head up in it and look out back. Tell me if you see anything coming at us from behind." His voice is light and friendly.

Scann, for a moment, feels part of this adventure. The only revenge is to join it. He unbuckles his harness and stands behind his seat with his head in the bubble. The view is frightening. The tail shakes and flutters. The wings flap up and down. Beyond is blackness. Nothing. The clouds are close above, and they look cold and annoyed. Mid-upper gunner Scann is terrified again. "Why?" he says loudly into his microphone. "Look why don't we land and tell someone who we are?" "No," Thrain says. "If you're going to write about it, you're damned well going to have a taste of it. You can't come to my squadron and sit at the bar and write your story." There is silence. Thrain flies. Scann watches and waits for him to speak again. But in the blackness, something blacker moves. "I see something," he screams. "Behind. Above. To your right." "Good boy. Are you sure?" Scann loses his vision; it fills with floating pinpoints of light. He blinks hard. When he sees again, there are tracer reds and greens suspended in arcs near the Oxford. The aircraft bucks, lifts Scann off his feet and jams his head into the glass dome. Then he feels heavy and cannot support his weight. His knees bend and he is down on the floor. He can't hang on. He gathers bruises. Then, Thrain's voice comes to him: "You see? He's no match for me. I'm so slow and can turn so tight that he over-shoots every time. If I'm not careful I'll make him fly into the ground." The bucking and turning continue, and then the aircraft is straight and level once more. Scann has seen nothing except one string of tracers. "You can come back to your seat now," Thrain says. "We're safe. I think those last two passes were friendly. Gerry hasn't got an aircraft that looks like this."

Scann sits again in his seat. Thrain's voice echoes: "We're safe." Vertigo. Tension. Safe. Scann wants to sleep, wants to fold into his mother's arms, feed at her left breast, wants to be in Stephanie's bed: he cries out her name, forgetting his intercom switch is flicked, and it stops his fear and his need to prove that he is safe by walking on earth again. He is not safe. Thrain says nothing; he flies; he pilots. What if Thrain, as Gladstone before him, comforts himself occasionally in Stephanie's special bed? Bullets and shells only intersect their targets by guess and by God: the most dangerous projectile is a man whose woman has been slept with. Scann sits on his seatpack and guards its release handle. He waits. "What," David Thrain says, "did you think you could find out from her?" "From?" Thrain says, "You talk, Scann, ask questions. You're not a reporter. You're an investigator." There is a silence and Scann waits again. Then Thrain's face turns toward him. "You won't write a feature when you go back to London. It will be a report with a recommendation that will go on file that contains a letter asking permission to relieve me of my command and take me home to try me for murder." "Of Germans?" Thrain's head looks forward again. "Don't be clever. They've found my father's wife and they think I did it." Reporter Scann memorizes what Thrain has said. "And you didn't?" "No." The aircraft banks and Scann shouts: "What are you doing? Straighten up." "Calm down, we've just crossed the beam and I'm taking us back on it so we can fly home." Scann leans close to Thrain to see him better. The aircraft levels. "I didn't even know she was dead until I got a letter from my brother Ro." Scann leans even closer. "Listen," he says. "Listen carefully. I don't want to hear any more. Do you understand? I am a reporter. This has been off the record. It will never pass my lips, ever. I am interested only in going back to Graydon. I want you to land this plane safely, and I want to be your friend." Scann feels foolish. And safer. Perhaps Thrain hasn't said anything to him at all. He looks at the instrument panel: the needles ride steady. Thrain says: "You're a coward, Scann. I never thought I'd see a real one, but you're it." "Yes," Scann says. Relief warms him. He sweats gently. A coward. A coward in an age of heroes, an unhappy stance that guarantees many mortalities. He hopes practise will make him perfect. How much better to be insane and a hero? Thrain flying a tinderbox training plane across the Channel and back again without a gun on board. And now, finally, Author Scann unzippers his flyingsuit and breaks a fingernail as he scratches among his clothing for his notebook and pencil. "Without guns. This is important. It is necessary here that one do what one must do to live, without guns, beyond sanity, without God. . . ."

Wing Commander Thrain begins to speak again. "You might note that my last trip put me at half a million pounds of bombs dropped on the enemy, mostly on his cities. In terms of people, my personal score couldn't be less than a hundred, but probably not more than a thousand." "That argument is as old as war," Rapid

Scann says. "The fact is you can always kill the state's enemies and feel neither guilt nor the hand of the law upon you." "You mistake me, Scann. I'm giving you ammunition for your report. Say, four or five hundred with bombs, and then I killed three Germans with my bare hands, with premeditation and considerable planning. I had no intention of just maiming them or knocking them out. I was a real killer then." "No, you had to." "Killing a man with your bare hands is an accomplishment. He doesn't die easy, you know. He wants to live. It takes a long time to make him give up." What kind of reply is possible: "Is that so?" It occurs to Scann that this man is more frightening than death, or even its process, dying. "He knows where I stand — or cower," Scann scribbles. "I want out, simply out. We may land soon. But even then, say we do, there is no real safety. He may kill me for any number of reasons. Contempt. If we were at war, this is how it would climax. He would win, and I would die learning that this is how wars are ended, not with guns, but because one knows the other will win whether he has guns or not. We will win this one with the Germans too. The truth is, we're nastier, insaner and more accomplished than they are in the real arts of war. The other truth is this: Thrain is our slave, and he will do what we want him to do: win. And the *meaning* of that act will escape us, perhaps forever. And now I need a drink." Scann stares out into the black. What a tremendous last half-dozen words to make up an epitaph. Nothing for mankind, family, friends or philosophy; only the statement that everything revelant to Amory Scann is known and finished: And now I need a drink. I do. "And now," Thrain says, "we're passing over the center of our runway." Scann leans against the window and looks out. The fog is there. The aircraft is encased. The wing on his side drops and then rises again. The motors cough, run free, then hack again as if the fog has finally made them sick. There is quiet, accented by the craft's steady mechanical wind. Scann smiles behind his facemask. There is peace in this descent. Thrain says, "We're out of petrol." Scann says nothing. He feels around inside himself but it is still peaceful there. He looks at Thrain. He is talking to the tower, telling them to stand by and to put every light they have on. The burst of orders is short, the reply is only, "Roger out." "Give me your hand, Scann," Thrain says. Shock bristles through him. "No. Why?" Surely he's not going to pray? Scann is embarrassed. The aircraft is turning. Thrain's hand reaches blind and finds Scann's, places it on a lever between them. "Pump." Scann moves the lever. "Fast! The engines are dead and our wheels won't lock if you don't pump hard." It is a very little lever. He moves sideways in his seat and pumps. He hears the wheels bump down and hang in the air. "They've got to lock, Scann, pump." He flicks the lever hard and fast. Fog. Flak. Bullets, no wheels. He has been in the air forever. He begins to curse and sweat splashes off his face. He can't see out. He has his head down. He changes hands. The left doesn't work well at all. He changes back. He feels pressure as the hydraulic begins to force the wheels locked. He looks up. The aircraft is diving steeply, and Thrain is simply sitting there with his head forward like a turtle, watching. The lever stops. He can't move it. A green light of ecstasy comes on in the cockpit. "Good boy," Thrain says. "Now watch." Scann sits up. A pale glow. "Lights," he cries out. Thrain's feet work their pedals. The Oxford slides like a crab over the runway and drops onto it roughly. The bounce is a long one. They float and settle again. Thrain brakes, and Scann feels himself pressing forward in his harness as they rumble to a halt. Thrain flicks on the radio. "Just the tractor, Stubbs, we've landed okay." He drops his mask and turns so that Scann can see his face. "You did all right," he says. "Someone who knew what was happening probably would have frozen." "Thanks," Scann says. He takes off his mask and harness. He feels only slightly tethered to earth. He wipes the sweat off his face. He can be angry now. "What the hell was all that supposed to prove?" "Think about Windham now, and figure it out for yourself." Scann tries to understand for a moment. "Now what?" "After they haul us in, we can go to the office and talk."

Old sweat Scann doesn't want to go to the office and talk. Quietly, he releases the harness on his parachute and asks, looking around, "Which way to the hangars?" Thrain points. "Funny," he says, "I would have thought they were in the other direction. Do you mind if I go outside and pee?" He rises and goes back down the short barrel of the aircraft and opens the door. The drop from the wing is longer than he expects. He is stiff and the shock of hitting the concrete hurts. He walks quickly away from the aircraft in the direction Thrain pointed. As he goes he turns his head and salutes over his shoulder. It is a gesture of relief. The man has saved his life. He is a great flier and properly mad. Scann hears the tractor coming and begins to run. But he thinks that this is not young reporter Scann running. He does not know who he is. Somebody who, in some way, has been freed. An enemy of both sides of the war. A truck, a lorry, Dolan. The words might be magic.

He travels fast through the thick blackness, as if he knows where he is going. The sound of the tractor fades and music takes over. It is a tune punctuated by a sunburst of trumpets as they ride high over the drone of saxophones and, beneath them both, onomato-poetic drums and a bull fiddle. In his flying clothes and helmet, and dangling an umbilical communications cord unplugged from Thrain, Scann begins to move, to swing toward the sound of the band. He is stuffed, a blundering blimp holding himself together with his arms and hands, swaying and stumbling in flightboots through Graydon's night to a party. It is a long time ago that he remembers having heard about it. He may have had an opinion: that it was too soon after the funeral to hold a party; or that it wasn't. He is happy the music is playing. It guides him across some grass and tarmack to an entrance of a hangar where he stands and tries to orient himself again to dimension and perspective, and to a cooperative world where agreements are made and useful constructions result. There is, for instance, the bandstand, where the musicians sit in three tiers. There is nothing permanent or even pleasing about it, but its inven-tion and erection are a prestidigitation he enjoys as evidence that he is back and safe. A muscle in his cheek twitches and he moves as if he has been stung. He shivers and sneezes. His whole involuntary system has been stopped up for the very long time he was Thrain's prisoner. It is another freedom to hiccough. He stares around the great room in front of him, and the only problem he has, the *only* problem, is to find the locker where he left his shoes and hat and greatcoat. He moves forward, the rubber soles of the flyingboots catching occasionally on rough patches of cement. Even his awk-wardness pleases him. Of course to have been *there* and to have come back does not guarantee safety. Nor does finding the locker where he left his clothes. He must find Dolan and a lorry.

He walks on the periphery of the crowd, looking for the young driver as he goes. The crowd is a peculiar beast that is mostly immobile. It lies curled around in front of the bandstand and along the long line of beerbarrels that split the hangar in two, and it watches a few people dancing and fewer roller skating beyond the barrels. It twitches here and there from tension. It is waiting for its master, who summoned it and then left. Scann wanders, still looking for Dolan, into the edge of the crowd. " 'Ere's a bloke what finks it's a bleeding masquerade." He is surrounded by 5A blues and polished buttons. "What's he supposed to be?" "A flyer, mate, remember? One of the ones 'oo flies against the 'itler gang." Scann grins and pushes to go beyond them. "Maybe he's a bloody hero." He is held. "Are you an 'ero, mate? By God, I think 'e is." He is lifted up and carried in triumphant procession. Scann sits on their shoulders, holding the tops of two heads through his slippy gloves, and sees faces turn to watch him. He must look stuffed, fake, in this suit that's too big for him. The irks beneath him begin to bounce him and sing. Scann shouts for them to put him down. He hopes they recognize an officer's voice when they hear one. But others are crowding around. He is passed from one set of hands to another. The crowd *is* a beast. It circles closer and all he can see are arms and upturned faces. They all want to hold him. The music stops at the end of a number. The band watches. The beast's cries of recognition are better heard, and he is held like an arrow and is passed and sometimes thrown. He bounces and rolls as if he is a piece of debris caught up in a flash flood. The crowd shouts for him, pushes and elbows to gain position. The noise level rises. The animal is fully awake and Flyer Scann has fixed its addled reason. He is King of Carnival, fool and idol at once, whose powers have unleashed madness and whose reign must now end in sacrifice. King Scann hurts. His ribs are bruised, his face is scratched, his arms wrenched. He cannot protect his genitals. There is a sick pain rising from them through his guts to his stomach. He is turned and turned again, from communicant faces to circular porcelain light shades gleaming from among steel girders near the roof. Round and back, round and back, he is the counterwheel in the mechanism of his own last moments. The lights and faces recede. King Scann begins to die. The noise is agony. The band plays again. The music is loud and fast, calling the beast whose faces are alive and laughing. Scann's consciousness is on the edge of guttering. He is sent rolling in another direction; the wave of noise subsides for a moment and there intrudes a single instrument whose glissando rises from the bottom of a scale to a note so high that all who follow it must certainly be allowed new vision. *Sfortz*: it flings itself beyond the beast's lunacy. The trumpeter leads and the band and the crowd attend. Scann hangs for a moment on hands and feels his bones bend and the animal release him. He is discard, and he lands hard across a barrel.

He wakes in the position he fled from. An airman is pouring beer over his head. Its bubbling rills over his ears to the concrete below and it disorients the moment of his return. But then he knows that he is safe. The party is a party. He has done what neither Thrain nor beer, nor roller skates, nor band could do. He has paid for his intrusion into the life of the station, and if he does not drown in beer, bleed to death or move and feel a broken bone force itself into his heart or brain, he will get down, take off his flying suit and go quickly from Thrain's squadron. "Do you repent?" the airman is shouting. The noise continues great. "Yes," cries Scann. "Do you believe on it, from where all bounties flow?" "Yes." "Then rise and lead us in the ceremony of the bung. You're lying on the airhole." The airman pushes him and he rolls and falls. Someone has put skates on him. He feels the floor beneath roller-bearing feet. It is smooth and helps him go forward, jerk, slide, jerk, swoop, glide. He does not want to fall. Skater Scann cuts through the crowd, a blunt knife. He is wet with beer and hurting. He is hot and greasy around his collar and between his thighs and beneath his arms. His stomach is sick. Someone is singing: Hut sut something on the rillerah. The trumpeter makes his glissando up to and beyond the polestar again. This time there is no meaning in the ride. Scann is grabbed and pulled and pushed and rolls erect and out of everyone's control again. A clown. He remembers that he has skated before and this is why he is still on his feet. He bends his knees a little, leans into his motion and fends off the hands that are trying to make him go faster. They believe in him now. He is theirs, and he understands that disguises don't belong to the wearer but only to the beholder. The wall comes closer, looms, he turns, crashes and falls alone among the debris from repaired aircraft. He cannot now be more hurt. He lies in the shadow of the wall and tries to calm at least his breathing. He wonders where all of his friends are, the ones he has talked, slept, beered with. Do they only know how to fight a war and never how to rescue a fellow creature? Stephanie, Esterby, Marie, Brannan even. Where's Thrain? He thinks he might like to be recaptured by Thrain and have to listen to the story of his step-mother's death. Murder. An interesting manifestation of war-guilt. Scann unzippers his flying suit. Cool air runs up over him and chills the damp beneath his clothes. He gets up and looks around. In the blue distance across the barrels and in the middle of the dancers going, swaying, but going forward, is the blade of a shovel. It comes closer, moving in the direction of the kegs and the skaters. Between the barrels, the padre walks. The crowd parts, skaters dodge and skid around him. He goes slowly, his own parade, the shovel-handle held close to his chest and the blade high. His uniform is muddy, rankless, and he wears no hat. He creates only a small quietness wherever he goes. People stand or pause for a moment, and then he is gone from in front of them. Thus history decays to event, and the enormity of it escapes even Author Scann, who only trusts it to his memory. The padre comes close to him, hesitates, anti-clown and clown see each other a moment, and then Digger Sweet moves on down the hangar to the door. Scann shivers. It is time to get out, to go.

He bends to unstrap the skates. They are on tight and he is too warm again before they are off. Back down on the cement floor he feels short, unfamiliar. The crowd, moving, drinking, active all around him is tall. His goal is the other side of the hangar where he sees the stairs to Thrain's mezzanine and the entrance to the flight rooms where his clothes are. He goes slowly along the line of barrels, his zipper undone to his knees, his helmet in his hand. Nor is he surprised now to see Esterby standing in front of him suddenly, with a beermug in each hand. "I thought it might have been you they were tossing around." Scann finds he doesn't want to talk to Esterby. He looks out and around him to the skaters and the dancers. "Where's everybody?" Scann asks. Esterby hands him his second beer. "Have it," he says, "I drew it for Geddings as a peace offering but he's disappeared." "After all this," Scann says, "the peace." "Of course," Esterby says, "you're right. We must all work for peace." "There seems a lot of it to make. Where's Brannan, and Marie?" "I'm glad you asked. I made them shake hands hours ago. That's all over now between them. You see, I've been working hard." "And Stephanie?" Scann finds himself petulant about her absence. "I'll tell you if you don't peach on her." Scann shakes his head and drinks deeply. The beer tastes very good. "She's taken the flight car and driven off." Scann tries to think it's possible the fog has suddenly cleared. He drinks again and finishes the glass. "Can she do that?" he asks stupidly. Esterby looks mysterious. "Dark, fog, all that sort of thing, just her element." "Alone, did she go alone?" And then it comes clear to him where she has gone. He remembers her saying a name. He can't recall it, but there is an image still with him of a rich, athletic, romantic Englishman sitting forever in a silent room. Part of the old team. The ranks were thinning. Last night, Scann himself had been sent in as a substitute. Substitutes are substitutes: he doesn't feel proud but, in a sense, he hadn't failed. He sees Stephanie at the hospital, walking down long white corridors and then standing at a door with a peephole. Scann draws another beer. Esterby says, "So you went with David?" "Yes." "And now you know." Scann is surprised but not shocked: Thrain tells everyone about his father's wife. That's his obsession. Stephanie goes to the silent hospital. Civil servant Geddings makes threats of violence. Marie attends wrecks and says she doesn't weep for dead lovers. Simms measures to find the exact distance he is from death. Brannan drinks and stays a child hoping that his innocence will attract God's help. Charlie talks about sexual conquest — he sees Charlie go by dancing with the beautiful girl who helped him at the bar last night — Charlie tells the truth. He drinks half a glass again and then the rest of it and turns from Esterby — who would take a searchlight with him to investigate Plato's cave — and goes to another barrel for a refill. He feels alone and inadequate among these citizens in whose Rome he is unable to act conventionally. He aches from it. He is homesick for a home. He limps down the line of barrels. The gallant twelve hundred around him dance and sing and bleed, and they love Thrain's alternate war, another that he is winning. Because he is right, knows how to be right. And in the shadows beneath Thrain's office, he finds the door through which he was led to dress for the trip in the Oxford. Beyond, the corridor holds two more doors on which are cardboard signs: A Flight, B Flight. He opens A Flight's door, trying to remember if it is the right one. There are unmistakable sounds of preparation by two for the act of love. The female is laughing softly, the male is mumbling, drunk but happy. Voyeur Scann's breath faults at the back of his throat, and the blood in his own loins make a little rush. His hold on the handle of his beermug tightens. He spends a long time closing the door and turning the knob so he won't make a noise. He hopes they won't be too long. He is still without his clothes. And he can't wait and listen.

He appears again among the dancers and skaters, feeling foolish now in a way that he had not before. His involuntary act is finished and he still lingers on stage. He drinks what's left of the beer in his mug and goes to the first barrel in the line to test its spigot. The noise is so loud now that it is beginning to pulse. He puts his helmet back on over his ears, and, as if the act is magic, a pale, freckled arm appears. Its hand is holding a glass that needs beer in it. Scann glances to look at who is holding the mug and sees only the tops of two precariously nested breasts: and a short, wide-skirted corduroy dress. Red. The face above them is a round bright party face bordered by naturally curly hair. "Quick," she says, "I'm escapin'." She looks, ducks in front of him. "That monkeysuit is good for somethin'." She makes herself small and he reaches around her to fill their mugs. "Don't get fresh now," she says, "I've had enough of that for one night." Her voice goes sarcastic: "The Wing Commander's birthday, they says. What a joke, 'es not even 'ere." She drinks, and Scann says, "Birthday party?" "Oh yes, and it's going to be a surprise. My God, they round you up like cattle. Come entertain the boys, there's good food, good drink, good band. And that's all right, but the admission price is too dear. I prefer the Yanks over on the other side of Woodhebrington. They're kind of gentle, like they was remembering their sisters at home. You Canadians, oh my Christ what a bunch. I do think you'd try to date a knothole if." Gently, he puts his hand over her mouth a moment and smiles to reassure her. "You're name?" She shakes her head. "Never give me name." "Mine's Scann," he tells her ear as he begins to dance with her ."Amory Scann." The music is slow and with a great beat. "What you doin' in this get-up?" "I was flying with Thrain. It's a borrowed suit . . . look it's a long story." She nods, and begins to sing. It is a big wretched voice. He joins her without knowing many of the words, following the articulation of her mouth, much as he does the rhythmic gestures of her hips. At the end of the chorus, the music stops, starts again. It is fast and she jitterbugs. He tries to follow. He does follow. He wouldn't miss it for anything. She jitters on the extreme edge of disaster. He improvises on heavy beer-wings, his unzipped flightsuit flying. He holds her, turns, sends her spinning out away from him. Her skirt spreads, rises, twirls up over lovely alabaster and, as she moves to return to him, a birthmark at the top of her thigh appears. He catches her as she goes by and holds her still. "Little lady in red," he shouts, "You're beautiful." "Your beautiful what?" she shouts back, and he knows that she knows that he knows; and during the next number she won't dance too close to him. He thinks he may faint anyway. The heat and the beer are making him weak. He dances them toward the door to the flight rooms. "I'll only be a minute," he tells her, and he leaves her to wait in the shadows beneath Thrain's mezzanine. He goes quickly to the proper door, hears only silence, opens it and listens again as he finds a switch to turn the light on. Three benches have been pushed together, and on them are Brannan and Marie. Marie's head hangs over the end. There are welts on her throat. Her hair hangs down. Her eyes are open. Brannan is alive. He sighs and stirs, and falls deeper into unconsciousness. He is on his back and his pants are buttoned. He has saved himself. Scann holds his wrist hard. He has been told this is the best way to wake a man. Brannan floats up to near the surface of his sleep. "Home in ten minutes," he says clearly and chuckles. "Everything's *just* fine." Slurrings. Quiet breathing again. And Scann is glad. He closes the door, locks it, takes off the boots, the suit, finds its locker and his clothes and puts them on: shoes, hat, greatcoat. Gloves. He looks now at Marie. Her blood is not circulating. It is draining down the slant of her body into her head. She stares in deep red embarrassment out of the precise rendering of her fate. "This has nothing to do with me," he tells her, standing still in the middle of the room. He doesn't want to run with the news, stop the party and make himself important. And he understands that this is an event he can't report: it has all the fragility of pure meaning. There is the problem, however, of Brannan waking alone and finding out what he has done. He might ruin the tableau, and Thrain must see it. For his protection. And for his edification. Scann stares around him, thinking. There is an alcove, and in it a desk untidy with papers and logbooks. He goes to it and understands that it is Brannan's desk. He takes out his copy-pencil to write, and then puts it away. He finds another pencil on the desk and a piece of scratchpaper. "Sir, please come to A Flight immediately." His hand inside his glove trembles. He prints the letters, a mixture of upper and lower case, folds the paper and looks up at Brannan and then at Marie's perplexed remains. She is more naked than if she were completely undressed. He reaches to cover the cold, black stiff triangle as he passes, but his emotions break through and he sobs once and lunges out of the door into the passageway. Then he must think, must stop and think, and he manages control. Should the light be out? The door closed? No and yes. He closes the door. And now he must deliver the note. He walks in his own shoes again, his feet too light, to the entrance and out to where his little lady in red is not waiting, and he climbs the stairs to David's office, stepping carefully over and around lovers and drunks. The hallway in front of Thrain's door is empty. He squats to shove the note through. "Cheers," Geddings is saying, "I take it all back. It's a grand success, what I've seen of it." "Much better than I expected. The day didn't start very well." "They understand about the padre, I think. He'll get a long rest." "Where'd you get this Johnny Walker?" "If I told you, you wouldn't believe me. When you've been here as long as I have, you've got to have contacts." "Have another," Thrain says, "I may have three or four myself." "I've got to go and find that fool Scann," Geddings says, "before he thinks he's on staff." "Well, just a short one then," Thrain says. Scann slips the note under the door, rises, taps very lightly on the panelling with his fingernails and goes down the stairs as fast as he can.

· He walks through the crowd. Out of the flying suit and in his greatcoat and hat he is in another disguise. He must look severe and official; he creates silences as he goes. "The war came back to Graydon-on-moor at 7.27 on a foggy night...." He looks for Dolan. There is pressure inside him expanding. "Jesus," he says out loud. They are all here, everyone of them, all, and he is the only one who knows that it really did come to Graydon-on-Moor at 7.27, that it finally arrived to make a game of the silk scarves and flak-holes and missing persons. Not a beginning or end, but a confrontation. He holds a beer mug under a spigot and watches it fill. Goddam us, he whispers. He drinks the pint. It settles in his stomach like tears. "The heart since proud," he says and draws another from the barrel, "it calls the calling manly, gives a guess that, hopes that, makes believe, the men must be no less." He shakes, drinking. "The heart," he says, "the heart, it makes love no matter what." He climbs up on the barrel, thinking that he is looking for Dolan, and sees them all doing what they're doing. "I love you," he shouts and doesn't know he's drunk. "I must. There's no one else." People wave. Someone whistles for the drunken officer. "Listen, listen please." He looks around for words. *Pretty soon there's going to be a silence. All the bombs are going to be duds and only the people will explode.* DO YOU UNDERSTAND ME?" There is no response. No one comprehends. He sways and crouches, holding the lip of the barrel for support. In front of him, frozen in a foxtrot position is his lady in red, and she is dancing with Dolan. Her face smiles and is puzzled. "You love us?" she asks, her voice barely reaching him through the noise. "Yes, you and Stephanie and

Thrain and Geddings, and Dolan I love you for being here right now, and I love lover Charlie and." He pauses because he thinks he might fall but doesn't. "And Squadron Leader Brannan and Marie who finally lost it for all the women in the world." He rises, strong again. "Where's Marie? Let's hear it for the biggest deflowering of them all." There is only small applause and into it Dolan says, "Here, let me help you down, sir." He reaches up and Scann takes the small hand in his and jumps from the barrel. His feet sting, his head clears a little. He looks into Dolan's face, with its Chinese red cheeks and is china-blue eyes. "I'm through here, Dolan. Done my stint, finished my tour, had my say, and I'm taking a vow of silence. Now, take me to the village, my friend, and close the circle of P.O. Scann's twenty-seven hour war." He puts his arm across the red lady's shoulders for support, but she stays closer to Dolan than to Scann. "Can you?" she asks. "Can you get your truck out of here now?" Dolan frowns. He is pensive. He will never make sergeant. "How'd we get through the gate." "It will be by Thrain's orders. The lady is ill," Scann tells him. "Go get your lorry, who's to stop you? And meet me at the mess. I shall be waiting."

They offer him no further help. They leave him, and he stands in front of his barrel and is tempted. Nor does he have the strength to resist. He makes his way down the wall of the hangar to the door behind the bandstand and goes along the outside until he sees light seeping out from around the blackout on A Flight's window. He stands against it for support and searches until he finds a peephole near its bottom edge. He puts his eye to it and sees Thrain and Geddings. They stand like a crowd around Brannan. The stiffness in them all is the electricity of shock. Marie has been moved. She lies, still embarrassed, looming into the spaces between the three men. Thrain is holding Brannan up. He slaps him back and forth across the cheeks and there is no protest. Brannan looks puzzled, caught out and perplexed. Thrain's muffled voice rises: "Someone sent the note, Brannan, who?" Brannan shakes his head and looks down at Marie and quickly back. They continue to stand, another tableau, and Scann wonders who will come to break it up. And then he understands that as long as he crouches at his peephole he is part of it. He rises and goes along the side of the hangar again, to the roadway where the funeral had passed and on up to the flagpole and then to the door to the mess. There is no one inside. He goes along the passage to the door opposite the bar marked Men and relieves himself. Standing liquid against the white coldness of the urinal, he feels better, but is not yet safe.

He goes with his luggage, his duffle, his suitcase, his camera and equipment, to wait for Dolan outside the door of the mess. The orange fog-lights of the lorry come around the flagpole and halt beside him. He puts his gear in the back and climbs into the cab. They arrange yet another tableau, this time for the policeman at the gate, and escape out into the blackness beyond the station. The little lady in red stirs. "I wonder if the wing commander will ever get to his party?" Scann thinks for a moment. "He's going to have to sooner or later." Dolan is driving. She leans close to Scann for warmth and allows him to touch her nesting birds. It is a great comfort.

And upstairs, in the room over the pub, the wireless on, they dance and violate every privacy but the one he thought they would. The struggle becomes final: he thinks she is ultimately stimulated by force. She breaks and runs, her coat grabbed around her for modesty as well as warmth, and he follows her down the stairs into the garden and along the wall until she stops and faces him again. "Okay Canada," she says with the old laughter effervescent just below her words, and all the way back to his room in Linden he feels the ache of their awkwardness and re-lives the long history of her most convertible truth. "Scann — " holding to him like a cat to a pole — "no one ever made me feel like this before." And then later: "You miss it too. Come on, admit it, admit it." She could remember Marie, a little of Brannan and gossip about Thrain. "That one was sent down, wasn' he?" Scann withdraws. He preserves carefully her smells and the taste of British beer that are still with him, and thinks that life is a discontinuous narrative surrounded and made durative by the habit of mere existence. He lies uncomfortable on his bed. And that humanitarian arrangement is disrupted by memory, a false consciousness which causes dangerous tranquility — the belief that from it we may learn, even understand. It makes social scientists of us all, complete with the cunning of objectivity and the cowardice of selection. Given Marie and Philippa, Stephanie and Amantha, little Red and Cecilia the processes follow easily: connections are managed, contexts are constructed, theories propounded, contingencies explained and *voila* what have we achieved? The past is made predictable. It is all very well to smile, but Scann has lived with this urge too, and has been often reduced to consistency, objectivity, the redundancy of history and obvious truth when the facts are only a review and fail to recreate those movements and moments that render the past perfectly unpredictable: his own war, for instance, is despite total recall still no certitude. It is as precise as a chronometer and tells its times exactly, but the function of the tick of its events is only to separate. The surprise of totality comes always at new intervals, or at the end of a continuum whose time is buried in the times. The facts. One had better not mind them. The fact is, life is one long embarrassment which occurs as if it is felicity itself while one is trying to make connections: construct contexts, perfect theories and explain contingencies. He rises from his bed and goes to the basin, voids (voids, for Christ's sake: precision is also found comedy), rinses, washes, brushes his teeth, combs his hair and aches a little for Stephanie whose response still echoes for him. He stares at the wreck of himself in the mirror. He had thought her strong. He had come to believe her, that she was alive, knew how to stay alive — say, do, be. He had begun to carry her lightly with him, disregarding the sentimentality of the act, her physicality gone, and his view finally reforged by the force of their encounter. She was not his invention. Every man needs one spirit that springs whole inside him like that, not necessarily to worship, but to give him confidence enough to continue inventing himself. But he had invented her madness. After the trial (in Linden, finally, when the war ended) he asked David about her. "She went insane, suddenly." He pictures it. She walks down the white hall, stops at a door, sees Robbie through the narrow window, finds the door open and goes in. They stay together, have their own space, get well. Nobody finds out. That insanity cancels out Stephanie's, and he understands the act is no longer hers, but it explains much about his own cowardice: he has never quite found the courage to let himself go finally mad. Marry, retreat to Linden, yes. A reasonable withdrawal to a place where mild freedoms are allowed, and his stance as general prosecutor has gone unnoticed while he has gathered evidence and has rehearsed the case against. What? His grey face in the mirror draws its lips back from its teeth, its nostrils flare and he works the flaps of his ears. "Despair," he cries, indignantly and undignified. The padre walks through with his shovel and creates a small silence. Scann is shamed once more and holds his breath against the noble decorum of that march. Its sanity charms him, gives him envy. *Hopes that, prays that.* But he has no shovel: only the license of this room where his own marches boldly lead away from effect toward cause and halt always against tangles of false emotion. Listen again.

David Thrain's father's wife's horse came home alone. Mrs. Thrain was not found for another five years. A skeleton whose height and teeth told what flesh it supported. David Thrain left for the war during the afternoon before the horse returned alone. And that morning he had driven his father's green 1936 Chev over the bridge across the Swifter, miles beyond which Mrs. Thrain was later found. All the rest was conjecture. The jury looked uncomfortable, impaled rather than impaneled. "The trouble," Scann wrote in the last of his seven dispatches from the trial (all of them unpublished and the reason he decided to quit and stay in Linden to become editor of the *Chronicle*), "seems to be that David Thrain let them down. Had he smiled, shaken hands, even swaggered a bit, the whole process would have been much easier. Linden has no great record for hanging murderers anyway. The last time the white gloves were not presented at the end of the assizes is barely remembered. This psychology is hard to pinpoint, but one suspects not frontier justice but its opposite. The hanging jury and summary justice have been replaced by the view that there but for the grace of God go I and anyone can make a mistake. And who's to say they're wrong? The murderer (except the mad dog and sexual varieties) is the least disruptive of citizens who come before the Supreme Court. On a number of occasions, the murderer may even be the instrument of public opinion. The claimjumper, the cuckold, the unfaithful wife, the sharper may also be fine people, but what if they are not, what if they offend the tribe in other ways? Murder has in Linden's eyes many degrees from 1st to manslaughter and on down to a five dollar fine and perhaps even covert applause. The jury system is not so finely tuned, but it can register its view by summary acquittal and Linden's juries have often done so. Mr. Justice DeWitt has presided before at such occasions, and only once has he vetoed a jury, and that was before he sent them off to their deliberations. He told them that he would accept no nonsense, the man was guilty beyond any shadow of doubt: "You must," he said, "do your duty." The jury went out for ten minutes and returned to tell him that it was hung. No verdict was possible. Mr. Justice DeWitt, probably calm, declared a mistrial, and the crown and defense had to do the whole thing over again. The proceedings, while somewhat different, achieved the same results. Mr. Justice DeWitt, at that point, made history himself. He said that the man had never taken out British citizenship, and therefore was eligible for deportation. The Crown, defense, the immigration people, the government and even the jury, sniffing a good solution when they heard one, did not object to the man being put on a quick boat back to his native land. Legend has it that he was met with blazing machineguns at the foot of the gangplank. His crime there was political, a hanging offense even in Linden. But the Thrain case was different. What do you do with a man who sits cool among his peers, accepts that justice will be done, presumes not at all on his Linden citizenship and is all but arrogant? And what do you do with his father who refuses to answer questions but prefers to make a speech until, to save him from contempt, the court declares him something like hostile to all sides and has him banned from the court? The judge didn't have to go that far. The jury knew old Thrain was more angry than bereaved and that he often yelled for much smaller reason. The tip of the iceberg of this case was a family quarrel, or perhaps worse: a father and son meeting head-on over the skeleton of their rivalry. It was a difficult situation. Old Thrain was their friend. David Thrain was a man of real substance, a hero, austere, remote — all qualities admired by Mr. Justice DeWitt whose own dignity was unflappable. There were too many forces at play. The jury, in the end, had to listen to the Crown Prosecutor and the lawyer for the defense, and came up with what anywhere in the world would be called a true verdict. The Thrain trial was somewhat unique in this, and one has the feeling that the whole course of justice in Linden may have changed. Still, the case seemed not to be a criminal one but a civil one between the two Thrains. David Thrain insisted on appearing in his own defense, being examined by the prosecution, and all of the time he may have been talking to old Thrain and not to the court at all. The intriguing thing about this part of the trial was that it seemed to be two things: a holding action and, between the lines, something quite different. The right questions, the philosophers tell us, will elicit the right answers. True. Providing both the questioner and the respondent have the same intention. Old Thrain stood at the door — the court attendants let him — and he listened. What happened to him and to his son is also conjecture. It was a *particular* performance. One must call it that, and fascinating.

" 'Did you love her?' 'No.' 'As a mother, perhaps?' 'She wasn't more than five years older than me.' 'Were you intimate?' 'Yes.' 'Just the once?' 'Yes.' 'Why at all?' 'Because I was weak, and she.' 'Was promiscuous?' 'Of course not.' 'Then how would you describe her?' Long pause. 'Like putty with rocks in it.' 'I didn't mean that. Was she in love with you?' 'She wanted both Thrains, maybe.' 'A matter of security?' 'No, of control — her own peculiar kind.' 'Was she beautiful?' 'You knew her.' 'Answer please. Was she beautiful?' 'Pretty.' 'Willful?' 'No, but beneath everything she knew what she was doing.' 'Then you say she died by legitimate accident?' 'Don't we all?' 'Murder is no accident.' 'Isn't it?' 'You drove out over the Swifter that day. Did you see her?' 'Yes.' 'Was it a meeting?' 'An interception.' 'For what reason?' 'When you're young, you want to talk.' 'Were you afraid of something?' 'Myself.' 'That you might love her?' 'No. That I might have harmed my father and that I might do it again. I wanted to be sure.' 'Sure of exactly what?' 'That I could think and not just feel.' The prosecutor smiles. "Could you elaborate? What happens if we only feel?" Mr. Justice DeWitt: 'Where are we going here? Is this relevant?' 'It is, m'Lord, if you'll allow me.' 'An odd line of questioning. Be quick to your point.' 'Yes m'Lord. Answer please Mr. Thrain. What happens when we only feel?' 'How about the depression and the war?' 'The war?' 'Yes.' 'Surely we had to fight the Germans?' 'In the end, yes.' 'You were against it?' 'Yes.' 'If I may say so, it was good to you, a young man of restricted opportunity from Linden.' 'I was good for it.' 'That's not an emotional statement, Wing Commander?' 'Not at all, Sergeant.' 'I was commissioned before discharge.' 'Congratulations.' Mr. Justice DeWitt: 'Round one to Wing Commander Thrain. This is not a debating society. What is the prosecution's point?' 'That the unfeeling arrogance of David Thrain allowed him to kill — we know that later he killed three men with his bare hands while escaping from being shot down in Germany, and his small regard for his men when he commanded them also underlines this arrogance — and that it was this irresponsible man who on the eve of his departure pursued his father's wife, with whom he had committed in the eyes of the law and custom incestuous adultery, and killed her simply because she threatened him with unwanted emotion and domestic entanglement, that, in short, he knowingly played God. You drove across the Swifter at approximately four o'clock on the afternoon that she died and intercepted her. Where?' 'About a mile down the Sunday Creek road.' 'How did you know she had gone that way?' 'I didn't, but there were the hoof-marks of a running horse at the turn-off.' 'She was happy to see you?' 'Momentarily.' 'Why momentarily?' 'Because I told her she was acting the bitch and if she harmed my father, or harmed him through me, I'd see that she suffered.' 'You told her that after what she'd done for you? What was her reply?' 'She simply looked at me and told me I'd be back sometime, maybe on leave, and we could talk then. I said no, we'd talk about it now.' 'So, you quarrelled.' 'No, we talked.' 'What did you say?' 'It was a private conversation.' 'You will not comment on it?' 'I'd prefer not.' 'Because it would incriminate you?' 'No. Because it's not relevant, except I told her I'd not be back.' 'And she accepted that?' 'Of course.' 'She intimated you weren't the man your father was, didn't she?' 'At that time it was a fact.' 'It angered you?' 'No. There are times when you're young that it's a relief not to be as good a man as your father.' 'It angered you nevertheless, and you killed her, put her body across the back of the horse and walked with it deep into the surrounding bush, where you threw it into a swamp and left the horse to return home at its will. Remember we have a report on the lamentable condition the poor horse was in that day, and the evidence of a witness that he heard a gunshot.' 'I believe that he did hear a gunshot. Only a horse suddenly bolting because of something like that could have unseated her. She was an experienced rider.' 'Now we must come to the hat.' The prosecutor was good and got better. He had information, gossip that came like flak and exploded ugly around the accused. The jury was fascinated, the defence annoyed and often sustained in its objections by Mr. Justice DeWitt. The prosecutor circled and circled and finally everything was finished, including the hat.

Then came Ro. He was still in uniform, but without rank. He told the court he had been a sergeant. 'When?' 'Lots of times.' The sweats from both wars in the jury box laughed, relaxed. The court rode its dignity through their ranks and decimated them. But Ro was real. Winners who win and become heroes make everyone uncomfortable. But winners who choose to be losers allow us all to dream that we, too, have made that choice. They are our true champions upon whom the fates seem to have only a slippery hold. Ro sat in the witness box, hardly obliging the chair's presence with his own, and his halfness was all about him: half in the army and half out, half Indian and half white, foster son and yet a brother, and, depending on what he said, a witness for either the defense or the prosecution. But the defence had called him and had brought him from the train directly to the court. He was asked three questions, none of which could have been rehearsed, and the brilliance of the examination lay in asking no others. 'Were you intimate with Mrs. Thrain, did you make love to her?' 'Yes, and before he did, too.' The relevance of this was doubtful, but the jury was all male. 'Did you see Wing Commander Thrain the day of the accident, before he left on the eastbound train for Edmonton?' 'We had an argument then is how I remember it. The old man was away in his plane again and we hadn't seen him since spring. David wanted me to stay around and look after her and the hotel until the old bugger got back. It didn't make any kind of difference though, because she went missing that day and Thrain flew in at the end of the week. I could leave then too.' 'Now, is there anything in your memory about a hat? A fedora, possibly blue or black.' Ro's eyes focused on the lawyer. The jury, the prosecution and Mr. Justice DeWitt could see them too. 'His hat?' The lawyer said nothing, nor did his expression change. 'Blue,' Ro said. 'It was blue and he was never without it. Slept in it, I bet, ever since he was about twelve. I couldn't remember seeing him without it, except at the train. I asked him, and he says she has it out riding and to get it from her when she came back and put it away for when the war was over.' And that was all. The prosecution's case had been propped on that hat, something of David's dropped at the scene of the crime. . . ." The civil case: whatever it meant to the father and the son (and to the foster son too), was over also. Mrs. Thrain, whomever she might have been, was more important to the Thrains than the trial or the possible verdict. Scann wrote more, suicide notes to his editor who thought that returning from the war had unhinged him: "The feeling I have is this: the Thrains are all of them released — from what I don't know — but they are not released whole. One senses that the woman's name need never again be mentioned because she had *happened* equally to them all, and her death, murder or not, is seen by the three of them as necessary now, not as revenge or some kind of restitution but as an indication, and an acceptance also, of a failure of something in themselves. Perhaps, on the other hand, what she and the trial have done for them is to allow them to separate. It seemed to me I was witnessing an explosion rather than the end of a trial. Ro Linden didn't stay in the courtroom after he had testified.

The old man has evidently disappeared from town altogether. . . ."

Editor Scann goes to the window and looks down on the street below him. It may be the same view he had stared at during the days of the trial and afterward until he had found a house for Marion and had considered his choice until he thought it was a good one. Until. The greatest of all romances is silence. Inside it all things are possible, remain possible. The ultimate drop-out; but the pressure builds. One begins to make bleeps, like a bat in the darkness, and believes them to be meaningful beyond giving simply a sense of direction. He leaves the window and walks to the door and back again, alone but unalienated — a pathetic condition. At the table he stops and finds old notes. He can still read his reporter's shorthand, his own transcript of David's trial. He had been sent to get sensation for his readers to immerse themselves in: pure gossip, petty and mindless. After six years of war, go back, go back. The enemy has been defeated; make sure nothing has been changed. No uniform suddenly: make sure that the old uniformity prevails again. After the thrill of violence, most of mankind achieves no greater euphoria than from imbibing anew the taste of the same old shit. Coming to Linden for the trial, being split off had given him expensive moments of clarity: war is not nearly so wounding as is returning from it. Back: what the hell is back? Old Thrain had gone back to the woods once more, David to the hotel and to the Marble Creek workings, Ro to the snooker tables. Kinds of silence: pretences at being back. But he himself had really believed in silence. So did most of the rest of his generation. In this he'd been a follower and not a leader; he'd given up hunting and finding, and he had no magics to perform to beguile his fellows. He begins to bleep again. Snicker. Not snigger. Old Rip Scann, back at last. Not too late. Old Thrain lives yet. David is back, and so is Ro. Scann looks around at his bed. He is still sleepy and possessed of other presences, and the manuscript on the table is remote. He goes to the closet and puts an eye to the hole in the wall, and greets the dawn of

THE FINAL DAY OF HIS CREATION. Nothing stirs in the swamped grey light beyond the portal of his eye. The TV at the other end of the room snows and hums, still relaying last night's prime-time message. The room looks occupied now. Clothing, shaving gear, cigarettes and ashtrays, orange peels and candy wrappers, a package of gum, the remains of room service. By his debris shall you know him and consider his passing. Here, there has been a party. Ro sleeps, gulping shallow drafts of time: another kind of waste, the black slag of oblivion for a third of each day. Scann's body aches for more of it, but his mind runs like a gyro somehow balancing need and renewed obsession. And he is rewarded. There is a knock at the door. Ro turns, wakes, coughs sleep out of his lungs and rises to stand by his bed, for a moment uncertain. Then he simply answers the knock, standing aside to let a female in. She is more copper than he is. Her skirt is black, wrinkled, spotted and uneven, short beneath a man's long-sleeved tee-shirt tucked in sometimes around her waist. Beneath it there is nothing to suggest a woman. Only her black hair, a rope of which she chews, identifies her sex. She is without flesh. Her face might one time have been pretty. If she weighed eighty pounds, Scann would be astounded. They don't speak. She coughs and looks at him out of a face half turned away. She stands slack in the middle of the room. Then she raises up her large handbag and begins to look into it. The door is still open, and Ro stares out. "What's this?" he says. A voice replies, "That's Mary Ann." Ro turns his head towards her again, and after a moment: "Murdoch's? The one Emma Murdoch had to look after her at her house?" "We didn't think you'd know about her." The voice appears. It is the faun, his daughter, Marilyn, and behind her her boy, Paul. Ro closes the door. "Why'd you bring her here?" The boy shrugs. "She needs a place." He touches her gently, as if she is precious. "She's a hype," Ro says, looking at her again, "and a pro too, every cop in town'll be here." "She's a human being," Marilyn says firmly, as if she is a recent convert to this special philosophy. "You keep her till we find a place. We just saw her getting off the bus." "No," Ro says, "you found her, you keep her." "We'll come back later for her," Paul says, taking Marilyn's hand. His black hat is a steeple above the chapel of his face. He gestures. "That's your sister and look what they've done to her. Last night we were just rapping about this kind of thing. Now it's real." He opens the door. "Now it's all relevant," Marilyn says. Ro watches them begin to go. Paul says, "Thrain's back from Ottawa. We're going to bring him and rub his nose in it." Suddenly Ro laughs and stands easy. "He don't go for clootches, but maybe he'll rap with you." Paul's face colours. "She's not a clootch, Ro. She's the whole evil thing they've done to the Indian nation." Ro speaks slowly, as if he is trying to make Paul understand something. "She's a clootch. When

245

she can stop being one, I'll let you know." Mary Ann's slow motion search in her handbag glides to a halt. She makes a movement toward Paul. "Hey," she says, and motions with her head. "Hey." She loses her moment of clarity and only gains another when she sees once more her hand in her purse. Paul comes close. There is wonderful concern in his face and in his gesture when he touches her again. Mary Ann looks at his hand on her arm as if it might be the one she has lost rummaging in her handbag, and then she grins. "It'll cost you, you keep doing that." Paul stops touching her. "You got to rest, right? When's the last time you slept?" Gradually Mary Ann's eyes come unstuck from his face and she frowns into her handbag. "Too much talking here. Let's go where it's quiet." Her eyes have tears, her nose runs. She bites her lip. Paul says quickly, "You stay," and as quickly leaves, holding Marilyn's elbow. The door closes. Its small slam echoes visibly along Mary Ann's bones. Scann watches her and then hears Ro. "Did you know his dad's a doctor?" Her head crouches dumb into the hunch of her shoulders. "Maybe he'll bring you some." He takes the handbag from her and empties it onto the bed. She smiles, not at him but at this ingenius solution. She picks and chooses from among the debris. She holds the capsule between thumb and forefinger, and her eyes go ravenous like an infant's seeing the promising tip of mother's breast. Her moment expands to a process, a progression. Spoon, water, needle. Ro watches. "It's been a little while," he says at last. She concentrates. The needle sucks up the fluid. She twists her scarf around her arm and after a moment holds it with her teeth. "They'll take you again, Mary Ann, and it'll be cold turkey," he says. "Shutup," she says, her voice a delighted gas escaping through the clench of her smile. She turns to show him she's found a vein and then puts the needle into it. The plunger works. She waits, the instrument by her side like a shot pistol. Then she lets the scarf go from between her teeth. Blood oozes down her arm. She closes her eyes slowly. Her infant's mouth sucks in and out, as if it counts certain private intervals. Scann changes eyes at his aperture. Ro rises slowly from the bed, but when the hit arrives he doesn't catch. She twists, her face is translated to beauty, opens, and her hands grab at the edges of the basin as if she might be violently sick, but after a long moment she floats up out of it and turns again, this time holding on to Ro. She laughs. "Smack," she says, looking up into his face. She leans back, her arms around his neck, her face to the ceiling and her hair hanging down her back. She leaves him and goes lightly around the room, but when she comes back near him she holds onto him again, leaning her head against his chest and gradually drawing in closer. Ro lets her. His small smile is a reflection of hers. Between them her hands begin to fumble and finally lift him free. Scann blinks. He has seen nothing before like her action now. She might be mounting a bicycle too tall for her. Ro stands stolid, then persuaded, then helpful. He holds her high. Her legs go nearly around him. Scann's tongue dries. He sees nothing, only a female clinging to a male. The rest, what he can't see, is real. But slowly, fighting ambivalence, Ro settles the darling beast she has made of them onto the bed. Scann is embarrassed by his watching. But he stays crouched at his small window looking out on this world he has not known before, and at last she floats and drifts beyond the long crack and lash of the ecstacy that began with the needle. And then Ro rolls free, stands by the bed, rubs his nose and looks down on the tiny heap of her, a lump of copper-coloured ambergris on the surface of the rumpled bed rendering now the perfume of paradise within itself. At the basin, Ro carefully washes himself and, from his bag retrieves an ointment which he applies. Scann is amazed. He has not seen the cosmetics of casual sex since the war. He had thought their disappearance part of the cessation of hostilities. Ro goes back to the bed. It is a sudden movement, as if he is prodded by memory, but she is not a woman anymore. She lies curled and smiling and with her hand gently to her face. She has become perhaps ten or twelve and holy, very holy, a saint lying among the longed-for ruins of her humanness. Scann feels the emanations of the peace within her. And so does Ro. He sits on the bed and watches her. He is affected, and looks as if he might worship and ask intercession by St. Mary Ann of Linden, patroness of old professionals everywhere. Scann chokes off his own moment of longing, coughs quietly and rises up out of the closet and away from the hole in his defences. He sits at his desk and takes up his pen to make it work again. There is, he writes, no loss greater than the loss of self, and no pleasure more intense. It is the great temptation, yet most of us cheat, concentrate on food and sex, relying on the egocentricity of the acts of eating and loving to keep us from totally losing ourselves, while at the same time giving the sensation of transport. And at the other side of the circle there is Celibacy and the Fast. Make continence a luxury and even an ordinary man may have religious experiences; and the true

Religious may, with self-denial as his passion, be visited by the very fists of heaven. Think, then, about Mary Ann. Author Scann can't, and knows he won't. He files his note. He must eat: eggs, ham, toast, jam, tea. He orders and breakfasts.

Then Scann, refueled, holds his ballpoint once more over the wilderness beyond the Toebroke where his own small continence has manufactured a vision that holds fast in the orange light thrown by the fire at the low end of Trapper Linden's Water Lake cabin. The peephole in Scann's closet is scaled over: his view now north and somewhat east. A scene grows into focus through the fisheye lens of his imagination. Thrain moves into the heavy-toned light and stands before Trapper Linden, who is sitting on the edge of his bunk. One pantleg hangs slack toward the floor. There is no hand beyond the cuff of his left sleeve. His white dandelion hair is long now and it layers down over scars that were once ears. His nostrils are long flat trenches that dig up toward his forehead. His eyes look out from behind ridges of scar-tissue. His tongue licks out over the mat of beard around his mouth. Then he gets up. God makes trees. Man makes crutches, and these Linden uses now are ingenious, if only for having been made with an axe and a knife. One fits the stump of his arm and straps over Linden's shoulder. He pulls on this small harness, grabs the other crutch and goes to the door. Thrain watches him. Except for his hair, he looks as old as Linden. The land outside is a cadaver and they have been feeding off it. Spruce tea, the occasional fish, anything Thrain can trap. It has been a long time since he has felt the triumph and omnipotence that came with the journey down from Mosquito Lake. He is not a trapper. Even starving, the calling bores him. He moves through trails across the landscape without seeing it. He fragments it. He counts the trees, divides them by kind and age, multiplies them by dollars, subtracts the cost of harvesting them and goes back to thinking of the creeks and streams that may hold in their bellies the answer he wants: he needs this virgin to reveal herself in a sudden passion for him, to *yield*. He believes in Trapper-Custodian Linden's gift to him. He believes it all the more now because he has, himself, resurrected Linden. Look, he walks, even if it is only uncertainly from the cabin to the edge of the lake. The door slants in. The day outside is flat grey. Thrain feels the air around his legs cool and freshen the cabin. He judges the temperature and finds it well above zero. He must go out. Linden doesn't talk any more. Since he began to crawl he has remained neutrally dumb. Thrain dresses and takes Linden's axe and begins to walk west and south toward the small jagged valley of the Moose. He turns quickly at the edge of the lake. Linden is back by the cabin watching him. He stands half-whole above his single foot, crutched nicely on the firm snow. "I'll be back," Thrain shouts, to hear a voice. The idiot words don't bother to echo. He wonders one more time what Linden would say if he did speak. Perhaps only commandments. Great givers are always austere, remote, inhumane. To receive is the cruelest fate, because with the gift always come the silences that demand worship after the noise of one's own thanks-giving has died away. Thrain has served Trapper Linden well, and now he tries to walk a little easier over his leasehold, travelling carefully to conserve his strength. He is hungry. He chews spruce gum and keeps to no particular trail. One step is only contingent upon another. Nothing moves, nor is there shadow or reflection. He humps along as if he might be a single prisoner in a horizonless exercise yard. Then there are no more trees in front of him. He has not been here before. The land clears, and it slopes easily down across a prairie of snow until after perhaps a quarter of a mile the forest begins again. Winds have blown across this empty corridor. On the east side there are drifts against the line of trees and on the west the snow is thin. An outcropping of bare rock and ground rises as if it might be some kind of promise: Noah saw a rainbow in a benigner climate.

Thrain sits on the head of his axe. The handle rises between his legs and he holds it with his hands to balance himself. It is a long time since he has seen a rock or a patch of ground. He crouches quietly; he is celibate and fasting, but he doesn't have a vision. Wildernesses are not for visions: they're for temptations. He has given in to the tempter, and the prize *is* the wilderness. The holy understand this and refuse, and are thought more holy. The rest pay out, unwrap their gifts and see the trick, the laughless joke: Welcome to Wilderness Camp, it's all yours; sit out in the weather, freeze a little to stop the pain, watch the sunset, do what you will and hear this from which all chaos flows: You're born and you have to die; pass it on. And revere the giver. Do not forget to revere the giver. And Thrain had spent a long time on his knees. Cleaning with boiled water and a boiled rag Linden's suppurating and swollen roasted joints. The kind of worship where it is possible to watch prayers being answered. The stumps begin to shine with new skin. Rotten, irridescent colours are still there, but Linden's body gradually breaks down the old blood behind wrist and thigh: a miracle of degeneration, out of which rises the living ashes of the man who delivered Thrain to these regions. But Thrain's worship has failed. In their time here they have gone from silence to violence, to revenge, to silence again, but they have not ever been brought together. Thrain once thought they might make contact. In the long time he had crouched evenings before the fireplace, learning with exactness the art of fitting wood to Linden's need, there grew in him a certainty that came near to making him happy: Linden would be grateful for his service. But there was no ceremony for the giving. The night Thrain finally finished the crutches he went to bed beneath his cougar skin, and then woke in the morning to the sound of Linden using them. Two short paces each way, over and over again. Then he pounded with the butt of the right crutch on the door as if he were demanding to be let in instead of out. Thrain opened it, steadied Linden on the step and watched him go down the path to the lake and stand there looking out over its blankness for a very long time. He turned, finally, looked across the clearing for a moment and then came back to the cabin, sat on the bunk and let the crutches fall away. Then he lay back in the dimness to sleep. The distance between them was no less empty, only greater.

Thrain sits on his axe and is tempted again. He need only double back and keep on walking until he finds the river. But that isn't enough. To go back alone is another kind of emptiness. Small uppercuts of anger hit at his diaphragm and he begins to laugh because he doesn't understand: neither Linden nor himself, or why the picture of his return to town bearing the old man across his shoulders is a steady portrait of victory and freedom. He feels tears dampen his laughter, and he looks up to where the sun should be. The great lid of the overcast is still clamped firm. He sits. He sits. Then out of the black treeness of the edge of the landscape comes a deer, a female deer. It hardly looks to see to its safety. At the bare rock it paws at the thin snow to get at grasses that might be beneath it. The deer is hungry too, starving maybe, this late in the season. But a pretty thing. Delicate. Thrain's hands slip from the handle of the axe and he slides back into the snow. The deer doesn't hear or see. It interests Thrain now, not just as food, but because it is unwary, a thing even weaker than he is that he may be able to kill without a gun.

Slowly he rises and fades back into the forest, circles, keeping the wind against the deer. Why is it alone? Too. Hunter Thrain's muscles wobble under the load of tension in his quiet walk. He begins to sweat. Why? He takes off his mitts. The air is warm as it touches his hands. The clouds above may hold rain, not snow. He bends and picks up a handful of crystals and they are not quite dry. He looks back. His footprints are more rigid than they've been all winter. He has not noticed. Why? He tries for concentration, and stares at the deer. The cruelty of last moments: before birth, before death. Very soon now it will be the last moment before spring. He throws the axe, more in despair than with intent. It catherinewheels over the feeding deer and lands beyond it. Its head comes up, looks at the handle in the snow and then, incredibly, it turns and leaps exactly at Thrain. It is a tiny thing, but its eyes are wide and steady: like a boxer's. Thrain watches and waits for it to swerve away to the left or right past him. He is surprised when the first hoof hits his chest. He is hurt. The sting and cut of the hoof is vicious. He falls. The eyes above him change colour from brown to black; they lust after his guts. Thrain rolls in the tough snow, gathers himself together to rise and fight, but the hooves won't let him. They trample sharp against his body. He feels the cage around his vitals begin to give, and the graceful death above him runs across him as if he is a dreadful landscape whose traverse means deliverance. He rolls and rolls again. He shouts and twists and leaps and dives until he is behind a deadfall and its stump. The deer leaps. He catches it by the head and twists it off its feet. It is all he can do. Pains in his ribs force his hands free of the deer. They lie together. It is the fullest moment of their fight. Thrain's heart backfires into his throat and halts his breathing. The deer accepts suddenly that it is victorious. It rises out of the sticks and stones of its legs and hooves: stands still, looks down at him and then leaps away. Maybe it has only hours to live. A rotten stench left behind by its breath still hangs over him. Thrain thinks about following it. He starts to get up but can't. Pain, blood, perhaps broken bones force him down behind the stump again. He sweats. The air around him feels warm and wet. An odd time for spring to begin, just at the moment when he is worse off than he has been since November. He rolls to a sitting position and opens his parka and shirt. He puts snow against the cuts and bruises to staunch the blood and dull the pain. He shivers and feels better. The steam of his breath finally begins to appear more steady. He gets to his knees and then stands up stiff against the stump. The trail he has made earlier runs back into the woods above him. He steps away from the stump and breathes as deep as his pain will let him, and he wonders how far he has come from the cabin. Surely not more than a mile in this new direction. He begins to walk slow and light, carrying his pain along as if it is a precious discovery, and refusing to examine the evidence against his chance of making it back to the cabin alone. Then he yells: it rises up out of him without his thinking, and it makes him feel good. He walks a dozen steps, slowly made and slowly counted, and then he shouts for help. But the pain increases and the light fades. He doesn't yell anymore. He speaks in a loud voice: When I go, you'll go too, Linden. He likes this thought. It makes Linden his creation. He says the sentence often. He stands against the trees to rest. He is afraid to sit in case he may not be able to get up. Then he becomes careless. He doesn't watch the trail and his foot slips into a soft hole. The new pain of it drags him down and over a dim line between light and darkness. He is conscious but he can't see. The sensation is pleasant. No pain, no weakness. He drifts on easily toward the cabin. He is sure he recognizes landmarks, blazes, even individual trees. But when he wakes it is dusk. His legs are folded bloodless beneath him. The temperature is below freezing again.

Linden is standing over him. "You like circles," he says distinctly, and Thrain knows he is conscious again. "You get in trouble and you go in circles." Linden is leaning into the snow on his crutches. Thrain says, "How far?" "Through there a hundred yards. Get up." Thrain tries and faints. When he comes to, Linden's face is looking down at him out of the gloom. The old man holds a crutch over Thrain's chest. "Move!" he shouts. "Get the hell up, goddamn you, get up."

Thrain gets up. He holds himself firm against the dark, against pain, against Linden's voice shouting: "Get me back to the cabin." His legs are still bloodless. He leans without thinking on Linden. They lean together and begin to fall. "Hold me, Thrain," Linden warns. Thrain shouts: "You got out here. Now get back." Linden yells: "If I go down we'll both die." "No we won't. Help me Henry, I've got broken ribs." Linden moves a step and they are separate again. "Is that all? I got one hand, one leg, no nose, no ears." They begin to move and each avoids the touch of the other. "You're lucky I bothered to keep you alive." "Thrain, you couldn't survive the night without me." "Who gave you the crutches?" "They hurt, Thrain, all they do is hurt." And he slips on the packed snow in front of the cabin and falls. Thrain leaves him there and goes inside. The fire is burning low. "Couldn't even keep the bloody fire going," he shouts, and begins to build it up again, stripping as he watches it make flames. Behind him, Linden flops across the threshold and then up onto the bed. "Food," he says. "Help yourself," Thrain says, and turns to face the old man. "And if you crap in the bed you can clean it up yourself." There is water in a tin pail by the fire that is warm, and he begins to bathe his cuts. But the silence between them is broken, and Linden can't stop talking. "What did you do, fall out of a tree? You're stupid enough." "I was attacked by a deer." Linden is silent for a moment, and then he laughs. "Only you," he says. "You're the only one it could happen to. I've decided, Thrain, I'm keeping this place. If a fool like you can stay alive here all winter then I can still run it." Thrain doesn't answer. The heat of the fire is beginning to relax his cold muscles. There may be bones broken but the sting of the cuts is receding. Linden settles back on the bunk. "Go find your own place. A year to rest up and Ro and me'll be back."

Thrain kneels before the fire and stares into it. "Spring's here," he says. "We got to get out pretty soon." He pushes the pan of rabbit meat a little closer to the fire, and pours water on it. "Down below it's been melting for days." He looks across at the old man in the bunk. "When will we be able to go down the river?" There is no answer. Thrain gets up and walks to the edge of the bunk. "Tell me," he says. Linden's eyes only stare at him. Thrain leans down. "You feel safe, don't you? That was a nasty moment there when you thought your servant was maybe hurt too bad to feed and keep you comfortable. Now it's all right. You can clam up again because you're home free. You just talk when you're in trouble. Let me tell you, you're in trouble now, so start talking. I left the axe out there, Henry. That's it for us. No gun, no axe, no nothing. We've got to move on down the river soon. When?" It's hard to look at Linden smiling. The scar where there was once a nose opens further and the holes in his face dilate. "Bring me the rabbit, Thrain. I ain't eaten all day." "When can we go down the river?" "When it's ready and you're ready and I'm ready. Why talk to you? You don't want to hear nothing except where the gold is. You'd forget all this and everything you're supposed to be doing if I said walk forty paces north and thirty west and twenty south and thirty east. Not talking to you is the only way to keep you headed in the right direction. Jesus, I don't know what'd happen if you really knew something. You're used to being ignorant, Thrain, and it keeps you out of the big mischiefs. Don't try for anything else. Now bind those ribs and cuts. They'll be sore a day or two, but I bet you'll be able to pull a sledge soon." "This place is mine, Henry. You're my guest." "Then feed me." "It's over there, if you want it." And when Linden is gone from the bunk, Thrain lies on it and then kicks Henry away when he crawls back from eating the rabbit. He takes the blanket and rips a foot-wide strip from it and nails one end to the wall. Then he binds himself by pulling the strip of blanket tight around his chest as he turns and turns toward the wall. He cuts the blanket loose from its nails and secures his bandaged ribs with rawhide lace. He turns to see Linden crouched among the folds of the cougar skin, watching him. He says nothing. He lies back and closes his eyes. The fire is a quiet glow. From somewhere water drips. After a while, Thrain gets up to try to find the leak in the roof. It is to the left of the door. He puts a pot under it and goes outside. The temperature is up again. A mild night wind is blowing across the lake. He feels too warm in his bandage. He gets Linden's ladder from against the front of the cabin and sets it beneath the eaves, but when he climbs it he can't see where the leak is or how to fix it. Maybe there will have to be a whole new layer of sod after the snow is gone. He climbs back down onto the ground. The sledge he built to transport Linden here from Mosquito Lake lies along the south side of the cabin. Thrain pulls it out toward the entrance to the Toebroke trail. It slides heavily along through the wet snow. He tries to remember the deadfalls and the rise and drop of the land. It is going to be a long trip. He decides to leave Linden to fend for himself, and he lets go of the sledge-lines and goes down the trail. In the dark, he loses the way and walks into trees, scraping his face and hands. He becomes weak again and staggers, feels ill: pauses, vomits easily onto the snow and holds to a treetrunk to keep from falling. He is lost in a lightless nightscape, and he doesn't care. He walks slow upwind away from the smell of himself, holding his arms out in front of him like catswhiskers. He wonders with humility if he is going in circles again. Perhaps. But in the blind dark what difference is there between a circle and a straight line?

Surely one is as good as the other. Is a man more a fool for circling than going straight? His ribs pain. He trips and falls over the sledge. His illness recedes as he lies among the sleigh's crusty furs. They had kept Linden safe on the trip from Mosquito Lake. He pulls them around him and sleeps until dawn. He is only a few yards from the clearing in which the cabin is set. Around him the trees are dripping and some are shedding loads of snow. It is too warm. The snow is melting too fast. Thrain stands. He is stiff and his chest hurts but he doesn't think now that his ribs are broken. He must eat, get his strength back. They must go before the spring turns on them and kills them.

At the lake, he walks out across the ice to his fishing hole. The big trout on the end of the line has been dead a day or so and his brothers have eaten half of him. He takes it from the hook and finishes cleaning it, and goes back into the cabin to cook it. He nibbles cautiously, letting his stomach reveal its intention in its own time. Gradually, as he eats, he becomes hungry. He chews down all of the fish and hopes for more. Linden is watching him. It adds relish to the meal. "I tried," Thrain says to him. "I saved your life, brought you here, fed you." He sucks at the spine of the fish. "I figured, sure, you had a right to be bitter, but even a madman would come round to reason. Who made the crutches? Must have taken a month, on and off, while I hunted and fished and trapped and snared and cut and chopped wood and cooked and washed and cleaned those rotten stumps of yours. Linden, the place is mine. I paid for it. And I paid more than it's worth, even if there's gold stones on the bottom of all the creeks." Linden sneezes. It is a ritual morning sneeze signifying that he is awake and that his body-passages are beginning to clear of their nightclog. "Gold," he says, "You cut off my pointing finger or I'd show you. You might not see it even then." He sits up. "How's your broken ribs?" Thrain looks over at him. The question is too friendly. "How was it when you pulled the sledge? I thought maybe you was gone for good when you didn't sleep here last night. What made you come back? Come on, Thrain, now it's your chance to talk. Where you been, out tellin' the trees your troubles?" Thrain stands up against the firelight so that it won't shine on Linden's noseless, earless, bearded face. He takes a deep breath and it causes him very little pain. He walks over to the overflowing pot beneath the leak in the roof and empties it out the door. The sun is up and flaring out of a clean blue sky. The snow dazzles. He goes back inside and dresses. Linden is up and leaning against the bunk like a crippled heron. The new light from the door illuminates his torn-up face. But it is his eyes Thrain sees suddenly. He has not been watched like this before. Then the mouth moves. "Don't try to turn the tables. Didn't I agree talking wasn't any good? Go get me a rabbit, there's a good lad." Then he laughs. "I don't know what you want my line for. You couldn't trap your own thumb." Thrain turns from him and goes out the door again. He walks slowly toward the trees to where the light won't blind his eyes. He goes from one snare to another. They are baitless pieces of fine wire suspended over the straight lines rabbits make in the snow. Nothing. Nothing. Nothing. He tries to make them better, more cunning traps. Then there is a rabbit snared by a hind leg. It is nearly severed, and the snow is pink all around. He kills the animal. He can bend now, run, breathe deep. He is sure his ribs are whole. The time to go is now.

Scann feels the tension of Thrain's decision. His pen shakes in his hand and he puts it down to pour the last of the cold tea out of the double pot he had ordered. He stands and drinks at it, bitter but distracting. He puts the cup back down on the room service cart and goes to his basin to rinse his mouth with water. His mind slips out of gear. He sees his face in the mirror. It is surrounded by lank hair. One eye is higher than the other. The ears are larger and more protuberant than they should be. His smile is like a dog's: it simply raises his upper lip and uncovers grey teeth. The skin beneath his eyes is badly-applied wallpaper. No wonder Mary Major doesn't succumb. He applauds her taste and wonders at his relationships with Marion and Shirley: how could he be at all attracted to females so debased they would associate with such stupefying ugliness? He wants to phone them and ask what the secret of their blindness is. Instead, he moistens and lathers his whiskers and stands like a point-headed St. Nicholas in front of the mirror. As he shaves, there is a knock at the door and a rattle of a key that lets in an aging waitress from the Linden House Grill. "Will that be all?" she asks, preparing to remove the cart. He nods his head and she goes. Her varicose veins are excrescent reptiles beneath her girlishly sheer nylons. The door closes, the mirror is empty again except for his half-clad face and he lets it weep for her who must dress her dying as if it is as enticing as fashion promises to make it, and for himself who also has sheer nylon dreams: of genius and consequence and conquest and craft. He does not cut himself with his platinum edged stainless steel razor blade. But he works swiftly, rinses and dries his face and refuses to look at it again in the mirror. The bellows of his spirit expand a little, sucking at more confident air. He cruises by the door, not yet ready to go back to work, and opens it. The blue roses are still there blooming up into linear silence. He likes them now. He is beginning to believe that roses are blue.

Inside again, he leans on the door and looks around the room. His room. Nothing in it is unfamiliar. He stands, loving it all, even the manuscript that lies scribbled and unfinished and without meaning. Even the hole in the back of the closet. He goes to it and looks out, resting his head against the pocked plaster and sees into Ro's room. Mary Ann is smiling a pretty smile. She turns over slowly onto her back and with her head turned in one-eyed Scann's direction. He remembers old Emma Murdoch, Royal's widowed chatelaine, phoning him at the paper and talking: "Mr. Scann, you are a man who has contacts in a number of places. Do you have any at the Coast? What I want to say is: Mary Ann has left me to go there, and she's alone. I couldn't stop her, you know. When they reach a certain age it's almost as if it isn't any of your business any more. And Mother Superior just shrugged her shoulders. Between you and me, I think they're just as happy when the bright ones disappear out of the parish. They *see*, the bright ones do, and I suppose that's dangerous. Anyway, do you think you could have someone meet the bus? It would be wrong of me to send one of my own friends. She'd feel betrayed. She left this morning, so you'll have a few hours to arrange something. Let them show her the place — you must know what I mean — give her a chance to keep herself safe. I gave her some extra money. I don't know whether that was right or not, but I thought she should have something to fall back on. She might be able to think straighter then. You know, it's the glamour she wants, Mr. Scann. I fear for someone in that position, don't you?" Her old old attenuated voice failed her still supple mind. No, he hadn't feared for her. Why fear for someone else's inevitables? But, for Emma, he had phoned a friend — a drinker but a puritan — and asked him to meet the bus, get Mary Ann a decent room and steer her in the direction of Mrs. Sprott's secretarial school. His daughter, Marilyn, would call that a white man's solution. Yes. It bears thinking about. Yet, it is possible that Mary Ann has not been treated with real respect since a sober MacDonald took her from the bus station and did what he had requested of him. Scann blinks. The rest is melodramatics: life. Or perhaps it's only a case history produced in imitation of the canons of sociology, that mule of a science manufactured by mating the donkeyhead of statistics with the horse's ass of philosophy, these parts being generally available to almost anyone bent on breeding a pet monster. Whatever it is, it can have nothing to do with Cultural Mosaics, or Male Egos, or Simple Alienation. And certainly nothing to do with specific ghettoes. The country itself is a Chinese boxful of them. The Canadian lives north of a border which has only cut him off and thus has given him a negative definition of himself. He is not an American. He lives, second, in a Region (there are five of them) whose paucity (in his eyes) of the goods and graces of the world causes him pain and, paradoxically, makes him a booster who tells wishful lies, harmless and somehow comforting, like real propaganda from real places to live — say Torremolinos or Las Vegas. He lives, also, in a city or town, walled in by inverted slabs of pride and longing, and from inside them he imports and luxuriates in a romantic squalor collected from bits and pieces of other civilisations: other people's literatures, sensibilities, heroes, politics, problems, money, goods and services. As there was the Roman eagle, the Chinese dragon, the British bulldog, the Russian bear, so there is the Canadian packrat. Yet, from out of the garbage and costly stench of his ghetto-nest there rises a banner of curious superior moralness on which words can be seen: From This Great Wisdom Of Our Own Some Advice To You. Awkwardly said, but then English and French badly spoken and blockheadedly lived are the true twin-heritages of the country. Not a mosaic, a labyrinth. How then does one join it? Monsieur Le Wildman Scann stares through the hole in the wall at Mary Ann and sees her smiling again. She knows that for a while yet the beast in her arm holds off another beast at a distance: but she does not know the other is only the packrat, lit up and disguised by magic lantern pictures provided at great cost to ourselves and our resources. Scann puts his experimental mouth to the hole and enunciates: "You're a nearly white Indian." Then he looks again. Already she is moving as if to offer her loins.

Delegate Scann rises, turns his back on the closet and sums up his report to the convention. Let me say at once that I'm a generalist and not a member of a specific discipline and so I will not place reliance on any such fragile edifice. On the other hand, among a variety of overlapping theories, a certain number of characteristics emerge which reflect a commonality of interests each to each within the theories themselves. You see. To begin, then, when the Canadian Government, in the name of Queen Victoria, gave the Indian a Reservation and a medicine chest his *peerness* was withdrawn. You understand that *peerness*, if we are to follow my theory, is basic to the elementary fact of joining. No peery, no joiny, as my Chinese laundryman used to say. So, it is useless to argue that the Indian is peerless. Nor is he without peer. Although some might now want to espouse this view. No. It is only that his peerness — that quality of being someone's peer — has been taken from him and bred out of him. It is perhaps one of the reasons he is dirty, shiftless, lazy, drunken, and his woman is an easy lay. In any event, when a female without peerness leaves the static non-society of the Reserve, or even a relatively stable up-country village, and goes to the city, Pandora's Paradox comes into play, and after that, what I call the Telephone Exchange Effect appears as it becomes ironically and experientially apparent to the girl that she *must* join. After the well-known Pandora's Paradox (where one, through the impress of faulty logic, loves the stings and poisons of the world) has been acted out in the early stages of contact with my labyrinth, then my Telephone Exchange Effect is produced. This is no more and no less than an analogy worked out on the human level after having observed carefully what happens to an electrical impulse when it enters a telephone exchange in search of a free line. Down the list of lines it goes. One, two, three and so on. All are engaged. The impulse is connected to a busy signal. Signal after signal is sent through and the same thing happens. The world *becomes* a busy signal. Now this, together with an absence of peerness brings us into contact with a further effect. It isn't, oddly enough, a primary one; it is based on an old (perhaps the only old) Canadian folksaying we've been able to uncover in researches extending back over decades. It goes like this: "Let's get drunk and be somebody else." It is not a wise saying like the Spanish one: To live well, that is the only revenge. The Canadian saying has no obvious ironies when it is acted out, no depths or breadths, no *piasano* waggishness, no civilized mock despair. It means simply what it says: "Let's get drunk (or rich or famous, or withit) and be somebody else." No. The irony, fellow researchers, is in the suggestion that, for Canadians, the action is feasible, even possible. While our citizen lives on other people's services, monies, etcetera, when it comes to the ultimate longing to *be* somebody else, there is simply nobody at home. This, I call the Dialtone Effect, which may, in fact, be worse than the busy signal. We don't know, of course, because there are not grants available to do this basic research. In any event, the net result, from observation, seems to be that when John Canuck gets drunk (or whatever) to try to be somebody else, he achieves (to put it positively) a lack of peerness too. Many, far more than we may realise, achieve this state and constantly believe that in fact they *are* someone else. And, at the lower end of the socio-economic scale, the middle-aged failure, the disaffected, the sociopath, the alienated, the weak, the hardcore second and third generation social welfare cases gather in loose groups in places where the Indian female eventually arrives in search of a way to silence her busy signal. The rest I leave to your imagination, except to say that my theory does expose the problem of *having* to join whether one is Indian, suburban, itinerant worker or stockbroker, although the latter seems somehow to relate, through some environmental evolvement perhaps, quite readily with other busy signals. During the whole of our social history we have had nothing to lose but our peerness, and that act itself, I think I've shown, identifies us more positively than most of our countrymen care to admit. Were there more time, I'd like to offer a few remarks on the problem of hyperbole in the Canadian character — the tendency he has to become a bigger junky, a wilder drunk, a more dedicated power-monger, a more fantastic ego, *etcetera, etcetera*. But that will have to wait, and I too will have to wait until next year, unless you would perhaps give me time tomorrow during the workshop on minorities because, you see, I can prove with my theory also that we have no minorities; our peculiar love, at once of other people's cultural artifacts and our own ghetto-nest, insures that our prejudices are *only material*, and therefore the importation of racist ideas and fashionable solutions to them are simply not relevant. But now, my thanks for your patience. I hope it's been amply rewarded. Success makes him reckless with his time and his security. He yearns for a larger view. He takes his chair from in front of his desk, moves it to the door and stands on it to look out through the vee of the transom. His chambermaid rounds the angle of the corridor from the top of the stairs and walks toward him. Her uniform is pert, fresh, her hair a golden golden golden light around her head and face. He wants to call softly to her — a morning call of great intimacy. But she takes out her key and faces Ro's door, inserts it, knocks twice and enters.

Scann waits. The door doesn't close. When Mary reappears it is as if something is ejecting her from the room. She exits. Then turns and closes the door with professional softness. She runs to his room, works the lock and pushes against it before he is able to move. But he manages to jump and the clatter of the chair fragments the focus she had achieved next door. "Goddamn," she says and stares at him in front of her without quite seeing him. She points. "He's got a girl in there." He nods and reaches to push the door closed behind her. "An Indian." Her face goes bloody with anger; Ro has betrayed her. "Lying there with no pants on." He watches her until her eyes quieten. "Does it excite you?" "What?" He persists with the treatment. "I said, does it excite you, awaken certain lustful feelings, start certain unnameable fluids oozing?" "Stop," she says. "Just stop it, stop it, stop it. All you do is talk. What's happening to Ro?" She plunges into the closet as if the hole there is as much hers as his. Her body crouches before it and is all angles and rigidities. "Don't just look," he says. "See. See hard." He waits for her to do it. "Who is it?" Silence. "Who is it? Come on, tell me." She stands and turns to him. "*You've* been looking too." Her eyes search his face to see whether he has seen everything she has, and more. "You know her," he says, "so tell me who she is." "Mary Ann whatshername. You know, she was at the Murdochs' until just before Emma died. It didn't help. She's an animal. They all are." "Even Ro?" "Well, I guess." "Except you're a bloody poor guesser. My daughter and her boyfriend brought her there, almost straight from jail, I should think. She was really strung out and fixed as soon as they left, and she's been out on the bed almost since then." "They brought her to Ro?" "Yes." "Why?" He thinks. "Maybe as exhibit A. Our new young are object-oriented and they believe as their mediaeval fore-fathers did that the real and true object has curative powers." It isn't what she wants to hear. "La-te-da, Mr. Scann. I just tidy up around here. Get out of the way and I'll do it before I go and unlock the alley door so she can be put out."

Scann sits on the desk and rests his feet on his chair while he watches her work at his bed and basin. "Would you," he says at last, "have her thrown out?" She is polishing. "Little slut. How long's it been since she was at Emma's — seven, eight years?" "All of that." "She was a sweet little thing while she was there. Demure."

"Demure?" "It's a word, isn't it?" She stands before him: "Then what happened? You're the expert on everybody. Is she another one of your stories, and all I'm seeing is the junky whore?" He nods his head and decides, without being able to understand the consequences, to save whatever it is that's happening next door. He tells her Mary Ann's story up to the point where her man says, "Now you make my friend here happy and he'll give us money for another bottle." Scann wishes the top of the truth weren't always so superficial. Mary Major dry-weeps a little. She sits on his bed and shakes her head as if she hadn't heard the story before. "Poor Mary Ann," she says now and then. "Goddam men." She says it twice and stands up. "Exploiters. The world is theirs and women are the last slaves." Scann is not prepared; he sits stiff on the desk trying to find this new direction. "I went to a woman's liberation meeting yesterday, Amory. A lady who's been to New York spoke to us. There's going to be one last revolution, she says. Just because we have to bear the children is no reason for us to be slaves." She walks stiffly towards him and stands close. "I'm not wearing a brassiere today, Scann, and the hair under my arms is never to be shaved again." Scann looks down at her chest. "I don't believe it. Let's see." "Oh, no you don't, Amory. You're not going to exploit my new freedom. I will not adorn myself for men and attract them with the products of Revlon and Dupont. We will meet as equals and I will let you know when. And you will be equally responsible for the fruits of our relationship, if any." "Will our representatives get together first to discuss the shape of the bed?" "Oh, you're funny. Laugh if you want, Amory, but it's happening. You're a lost cause." Scann pushes past her and stands pointing dramatically at the hole in the back of the closet. "A minute ago, for Christ's sake, you were going to throw out one of your own into the street." Mary sits again on the bed. "The lady said it would take time to react right in every situation. She said we've got thousands of years of slave thinking to live down." She sits with her hands clasped in her lap and stares away into the closet, and then she looks up at Scann and smiles. "No, I won't kick her out. But I'll liberate her." For Scann this is a moment of fear. Her smile, her delight in reversing the meaning of the act, her understanding of its effectiveness makes him search her face as he hasn't before, and he thinks: you go away for a few days and they hold a meeting to plot destruction of the world. She can't be serious, but she is, and he sees that she may be a natural revolutionary, one of the saints of the cause. He stops staring at her and begins to move and crawl inside his skin like a horse hobbled and frantic with flies. He is no longer in control. One moment she is Mary Chambermaid, well in hand, dissolved in tears of his making, and then suddenly down comes the lightning of her conversion, and of their days at Linden House together there is nothing left but the spent smell of ammonia and oxides — faint remembrances of things past. And, he thinks, conscious of enunciating Scann's cornerstone paradox, the past is farthest away and least graspable at its nearest edge. He tries to begin to speak to her, but as in other famous scenes, her eyes stop him. They are clear and frank and steady and compassionate and proud, and they have been wounded by sudden knowledge and understanding so that they are also wary and unapproachable. "Amory," she says, "you look like your face has just been stepped on." Slowly, he squats before her and tries again. "I've only now seen you. Before I thought you were just pretty, but you're really quite beautiful." There is a long pause. Her face is not illuminated by his words. Nor does she smile. He watches. Her eyes reflect only careful consideration. He wants to yell into the silence she is making. Finally she says directly to him: "That was a very nice thing to say." He can shout now. He stands stage-centre: "Say? *Say*, for God's sake? Do you think I just said it?" She looks at her watch. It is her answer. "Amory, this has been the biggest weekend of my life, and you were part of it. I don't know how to thank you." He stops the gesture he was going to make and puts his hands in his pockets. He wonders if communication for him is perfectly impaired, a scrambled transmission for which no receiver has been built. Yet, her broadcasts get through happily and well: Amory Scann, I have nothing for you and this makes me conventionally sad. Over and out.

Courtier Scann paces a little. It hurts. His muscles are rigid. He tries again. "Queen Catherine," he says to her. Her face brightens as she recognizes the allusion. It is as if she had acquired by some miracle a dispatch case full of intelligence overnight. He may, in fact, be partially responsible. "You've killed off your courtier and sent for the hurly-burly of the revolution." She nods. "Oh, yes, and suddenly I'm so very much alive." He muses, and reaches to dazzle her once again. "The rough prick of these moral times rather than the lapidary tool of that old technician and hedonist, Time himself?" But she doesn't even bother to listen. "Queen Catherine wasn't great," she said. "I knew that when you first told me about her. No woman would've bothered with the story, only a man would." "Because it's dirty?" "No, because for him it's about the worst monster of all." Her face opens out now and holds compassion and humour and tenderness and a knowledge for which there are no words. He is irradiated. Warmed. She reaches and takes his hand. "Oh Amory, you've been such a temptation. Think how awful and what a waste it would have been. We'd've just gone to bed and *screwed*. Instead there, well, there's what's happened." She lets his hand go, and the warmth sinks deeper into him, and lower. He feels around in himself for defences. "But isn't *that* part of life too?" She hears. He feels delight in having got through. "Yes." Her face doesn't tell him what the answer means. "A good part?" "I don't know, I don't think so." He tries to feel hope; but she stands and goes to the window and looks out around the blind: "Billy took me for a ride on his motorcycle yesterday morning," she says, and turns toward him again. "Out beyond Rainford we saw old Mr. Thrain walking along. I thought he was sick or dying or dead. Anyway, I made Billy stop." She looks down into the silence, and then: "Why do you lie so, Amory?" A feather-tickle of laughter in him forces diversionary action. He sits on the bed and blows his nose into one of Marion's neatly ironed handkerchiefs. She comes in closer toward him. "Mr. Thrain said Philippa was crazy, had been for years. They had to keep her locked up in her room and trained a dog to be with her. He shouted it at me, 'like a goat in a horsestall.' He shouts instead of talks. He's a bit deaf. It was kind of hard to ask him about I.J. I don't have the scientific words and Billy was there all ears, but Mr. Thrain seemed to catch on all right and he hollered at me: 'Girlie, if you're trying to get me to tell you he was the most peculiar slavey I ever saw in my life then I'll agree, but as for him being gelded, I couldn't say. He laughed like hell when the dog came at me, I know that.' "

Scann is up and facing her. He also hollers. "Just where do the facts differ? Did I say Philippa was sane? Have I ever said anyone was sane?" "But all that about cutting the men and freeing them." "You think that's a lie?" "Yes." "Then why so many ball-less men walking around thinking they're free? Answer me that. Did Moses come down off the mountain with God's handwriting on polished stone tablets?" "I don't know. It's in the Bible." "Or did his going up the mountain and coming back down with some rules of conduct only mean there was a new and necessary concern for a specific morality all around him in the air, and when he disappeared from his wandering tribe for awhile and left them leaderless (fact one) and then after awhile came back (fact two) with some rules for living together as refugees looking for a home (fact three, and aren't we all refugees?) didn't the truth of his return and the effectiveness of his moral solutions become as if divine? Is it so far then from there to the mountain again, to the hand of God and the tablets of stone?" "Moses wrote the book," she says. "And *he* wasn't a liar. Does it say too much? Does it celebrate too much? Not at all. The Jews carried the happy and pathetic and noble and consequential tablets out into the great mix of civilization where they became our kidney and gall and bladder stones whose pain reminded us of the stretch between what we had to do to stay alive and what we thought we must do to be content and just. We have hated the Jews for their tablet-stones too, and now they have expropriated, with our blessing, their old home and have gone full circle back to the deserts and a new kind of wilderness, led by a half-blind general and an old lioness of Judah, to their final tragedy, which is that at last they are able not just to *die* but to *die out*. The spectacle of old Ben, with Moishe and Golda strung out behind, marching out into Sinai and coming back with nationhood and all that *that* means signals our final insult upon the scapegoats of the western world: we have allowed them to render themselves *ordinary*. But," Scann says loudly, and Mary wakes from her trance, "very few stories have such force or duration or universal significance." He sits beside her on the bed. She smiles a little. "Does it make you feel better to do things like that? Shoot a robin with a rifle?" "All my life," he says, "I've had trouble with audiences. Never the right one at the right time." "Are you sure we aren't the only one you've ever had?" He can only laugh. "Look," he says, "Philippa is not a bad find. When I discovered her, I remember being all atremble. And when I dug deeper and her companion pieces showed up I thought one of my best days had dawned." "But they're all lies." Her voice is without inflection. He waits for her to go on, but she only folds and unfolds her hands; and then looks up at him. He tries to think about her. It isn't easy. "Do you think old Thrain could tell the truth about them?" "He had nothing to hold back." She gets up and goes to the door, then she turns again as people do at doors. Her eyes look at him, and even from that distance he can see a wave of shock and recognition pass over their clear surfaces. She makes a small aborted movement toward him. Moondust and ennui float up between them: a giant step for art. She's leaving and he feels no honest sorrow. He drags out his only real defence and closes himself off. Then he runs her through his mind: the exercise renders out sentimentality and even lust. He sees her standing there, brassiereless, fumbling for words to express the small regrets of her parting. But she only says, "I guess it's finished," and he decides for their time's sake to save her from the pretension of that sentiment.

"Not at all. There's the rest of the pilgrim's march. Remember the pilgrim's march?" She hesitates and doesn't turn the doorknob. "During which each gradually discovers the soothing madness of the rôles they played until Thrain arrived — which is a truth he could never tell you now." "Amory, I know the ending." "Of course you do. It's a matter of public record. But before that, what about the great encounter between Thrain and Philippa? Their gigantic contest of wills and their last bone-splitting orgiastic moment before she dies? Imagine the dexterity of that earlier Thrain, the exploiter of moments, as well as the land he lived in, when he dodged the dog and managed Philippa too. And then the fight between Master II and Thrain, after which the death march to the aircraft where the dead but still smiling Philippa is strapped beneath the tailplane to be flown to Linden for burial, after the inquest had rendered the verdict that she had died of natural causes. And that is the great moment of the story: they stand in a small slipped knot of humanity around Thrain's flying machine, each recognizing, each understanding the odd fuels that have been firing their private engines. And then the aftermath. How Cecilia killed herself and I.J. packed her out wrapped in two tattered gunnysacks so that she could join her mother at the cemetery here in Linden; and how later I.J. went east to Ottawa to work as hall porter in the House of Commons where he was a great favourite of all parties and was called George because some of the legislators had been to see the Big Time in Washington, D.C. and knew how to address a nigger. And so he changed his calling from prime administrator and dog trainer to precursor and in a sense did not lose his balls in vain, because there are many now who remember George and, even as they think fondly of him, wonder if there isn't some connection between him and the new uprisings and revolutions that are making life in Ottawa grimmer than it once used to be. And, of course, there may be a connection.

There were times when George didn't always smile. You know that Thrain married Amantha and lived miserably with her, disappeared again in his aircraft and didn't come back until after her mysterious death." He stops his pacing and sees her once more. Her face is very sad. Perhaps his signal has been scrambled again. "What's the matter?" She shakes her head. "I don't know. I guess it's just that you're such a big failure about the thing you want to be the most." "Which is?" Scann stands tall. She takes a deep breath. "You want to be serious. That's it." "Serious? Aren't I serious?" She looks past him, perhaps out beyond the windowblind again. "You talk a lot too. When Mr. Thrain stares you in the eye and shouts, he's so — you know — earnest and true that you begin to make up the story along with him. Seduce yourself, if you know what I mean. But not with you, you don't look me in the eye, and you rub my nose in it." She can't stop a smile from appearing on her face. "We couldn't have made love. You'd have to *tell* me that every little movement had a meaning all its own." And now she is laughing, and he must not let her take any more moments from him. He moves toward her, but she sees, and believes his intention and she opens the door, goes through, locks it and holds the key inserted. He rattles the knob but there is nothing he can do about it. He backs away. The welt she has laid across his ego swells in the new silence and chokes the beat of his heart. Somehow, this has become war. He lies down on the bed to think. Then he hears her voice through the transom. "Amory, please, I'm sorry, can I come back in for a minute?" He nods as if she can see him, and the door splits open a little. He sees her eyes watching him. They are solemn. She comes in and crosses to the bed, and he gathers his defences around him. (The actress, at this point, should make no large melodramatic gesture. She should quite simply and elegantly remove her clothes, take her diaphragm from her purse, insert it delicately, with her back to the audience, and then, as the curtain falls, she should go directly, as it were, to the point of the matter.) "What you want to be most," Mary says, "isn't happening now. But what you do do; you know Amory, what you can't help doing, that's important and I'll always like and remember you for it." Sir Ralph (Rafe) Scann looks at her out of hollow sockets. "What?" he asks. She smiles and leans to touch his upper arm: "You really rattle a girl's brains." He nods and turns his face away. Ralph looks at his white feather and goes to Egypt. "That's good." "And you *believe*, Amory. That's important." He struggles visibly for a moment to find an image of her behind closed eyelids and then revolves his head on the pillow to see her again. He rises up on one elbow. "Who the *hell* are you?" he says. "I am serious. Very serious." He sits up, forcing her away from him and the bed as he gets to his feet. "Precisely because I so strongly don't believe." The words he has spoken tip up their old relationship and the new slant forces another perspective. "By God," he says, "you try a man's patience. You're mad to do it. Anything might happen." He sees in slow motion the welter of movement that follows: his hands drift up to hold the material of her smock just above and behind her clavicles; then a sudden sharp pull and his pride is ransomed with her humiliation. She stands naked to the navel before him. Breasts like small wineskins dangle only slightly. Slowly, he sits down on the bed and contemplates. "The price of your liberation was small," he murmurs. Only George Sanders could have served the line better. He looks into her eyes: perhaps she knows, even believes, that the real fiction they have manufactured was that there could have been any attraction between them; and that that tension was the only ingredient she had contributed to it. He wonders at her not covering herself, not hitting him, not running away. But it's as if she has not understood that she is exposed; she stands in front of him as if she is an abandoned and unsuccessful study in stone. She might have been beautiful. He holds to that, and he wants to touch, that's all. Touch. The back of his tongue makes the noise. His hand levitates, and he brings it hard against his chin as if to smash a fly. His struggle wakes her. She moves, but the wineskins don't. "You're right. I owe you," she says. "I didn't say that." He watches her look down at where her clothes should be. "What were you saying then?" He thinks and can't remember, but refuses to give up his advantage; he remains silent, and after awhile she speaks. "I can't, Amory, not now or ever. With all your talk, you've let me be my own person." She covers herself with her ripped smock and moves closer to him. She smiles. "See what you've done?" Her sudden languishing falls cold around him. He shivers and rises to stand beside her. "Hush," he says, and tries not to take out the great spike of his anger and impale her on it. He walks slowly to the closet, removes his war correspondent's raincoat and brings it to her. She turns her back against him and he slips it across her shoulders, but at the door she stops and looks down at herself. She takes off the coat and gives it back to him.

"I think I'd better not." The scene is over, yet she continues on, stretching up to kiss his cheek. "You're really a very good person." He grabs her and shouts "No!" straight down into her being. "No one who produces a monster can be good," he says, faltering and turning away. He feels witling tears swelling against the back of his throat and eyes, and he doesn't see her go. There is only the little shatter of her laughing at him and, in a moment, the door opens and closes. She has won.

Beaver Scann (the beaver is one of the country's national symbols and, according to Apuleius in *The Golden Ass*, when alarmed by the hunt, bites off its testicles and leaves them lying by the river bank to put the hounds off the scent) Beaver Scann has only one precious stone, and he has given it to the chase. Still mad with it, he knows that he is running hard against time and that his own animals of refutation are answering echoes of their own snarling in the near distance. He stands with his back to the door, is perplexed and his mind will not stop leaping and searching in a great circle that may or may not lead back to the manuscript on the desk. He knows there is colour in his cheeks. The sheer sheltering walls around him hold only his fool and not his genius. Mary, Mary quite contrary, in my garden you grow to gull my oaf, my sap, my gawk, my clod, my doltish pale Pierrot. Yes. Oh yes. He is transposed from tears to gaseous laughter, and he puts the chair once more to the door, climbs up on it and, with his mouth to the transom, makes confession: "I have been gentle," he says, "kind, considerate, indulgent, lenient, benign, obliging, tasty, tender, juicy, mild and sweet. I have sucked from the honeycomb of humanity, ghouled the casket of convention and believed for moments on end in the wonders of old philosophies. Forgive me, forgive me." He serves. He stands and waits. Out there the blue roses lie quiet, the brown walls support no shadows. Nothing. He calls out: "And I have believed in the silences, too, Peckerhead."

He steps back to get down. The chair tips, cracks, collapses in a bundle of kindling around his feet. The moment of accident, the accident of moment: his mind turns over, fires, catches its energy again. The conjunction of defiance and accident causes that terror for which faith seems the only palliative. He stands among the chair's splinters and contemplates the theologies of chaos. Certainly they are powerful. The great thinkers have found no other alternative to faith than disarray. The whole matter is of prime seriousness. It is possible that the Ultimate Good is the Other Alternative: some vehicle that will run smoothly over the interstices between actuality and the mystical Real without becoming political: anarchist, fascist, communist — the anal, oral and genital of social religiosity. The search for the answer always degenerates to depravity. Penitent Scann kneels among the fragments of his chair. "And what stage of depravity are you at now, Scann?" he asks himself. "My own, my very own!" He tries to piece the chair together as if it were a game newly delivered to distract him. There are vehicles, real and practical ones. Thrain's aircraft, Linden's feet, and Philippa's. No, perhaps not Philippa's. We must confess that research into the origins and the writing and the reality of Scann's first novella have turned up oddly significant shards from the dump of his waste materials. There is, for instance, the scrawled outline of a story about a family called Morton who lived on a ranch not far, one gathers, from Linden, though whether it is the actual or the metaphorical Linden is difficult to tell. However, it is a most engaging little tale, trenchant, to the point, interesting and illuminating. Philippa, a matriarch, has been left alone with her brood on the ranch her husband had built before he died. There are two girls, Cecilia and Amantha, and a great number of "Zed's people," brought from his old home in the south. Philippa feels responsible for them all, but her frailness of mind does her in. The story gradually becomes a study in physical, moral, mental, religious and political depravity, and beneath all of its turbulence, neatly woven in, is the quiet beauty and strength of nature, so basic to Canadian writing: the dark but brightly pollinated waters of Morton Lake, the lovely browns and greens of the countryside, and the noble dogs of the ranch whose perversion by man signals our descent with Philippa, I.J. (her negro "slave"), the daughters and the others into one of the most intriguing and labyrinthine hells created inside the confines of our small literature. The writing, as it stands, in these rather full notes, is crude, as are the sentiments and emphases from time to time. Apropos of the latter, there is Scann's rather sumptuous employment of Cecilia's large, long, lolling, unfettered and softly promising, but scarred and nippleless (they have been bitten off by rapists when she was an overwhelming fifteen years old) breasts. Still, one is bombarded with meaning and buoyed up by a complexity and candour of motive that moves along on the simple rollerbearings of the narrative in such a way that one regrets extremely the fact that it is an unfinished work. One wonders what the climax will yield when Thrain (yes, this is another Thrain story) meets — perhaps clashes would be a better word — with Philippa. For this meeting it is not just the simple aim of the narrative, but must also be the culmination of the socio-religious-sub-structure of the story: Thrain, the naked and naive native-Canadian force thundering up against the regressed religious nymphomaniac female principle whose guilt regarding her fearful drives demands that she train her half-wolf dog to geld her sexual partners during coition, thus "freeing" them to become, one supposes, Good Citizens, but (and this must surely be Scann's point about the "Negro", the "Indian", the slave mentality latent in all of us) incapable of love and, as Scann tells us elsewhere, victims of "a ball-less mentality." Had the story been completed and published, one might have been tempted to shout, not with just a little pride, "Authors of the world, watch out!" Still, there are other interests, other pointers, to be gleaned from this incomplete first draft: Thrain's fabled aircraft, for instance, his flying boat built with his own hands and used by him to move swiftly across the land so that it's secrets can be observed unawares. It is with this machine, Scann tells us in another set of notes, that Thrain "transports Linden piece by piece into the present century." But it is also the machine that Thrain uses to carry off Amantha, Philippa's acolyte, to be his second wife. Surely no man ever made a more bitter choice. What must her picture of the male have been? What, for that matter, must the picture of herself have been? Scann does not tell us either in these notes or elsewhere, missing, as he often does, the peaks while head-down on his knees in the valleys. But we must gather from the testimony of David and Ro at David's trial (even though the trial in the war novel is rather weak) for her "murder" that her relationship with the Thrain men was but an harmonic echo of her mother's hellish sickness. And, one asks oneself, by rather crude extension, whether Scann intended her actions to throw some kind of light onto the motivational behaviour of Canadians in general. After she passes through the lives of the Thrain's, the men are less than whole. But perhaps Scann only intends her passing to give some shape to the sentiments they all have for Erica in whose memory and for whose loss they light their candles and trim their wicks. There are flashes here, points of light. Scann rises from among the bones of his chair, shriven, his peeled eye bleak among these sudden ruins. There is no other chair, and

Mary, who could bring one, Mary, the mother of his crippled invention, is gone brassiereless and with darkening armpits, probably to peach on him. A wildness is upon this simple word-carpenter, who must forgive according to his own habit, and the devil of his mind refuses to stop offering up temptations. He feels a steady dying within him, the final temptation of them all. He takes his pen and writes to her on the wall above the lightswitch just inside the door: "Here lies an evil man who was forced all his life to do good. And whose bladder of resentment leaked constantly, uncontrollably."

From the bed, propped on three pillows, he can see only lines of ink, no words. His long-sightedness that has come with middle age is not enough. What he sees most clearly is the doorknob. Its brassy seductiveness reflects light, even hope, from a ray of sunshine beaming through a crack in the windowblind. The ancient serpent of his unconsciousness unwinds and prepares to sting. His mind fights from shadow to penumbra, a rearguard action out into the light, and twists to grab at any line of thought. Beyond the door there must be a chair. He thinks of its possible location. The bathroom is empty, except for its proper instruments. The lobby has chairs, but only grand overstuffed leather ones. He could go next door: in the closet once more he sees through into Ro's room. The twin to his broken one sits before an identical desk littered with Ro's belongings, and Mary Ann's purse. She has collected its contents and now she is rummaging in it. He puts his ear to the aperture. She is humming. He looks again. The floor in front of the basin is wet. Perhaps she has spongebathed. Her face is hidden by a long wave of hair that hangs. Her feet move, a shambles beneath her. The walls of heaven surround her and make her safe, and in her hands now are the tools of Elysium. He wonders if she would share a capsule, for old time's sake. She might remember him, and can an author ever forsake the great guide of experience? He rests on his heels, the hole in the wall a blur before him, and lets this new excitement drain away into the neglected sands at the edge of necessary knowledge. Pure pain, pleasure, prejudice, ecstacy, belief: each their own unconsciousness. And in an antipodean desert on the other side of that circle is the ultimate perversion: absolute control. He feels the slow motion of longing drag at his mind. These final temptations coil around him, bold and sure, knowing he has given in to all the petty others, whose emergency handouts distributed by the bureaucracy of the emotions to try to alleviate pockets of poverty in the soul: contingent nightmares dreamed at the point where pitch becomes catch, and elides the miracle of endurance with the times, to make endtimes. He rises, fearful of having fabricated Apocalypse. Out in the middle of the room, he feels the old serpent uncoil and drop, but his sense that endtimes are now with him is sure. And they are the continuing result of absolute possibilities, the original consummations: earth, air, fire, water, which lie inert, or decay, or become, between their own pitch and catch, something living — a simplicity of movement; a complexity of route; a bravery of intention; a simulation of chaos: vague proof of the accident of beginning, a denial of Apocalypse, and even in the end, perhaps, a refutation of the end. Scann smiles at himself. But, still, there is something wrong with contingency and its demands for circles and the game of revenge. It explains only another sentimental faith: the belief in Nil. Lucubrator Scann catches at the wreck of philosophy. Only pitch and catch float free, and that other moment between, where confusion makes the mind miss its trajectory and allows it only the whirlpool of history and biography, those ultimate and petty responses of sentient life to the personal tragedy of the future. He stands on his 8 X 9 carpet with his arms at his sides and his head raises like a dog's at the moon. He makes a dumb prayer that speaks in another tongue, and which only he could possibly answer at some point beyond discovering the key to its translation. And so the pitch of his romance culminates and he must wait and see whether he is caught again and slung back into the arms of the old faiths. He suspects his strength and fears derangement. It seems a very long time, perhaps days, since Mary closed the door and died quickly. He surveys again the room, the bed (double, empty) the blind window, the pissed basin, the locked and confessional door, the closet where the finger of his purpose now blocks the drain of his concentration, the chest-high bureau unlittered with any artifacts to prove his having civilized the place. And then the ruined chair, and the desk with his book of diversionary tactics upon it. There is nowhere to sit. He has a choice between emulating Edith Sitwell and writing in bed or joining Thomas Wolfe and standing at the bureau. He focuses on Dame Edith, an old mediaeval vulture squatting among the fetid rot of bad English and cleaning it to its bones. He sits on the bed. Churchill was a bedauthor too, a gigantic infant, a bald cherub come to lead us through acts of praise and violence, lying propped with his mother's foot-long black nipple stuck in his mouth and a stream of clerks running to him with his slant of our furious time balanced on their heads to throw into his rumbling camouflage machine. History. Scann gets up, promises Big Tom he will try to think better of him in the future if he will now move over to make room for another standee. A little better. He crosses his fingers behind his back. He approaches the bureau warily, manuscript in hand. The time has come, the deathrow padre says, just rise slowly and walk in measured steps beside me while I read to you. Concentrate on the words and be prepared for loud noises that echo. They are testing continually. It's for your own good. Only a few paces. There, now our guards will close the door. "The Lord is my shepherd, I shall not want. . . ." Will I? Will I? This foot in front of that other, one little scuff and then one more along the cement of God's *Camino Real*. Light a candle for me. It's all so exciting. For me. All this for me. Scann's pen won't write; his Canada, Eagle, Stickpen, Erasall, Medium makes an inkless dent on the lined yellow pages. Even, he thinks, the pen's a bloody censor. He tries not to shout; the passage of time, intimations of a hernia and tight shoes madden him. Slowly, with care, he selects another pen from his sportsjacket and puts it beside the dead one so that it may ingest its good spirit. Then wraps the old one in a piece of discarded manuscript and puts it in an envelope addressed to Sothebys in London, for auction sometime after the turn of the century. He is done. He is finished. He gives himself up to that place where the rhythms of his prepared endtimes keep him on his feet at the bureau, and he writes as if there is one gasp of air left, and when its chemistry is broken, only a long exhalation to oblivion will remain.

Thrain comes back from the forest and out into the impress of sun and snow near the cabin. The dead rabbit hangs white in his hand. He sits on the chopping block and holds it steady between his feet while he makes a long incision from chest to tail so that he can gut it. This is a big buck who has wintered well. Plump. He feels the legs and breast and hears the sudden chatter of a squirrel. It is later than he had imagined it could be. The time of his two-week trip has ballooned into comatose months of waiting and now it bursts. It becomes physical pain. In the warmth of the sun reflecting from the side of the cabin he hurts and tears loose. There is no possibility that he will see the lake in front of him take colour from another sunset. He throws the entrails of the rabbit in a broadcast circle around him, but he doesn't get up. There is Linden to think about. It occurs to him that Henry is dead. He is old, completely used and gone. And empty *gone* echoes with done, with the relief of completion. Everything is done that can be done. He stands up strong against the wall of the cabin, leaving the rabbit on a melting drift where he can pick it up on the way out. He opens the door. Linden is dead. Or nearly so. A matter of minutes, hours perhaps, but he will not wake again. Thrain looks around, waiting for his eyes to dilate in the dimness. Objects grow in his vision. A can for boiling water. He picks it up. The last of the beans. A twist of salt. A cloth bag in which to carry these first and last things. Then he turns and turns again in excitement and fear. His heart pumps solid in his throat. On the bunk, the old man's noseless, earless face is carved stiff in the shadows. He stands looking and waiting for something to understand or even feel about him. It seems wrong that there is nothing, and he sits on the edge of the bunk to wait for the moment when he can go. He feels Linden's stumps and arm go around him; he thinks at first he is embraced, and then he understands what has happened. He thinks, he thinks slowly: we have been at war, and it has kept us alive. He rises and slams his burden against the wall, but its grip only tightens and chokes him. Its strength is great for something that weighs now not much more than a hundred pounds. And it has a knife he didn't know about in its one hand at his throat. "Walk on out," it says. All the rest is totally understood. Thrain stands, stoops under the low ceiling and sees the rabbit lying out beyond the door. The knife pricks and prods. "Where did you get it?" Thrain asks, and knows by the sound of his own voice that he will walk, that there will be no bargaining. "I'll put you on the sled," he says, still not moving. "That'd be fine if I had a gun," old Linden says. Thrain has the bag of beans and salt in one hand, and the other is free for the rabbit. He goes out the door and crouches for it, sommersaults in the snow and grabs for the knife. His hand closes over the blade and springs open as if the steel is hot. Linden still clings. "Goddam," he shouts like shock in his ear, "how much strength do you think you got?" Thrain lies cold on the snow. It doesn't matter whether he has enough or not. It has never mattered, but there has not been a time like this before. He gets to his knees and then up, feeling all of his muscles pulling dry against Linden's weight. He goes to the chopping block for his mitts and then to the rabbit again and past the end of the cabin and across the clearing to the entrance of the trail where the sled is. He pauses and sees ahead of them the windfall where Linden had leaped over and shot the cougar. And it is only the first windfall, with bush on either side and dead logs humped with snow. Beyond are dozens, maybe fifty, and he can't remember them or the directions of the trail. "You ain't got a hope." "*I* haven't?" "I just want to watch, Thrain." Thrain sees the full picture painted with one stroke. He moves fast, like a hiccough, toward the nearest tree, twisting his body for leverage, and Linden shouts, "No, by God, I won't kill you now." Thrain stops, holding to the spruce to halt his action. He makes a promise: after this he will never walk again. After this. He watches down the trail as if it might become shorter by an effort of will. Linden uses the point of his knife to dislodge a lump of spruce gum and puts it in his mouth. "Now," he says, chewing, "let's see you go." He still has the rabbit, the beans and the can. The beauty of sanity overcomes him. He begins to walk. Only in the walking will Linden suffer. He climbs the first deadfall and jumps, as Linden had, down on the other side. He feels a kind of strength in him which he knows is false and will pass when his emotions die under the strain of moving. The trail goes downward, slopes even while rising and dipping over the narrow folds of the ground. The crust on the snow gives. He walks in holes his feet make for themselves. A great warm wind blows in the tops of the evergreens and rattles the branches of the tall birches around him as he goes. Linden's spruced breath blows around his ear and up his nose. Its wry acridness sucks at his emptying gut, and the bone-cornered weight on his back and around his waist and shoulders rub sores into his flesh. He walks and scales windfalls as if it is a chosen career, and wonders about Linden, and he thinks how so much of life is impossible, why must death also be impossible? He has not thought like this before. He considers falling; simply lying down until the disease of Linden abandons him for dead. But it is easier to keep walking, safer. He wonders about Linden again. His grip is firm, hard. It is something almost to be admired. He thinks back to the beginning of their trip, with Linden sprinting ahead, and he tries to understand what there was then that is now giving birth to this. He goes forward, the muscles in the fronts of his thighs trembling against a slope. His ears stretch their hearing through the hours for the sound of Toebroke Falls. The rabbit is a skin at his side, the beans balance it, and him. He is no longer walking. He is following himself like a man in the dark might follow a stranger he thinks knows the way. The sun is the shadows it makes, his breathing is separated noises, and his eyes are distant cameras whose pictures are ill-lit and off-focus. Yet, he stops when he sees the deer. It is wrong to stop. The rhythms of his going continue on and make vertigo in his head. The deer is beyond them in the cave of a natural clearing, the whole of the forest behind it, and it is down. Not resting. Down. A gentle thing, but animal still. It moves slowly, its eyes large and their beauty stolen by puzzlement. It rises and tries to leap, a formless struggle with direction. Then it turns to go, but its legs crumble, and the death it had hoped would come calmly when it was down assaults it as it falls. Thrain sees meat, food before him. He drops the rabbit and reaches for his knife, and is a fool. He has always had his knife to answer the one at his throat. He takes it out and holds it in front of him, forgetting the deer and his weakness. "We're even, Linden," he says. Linden's voice is calm. "Mine's where it should be, and yours is only in your hand. Are you going to die now, or do you want to walk a little farther?" "It's you who's dying," Thrain says. "Not by that knife and you know it." "You're getting weak, Linden, losing your grip. I can feel it." "Thrain, I can cut your head off right now and there's enough meat lying over there to keep me 'til I can crawl out and take the canoe home." Thrain looks again at the deer. "It's dead of some disease." "A little fire'll fix that. Use that knife of yours and get us a steak or two." "Then let go," Thrain says and shrugs at Linden's weight. But there is no answer. He holds to a tree and forces a leg forward. The extra strength in the one that carries his clubbed foot holds him. The other leg follows. It is a rest to crouch beside the deer, skin a leg and cut meat for them. His muscles cease their twitching. Linden clings. It is good to feel his discomfort, but he can only hope for a complaint. He works in silence and then rises again with the rabbit and the dripping venison in one hand and the bag and can in the other. "Where'll we eat it?" he asks, surprised at his deference. "The falls." "That's a long way." He listens for the run of the creek. It's there, if the noise he hears isn't the breeze above them in the tops of the spruce and firs. He begins again to walk, now in pain and using his will for the first time as a prod. Linden will not get down. Thrain is strung like a bead on a long string over chaos. He walks and they cross the creek where he had fallen months ago. He is careful this time. The trail moves now in a great arc, over and down, through bigger timber that is shedding its snow like footfalls near them. His legs hold, his feet go past pain to a kind of cool numbness. Linden clings like a three-clawed cat, the stump of his leg and the knife prodding behind and before. The noise of the falls spreads until it surrounds them. Linden will not let go. Perhaps he can't now, but Thrain suspects he does not know how to suffer. Or is past it now, and simply being alive is the last revenge. He feels a sentiment rise like a bubble up through his own pain, but he does not prick it as he gathers deadfall for a fire, and stones from the exposed waters of the creek above the falls on which to cook the rabbit. In the tin he boils some beans. Linden is quiet, almost a dead weight on him. He lies in the snow away from the fire to rest, and smiles at the sight they must be, an unnatural double-humped animal, or a man with his buggering past locked onto his backside. Perhaps he sleeps. He hopes that Linden falls asleep, and he dreams of walking light without him, gliding down the steep ridge they must negotiate after they eat and begin the rest of their trip. But he is prodded by Linden, who must by now be feeling the assaults of hope. The rabbit is cooked badly, the beans are only hot. Linden eats in his ear, slobbering as he always does. Thrain's shoulder is wet with beanjuice and rabbit grease. But the damp sickness of hunger in him is cured and he moves continually to keep his muscles from locking. They stand: he knows it is "they" now and not just him: a frail construction that can't bear the anchoring filaments of faith or trust — and at the edge of their descent he looks back at Linden for the first time since the cabin. There are only eyes in the slit face; they measure, and behind the measuring is a hard colourless fear. "You think we're going to make it?" Thrain asks. "We? Without you I could hop it from here," and Linden looks up and away. "How are you in the dark?" The sun is going down. Thrain stands as if waiting for that final act to stop. "We can sleep through it." Linden's knife becomes a little alive. "Not in the cold. Move." Thrain backs down most of the steep slope, holding dry berry bushes and alder branches when he can, forcing his feet into always more solid snow. At the bottom, the snow is wet, without its old crust, and it is slippery. The muscles in his groin pull and burn, and he must bend down under Linden's weight to balance their forward motion. Often he must go down, pain in his back forcing him to lie and stretch until he can get up again. The dark comes slower than he had expected. On the flats beside the Bear River there is a long moment of twilight. Linden begins to sing in a foreign language. Thrain stops, unsure, and then he laughs as loud as Linden sings, and the old man's weight is not as heavy as it used to be. He has him now. Hope has geysered up anticipation in old Henry. He runs suddenly into a tree, swinging Linden against it. Knife and man fall to the ground, and Thrain stumbles, his knees buckle oddly as if he is carrying more weight than before. Yet, he runs somehow, laughing still, and then he stops both running and laughing in order to hear Linden's cry. It comes. No words. A rage, a bellow that knocks Thrain to the ground in an ecstasy. He listens, and then listens again to its echoes, and then with a terrible acuteness he hears the silence, beyond which he finds strength to get up and run back to the bundle on the ground. He stands above it, breathing as if he had come a mile. Linden says: "Jesus, man, you're not going to leave me?" Thrain doesn't have to ask to hear it again. Linden repeats himself, and throws his knife into the Bear. Finally, Thrain gathers some words: "It must have been a long winter for you, Henry." He utters them, and hears them come gentle, what he had meant to say boiled away by the hot rave within him. "Say this, Henry: Thrain you've saved me. I owe you my life." He listens. Linden speaks: "More than that, Thrain, more than that." He kneels by Linden and holds his stump arm. "No, say it right. It's not more than that you pile of shit. I only saved your life and that's all you owe me." "All right," Linden says, and repeats the words. "But the other I said had to do with you, not me." "No last words, goddamn you, Henry. I'm the one with the last words. I'm free now to carry you or not, however I will." "But you'll carry me." Thrain stands again, wondering now whether he has made a decision before. It doesn't matter. The war is over and he feels sorrow. And like all wars, it has ended in the middle of things with only the fighting stopped. He begins again, without promulgating the decision, resuming his dumb donkey movements down the trail with Linden on his back. Darkness has all but arrived. The snow is a pale slippery plate he walks across into the black beyond. Linden does know the way, and he tries to ride lightly, but it is no less painful than before. And it is slow, this walking with only physical tension to hold his muscles true. A mile is three thousand steps, and he runs into trees and is hung up in blinding bushes, and is helpless against the wall of a deadfall, even with Linden saying and saying the way to go. The wind has calmed. The woods make no noises loud enough to be heard above the rumbling of the Bear. He walks and then rests, with Linden nervous off his back. They go right, away from the Bear, and through a long mile of alder and cottonwood that Thrain has no memory of, and then they are at Linden's river. Safe. Not a miracle. Simple attrition against space. Here there is a wind, small and cold, running down the white surface of the river. It is frozen still. In the narrow moonlight they can see a kind of vastness before them of heaved-up ice. It takes some time to understand that it is not the night that is hiding their escape, but it is the river that is so clogged that its jungle has overcome the darkness to reveal itself to them. Thrain can't think, or stand still. He finds the canoe, an ovoid of half-melted ice. Somehow he had expected it to be ready to sail. He chips at it with his knife and manages to make a chunk fall off near the bow. A half-day's work and no water to paddle it in. It occurs to him that he has come this far, packed this much, simply to die. He collects alder branches and builds a fire, cuts the venison into squares and roasts them on sharp sticks. They feed. Linden chooses to say nothing. The moon climbs higher, the shadows of the piled-up ice are not so long. "How are you about ice, Henry?" "I never come out this time of year." "So, now what?" "Keep moving. There's a stump ranch over on the other side somewhere, and about four miles back through the bush is the railway grade." "I'd need corked boots to get up and down all that ice." Linden chews venison, and in the firelight his frosty eyes blink slowly. "What we need to do is not die now," he says. He looks at Thrain and laughs as if he's just received permission. "Anyway, I don't want to go not trying," and he heaves with his one hand the end of an alder log into the fire. "Let's leave it burning bright in case some damn fool sees it. Maybe they'll meet us over there. Who knows?" And they begin, although Thrain can see no real reason why. As far as the river is all he'd planned for and neither his will nor his muscles can stand much more. He might make it alone. He thinks about that. From the shore there is a slope down to river ice proper. Thrain slides first, and turns to catch Linden. Then they couple once more and in the moonlight Thrain searches for hand and footholds between the slabs of ice. The icescape before him looks like a blown-up graveyard, a jumble of wrecked markers, cold and pale against the darkness ahead. Still, every now and then, they break out into a small prairie of level ice the size of a small ship's poopdeck and they rest, Linden down on his one leg like a heron, and Thrain exploring for crevasses and listening for the sound of naked running water. Behind them, the light of their fire is gone, and in front to guide them, nothing. They simply travel, Linden silent, Thrain cursing. They go up for a while, slipping and falling and bruising, and then they stare almost too quickly into open water that carries with it pans of ice. There is a long moment of realisation. It breaks slowly. Thrain looks back toward the canoe and then down into the water again. "She's always open somewheres," Linden says. "Boils up even in the coldest weather." "But this is spring," Thrain says. He can see nothing now but the whiteness of his breath. He lies still on the ice and feels himself going to sleep. "Thrain," Linden says, touching him, "I'd say she hasn't been open here more'n a little while. See above there? We can cross." Thrain looks left beyond the steam of his breath, and then begins to crawl, leaving Linden to do the same. It is a relief to be free of him. The ice needles him awake. At the ice bridge across the running water, he feels forward with his hands, looking at the same time upstream. There is open water there too. They both slide out onto suspended ice. It is perhaps twenty yards to the other side. When it breaks it goes softly at first, like a liner launching, and then fast and inevitable. Thrain comes to his feet to jump and sees Linden crumple in the middle of the floating ice. Then it is too late. The sides of the pan scrape the hard edges of the open stream, break, float free. Almost half of their raft is gone by the time they pass the point where they had first seen the water. Even if he ran and jumped now he'd never make it. "Sit in the goddamned middle," Linden shouts as if he is trying to be heard over the churn of engines. But their motion is silent and fast. Thrain moves carefully over the rotting ice and sits close to Linden. "How long?" Linden computes, his ruined face a horror in the moonlight. "This is a twelve, thirteen mile an hour river. Four hours, maybe." Another chunk breaks away. Thrain stands up. "Get on my back," he says, reaching for Linden's good hand. "Next time it goes close to the edge we'll get off." But Linden doesn't move. "Thrain," he says, "you can't go to the edge because when you get there it won't be the edge any more, it'll be broke off, and the shore'll be as far away as it ever was. Just sit here where it's thickest." His voice stops. Thrain turns. The channel is getting wider as they go. It seems very far to the shore. "Sit and what?" he asks. Linden's mouth works until it is a hairy moonlit doughnut and Thrain knows what he is thinking about saying. They bump a smaller pan and more of their own floats away. The ice-raft is longer than it is wide. "Sit down," Linden says. "The least we move, the safer we'll be." Thrain sits beside him and laughs. "I said I'd never walk again, Henry. I swore it up there this side of the cabin with you on my back. I said when this is all over I'll never walk again, and you're off my back and I'm not walking." Linden's face grins. "Well, it's nice you asked for it." Thrain shifts his position on the ice. They may freeze. He wonders at the endurance of Linden sitting there before him like a limbless beggar on a white pavement. In the moonlight he can see the shore moving backwards, piled-up slabs of white ice and black stands of timber making indifferent patterns against further darkness. The moon is nearly before them now and setting in the southwest, and above it more indecipherable patterns made by the stars. He sits silent for a long time, looking at objects but trying to discover words that he can say to Linden to make this real. He begins where he doesn't want to. "You scared?" The old trapper shifts and coughs. "Yes." "That's good to know. I never figured it'd occur to you." "Just when I need to be. When there's nothing else to do." The channel they are going down is growing still wider, and the water tearing the ice at its edge is vicious. Their pan begins, finally, to turn end for end, knocked by other chunks of ice and grabbed by cross-currents in the water. Both bow and stern break off, and they sit on a raft not more than twenty-five feet across. Thrain thinks of David's birth in the paddlewheeler going end for end down the rapids thirty miles east of here. He says Erica's name out loud. Their pan dips and sways in a whirlpool and is swept around a shallow curve in the channel. "Christ," he says, and feels Linden hold onto him for balance. "It seems like one long accident that won't stop happening." Linden is still holding on to him, and is up on his one knee watching ahead. The channel is directly into the low moon now, and they can see nearly a mile down the straight gut of the river. It is a jigsaw puzzle of ice jumbling on into the distance. "If it jams we ain't got a hope," Linden says. "You jump if you can." "And leave you," Thrain says, "with a chance of making it? To hell with you, Linden, I'm not getting off." "I didn't say now, goddamn it. If you have to." He sits again, folding his one unnaturally long leg beneath him. "You don't deserve better'n you get, Thrain. This ain't no accident. You spent your whole life getting here. You never know what the hell's happening to you, just what you think's going to happen. Ain't that so? You're here now, and that's a fact. You might as well enjoy the scenery. I'll tell you when to jump and you will. You're a jumper, Thrain, it's in your nature." And Linden lies full out on the ice, his head on his half-empty sleeve. Thrain knows he is alone now: his months with Linden have taught him this much at least. Silence is the weapon he's used since the beginning, and his grin which even a knife hadn't been able to fix. "I won't jump, but I might throw you," Thrain says, and stands as if on watch. The ice pan begins to turn again on its axis, slowly, as the current hurries it along the edge of the channel. It touches, turns, jams against immoveable ice, breaks another fraction of itself off, which disappears into the tug of the current. It turns again, and nearly a third of their island severs, gradually separates from them. Their weight tips the pan. Thrain skids to his knees and crawls up the delicate slope to the farther side of Linden. He shouts at the old man: Linden rolls up toward Thrain. They make a balance together. By a process of elimination they have found where the ice is thickest: at the southern edge. Linden lies on his stomach and looks downstream. Thrain watches too: the clutter ahead of them is perhaps no thicker than before. The real danger is that the frozen cake they are on will capsize and float on its other surface for a while. Occasionally, as they watch, smaller pans upend at the edge of the current and dive like sinking ships to the bottom. The moon goes under. Clouds cross the sky and become solid. When the moon was up they had come to know their enemies and now the dark is honestly frightening. Thrain believes that Linden doesn't care. It is something to think about instead of counting minutes. He moves to see the old man better. He might be asleep with his chin on his mitt. He doesn't care. He should understand what it is to care. Ahead is blackness, a blank. They crash again and spin. A small piece of their ice drifts away, but then there is a crash beside them. Thrain rises up to see better. A pan surfaces whitely, pushing them with its bow-wave out into the centre of the current. The two pans float in tandem. Thrain stoops and picks up Linden by his collar and rawhide belt and heaves him as far as he can. Solid ice receives him. He crashes, a wingless bird on the other pan. It tips, rights itself and continues to float. Thrain breathes again. Linden crawls as if he is going up a cliff to the centre of his new pan and sits holding a bruised shoulder. They are not ten feet apart. Thrain watches, waiting for his own answer to his decision. It comes: a fine gladness. Their lot is separate. "Who gets the short stick, Henry?" It's suddenly easy to laugh, to invent a game: no guns, no knives, no physical touching, no wily woodcraft. Just chance. He feels safe. "Now," he shouts, not needing to, "let whoever gets there tell the story and see if anyone believes it." Quietly, Linden replies, "You got a couple of extra things going for you." "Crawling's as good as walking now." "You ain't the one who can only crawl." "You taught me, Henry: no quarter." "That's only when you got something to fight, Thrain." "You've been asking for one last one ever since we met." Linden is drifting away in the rip of the current. They watch in silence, the darkness dimming them each to each. Then Linden is gone, and Thrain goes down on his knees and watches out into the nothing around him. In this new dimensionless place he has to put his hands down on the ice in front of him to save his balance. The shapes he sees are only behind his eyes. He lies down to try to stop the sensation of falling. The pan is unstable. It rides the current like a chip now, and from minute to minute he waits for the soft effervescent sound of another chunk of his raft dropping off into the water. He cannot relax his muscles: they wait, permanently tense, for the collision with either floating or solid ice. Then it occurs to him that he doesn't know where he is going. Or, he knows a place where he wants to go, but has no way of recognizing it if he happens to get there. Nor is there a game to be played any more. Linden is not playing it. He is either close or he isn't. The difference is small: he is silent. Only the river runs its octaves of noise from a high suck to a vibrating boom, punctuated always by long descending cracks of river ice breaking up. The din of the unseen is chaos, and it forces his mind open. He wants to hear from himself. "I am moving," he says aloud and is embarrassed by the sound of his voice. He listens for Linden's laughter and is relieved when it doesn't come. His ice-raft bumps and shudders. No, he, himself, is not moving; just the pan of ice moves through the dark. Where he is is unknowable, except that it is no one place because of where he is. The circle closes, swallows him. There is a wind against the back of his neck. "Linden," he says without force. "Linden?" He is out there on the river somewhere. Thrain moves around the points of the compass saying his name. But above the noise of the river there is only a special kind of silence that he had thought ordinary before. "Linden," he says sure he is near and only disciplining him with silence, "Linden, you're going to know when we get there, even in the dark. Now, look, you *say*. It can't be far now." He listens, stands up in a confused blackness and tries once more to see. There are useless shapes. He is careful not to shift his feet. If he moves it might be to where the ice is thin, or over the side altogether. He shouts once as loud as he can, and listens. He thinks he hears a reply. The fear that he may have heard a voice, and therefore can hope, or that it may have only been in his mind, and therefore cannot hope, silences him. He lies down and feels with his fingers through the hide of his mitts for roughnesses to hold to. For a long time he floats and falls, floats and falls, and feels himself jerked up again. His mind is as big as the dark around it. Nothing escapes his notice: a more intense dip, a soft crash and a falling away of more supporting ice, a rise or fall in the noise the river makes, the ultimate understanding that as the pan becomes smaller its ability to float must decrease in absolute proportion. He tries for Linden again. It is no comfort. And then he understands that he has an alternative. He can get off. He can roll once, or perhaps twice, and become his own pan for the moments the river will let him. Or he can stand and walk off. He can crawl. There are many ways. Two steps forward and one back. A dance until the pan collapses around him. He is free to choose. Why only this for him? Linden, he knows, is safe, this is his river and it will not harm him. His own failure, during the winter, to earn that gift, or another as valuable confuses the dark again. He rides the small greyness beneath him and feels it ship water and begin to buck in the current. "Linden," he says again without thinking, "tell me to jump now and I will." The faintness of his voice is a measure of the rising noise of the river. He raises his head. The ice he is on slopes up and shudders. Thrain knows it is turning: the wind is on his neck and then his ear and then his face. Alternatives are cancelled. The thing he is riding is trying to shake him free. The pan is sinking under his weight. He gets to his hands and knees and feels the wind blowing hard behind him. Below is a solid edge of grey. Two things: the water is flowing in a different direction and the ice is packing. He has stopped going forward. His pan is being ground to slush. From a distance he hears Linden's voice, tattered by the wind, calling him. His feet are wet and he moves. What he steps on sinks, and he begins to run toward the sound of his name, his feet finding, holding, submerging and his arms making a kind of balance above. Nothing is firm enough to stand on. He slips and goes down to his waist. His hands find an edge of ice to hold to and the current swings his legs and tries to suck him under. He lets go because he has to, and the water twists him and slams his chest against a solid ledge that his hands can grab. He is sweating. The water on his face and in his eyes is his own. He is jacknifed around the edge of a pan and his legs flutter like bunting beneath the water — which means the ice is not moving. He knows that he is shouting and laughing. Maybe Linden is doing it too. He tries to listen but his own voice roars words into his ears as if it is the exhaust of a runaway engine. The water rises over the curve of his buttocks and he feels it winning. Then it flows between his clothes and his skin. His pants and his moccasins loosen and are dragged off. In that moment, as if the river has forgotten his actual flesh, he feels light and free and he heaves himself up onto a solid ledge. He stands and is scalded by the touch of the ice on his bare feet. His voice is shouting once more and he tries to stop its bark to listen for Linden. Without him there is no direction, and his fate each time he has left the old man has only been circles. Even a curve right now might break his luck. He waits, calls again, and hears Linden reply, and his held breath begins to sob. He takes a step. The toes of his good foot grab at sharp pebbles of ice but he begins to fall. He crouches and understands that he must go, if he is to go at all, on all fours. He tries to make his mitted hands take his weight and find moments of traction. The pack is solid. He goes forward, downwind, between upended pans of ice, keeping what he can hear of Trapper Linden's voice ahead of him. The sound of the river is beneath him now: and seems more dangerous than before. His feet stop feeling. His skin shrivels to numbness. His hands find and hold quickly as if they suddenly understand a new skill. He knows he is hurting himself. The bunch of his clubbed foot poles him along too fast, and he falls down between slabs of ice, is wedged and cries out for help. "I can't move," he tells Linden. "I'm stuck." He hears a voice far away. "Henry," he says, "Henry, I'm done for." He feels himself freezing. "Hurry, Henry," he calls as if to a pet dog. But Linden isn't coming, and he can't wait to think how to make him understand. While there is feeling in his naked legs he must try to move them. He braces his arms against the wall of ice in front of him and forces his back onto the one behind him. He can lift his feet free. He hangs, turns his hips, spreads his knees and legs against the walls of ice, shifts his body around quick so that his shoulders are holding him up and he begins to climb with mitts and toes, shouting again, making calls as if he is a man hammering heavy steel fast. He rises one hunch at a time out of the crevice. He doesn't know what he is doing to himself, only what he is not. There may be light above him now, but his head hangs down between his shoulders as he heaves and he can't be sure of it. As he goes, the depth he is making below him becomes more and more terrifying. A minute before he had thought he could never be worse off. Now his progress upward is both salvation and the enemy. He holds with his elbows and forces his hands high. On his left there is a depression. It might be the top. He twists his head around to see. It is only a ledge. But he can see the top, an edge blacker than the space beyond. He turns again, forces his feet up as high as they will go and levers his back up the ice behind him. At the ledge he puts his arms and hands behind him and forces himself forward. He stands free, head and shoulders out into the wind again. There is small light. He can see that his mitts are torn, and the ends of his fingers are exposed. He rises slowly over the edge and crouches, refusing the temptation to find out how hurt he is. He may never move again. There might be another hole in the grinding ice only a foot away. The wind gusts against him and then stops. Into the dead air he shouts Linden's name. The wind rises again before he can hear a reply. Thrain curses. Then he looks left and sees the dim outlines of the bridge across the water where the Swifter and the Linden meet. The direction he is facing, then, is the bank of the river. The bluff above him is a black shape in the slowly strengthening light. He feels forward with his hands along the beaded ice. He has crouched too long. The muscles of his legs and bare haunches feel locked. He falls onto his elbows and the side of his face. The pain makes him angry, and he moves against it, crying and shouting. The moment forces progress. He rises once more to a crouch and his mind directs his hands and then his feet to begin to carry him toward the bluff. It rises in front of him, taller and taller. He ignores the implications. On a sheet of ice that juts out from the edge of the water, he stands. It holds him. In the better light he can see it is smooth. He begins to walk, spastic on feet he knows leave bloody footprints behind him. He reaches land. It is flat against his face and stands five times his height above him. He hangs on and looks toward the bridge. It seems very far away. He tries to think whether it should be. He turns his head to look behind him. It is only dark there. He might have to go all the way to the bridge. Thrain's muscles are beginning to go slack now, and his guts roll gas like pebbles around in them. He has to move. He counts his steps, leaning against the cliff, and at eighteen the fall of the bluff fades away. He falls and hears himself begin to scream. He tries not to. What he is holding to is a step cut into the hard clay. He looks up. There must be an end. He sees Linden's fence. He doesn't wait to think. He stands, with all the strength he has, and takes a step. The foot doesn't rise high enough. He trips and crawls once more. But it is up. He hears his breath again, hollow across the drums of his ears. Then there is another sound. He thinks it is an animal coming toward the fence above him. He grabs for the bottom railing and waits, looking up. The light waxes, perhaps suddenly. He doesn't know. The animal is Linden. He can see his grin. "Jumped by yourself." Linden begins to laugh. "Made it up here bare-assed too. By God, she really got to you. Lucky it's spring or you'd be cold." Seeing Linden, hearing him, Thrain begins to laugh too. It is a peculiar sound that turns sour in the still-gusting wind. He pulls himself up and through the fence, rising all the time until he is beside Trapper Linden and staring into his carved face. He can feel his body shiver, his skin shrink and then go warm. "You son of a bitch," he says, "you didn't holler me in." "Careful," Linden says, "we ain't either one of us in top shape." But Thrain keeps raising one arm and then the other, understanding that it is reasonable now to be angry and that his strength has returned. Even his feet feel easy in the snow. He watches Linden, sees him standing on one leg and leaning on the fence, and then he smashes both fists against the old man's head, but he doesn't fall. "When I shout you answer," he tells him as loud as he can. "Linden," he yells into his face. The light from the dawn is clear; he can see Linden's eyes stare back. Thrain remembers everything about the winter, everything necessary. He has been on his own since they crossed the creek above Toebroke Falls, going in. He looks away toward the cabin and beyond it. "Without you, I'd be home." He turns again. Linden is going down of his own accord. The movement makes Thrain unsure of his own balance. He grabs with his hands at the railing, but he goes down too. The crusted snow breaks beneath him, hurting him and keeping him conscious. From this angle he can see smoke rising from the cabin's chimney up into a grey-blue sky. He is not going to make it. Fifty feet. With what struggle there is left in him, he tries to force himself upright. Linden is all there is to hold on to. He thinks he can smell the smoke now. It is that close. His mind drifts beyond his floundering. He thinks Linden still may be on his back. Another transfer has been made. He tries to throw him off, but then he is lifted up, and he understands that it is Linden who is doing it. That is right, proper. Everything else that has happened has been impossible. The sting of rotting snow is no longer on his skin. All of his muscles stop working, even his breathing. The struggle is forced inside himself and it is against blackness, against wanting it. "Thrain?" The voice is not Linden's, but it is familiar. A surprise. He manages a breath, and sees. He is in Ole's arms. "You come back?" Ole's voice hardly reaches him. Thrain takes another breath, and then another. Ole is turning Linden with his foot. Thrain watches. Soon he is lying face up in the snow. And now Ole is crouching down. Thrain says: "Take me in." Perhaps he hasn't spoken. Ole doesn't move. "Get me in," Thrain says. "Yeah," Ole says, "but I think that was a lot of work for nothing. He's dead, ain't he?" Thrain, as if he had been going somewhere, stops. He looks down on Linden lying half-there and surrounded by broken snow. Ole says, "You packed him down the river?" His voice doesn't believe. "Linden," Thrain says. Ole's body hunched over him is holding and warming him. The old man doesn't reply. It doesn't mean he's dead. "Put me down," Thrain says. Ole is touching the noseless face with his hands. "No, you done enough already." He stands and goes quick across the yard. Thrain has no struggle in him, and no sense of peace, either. "He isn't dead," he tells Ole. He believes it, now that he knows it's happened. Inside the door a lantern burns on the table; the fire is high and hot. The room is light, lighter than he's seen one since he left home, but his own light is nearly gone. Ole puts him down carefully on the bed and covers him with blankets. There is somebody else sleeping beside him. It takes moments of concentration to see that it is Erica. She has come here to wait for him. He can't move now, and he tries to think how to wake her with only his presence, but his eyes close, and when he opens them again he is near the wall, where Erica had been. He feels caught, held, even suspended as if only his brain is able to work and the rest of him is inert. He is on his back staring at the place where the ceiling meets the rise of the log wall. He has never been here before, but it doesn't look like Linden's place. It is clean. The air he breathes smells only of earth and old timber and water, the keen damp smell of melting snow. There is sound too. Above Toebroke Falls at the Water Lake cabin (he begins to remember) there was silence. The noise here is the river going by, tearing itself open and breaking up. Thrain moves his hands beneath the blankets. They still have their mitts on them. The last moments of his time on the ice come back to him, but a weakness inside of himself cannot stand the force of the memory. His guts begin to tremble. But he has started to think and there is no way of stopping. It is a kind of violence he hasn't experienced before. His mind makes scenes of himself going toward death, and then it tries to destroy them. They are made of tough fabrics. He cries out with the effort. The cougar falls limp across his body. The wolverine chews at his arm. The deer runs across his chest and dies staring at him. Linden is on his back and the muscles in his legs and shoulders bunch and pain. "He's coming round," a quiet voice says. It isn't Erica's. He tries to turn his head but only his eyes will shift. Currie is standing near the other side of the bed; Ole is sitting on the bench at the table. The door is open, the fire is still burning and the light from each affects the other. Everything has a hard shadowless edge; even their faces would hurt him if he had to touch them. Then he sees Linden. He is lying beside him. His hair is frost above the scar where an ear should be. There is no profile. Just a forehead and a beard. The stumps of his arm and his leg have been laid bare. Currie looks down at them. Thrain wants there to be an end to it ."Take me home," he says. Currie shakes his head. "I don't think we'd better risk it. Not yet." Thrain struggles to sit up, but there is only struggle. Nothing happens. "I'm down," he says to Currie, "you and Ole can move me." Currie covers Linden and comes around the bed. He sits and brings Thrain's wrist out from under the blankets. There isn't a mitt on his hand. His fingers are bandaged. Currie feels for the pulse. "You're a strong one, Thrain. No one else could've done it." "I wish," Thrain says, but Currie tells him, "You needn't've brought him out. We'd have believed you didn't kill him." Thrain feels his voice failing him. He forces it. "I chose to." Currie's eyes are questions. "He must've been more than half-dead when you started." Thrain doesn't answer. He manages to roll his head so he can see Linden again, but he is covered with the blanket. "Tell me," Currie says, "do you remember?" Thrain thinks. Images shift, separate. He looks beyond Linden out through the door. He sees the fence, cottonwoods beyond, and beyond them the high clay cuts where the two rivers turn south to the sea. "Who the hell wants to remember? I got it in me now." "What?" "The best way to kill a man is not to give a damn about him one way or another. It's the only way." Currie doesn't answer. He gets up and goes around the bed and says to Ole, "It's too soon for him to talk." Then he turns to Linden again and takes the blanket from his face. Ole stands too, looking down. His face is white, as if he is exhausted, Thrain thinks, or sick, or both. Currie says, "You brought another box?" Ole nods. He doesn't seem to want to talk. Currie doesn't drop the blanket. "He's not very pretty. Thrain, did you have to do that to his face?" Thrain feels himself touched for the first time since he's been back. "You weren't there, Currie," he says. He is shouting again. Everything about Linden makes him want to shout. And yet the violence is gone. He lives with echoes. "It's not usual," Currie says mildly, "but I suppose you didn't know." "I knew," Thrain tells him. "I knew." And Ole interrupts: "It don't make any difference." His voice is high. "We buried enough now so nothing makes any difference." He takes the blanket out of Currie's hand and wraps it around Linden. Then he lifts him from the bed in his arms. "We had the flu here, Thrain," he says. "Maybe a hundred died. You missed that anyway." "Hush," Currie says. "Just let him get well. Go on, I'll stay till you get back." Thrain looks at them looking at each other. Erica's been gone a long time. "Where is she?" he asks. "At the hotel," Currie says, but it is Ole Thrain sees begin to tremble as if the load he's carrying is inside him and not in his arms. The skin of his face blotches with colour. "Godamn," he cries. "Oh godamn," and he sits on the bench with Linden across his knees, holding him like a baby. Currie says, very calm, "Get out of here, Ole." Thrain stops watching. It isn't finished. Nothing's finished and he's not ready to go on. He knows Ole stands again. The light changes. Perhaps he's at the door taking Linden away. It is only a short distance from here to there, but it is a line he cannot walk. For fear and for knowing. There is a lot of country to travel before anything more is possible. "She's at the hotel," he listens to himself say, "and I'm here." "For a while," Currie says. He hears only one more curse, fading, as Ole goes out the door.

EDITORIAL INSIGHTS. Four: moments of solemnity. Scann holds Thrain complete in his mind while he stands stiff in front of the bureau where his hand, pen and manuscript lie inert. His muscles are sore; his feet are swollen in his shoes; his head floats tethered lightly somewhere above his shoulders, a thing apart. He thinks for a moment that he is home-free, but as with all homecomings the sense of things being at rest is false. There is a tension in him, and in the room. He might in fact be on Linden's river with the ice shattering and his handhold on existence unsure. He has never been in this space before, inside this time where what has been made runs out and takes form all at once. What has been a tangle of visions has become a single strand. He looks down on Thrain unconscious. It is a serious moment. There are many ways to inherit a country. Scann gathers the pages of his book together and sits on the bed with them resting on his knees. But he is not ready for them yet. He wishes a time of unconsciousness for himself. At least Thrain had that. But there is only rigidity in Scann, and he can feel beneath his skin the motor of his days at Linden House labour and ping against the tiny late spark of his soul. He stands again and places the manuscript carefully on the bureau. He feels caught out; or perhaps found in: the policemen of his own judgment are loud at the doors of his mind. He musters defenses. But they are overwhelmed by this simple standing upright. The effort forces his heart to throb, his tender tooth to pain in time with his blood's beat. The light in the room goes dim. He moves across the carpet and around his bed to the window. He breaks the seal of the blind and looks out. There is a fine rain falling. The streetlight at the corner has a suggestion of a halo. An umbrella passes. He wonders who she is. If he could see her face he would know her name. There is comfort in that. He waits. Monday night. There is no one else. The cement below is black with water. It reflects the streetlight. He goes from the window to the basin and washes his hands. He is surprised to see how dirty the water is when he is finished. He looks in the mirror, and his face is empty, quiet. It might be an old portrait suddenly found and not yet restored. He smiles. It is a failure. If this moment were real life this might be the cue for a soliloquy, but it is only closet drama staged for himself. He grins. Linden knew how to grin. Thrain didn't. Neither does he. His teeth are bad, but not bad enough. He remembers that Linden cured toothache by plunging a red-hot needle into the offending hole. The thought stops the pain in George's tooth. He leans forward, soaps his face, rinses it under the clear run of the tap and then dries it. A good Linden grin is a straight line. *Via Dolorosas* are straight lines also. There is never any mention of them circling. He drops the towel in the basin and gathers what is his in the room. It fills one compartment of his briefcase. Then he goes to the bureau for the manuscript. The used leaves of the big compact pad he had brought with him are loose and thick. They feel, godamn it, good in his hand. He leans against the bureau and doesn't feel the protection of audacity. The words on the green-lined pages shelter Thrain, but they expose Scann. He floats in generative silence. Images gather and refuse dismissal. He sits carefully in the plastic, formfitting swivel chair and watches t/v interviewer Farstead. It is easier than looking at the cameras. They are hooded birds with tumescent beaks, and when one of them preys it affects a red running sore in the middle of its forehead.

"It finishes very abruptly. Is this a technique, or does the story just not end?" Farstead has his fashionable clipboard on his knee which a script assistant has given him. All the questions are there. The easy ones. This boy with a head shaped like a man's lounges sidewise in his chair facing Scann, half his ass and all of his profile to the cameras. "There are no endings," Scann says. "Ends of worlds are not our business. Only bad writers go in for endings. Or beginnings. Beginnings are gardens. Endings are revelations, and apocalypses are for the weary of mind." His interlocutor smiles coolly. "Really?" he says. "How very interesting." Scann watches him reveal what he is thinking.

In solid print — where it really counts — the next morning: "There are t/v interviewers and t/v interviewers, and in case you hadn't noticed, Robin Farstead is becoming one of the best. Last night on *Program* he put one of those ageing neophyte authors, whose name I didn't catch, through enough hoops to last a lifetime."

A fine hard line of pain defines absolutely the center of his being just three teeth back in the row of molars along his left jaw. Complete integration: there is only one Scann. He stands in the centre of his room at Linden House visionless and unable to breathe or move. The tooth is a cold flame in his mouth. He might be unconscious, except it is not that but rather intense concentration. He leans forward as if into a wind and his hand rises up toward his open mouth. He reaches in with thumb and forefinger and holds the tooth firm. He is sure it is moving. The alarm in the nerve subsides, stabs hard again. He begins to moan, cry out. He walks around the wreck of his chair and opens the door. The pain stops as it had started, suddenly. The tooth is simply tender again. He stands uncertain looking out into the hallway where blue roses bloom quietly and the air he breathes is different. It occurs to him that he is free to leave now. Carefully, he turns and goes to the closet for his war correspondent's raincoat. He shrugs it on gently and stares up at the narrow triangle of the open transom. That's where fiction culminates. He is calm again. His mind can link up thoughts. His view of himself comes into focus once more. There is a little laughter in him, the kind that comes when one has thieved successfully. He wants to share it. The phone is by the door. He should call Marion and tell her he is back. Perhaps even confess, let her in on the joke. He lifts the instrument from its cradle and puts it to his ear. Someone asks a question. He is not ready for it, but he is glad things are normal out there. He holds the phone and stares at it as if he might see who is speaking and then hangs up. He steps out into the hallway, standing on the roses, and shuts the door behind him. Perhaps shutting it jars the nerve in his tooth. He forces his tongue against the pain. He is in the lobby before he remembers that he has not brought his briefcase or the manuscript.

"Amory," Alderman Brixton Potter says from his chair by the window. Scann sees the old man through a haze. His eyes have begun to water. "Can you give me a moment?" Potter asks. "I suppose you know it's Thrain's eightieth birthday? You didn't do a damned thing about him in that anniversary issue of yours."

"His birthday's in November," Scann says, and puts his tongue back hard against the tooth.

"Tonight," Brixton says, as if he's at a council meeting. "Not that he's allowing a celebration, but he deserves a picture and a story. We can't let our pioneers just fade away." He stops. "What's the matter, Amory? You look done in."

"It's this tooth. I have this tooth," Scann says. "I'm on my way to George Dockerly's to have it looked at."

Potter gets up. Scann wishes he wouldn't. Now that he knows he's going to George's he feels better. He begins to move away.

"Sorry," Brixton says. "I'd drive you but my car's not here."

"I'll get Crawley to taxi me." He pushes out the door while Brixton Potter is saying, "Had mine out when I was twenty, right after the first war. Best thing I ever did." Scann goes out into the street, but there isn't a taxi there. He begins to walk south and then west through the fine spring rain, holding his head over to one side in a position where the pain is least intense. The sharpness has gone from it. He holds his tongue gentle against it and walks lightly hoping not to disturb the savage nerve. He is among hedges and goes along straight streets with wide boulevards lined with planted birches. In one of the pockets of his raincoat there is a notebook and in the other a copy-pencil. He holds them firm in his hands, and his mind begins to function again. He notices that Linden is beautiful beneath the streetlights and the dripping leaves. He feels calm. The near edge of the future is just visible, a miracle made possible, he thinks, by having eschewed the present across the space of four days. The violence of that exorcising is gone, and he forgives twenty-five years of trespassers their importunities. Odd that Thrain's birthday is in April. A small matter. The pain is dying again to tenderness.

Amory Scann's books are acts of love. A regionalist, yes; but he rises up out of those literary restrictions, a phoenix from the fires of his passion for place. His own place: for him Linden is the point at which man and nature join, that cruel moment outside of time (but very much of our own times) which yields the profound and enduring strengths of both.

If it weren't for George's tooth he would be walking in the opposite direction, east and then north along Traverse Road to the place where Linden's cabin was. The ice is not all out of the river yet. Great pans are still floating down from the high mountains and cracking up against the piers of the bridge. He had planned to go there when the manuscript was done to check out the sight and sound and smell of what he had put on paper. Even in this rain it would be possible. But there is pain again. The tooth is sick and there is no hope for it. He will need pills to damp down the pain so that he can sleep until morning when it will have to come out. He looks for George's house among those he is passing, and finds it surrounded by its high barbered hedge and planted evergreens; and inside its wrought iron gate is the lawn, the fish pool, the rockeries on artificial mounds near the house. George lives well. He pulls teeth, weeds gardens, loves his wife and child. He doesn't worry about the mysteries of inheritance or birth and doesn't run a newspaper. The porch light is on. He pushes the bellbutton. Chimes ring out, and George himself answers. He peers out from the doorway anxiously, then releases a smile. "My tooth," Scann says before George can speak. George laughs. "Come in come in, you look like some waif out there Amory. When did you get back?" "An hour ago." Scann stands just inside the door, disoriented. "Come in come in," George says again. "Helen's at a PTA meeting and Johnny's out." Scann looks up into George's tall face. It is tall. It is the kind of face one speaks up into, a slab of professional friendliness. Does one confide in a dentist? "George," he says. "It hurts like hell." He is led to a light. "Open up." "I thought you might give me some pills," Scann says and opens. "No swelling. Come on down stairs," he says, and leads the way. Scann's tooth stops aching. The steps are carpeted in red and they lead not to the basement but to another world. The red carpeting stops and black tiles begin, and they lie precisely beneath solid lighting that allows neither glare nor shadows. A large room, not divided by partitions but by functions. It is a place of things, orderly, disciplined, logical extensions of drills and X-ray machines and the tools of dental mechanics, and of George. Cameras, lights, tripods, screens, projectors, a curtained darkroom open now and displaying a gigantic enlarger; half-built high fidelity components neat as war games, a ham radio station built into a U-shaped desk in one corner, complete with log book and typewriter; skis (water and snow); three outboard motors on brackets on the wall; and farther away a room into which George walks. It is a peculiar moment. Scann feels envy and fascination, and inadequate. By a trick of light, George seems taller in his room standing beside his chair, a beckoning force with no need for gestures. Scann goes slowly toward the doorway, and holds his notebooks and pencil firm in his hands. He feels reproached. The artifacts of this other reality surround him — moulded, manipulable surfaces that can be got at, arranged, summed into wholes not greater than their parts. Discretely manageable. No metaphysics. A new frontier of pure physicals. He looks at George wanting him to sit in the chair. "My first one," he says. "Had it in the old office over on Second Street, remember?" Scann sees it again. George says, "Still serviceable. I may retire early when Johnny's through school and keep my hand in with a few selected patients. Old faithfuls like yourself." Scann enters and sits down on the edge of the chair. George opens a drawer and the door of a cabinet, puts out his tools and turns on the overhead light. Scann's head is very clear. George moves in front of him, lined up against the rigid background beyond the door. Scann thinks that he has never been in a place like this before, not quite ever inside this new cave, with its artificial sunlight and hardware instead of shadows on the walls. Something that ancient Greek, thinking of man and the problems of reality, could not have foreseen. Scann feels the ache of the tooth inside his mouth again, a kind of consciousness linked with his life of long-distance dispatches and cut-lines under reproductions of disasters. No revelations, only a continuing sense of occurrence.

"Let's see it again, Amory." The light is adjusted so that it shines in his mouth. George holds a pick and a mirror in his hand and leans close. It is a moment and a place in which Scann must define himself too. "I didn't go to Banff. I spent the last four days at Linden House writing on a book." He looks past George and at the bright surfaces. George says, "Linden House?" "It was relevant to the project," Scann tells him. George stands back and grins. It is a pretty good one, hauled up over shining teeth. "That right? You old fox. I wondered about our phonecall." "A slip of the finger," Scann says. George approaches again with his instruments; he doesn't want to know about the book. "It's not a work I dislike," Scann says, happy with the phrase, and then he opens his mouth to let George in. "I believe that, Amory. You've got the knack. I see it in your editorials." The pick picks. "You write like you speak. I heard somewhere that's the secret." The prong finds the nerve. Scann twitches. "Godamn," he chokes. George withdraws: "Hurts a bit." He straightens up. "It'll abscess. Going to let me fix it this time?" "Right now? Pull it?" George is already unlimbering a needle and a vial over by the cabinet. "You better be careful, Amory." He has never heard George's voice tease before. "Or you'll give cowardice a bad name." "Or make it a bad joke." "You did walk out on me the other day," George says, and he takes cotton in tweezers and dunks it in alcohol. "Open wide. Wide. That's it." He swabs, puts down the cotton, takes up the needle and pinches the slack in Scann's cheek between thumb and forefinger. He shakes it while the needle goes in, far back, discharges. Another vial. George needles the gum around the tooth. Scann closes his eyes. He hears the instrument drop into the glass tray. "We'll give it a minute or two," George says. Scann opens his eyes again and sees George standing with his arms folded by the chair looking down at him. His heavy lips are pursed. "What's the matter?" Scann asks. George shakes his head, but his eyes are merry. Scann knows his face is smiling uncertainly. It is a kind of intimidation.

"A classic case, Amory. All wrapped up in your work." Scann's jaw and tongue are dying. "Come on George, say it." "Helen tells me she heard from Jackie Purvis that Marion told her you'd gone off and completely forgotten last Saturday was your anniversary." He rubs Scann's jaw a little with his finger. "Feel that?" Scann shakes his head. George's eyes still aren't serious. "Been home yet?" "No," Scann says and sits up. George tells him, "With this tooth out maybe it'll go better for you." George does laugh now. He can't seem to help it. A man who forgets twenty-five years of marriage and only has a notebook and a pencil to defend himself against the world is funny.

"George," he says, to stop him laughing, and then he stands up. The freezing is taking hold all the down the back of his throat. It may be blocking his stomach. George's hands are on his arm and shoulder. Scann looks at him. His eyes are astounded. "Is it that serious?" "Everything's serious." He remembers Mary Major telling him, "You can't be serious." But he is, and Marion is going to be. Only George doesn't need to be. He allows himself to be sat down again. "I'm surprised," George says. "I always thought you were a fellow with everything under control. Lie back. We can't have you running off again." His voice is edging toward the professional's.

"Take it out." He gives the order to George and lies back and looks up at the ceiling. His heart floods, knocks, and ebbs. He can't stand cold decisions about his own person, but George's voice is soothing. "Open a moment and let's see that tooth, Amory." Scann does as he is told. He sees nothing in George's hand, but suddenly he feels hooked. He can sense steel on the dead tooth, and George is working it loose. He struggles, but his head is pulled against George's chest and he feels the tooth rise up out of its socket with its numbed nerves frantically trying to signal distress. The tooth is dropped in a metal tray. A voice close to him tells of success: "There, that's done." Scann opens his eyes. "Thanks George." He lies exhausted. He may weep. George is in his mouth again, swabbing, laying cotton wads in the hole he has made. "Bite down on that, it'll stop the bleeding." Scann bites, feels nothing. "Very clean, very simple. I'll give you a couple of pills for tonight and in a day or two you won't remember you ever had it."

Scann sits up, accepts the pills, wipes his mouth and asks through clenched jaws, "Can I go now?" George nods, and when Scann climbs up out of the chair the hand that took his tooth is held out for him to shake. He looks up into friendly eyes. "Give Marion my best. I wish I could think of what you might buy at this hour for a peace offering." They go together through the doorway and out into the order of George's basement. He feels too calm. He watches himself look at George. His animal is out again, weakly perhaps, but it is prowling beyond the perimeters of his consciousness. He wants to be back at Linden House and begin the night again. "I can find my own way out," he says. "I guess you'll have to clean up in there," and he goes fast up the stairs and through the living-room out into the garden, but George is behind him at the door. "If that extraction acts up, you call me, Amory." Scann halts. What people like George have.is a sense of serving, that decent feeling that keeps bankers and plumbers and salesmen, the whole remarkable world of enterprise at work for itself while doing holy office for dependent others. Scann feels ungrateful. He returns to the porch steps and looks up into George's face. "My apologies," he says, through clenched teeth and with half-dead tongue, "I've been a bloody nuisance." "Think nothing of it, Amory." "Well, we got it done, anyway." "Yes, we did." George is genuine. That is the road to contentment, perhaps even happiness. There are no straight lines for him, only an equation, balance, a stunning act of faith that order and ancient logic will solve the X-factors in life. Scann moves back down the stairs. He doesn't even know the formula for parting. He waves, and then puts the offending hand in his pocket as he goes toward George's gate and walks out into the street again.

Things are clearer now, the rain has nearly stopped and he keeps walking, occasionally spitting a little blood into the gutter. His footsteps splash. He remembers that Trapper Linden walked all of his life. He believed it kept the land from folding up. Scann believes it. Philippa Morton didn't. He knows about her now. She could not leave for south because the horizon quit on her. George isn't walking either. Already he is in his basement, surrounded, planning to retire there. A male Marion, whose cloister will soon only admit of anniversaries. He turns right, then right again to his own street. His houselights are off. The gate needs fixing. He goes down the walkway, feeling in his pockets for his keys, and while he is sorting them to find the right one, he puts his elbow on the bell-button. George's chimes ring out. Bong-bong. They are watching t/v behind drawn drapes. Homecomings require tolerance. On both sides. He inserts the right key in the lock and goes through the door. The dark seems for a moment absolute. He stands in the black foyer and calls all of his family's names in reverse order of age. He expects Marion to rise like a grampus from an ocean of early sleep and be frightened he is a prowler. Nothing happens. He finds a light switch and flips it. The light is a shock. His skin shrinks. He calls again to enforce his presence in this illuminated emptiness. Then he begins to walk through the house, turning on lights, spitting blood in the toilet, looking, he realizes, for a note. He feels the top of the t/v set. It is cold. The house is cold. Very cold, and neat. Housekept. There is nothing for him in it. The clock on the mantel says eight minutes after nine. Which one? Yesterday's? This morning's? Or has it just stopped? He sits on the edge of his lazyboy chair and looks around. Hard lumps of insensate flesh lie dumb in his mouth. In the quiet, he feels how pristinely personal it is to be left alone. For him it is a dream that has rotted through years of not having come true. He needs Marion. She is part of him, but not a part that makes big decisions. He sits, thinking what has happened.

They have gone to the airport to meet him. She has driven out to pick him up. Add that to the forgotten anniversary. He is in trouble. But his half-dead throat heaves and the tension in him gradually subsides. He goes through the diningroom to the kitchen and turns on the carport light. No car. He faces again her white walls all set about with avocado appliances, a closed system she designed herself, but clever and mindless. She could manage a natural resource, a coal mine, say, or an oil pipeline, except that her cool eye for efficiency would bring about an immediate general strike. He opens the refrigerator, the kind whose light goes out before the door closes. The mysteries here are all resolved. It is empty but for a half-bottle of milk and a note. He picks the milk bottle up in one hand, but the other is amazingly modest about touching the piece of paper with her writing on it. He holds the milk and stoops to read. His legs tremble. Amory, you aren't at Banff. I phoned and they said you had never registered at the conference. Where you are celebrating our silver anniversary, I don't know. I sat down and thought about us. There wasn't much to think, and not much to say either, but it's better I put it down in writing, because you can't hear what people try to tell you, at least not me anyway. Amory, I didn't stay twenty-five years and work like a dog for no pay, bring up three children because it was what I wanted to do with all of the best part of my life. I mean it isn't even the life I would have chosen. I did it because I *loved*. You don't do those things for any other reason. You would argue me out of that if you were here. That's been our life, you arguing me out of my half of it. I'm going back home. I have Diane and Carol with me. Marilyn has begun her own life and her own job. Protect her if you can. He reads it again, and is able then to pick it out of the cold, shut the door and bring it into the bright fluorescence of the kitchen. Her ballpoint is still on the breakfastnook table. It is all he can see or feel. He knows he is standing. The blood from the tooth is cementing his tongue to the roof of his mouth. He holds the paper up in front of his eyes. There is no way into it or past it, no cracks or crevices. He reads the words again. They make a particular sound: perhaps the fall of a coffin lid. Everything has been stated, proved. He puts the milk bottle on the table beside her pen. "What," he says, breaking his tongue loose, "makes you so sure?" The words squeeze out from among the facts. He folds them up and puts her note in his pocket. One item will not fold and be put away. The habit of her. His eyes water and his nose plugs: cold, sudden withdrawal. The supply of Marion has dried up. Habits form. One makes love. He has formulated that with the pencil in his pocket. He holds onto it, and begins to move again through the house, uncertain. He may not have seen it before, and it frightens him. The photographs on the piano stun him. Their wedding picture stands among her gallery of portraits of the children alone and together. It is hand-tinted, and their faces blanked by the cosmetic art of the photofinisher. She is in her mother's wedding dress and he is in uniform. The doors of the church at Andover arch smally over them. This is as far as he can go. His muscles begin to shake as if he is trying to hold himself together in a vacuum.

Scann manages the door and negotiates the walkway to the gate and the street beyond. The car is at the airport. He could phone and have someone there bring it in, but even that is complicated now by awkward questions. Shirley might do it, not an unnatural service. He can feel the cotton in his mouth, and his tongue is nearly freed of anaesthetic. Soon he may have a variety of pains instead of one. He walks quickly, takes shortcuts through lanes and alleyways. He might be running to someone's rescue. There are three cement steps up to the door of the *Chronicle* offices, and lights are on as usual inside. He sees Downey, the contract janitor, making the rounds of the wastepaper baskets. He does five buildings a night and speaks to no one. His face is stiff, his eyes burn with anger all the time he works. Scann smiles. He is able to smile, and the hole in his jaw is beginning to throb. Downey makes a great noise and plunges into the printshop with his wheeled garbage collector. The simple life. Scann goes with alacrity into his office. It is as he left it. He closes the door, sits down at his desk and swings his typewriter around to face him. The words are routine. "Mrs. Amory Scann is off to England for her first visit to her homeland in twenty-five years. She left . . ." The street door opens and through the glass window in his own he can see Shirley come in and stand her umbrella in her empty wastebasket. He is safe. Even at this hour, she catches vibrations in her antennae that tell her he needs help. He sits and watches. She doesn't take off her coat but only opens a lower drawer in her desk and takes out a pair of shoes which she exchanges for the wet ones she is wearing.

Editor Scann begins to get up to go to her, perhaps to tell her about Marion, show her the note, make peace between them by drawing out her sympathies. He finds himself hesitating, and the moment is left with himself for himself. He deals with it carefully while he watches Shirley fumble beneath her skirt to smooth her stockings. She, at least, will not go, nor will Marion's leaving necessarily make her unhappy. He suffers a moment on both counts, and then he thinks that he is glad she has come by and is leaving again. Until now there has been no foreground to his view of the present, nothing to catch the focus or help make the perspective his own. Whom he must see is his daughter. Shirley moves away from her desk, and he faces his typewriter again, listening for the door to open and close. "She left with two of her three daughters, Carol and Diane, by air and will stay with her mother, Mrs. R. D. Stone, The Cottage, Hart Lane, Middle Wallup, Hants., for an extended spring holiday." He pulls the paper out of the typewriter and goes out into the general office to put it on Dorothy's desk. All of that particular news that's fit to print. He is going in circles. He knows it. He stands at the door and looks out. He knows too much suddenly; that, for instance; there is a danger of knowing now where he's been and only sensing the logjam of the future pressing at his back.

PRACTICE SESSION. Three: catching and pitching. Editor Amory Scann opens the door to room 322 of Linden House and breathes its familiar air once more. He puts the light on and looks around.

His briefcase is on the writing-table and the manuscript carefully on top of the bureau. He might not have left, but his tooth is gone and so have Marion and Carol and Diane. There have been changes. Movement. The slow, honest struggle of Goody Goodfellow away from the theory and toward the practice of pathetics. He feels better, a little anyway. He has gone beyond Thrain. Thrain knew only of the necessities of going and returning: the exploitation of straight lines in order to amass a legacy of circles. Scann sits again at his desk, and pulls out his pencil and notebook from his pockets. Visions are expensive, he writes. A vision acted upon is insupportable. Among the tosses and grabs and small hostilities of existence it embarrasses totally, ensuring that the inadequate arrangements in one's life will go brittle and fall away to expose not the fecund question but the suicidal answer: visions are only possibilities, other contingencies. Scann tries not to think what follows. Something else insupportable. Go quiet and pursue the vision, like Stephanie. Become like Thrain, and shout denials. Ask intercession from Saint George and Lady Marion. He still knows too much. He knows what he will do. It is the past that's detailed and inscrutable, not the future. He has never willingly been in the present. He rises, dodging revelation, puts away his notebook and his pencil, and allows himself a final temptation, a small thing to divert him before he goes. In the closet he crouches before the hole in the wall.

He sees his daughter. That is enough. He should not be surprised. He might have made this hole in the wall specifically to find her. He allows himself a moment of sentiment, and then looks again. She is dressed in her other uniform, a granny dress whose material is pulled thin across her back and shoulders as she hunches over, close to Paul, listening to him talk. He can see she wears no brassiere. He tries to think what that means, or even if she needs one. Yes. Her china doll body has matured and, secure, she no longer cares about it. Other realities begin to impinge. Paul is talking. He is always talking. What does he do when he isn't? There are other moments in his life. Scann hasn't seen them, but he supposes his daughter participates. The old bull stirs in him. He regrets that fatherhood has never been more than a nagging bruise on the edge of his life while he pursued other immortalities. He sees her listening. She listens well. He wants her to listen to him too. He adjusts his eye so he can see the others in the room. David is there, and his father. Ro. Mary Ann is asleep on the bed. There are others out of range of his eye.

He walks out of the closet and puts his manuscript in his brief-case. No strategy is required. Simply knock and ask for her. He goes to the door and opens it, and then turns once more to look at where he has been. A man's world can ask just so much of him. He would do it again. And again. He breathes deeply of his room's air, a final gesture, like all his others, that he makes even though they embarrass him, and he is disturbed to see Burke at his side, watching. "Leaving Mr. Scann?" He lifts one eyebrow, and then he sees the broken chair. Scann bends down and picks up its tangle by one leg. He holds it carefully for Burke to view, and then he forces him to take it. "Yes, I'm leaving," he says. "The coast is clear, Burke." He finds he has very little interest in either managers or chambermaids any-more. "We hold guests responsible," Burke begins. Scann turns and walks toward Ro's room. "Put it on the bill. I'll be down to pay it in a moment." He knocks on the door. Burke may or may not have passed behind him. His sense of another event beginning to take form is strong. The noise inside the room is argument. Ro's face appears, looks puzzled. "Scann," Scann says, "of the *Chronicle*. Could I speak with my daughter?" He sees her. They don't need Ro to relay the message. She comes, suddenly awkward, to the door. Paul is talking up into David's face. Others are trying to speak at the same time. They are haranguing David about Mary Ann.

Marilyn's face tells him nothing. It hides even surprise. "What do you want?" she asks. "To talk to you." "Mummy's gone." "I know." "Then you've been home." "Marilyn, we should talk." "Not here. Later." He struggles with impatience. "Of course not here. I've come for you." "I'm with Paul." "I can see that. He can wait." "No, this is important." He forces himself to look away from her shut face, and he sees David gesturing for him to come into the room. He doesn't hear what he says. "Important to whom?" "To me," she says, and turns, a little uncertainly, defying him. He follows her, and sees her go to Paul whose body is articulating every word he says. He closes the door behind him and stands with his briefcase in his hand. He has no plan except that his daughter should come home with him. Old Thrain is sitting on a chair between the closet and the bureau. Scann focuses a moment on him. He is playing with a book of hotel matches, folding the cover back little by little and tearing strips from it. His face has that blank seriousness of a baby. Thrain always was active. Scann goes to him and puts his briefcase down as he yells into his ear. "Happy Birthday." Thrain looks up. "I'm not tired," he says. Scann stands beside him. The old man is a sturdy wreck, but he probably is tired. He wonders how Paul and the others dragged David here. He turns away toward Marilyn. She is listening again, but she is agitated. Her hands are clenched in front of her. He sees her begin to speak. "Cultural murder," he hears her say. "And Mary Ann's not the only Indian here. We're all getting to be Indians, special citizens with very special choices to make." Scann admires her rhetoric. He watches David looking at her and admiring too, but he is losing his parliamentary manner. "Time to go," he tells them in a moment of silence. But Paul shouts, "Bullshit, Mr. Member of Parliament. We've got you here and you're going to listen." He puts his back to the door. Marilyn doesn't go with him, and Scann moves to be near her, to cut her off from joining the half-dozen others who are pressing David harder now. She watches him confront her. "Look," he says, "I'm your father. Come home with me so we can talk." "It's a little late, isn't it? I mean, you go away and do whatever you were doing and when you find out what's really happening — daddy, I'm not going to let you make it hurt anymore than it does already." "Believe me," Scann tells her, "I don't want it to hurt anyone, least of all you." Her face cracks and puckers as if he'd hit her. "You're embarrassing me in front of my friends. You did your thing, and if you feel unfree about it, what can I do? You can lie about Banff, so maybe everything else is a lie too. I don't have any answers." She leaves him, and then somebody by the bed shouts "Mary Ann" into the noise. Ro goes over to the bed and Scann watches him bend over the young man already there. It occurs to him that there are five Indians in the room, and five whites. He and Thrain and Mary Ann are non-combatants. His mouth has blood in it again. He spits into the basin and runs water to wash the pink away. A quiet has formed around him. He looks through it with some curiosity at the action by the bed. Then he watches David go to the phone, and he hears him ask for an ambulance. Paul is swearing, accusing, and Marilyn is trying to calm him. Scann thinks the boy may be crying.

Then he smells smoke. Thinking of Marilyn, he smells smoke. His animal is asleep. He leans against the basin and watches all of them watch Mary Ann. In a moment, he sees flames and then Thrain feeding his manuscript into the wastebasket, a few pages at a time and then finally all of them. The old man is frowning seriously into the heat he is making, and Scann runs and grabs at the metal can. It is too hot. He puts his foot into it and tramps down hard. The flames subside; his shoe may be burning. He tries to take it out, but it won't come. It is stuck. He looks around for help. They are holding Mary Ann over the edge of the bed. Marilyn has her finger down the woman's throat. Vomit flies. Scann bends and holds the metal between his sleeved arms and tries to lift his foot out, but he is doubled over and his knee is in his chest. He hops, holds the can near the edge perilously close to his wrists. There are tears in his eyes because of the smoke. He is near the basin, hopping and heaving, and then the foot comes loose. He tries to force the basket into the sink so he can get water into it, but it's no use. The can's too big. He sits it on the floor and sprays water out over the flames by holding his hand against the tap's flow. The water splashes down, in and around the burning manuscript. He concentrates the stream of water, willing it into the basket. Smoke becomes steam. He turns off the tap. He is reduced beyond quiet. Everything is final. He peers down into the debris and sees wet ash, scorched paper and some yellow green-lined sheets appear as the steam fades. He raises his eyes. They are still busy at the bed wrapping Mary Ann in blankets. He hears that she may be dying. People shout precious instructions at one another. He picks up his can and goes across the room to where his briefcase lies on its side beneath the chair where Thrain sleeps. Forgive him: of course forgive him for trying to make an ending. "Thrain," he says to him, "everything here is yours, the room, the sick Indian whore, my daughter." He looks at the old man more closely. He *is* dead. Scann shouts, as if he might be heard across that barrier: "You tried to burn the evidence, goddamn you, but it's here" (he is pointing to his own high forehead) "and you've just released it for publication." Scann is laughing. The hole where George's tooth once was is a metallic taste in his mouth. A siren hollers for action. He turns from Thrain and sees them lift Mary Ann from the bed, her tiny body supported by many hands. They make a gaggle crowding through the door. "Extras," he shouts after them, and then he reaches down into the can and picks out what is whole and half-whole and fragments burned and wet. "There are no beginnings and endings, Thrain," he says, stuffing his briefcase and closing it. "But there are responsibilities." He stands before Thrain's absolute quiet. The urge to dance is upon him — his animal maybe. Or it may be the result of a moment of new consciousness. Hardwon. He does not dance. Writer Novelist Scann goes carefully, husbanding that moment, through the door, tramples blue roses and walks with tenderness on his left foot, the one that put out the fire.

THE NEW CANADIAN LIBRARY LIST